Fiction
Thane, Elswyth.
Ever after.

Ever After

Also Available in Large Print
by Elswyth Thane:

Dawn's Early Light
Yankee Stranger
The Light Heart
Kissing Kin
This Was Tomorrow
Homing

Ever After

ELSWYTH THANE

G.K. HALL &CO.

Boston, Massachusetts

1981

FICTION
C 1
LT

Library of Congress Cataloging in Publication Data

Thane, Elswyth, 1900–
  Ever after.

  Large print ed.
  1. Large type books. I. Title.
[PS3539.H143E9 1981]   813′.52   80–25631
ISBN 0–8161–3165–1

Published in Large Print by arrangement with Elsevier / Nelson Books.

Set in Linotron 202 16 pt Times Roman

To
The Bright Memory
of Sam Sloan

Acknowledgments

Once more I take this opportunity to thank Mrs. F. G. King and the staff of the New York Seymour of the Museum of the City of New York. At Williamsburg, Miss Mary Seymour of the Museum of the City of New York. At Williamsburg, Miss Mary McWilliams continues to be my dear friend in need and I am indebted for time and hospitality to Mr. and Mrs. Kenneth Chorley, Mr. and Mrs. Gerald Bath, Mrs. George Coleman, Mrs. Isobel Hubbard, Judge Frank Armistead, Dr. W. G. Swem, Mr. Rutherford Goodwin, Mr. A. T. Love, and Mrs. Eleanor Duncan. Colonel Arthur F. Cosby, Officers Reserve Corps, U.S. Army, retired, very kindly lent me personal letters and files regarding the Rough Riders, and I am grateful to Lieutenant-Colonel W. E. G. Ord-Statter of the British Army, Major C. B. Ormerod of the British Information Services, Captain G. M. Game of the British Territorial Army, Dr. K. C. Waddell of the Henry Ford Hospital, Mr.

Herbert Satterlee, and Miss Elizabeth Garthwaite for the trouble they have taken to answer by letter and in consultation what must often have seemed to them foolish questions about Kitchener's Egyptian Army, Court presentations, English divorce laws and Scotland Yard procedure, malaria and yellow fever, the Cuban campaign, and the half-forgotten, spacious days of the Nineties, which were not altogether gay. To those of us who cannot quite remember, I hope the book will bring glimpses of a vanished world. And I hope that those who lived in it will feel at home again.

E.T.

Contents

Contents

All the characters
in this book, except those
obviously connected by history to the
war in Cuba, are entirely fictitious and any
resemblance to any actual person is
coincidental.

The Days AND

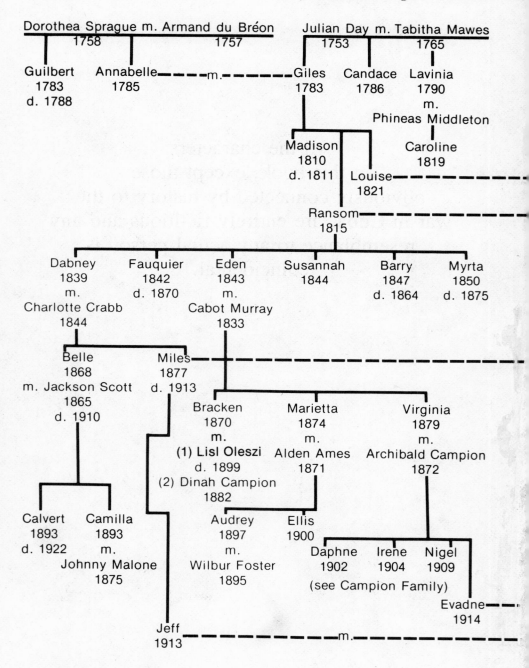

Dorothea Sprague m. Armand du Bréon
1758   1757

Guilbert   Annabelle - - - - m. - - - - Giles
1783   1785   1783
d. 1788

Julian Day m. Tabitha Mawes
1753   1765

Giles   Candace   Lavinia
1783   1786   1790
                      m.
           Phineas Middleton

Madison   Caroline
1810   1819
d. 1811   Louise
             1821

Ransom - - - - - - -
1815

Dabney   Fauquier   Eden   Susannah   Barry   Myrta
1839   1842   1843   1844   1847   1850
m.   d. 1870   m.   d. 1864   d. 1875
Charlotte Crabb   Cabot Murray
1844   1833

Belle   Miles - - - - - - - - - - - - - - - -
1868   1877
m. Jackson Scott d. 1913
1865
d. 1910

Bracken   Marietta   Virginia
1870   1874   1879
m.   m.   m.
(1) Lisl Oleszi   Alden Ames   Archibald Campion
d. 1899   1871   1872
(2) Dinah Campion
1882

Calvert   Camilla
1893   1893
d. 1922   m.
           Johnny Malone   Audrey   Ellis
           1875   1897   1900
                              m.
                              Wilbur Foster
                              1895   Daphne   Irene   Nigel
                                               1902   1904   1909
                                               (see Campion Family)

Evadne - - -
1914

Jeff - - - - - - - - - - - - - - - - - m. - - - - - - - - -
1913

The Spragues

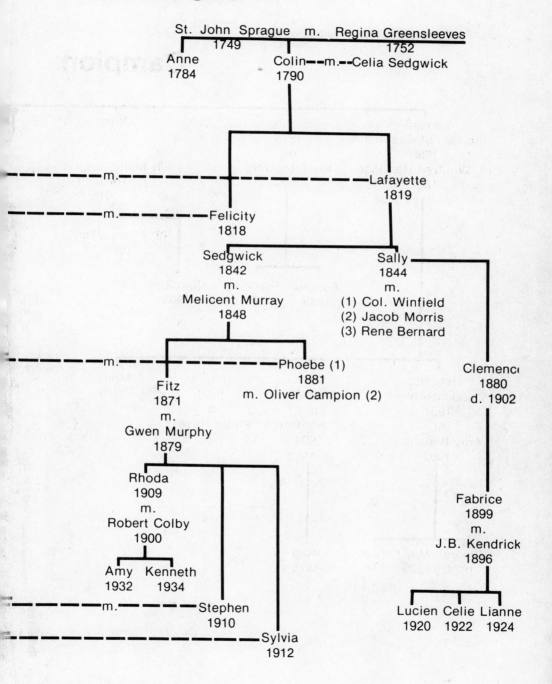

Campion

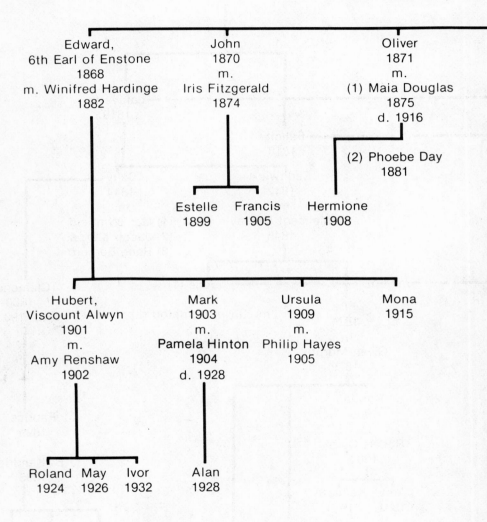

Edward,
6th Earl of Enstone
1868
m. Winifred Hardinge
1882

John
1870
m.
Iris Fitzgerald
1874

Oliver
1871
m.
(1) Maia Douglas
1875
d. 1916

(2) Phoebe Day
1881

Estelle
1899

Francis
1905

Hermione
1908

Hubert,
Viscount Alwyn
1901
m.
Amy Renshaw
1902

Mark
1903
m.
Pamela Hinton
1904
d. 1928

Ursula
1909
m.
Philip Hayes
1905

Mona
1915

Roland
1924

May
1926

Ivor
1932

Alan
1928

Family

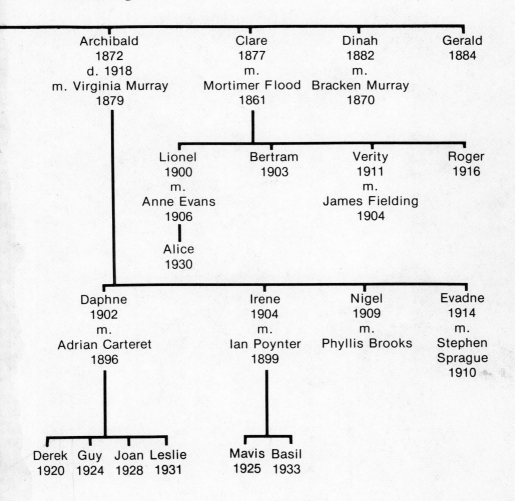

PART ONE
SUSANNAH

Williamsburg.   *Christmas, 1896.*

1

The letter from Miss Eden had come.

Pharaoh, the old colored butler, carried it eagerly towards his master's bedroom upstairs, where Miss Susannah sat reading to her father in front of the fire. Marse Ransom, he knew, had been fretting to hear. Time was getting short, till Christmas. If Miss Eden was coming home she better get a move on. Hardly missed a year, she hadn't, since she married the Yankee gentleman and went up North to live. Once when young Marse Bracken was getting born, back about '69, it was, she didn't come, and that time along early in the '80's when little Miss Virginia almost died of diphtheria — that kept them home, and one other time — Pharaoh's dimming memory fumbled at it — must be three times she'd missed, maybe four — four Christmases out of round about thirty — that

1

was pretty good. It never seemed rightly Christmas without Miss Eden there, and her children. Turned out real well, Miss Eden's marriage had, for all Captain Murray was a Yankee and took her away to Washington and New York with him. Captain Murray was rich too, which was something nobody hereabouts was any more. . . .

Pharaoh's long, spindly legs in narrow trousers strapped under the instep, and his tail coat, and his thin black neck inside the stiff white collar, gave him the look of an elderly insect as he ascended the broad stairs, but his progress was full of purpose, and the square envelope with its New York postmark was tenderly held in his gnarled fingers. He paused outside Ransom Day's door and cocked an ear to the panel. The room was quiet, as it would be if the old man had dropped off to sleep. Sue often sat patiently, the book in her lap, waiting till he roused again rather than disturb his light slumber by trying to tiptoe away.

Her care of him was infinitely loving, for she never ceased trying to make up to him for her mother's death in fever-stricken Richmond during the war. It seemed sometimes that he did not want to live — but here he was at eighty-one, the last of his generation, frail, sad, broken, but with a mind quite clear, and a lively interest in his surviving children and their offspring. There were three of them left to call him Father — Susannah, and her sister Eden, and their eldest brother Dabney, who had lost a leg at Drewry's Bluff in '64.

Pharaoh's soft scratch on the door did not rouse his master, and he opened to Sue's quick gesture for silence. He put the letter in her hand and departed soundlessly, thinking as he often did how pretty she still was, with only a few silver threads in her coppery hair, and the most elegant shape in Williamsburg even with the outlandish way styles were nowadays since they left off their hoops; not weighing a pound more than she had when she was a girl, seemed like, and that smile that showed her little white teeth and the dimple at the corner of her mouth — for the thousandth time Pharaoh mourned the incomprehensible fact that Miss Sue, the darling of them all, had never married.

Sue opened the letter softly, with an eye on her father's bent head.

Dearest Sue — [Eden had written]
You must be fit to kill me for so much delay and uncertainty, but things have really been at sixes and sevens here, and I could not look ahead. I may

as well break it to you at once, I suppose — Bracken's wife has left him.

There, and doesn't it look awful, down in black and white! My only son's marriage gone on the rocks, and his life smashed up by a creature we none of us ever liked or trusted, though our worst suspicions of her never quite equalled the facts. I won't say Lisl has broken his heart, because for that to happen he would have had to love her very dearly, and I am sure he stopped doing that some time ago.

You will ask me how he takes it, and I can only say — like Bracken. He is defiant to the point of flippancy, lest we pity him. And he is close-mouthed to the point of rudeness, lest we come at the truth, which I fear is far worse than I can imagine. We all knew that Lisl was wildly extravagant, of course, because Bracken has twice had to ask his father for help with debts, though Cabot made him a very generous arrangement in the partnership, and he has had his pay as Special Correspondent to the paper as well, with travelling expenses extra. Lisl has a passion for diamonds, she is really mad about them, and he gave her all he could afford, but she would buy more and send the bills to him. She entertained on a scale suitable for Royalty — one evening party could swallow a month of Bracken's income. Her gowns, of course, were famous, and the dressmaker's bills naturally came home to roost. Well, we knew all that, it went with her type of beauty and her European ideas of high society — and her notorious indiscretions of speech! But there was something *more,* towards the end, and he does not mean for us to know what it was.

We are giving out here that she has returned to Vienna for a family visit, and that Bracken finds it impossible to take a holiday abroad just now. But we know that she will never set foot in his house again, and her religion does not sanction divorce, and what future does that leave Bracken, at twenty-seven? No wife, no home, no children — and he is not the celibate type, I don't have to tell you, he's like Sedgwick, quick and kind and loving, and always irresistible to women. It seems almost more than I can *bear,* but then, Lisl has always been that!

So now I shall pack up the pieces of Bracken and bring them down to you all for healing. Cabot is in a towering rage about the whole thing, and is convinced that Bracken must have a stiff job at once to occupy his mind, and has decided to send him to London in the spring to open an office in Fleet Street for the newspaper. It is almost too much responsibility, but with the election over, and lacking a good war at the moment, Cabot considers London the next best thing for keeping Bracken absorbed and leaving him no time to brood. He will have to be in Washington for the inauguration in March, and we sail immediately after that, in time to have Virginia presented at one of the May Drawing-Rooms.

Now, Sue, honey, seriously — this is the year for you to come with us! Each time before when I have asked you to go abroad you have had some reason for refusing — Dabney and Charl were having a baby, or Sedgwick's boy was coming of age, or Father had had an illness. This time we won't take No for an answer. You owe it to yourself to see something of the world while you are still young enough to enjoy it, and next summer in England will be exciting, with special doings on account of the Jubilee. Moreover, launching my daughter Virginia into society is going to be fun.

She is rather a beauty if I do say it as shouldn't! Please come, Sue. I shall argue it out with you when I get there.

As our plans stand now, we shall arrive there on Thursday evening. Please inform the family of the situation and beg them to use all possible tact with Bracken, as I'm sure they will. Give my love to everybody — no one knows how good it will seem to be in Williamsburg again, where there are no Lisls and no upheavals, and where Bracken can draw a long breath. Why on earth couldn't he have chosen some nice Virginia girl (like ourselves when we were young!) instead of this exotic Austrian, who has meant nothing but trouble, one way or another, ever since he first set eyes on her!

Love,
EDEN

Sue read the letter twice through and then sat with it in her fingers, frowning at the fire. Poor Bracken — not because his foreign wife had left him, but because he would still not be free of her, to make a new start and live the life he was meant to. But surely there must be some way, even though Lisl did say she was a Catholic. Precious little she cared about religion, except as an excuse!

Sedgwick would know, Sue thought. She must go and tell Sedgwick about this at once.

Moving very cautiously, holding her full poplin skirts close to keep them from rustling, she rose and slipped across the room and whisked out the door before her father roused. Sometimes one was justified in taking advantage of his feebleness, she considered, especially when something came up about which she wished to consult her cousin Sedgwick, who was a lawyer and therefore knew everything. Besides, as Eden had mentioned in her letter, Bracken was more like Sedgwick Sprague than like his own father. Somehow in Bracken the Sprague strain, three times bred into his mother's family through the marriage of first cousins, was dominant; while by a freak of heredity, Sedgwick's own son was a changeling, unaccountable anywhere in the family history.

Sue put on her hat and the little fur jacket which Eden had given her for Christmas two years before, and set off for Sedgwick's office, which was up over the bank in the Duke of Gloucester Street. It was a grey, chilly day in December, and the shabby little town looked derelict and bleak. Williamsburg had been the capital of Virginia once, with a Governor's Palace and a State House and a famous tavern called the Raleigh where Sue's great grandmother had danced and dined as a bride after Yorktown — Grandmother Tabitha Day, who could remember when George Washington was only a Burgess and went to dine with the British Royal Governor, wearing powder and his blue Virginia militia uniform with red facings. It was all gone now. The capital had moved to Richmond during the war with England, and even the young ladies' Academy which in the Sixties had stood on the ground had been torn down so that its bricks could be used by the railway, leaving the upper end of the Duke of Gloucester Street barren and empty. The Palace had burned down after Yorktown and was further demolished by the Federal troops in '62. A modest residence or two occupied its site, and the depot encroached where once the pleached walks and clipped yews of the Royal gardens had been. Fire had destroyed the Raleigh in '59, and Lane's store had taken its place. The College, which remained closed for some years after Lee's surrender, was running again, with seven professors and more than a hundred students, but for the professional courses like Law and Medicine everybody had to go to the new University at Charlottesville — new, that is, in Thomas Jefferson's time.

9

The town was poverty-pinched and forgotten and forlorn, the last of its prosperity swept away by the War Between the States. Chickens foraged undisturbed in the wide, unpaved Duke of Gloucester Street — Sue was one of those who refused to call it Main Street as the careless younger generation did — and cows were let graze in the shade of the old mulberry trees which lined each side of the road. The Palace Green, once a well-kept lawn, was weed-grown and never got mowed. Everybody was poor since the war, even the Spragues, though Sedgwick was the best lawyer on the Peninsula and kept pretty busy — and of course there was his wife's legacy from her father's estate, which he would never touch for himself. . . .

The doctor's sagging buggy went by, bumping over the frost-hardened ruts of the road, and Sue responded to his greeting absent-mindedly, and walked on, thinking about Bracken.

Somewhere there must be a girl who was meant for him, and who but for this hasty, hectic marriage with Lisl Oleszi might still come to reign in his luxurious little house just around the corner from his father's brownstone mansion on Madison Avenue — the house Bracken had bought and lavishly furnished for his lovely, exacting bride four years ago. The family had always called her "the Austrian" — in the same hostile tone the French had once used, Sue always thought, in speaking of Marie Antoinette by the same term, though strictly speaking Lisl was half Hungarian. Bracken had met her at the Austrian Embassy while he was Washington Correspondent to his father's New York newspaper. She was cousin or niece to somebody there, and must have come fortune-hunting to America. When anyone so good-looking and — his mother's word was no exaggeration — irresistible as Bracken was actually had money as well, Lisl was sure to try for him.

Whether his very substantial income had proved to be less than she supposed, or whether she had always meant to tap his father's resources as well, or whether she merely had a heedless passion for spending money, it was not long before Bracken had been forced to remonstrate, diffidently at first, then more firmly, and finally — he was not a meek man — with justifiable heat. Lisl had called him stingy, and a lot of other things, in that lisping accent he had once found so charming — she could never even manage the *r* in his given name correctly, and it was strange how irritating a thing like that could become. There were sulks and scenes and passionate reconciliations, and then always the confession, sometimes tearful and contrite, sometimes bold and arrogant, of new expenditures. She was beautiful, and deserved to be adorned. She was artful with her loving — *experienced,* said Eden, her nose very high — and after each quarrel knew how to enslave him again.

So much Sue had known for some time now. She had seen Lisl just once, when Bracken brought her to Williamsburg for Christmas the year they were married, and Sue had decided then that Lisl had no tenderness and no sense of humor, and hence was no wife for Bracken. The next year Lisl had contrived to be ill at Christmas time — too ill to travel, not too ill for the gaieties of the season in New York. And for the two years after that she had kept Bracken abroad through December. Now she had gone to Europe again — and alone.

Sue came to the narrow dark stairs beside the entrance to the bank and went up them, holding her blue poplin skirts daintily, and turned to the right, and there was the familiar door with SEDGWICK SPRAGUE, ATTORNEY-AT-LAW, on it in faded black and gold letters. The office was rather faded-looking too, and the once handsome stuffed black leather furniture was worn and patched and came off on your clothes in a fine brown powder, like the old calf bindings of the thick books that lined the walls. The mahogany desk to the right of the door as you went in was empty. Sedgwick had sat there once, when his father was the senior partner, and Sedgwick's son should be sitting there now. Sedgwick refused to accept another apprentice, though he needed help. The job was Fitz's if ever he wanted it. But the desk remained empty.

Sedgwick was alone and rose to meet her with both hands extended in welcome — placed her tenderly in the visitor's chair facing his desk, lowered the blind an inch lest the light strike into her eyes, and returned to her side to receive her gloves and hand-bag before she could be put to the trouble of laying them down herself. It was always that way when she came to the office. Whatever he was doing stopped. Everything was set aside in order that she might find herself the center of the universe, empress of his world.

They were double first cousins — her father and his mother both Days, her mother and his father both Spragues — and they had grown up together. Once, a long time ago before the war, they had been in love and were forbidden to marry because of the close relationship. Faithfully they had kept their resolution never to speak of it again. They didn't have to. His face, when she came unexpectedly upon his sight — her smile, when they looked at each other as they did now in their wordless satisfaction at being together — that was enough. She had never grudged him his peaceful marriage with the sister of Eden's Yankee husband, his well-run home, his son and daughter. She had made up her mind long before it happened that he must marry some day and not go maimed and lacking all his life for love of herself. And as for her, she had never left Williamsburg, and no man had ever crossed her horizon who could disturb the deep serenity of her lifelong devotion to Sedgwick. Since the first blinding shock of rebellion that day so long ago when she was sixteen, there had been no repining and no bitterness. After all, they saw each other nearly every day, and Melicent was her dear friend, the very person she had hoped he would marry since marry he must, and the children were almost like her own. . . .

Her life on those terms had made her a mysteriously enchanting creature, a girl playing at womanhood even while her hair turned grey — a girl untouched and virginal and yet awakened and chastened by love. It was impossible to think of Susannah Day as a spinster, or to realize that she was now passing imperceptibly from her forties into her fifties, still slender, with a rounded high bosom and that misplaced dimple in her ready smile. And the books she wrote and published every two or three years were mature and knowing and warm-blooded, and had kept the simple household running in comparative comfort during the long years of her father's invalidism.

She held fast to her hand-bag as Sedgwick's hands closed on it, delaying to extract Eden's letter and give it to him.

"You'd better read it yourself," she told him. "It's all about Bracken." And she added as his expressive eyebrows rose — "They'll be here in time for Christmas. *That* part's all right."

She sat watching him while he read, telling over again to herself the familiar sum of the things she loved best about him; his fine head bent now above Eden's letter, the thick straight hair greying at the edges and left long to the top of his collar in the back; the old-fashioned black stock he still wore with such an air; his crisp white linen and brushed broadcloth frock coat — people had begun to call him Colonel now when he travelled, but he had been only a captain of cavalry when

Lee surrendered at Appomattox. His long hands held the letter lightly, flipping over its pages — he always moved so neatly. Watching his hands today, Sue was hardly aware that at the back of her memory lay a rainswept night in '62 when she had passed along rows of wounded, bandaged men on stretchers, here in Williamsburg, sure that she would be able to pick out Sedgwick even though his face should be covered or unrecognizable, if she could just see his hands. . . .

At last Sedgwick folded the letter tidily and replaced it in its envelope and laid it on top of Sue's hand-bag which was on the corner of the desk. Her eyes waited on his face. As usual, he began where she might least expect his attention to focus.

"*Am* I irresistible to women? he queried, with a sidelong look, his brows askew.

"Oh, Sedgie! *Inevitably!*" Her dimple showed.

"You mean you had noticed it yourself?" He inquired in feigned surprise, leaning towards her across the desk with wistful eyes on her ever-changing face.

"A long time ago," she answered steadily. It was the nearest allusion they had made for years to the tragedy of their youth, and her gaze as it met his was smiling, and sweet.

"Still?" he asked briefly, and —

"Always," she nodded.

He sat a moment, looking down at his clasped hands on the desk in front of him.

"It oughtn't to be like that," he said finally. "I've gone on — I married little saint Melicent, I've got my children —"

"I've got them too, Sedgie," she reminded him. "And that was the way it had to be. You see, I'm still thanking God you weren't killed in the war. I've had all these years since then to see you — and tell you things — I've been very happy, Sedgie, really I have."

"I believe by some miracle you have been," he said, and raised another point in Eden's letter which it had not occurred to her to discuss. "Now, about your going abroad in the spring," he began. "I think you ought to, you know."

"My book won't be done," she said at once.

"Well, leave it undone. You won't need the money, Eden will see to all that."

"D-don't you think it — seems a good deal —"

"My dear child, Cabot is rolling in the stuff! We're all so used to being poor down here, it is beyond our conception that a man may have, not just enough, but more than enough! Cabot has steel mills and Cabot has a flourishing newspaper, don't forget! No doubt Eden's dress allowance would pay all my expenses for a year. You will go with her, won't you, Sue?''

''You're awfully anxious to be rid of me, all of a sudden,'' she complained.

''It's as Eden says — you must see something of the world while you are still young enough to enjoy it.''

''This is my world,'' said Sue. ''Here in Williamsburg.''

He shook his head.

''It's not enough,'' he said.

''It's all you've had, Sedgie.''

''To my regret.''

''You mean *you* wanted to go abroad?''

He shifted impatiently in his chair.

''If this is our day for telling the truth to each other, I haven't been a country lawyer by choice, all my life,'' he confessed. ''I always coveted Dabney's year at the Legation before the war. Later I envied Cabot his vagabond existence as a reporter, before he married Eden.''

''Why, Sedgie, I never dreamed —''

''I particularly wanted to go to England, you always knew that.''

''Well, yes, in a way, we all talked about it, but —''

"Suppose you go to England for me, in the spring."

"But, Sedgie, I —"

"Go down to Gloucestershire and see the old family place — the place our great grandfather St. John came from, the house the plantation here was named for — Farthingale. Find out who is living there now and what it looks like. I've often wondered. Besides, you might get a new book out of it, you never know."

"Yes," she said thoughtfully. "I might."

"You will go, then?"

"Well, I — I'll talk to Father. I'll see how he is when the time comes. Sedgie — what about Bracken?"

"Oh, Bracken, poor devil, he's in for a bad time. But I'm not surprised, are you?"

"Except for one thing."

"What's that?" he asked.

"Well — women don't, as a rule, leave men who are irresistible."

Sedgwick made a small rude sound.

"Don't you see the answer to that?"

"What answer? Eden doesn't say —"

"She doesn't say anything about a financial settlement, does she?"

"I d-didn't think there was one."

"And if there wasn't one, what is the expensive Lisl going to live on after she is no longer under Bracken's roof? Not her precious diamonds!''

"But I still don't see —"

"Why, Miss Innocence, it's plain as the nose on your funny little face, if Eden can't see it for herself! Lisl has found somebody who can buy her more diamonds than Bracken ever can, and Bracken is resigning in his favor!"

Sue gazed at him in awe.

"What it is to be a lawyer!" she marvelled. "Is *that* what he is so afraid they'll find out?"

"Bracken can be as close-mouthed as he likes, but I'll bet Cabot knows the other fellow's name and even the amount of his income!" His eyes sharpened, his lazy pose drew together, his lips slipped into a small sardonic smile. "I wonder," he murmured.

"What?"

"Nothing." But their eyes met, and now Sue was not far behind him.

"Oh, Sedgie, you don't think Cabot would ever —"

"Cabot tried to buy her off in the beginning."

"I didn't know that."

"Nobody was supposed to," he admitted. "But that's where Bracken's being so irresistible came in. She wouldn't let go of him for any sum Cabot offered. He's always hated her very — bootlaces, and I was just thinking, if Cabot found a way to sic her on to some sucker with a diamond mine, as it were, that would be another way of buying her off, wouldn't it!''

''But Cabot would never deliberately break up the marriage —''

''The marriage was already broken up, long since. It was only a question of getting rid of her.''

''But if she won't divorce him —'' Sue began.

''Ah, but he can divorce her if he can prove infidelity! Cabot may be counting on something like that.''

''Do you think Eden suspects?''

''Darling Eden. You can never be sure what she knows and what she misses. Anyway, I shouldn't have mentioned it. Don't dwell on it, will you. As for Bracken — he'll want handling for a while.''

''Yes, even if he's stopped loving her, it must be so *humiliating* to a man when his wife leaves him!'' Sue ruminated. ''Even if he hated her, it must be such a blow to his *pride* — ''

''Don't envy lawyers for their wisdom, my dear,'' he said with a smile. ''You have put your finger on Bracken's trouble. It's the insult to his manhood he's feeling now. What a trollop that woman is! It always stuck out of her a mile. Bracken was a fool, anyone could see what she was! Why did he have to marry her, anyway, he could have had her, if he'd tried, enough to cure him, right there in Washington!''

"*Sedgie,* how you talk! Perhaps she was too clever for that."

"No doubt she was. And no doubt this fellow with the diamond mine, whoever he is, lacks Bracken's chivalrous feelings. If he were proposing marriage, we'd hear about divorce fast enough!''

Sue looked horrified.

"Oh, Sedgie, this is awful! I didn't *realize!* Can't you do something?''

"Honey, I'm not a wizard, though I've often wished I were. In a case like this, Cabot's bankroll can probably do more than the Law. He may have something up his sleeve, it's hard to beat Cabot forever."

"I dread having to tell Father," she reflected.

"It won't be any surprise to him either," said Sedgwick philosophically. "He's seen her. He knows. Tell me what you've been doing." They hadn't had a talk since the day before yesterday and were in arrears. Their eyes held without effort or urgency, drawing comfort and serenity from each other. Their lost dream had died peacefully in his careful hands a long time ago, leaving behind it only an abiding need, disciplined and docile now, but never icebound. They were infinitely contented together, that was all. Nearly all. "Tell me things," he said affectionately.

"Well — let's see." It was an old game they had got very good at. "Mammy and I have been turning out the rooms to get ready for the guests. And I'm trying to finish my chapter before everybody arrives and catches me at the wrong place. And I'm fixing over my black velvet to wear at the party. I reckon that's about all. At breakfast we were counting up the ones who are coming this year and the ones who — won't be here. One list is very short and the other one is lengthening. Sedgie, have you heard from Sally?"

"Not a line. Our Sally done flew de coop, Sue."

"Forever?"

"It looks like it."

They both paused to consider his sister Sally, the beauty of the family, who had married and buried three elderly husbands in quick succession and gone to live on their combined bequests in a large gaudy villa on the French Riviera. Once when Eden was abroad she had gone to see Sally and confessed to Sedgwick afterwards that she had been a little scandalized. The house was full of foreigners and small yapping dogs, said Eden, and Sally had begun to speak English with a French accent, and — Sally painted her face. There was more, which Sue as an unmarried woman was not supposed to suspect.

''I was wondering what her Christmas gifts this year would be,'' Sue said. At Christmas time and for birthdays and coming-of-age parties, Sally's presents were magnificent and unexpected and seldom arrived on time. For Bracken's twenty-first birthday she had sent a check with instructions that it was to buy him the best Virginia-bred saddle horse to be found. For Fitz's coming-of-age she had sent a Swiss watch of such splendor that he wasn't allowed to wear it on weekdays. For the girls she usually sent gowns from Worth or Paquin, too elaborate to be of any use. Sue had a special interest in Sally's presents this year, because for the first time she had interfered by giving a hint. She was wishing now that she hadn't. Sedgwick might not be pleased.

''Just because she's so stinkin' rich, Sally thinks she needn't bother to write anything but checks any more,'' Sedgwick said rather huffily.

It was nearly lunch time and when Sue rose to go Sedgwick said he would walk along with her. She stood waiting in the dingy hall while he turned to lock the door behind him. There was the sound of running feet on the stairs and a small colored boy came into view at headlong speed. When he saw them he halted on the top step, holding to the newel-post and gasping for breath.

"Oh, Marse Sedgwick — Miss Melicent say please you come home dis minute, suh!"

"Something wrong at home?"

"No, suh. Essept Miss Sally's Chris'mas gif' fo' Marse Fitz done come."

"Well, what is it?"

"A pinano, suh."

"Piano!"

"Bigges' ole pinano you all eveh did see!" His eyes rolled to include Susannah, his small arms flung wide to include all space. "Miss Melicent say no room in de parloh — no room in de po'ch — no room in de kerridge-house, even, foh any sech pinano. She say eff'n you all move out, bag an' baggage, de pinano kin come in, no ways else."

Sue was shaking with laughter, and Sedgwick turned on her accusingly.

"Well, it was you that brought up these

presents from Sally," he said. "Now come and see one!"

"Fitz did want a piano, Sedgie."

"What's the matter with the one he's always had?"

"It's old. It belonged to your mother. He wants one of those new grand pianos."

"You don't suppose he had the cheek to write and tell her so!"

"No. I did."

2

There had never been anyone in the family like Sedgwick's son Fitz, and nobody knew what to do about him. Easy enough to say it was the Yankee blood in him, his mother being Cabot Murray's sister. But while the son born to Cabot and Eden was oddly all Sprague, Fitz was neither Murray nor Sprague to any visible degree.

The Sprague men were strong and gay and unruly, enterprising, virile, and irresistible (even as Eden said) to women. The Murrays were a tough, adventurous, passionate, intensely masculine breed of men with a flair for making money. And the Days were likely to be bookish, thoughtful, homekeeping, loving people. Fitz didn't fit in anywhere. He was lazy and easygoing and idle, he never studied, he had never earned a penny, he had no ambition or aim in life, and he liked it that way. He didn't even fall in love, he said it was too much trouble. He had a strange sort of hobby, though. He collected songs.

He had learned how to write music on blank score paper, he had a true ear and a pleasant untrained voice, and he spent hours among the darkies learning and setting down their songs. More than once he had mentioned that he would like to go to New Orleans and Memphis and Charleston just to see what songs he could find there. But travel cost money, and Fitz never had a cent of his own, and Sedgwick wouldn't allow him to take money from his mother for any such nonsense as that. And so Fitz drifted, and sang his darky songs, and played any instrument he got hold of, and now and then he sulked a bit, and the girls were all disgusted with him.

It was very worrying for Sedgwick, who had gone into his own father's law office as a partner when the war ended, and by perpetual diligence and unlimited natural charm had contrived to make a living. Not that Fitz wasn't charming. He was. But it was a charm which sat amiably on its spine with its feet up, so to speak. Fitz hadn't an enemy in the world. Which just showed you, said his father, who had plenty and loved them all for adding zest to life.

When they reached the Sprague house in England Street the grand piano, still enclosed, legs and all, in its raw pine packing-case, stood impressively blocking the path which led from the gate between low clipped box hedges to the porch steps. Three men from the express company, Micah the Spragues' colored butler, Shadrach their gardener, and two little colored boys stood around it in attitudes of patient despair.

They all brightened visibly when Sedgwick and Sue appeared at the gate, and they watched the approach of the master of the house with cautious hope. The small colored child who attended him ran ahead into the house to announce his arrival, and Melicent came out on to the porch with a shawl around her shoulders. She was followed by Phoebe, who looked just like her mother and was nearly sixteen. Fitz was nowhere.

Melicent, who had once or twice rather wished for a grand piano herself, was not so sure now. She was pretty and brown-haired, and her mouth turned up at the corners and she was the first to admit that she adored Sedgwick to the verge of lunacy.

''Hello, darling!'' she cried at sight of him. ''Hello, Sue! What-*ever* are we going to do with this thing?''But even while she tried to look vexed it was plain that she thought the grand piano great fun. To Melicent almost everything was fun that had happened to her since her marriage to Sedgwick had rescued her from the gloomy household which had imprisoned her childhood. Both she and Phoebe looked to him for the instant solution of any dilemma. Their bright, waiting eyes were now full of confidence that a grand piano more or less would be nothing to him.

"Where's Fitz?" asked Sedgwick, eyeing the packing-case warily. "It's his problem, after all."

"He's gone down to the Carters', I think. He didn't say when he would come. But it can't just go on *sitting* there, can it!"

"And of course it won't be *quite* so big when it's been uncrated," Sue murmured at his elbow.

Sedgwick sent for tools and the men from the express company began to knock the crate apart, there in the path, while the family went in to look at the parlor and see what could be done there. It was not a small room, but it had been lived in a great many years, and things had accumulated. By actual measurement Sedgwick discovered that the piano would fit nicely into the corner to the left of the bow window, provided that several familiar pieces of furniture, including the old upright, were done away with. These were removed by Micah and Shadrach to stand somewhat at random in the middle of the library floor, and a way was cleared for Sally's gift.

Before these arrangements could be completed, however, Fitz turned in at the gate and came rather dazedly up the path. Sue was the first to see him, and she went out on to the porch and then, instead of hailing him, stood watching the lad who was, in spite of everything, her favorite of all the younger generation.

Fitz stood in the brick path between the low box hedges, gazing at the grand piano, most of whose dark glossy surface was now uncovered. He stood quite motionless, with his hat pushed back on his high, round forehead, just taking it in. Fitz was of average height, and slouched a little, not making the most of his inches. His eyes were a clear grey, with a dark-ringed iris, and long curving lashes enhanced their natural candor. His nose was straight and good, his lips sensitive yet firm, his face, broad at the eye level, narrowed to a boyish chin. His clothes were always casual, and yet he always looked exceedingly clean. Because his gentle voice drawled more than the rest of them did, they told him he talked like a darky, but nobody had ever heard him raise it for emphasis. As always, Sue's heart crinkled with foolish love of him.

Hypnotized by the piano, he failed to see her standing there on the porch looking down at him. With a last crack of wood and the scream of long nails wrenched loose, the pine case came away, and the men with the hammers and screw-drivers paused to regard him curiously.

"Would you be Mr. Fitzhugh Sprague, then?" one of them asked, with reference to the label on the board in his hand.

Fitz nodded, not taking his eyes from the piano.

"Then you're the feller it belongs to."

"Yes," Fitz agreed like a sleepwalker. "Oh, yes, we belong to each other." His thin, blunt-tipped fingers touched the shining mahogany lid which covered the keys. It rose on hidden hinges and dropped back soundlessly on little rubber knobs, and the harlequin keyboard was there. His right hand hovered and then came to rest almost timidly, and the piano awoke to sweet treble harmony in G. "Lordy," he muttered to himself. "Oh, Lord-a-massy, hear that tone." His left hand came home to the bass.

"How about givin' us a tune, sir?" suggested one of the men from the express company.

"Sure, what'll you have?" Fitz edged the still crated piano bench crosswise in the path with his foot and sat down on the end of it, his fingers wandering among the keys.

"Under the Bamboo Tree, maybe," said the man, and winked at his companions, deluded that the owner of so elegant an instrument would be unable to play anything less than a nocturne at best. But —

> "If I like-a you and you like-a me,
> And we like-a both the same,
> *I'd* like to say, *this* very day,
> *I'd* like to change your name —"

obliged the piano promptly, and their faces lighted up and they began to hum, and one of them beat time with his hat as though leading a whole orchestra. At first Fitz whistled softly under his breath. Then his crooning, plaintive baritone emerged almost imperceptibly into the open, and soon they were a fine quartette with the pedal going, and the three little colored boys piping up in perfect key.

> "If *I* love-a you and *you* love-a me,
> And *we* love-a both the same,
> One live as two, two live as one,
> *Un*-der the bamboo tree —"

33

It was purest ragtime magnificently played, and passersby on their way home to lunch began to linger, while Sue stood laughing on the porch and Melicent came out of the house to find that the song had spread to a cluster of beaming faces at the gate and was being echoed from within, where Micah and Shadrach under Phoebe's supervision were rolling the old upright along the hall towards its exile in the library.

The Bamboo Tree ended with a full choral effect, and Melicent ran down the steps and caught Fitz's arm.

"Do stop, darling, you're disturbing the whole neighborhood! Besides, the men can bring it in now, we've made room."

"Listen," said Fitz, his young face brooding and serious above the keys like a mother's above a cradle, and he played a major chord and allowed the strings to vibrate to the vanishing point on the still, cold air. "Listen to this," he said, and began a series of *arpeggi,* his fingers caressing ripples of crystal sound from the keys.

"Yes, dear, it's beautiful," his mother agreed affectionately. "But do come away now so the men can —"

"Isn't she a lady," he marvelled, slipping into a progression of chords in the whole tone scale. "Isn't she an angel? Listen to that —!"

"Fitz!" shouted Sedgwick from the porch, where Micah and Shadrach stood grinning behind him. "Leave it alone now, and let's get it into the house." At a sign from him the two colored men came down the steps and joined the express men, and they all laid hold on the glossy mahogany and drew the grand piano slowly from under Fitz's hands. He sat there on the crated bench and watched it go.

"Careful, now," he admonished them gently, and looked up at his mother. "Where did it come from? Is it you I thank?"

"Your Aunt Sally sent it."

"From *France?* How did she know that was what I wanted?"

"I told her," said Sue, joining them in the path. "It's from New York, she must have cabled. And it's your Christmas present, Fitz, you're not supposed to have it now."

"It's a little late to try and hide it," he remarked, watching its dignified progress up the steps of the porch.

"Fitz, darling, thank your Cousin Sue for going to so much trouble for you," his mother prodded him lovingly.

"I do," he said, and his grey eyes left the piano reluctantly again and came to Sue's face. "I always thank my Cousin Sue —

35

even without grand pianos. I'll thank her any day for just being around where we can look at her.'' And he rose from the crate and kissed Sue warmly on both cheeks, and then drifted away down the path to watch the piano being maneuvered through the front door.

''He's in a sort of trance,'' said Melicent with understanding and strolled towards the gate, her arm around Sue's waist.

''If I don't get along home fast,'' Sue said, ''Father will be sitting down to lunch without me. Dabney and Charl arrive this evening, you know. Miles is coming with them, but not Belle, her babies are still whooping.''

''Our Christmases get smaller and smaller,'' Melicent sighed. ''Each year now it seems as though somebody's babies are sick, or somebody has got married and can't come. This time we'll have Dabney's three, and five Murrays, and us four Spragues, and you and Uncle Ransom — that's not very many.''

''Four Murrays,'' Sue corrected her. ''Lisl isn't coming.''

''What, *again?* D'you mean to say Bracken is coming *without* her?''

''Sedgwick will tell you about it,'' said Sue, edging out the gate. ''I really must get home to lunch.''

3

It was true that the family parties seemed to diminish in size, in spite of the new babies.

Eden's eldest girl, Marietta, had married a professor at Princeton in September and was spending the holidays getting acquainted with his parents somewhere in Pennsylvania. Dabney's married daughter Belle had twins down with whooping-cough, in Richmond. His son Miles was nineteen, and a student at Charlottesville where Dabney himself had been teaching classes in mathematics ever since the school Ransom had once kept in Williamsburg went to pieces after the war. Dabney had learned to manage his artificial leg so well you could hardly notice, but pretty Charlotte Crabb had been glad to marry him while he still went on crutches during the siege of Richmond.

Dabney's Miles and Sedgwick's Phoebe

were cousins and had been playmates since babyhood. And while Sedgwick might in moments of discouragement compare his own changeling boy unfavorably with Eden's Bracken, Dabney had no complaints about Miles. Miles was a Day, through and through — tall and lanky, with a large humorous mouth and thoughtful ways, a natural student — a schoolmaster's son. He had taught Phoebe her letters, and then taught her to read, and they always gave each other books as presents, and watched the growth of their personal libraries with a miserly eye. Melicent, who had once known a great deal of Tennyson by heart, regarded her intellectual daughter almost with awe, and Sedgwick hoped fervently that Phoebe would outgrow it.

The Murrays arrived in Williamsburg at the end of the week, to find Dabney's family from Charlottesville already established in Ransom's house, and there was a great deal of kissing and laughter and reminiscence and the heartwarming, bloodstirring upsurge of kinship that family reunions can bring.

The Spragues came to supper the first evening, completing the circle which Ransom Day surveyed fondly from his armchair at the head of the table. He noted with regret the absence of babies from the festivities. There used always to be babies, it seemed to him. Who would be getting married next, he wondered. His clear, serene gaze came to rest on Miles and Phoebe, seated together on the righthand side of the table. Perhaps. They were only second cousins. But Miles was devoting himself tonight to his cousin Virginia Murray, who sat on his other hand. She came between Phoebe and Miles in age, as she would turn eighteen in the spring, and with a Court presentation in view she had suddenly become a young lady. Virginia was dark like her father, with a heart-shaped, minxish face, long, slender, soaring eyebrows, and a closed, mysterious, "grown up" smile. Ransom beheld her with a mild concern. A heartbreaker. Eden's daughter was bound to be that, but he was sure that Eden herself at seventeen had been less aware of her own potentialities. Virginia was wrapping Miles around her little finger just for the fun of it. Would Phoebe mind? Ransom brooded gently at his descendants and relations, silent himself in the candlelit merriment which ran up and down the long, glittering table.

His gaze caught the glance of Eden's husband, the Yankee Cabot Murray, and a look flashed between them — friendly, full of comprehension. Each of them recalled in that instant the first time Cabot had sat at this table, a stranger, but with Eden's heart already in his possession, and the long, bitter years of civil war still to come. Ransom smiled into his son-in-law's eyes, and Cabot smiled back affectionately. Once they had not known how to take this fellow, Ransom thought, but that was over now. A blind man could see that Eden was happy and content and still in love with her husband.

Ransom sought and found the face of their son Bracken, who had come with the shadow of his broken marriage upon him. The family were all being very careful not to stare at Bracken, the first among them ever to be deserted by his wife. Bracken seemed anything but self-conscious. He sat at the corner of the table between Phoebe and Sue and obviously entertained them both. How he resembles Sedgwick, Ransom thought, and what a queer thing inheritance is — or do I mean heredity? — but then, he thought, ours is a queer family, three lines all juggled in together — we've even got French blood, 'way back — perhaps it came out in Sally — perhaps it's in Virginia too — that smile, as though she knew something you didn't know — provocative — at her age — dear, dear, thought Ransom, poor Miles — poor lots of people, before she's safely married — and as for Fitz, something on his mother's side, I suppose, that we'll never know — music — yes, of course, music up to a point in all of us, and his mother did have a lovely singing voice as a girl — but music like a disease — that's not accountable —

"Tired, Father?" asked Eden's voice on his left, and her soft, warm hand was laid on his beside his plate.

"With all this fun going on?" he asked wistfully. "How could I be tired? You're very beautiful tonight, my dear," he added with his childlike, searching scrutiny.

"Thank you, Father." Her fingers pressed his. "My husband said the same thing, just before we came down stairs to supper. I'll begin to think it's true!"

"You were always prettier than Sally, I thought," he said, slipping back thirty-five years between breaths.

"You never said so before!"

"Didn't want to turn your head. Cabot knew it, though — didn't he!"

Cabot, who sat next to his wife as the custom was at these family parties, looked round at the sound of his name and demanded to know what it was that he knew.

"The difference between Sally and Eden when they were girls," said Ransom.

"Ho!" said Cabot with something like a

snort. *"What* a difference!"

"That's our beauty now," Ransom continued, nodding towards Virginia, and Eden's eyes were proud. "You've got your work cut out, giving that girl a London season. D'you want her to marry a duke?"

"Heavens, no!" cried Eden. "We'll bring her back, never fear! She's not like Sally either!"

"She's a flirt," Ransom warned them. "You wait. She even makes eyes at Sedgwick at his age, and he laps it up. Look at them!"

"Don't you worry about her, sir." Cabot smiled at his father-in-law's forebodings. "She's an honest little soul, and always thinks straight and for keeps like her mother."

"Aren't you pleased with us, Father?" Eden teased him. "Don't you think we're a credit to you, on the whole?"

"Yes, you are," he nodded, and his withered fingers clung to her hand while his gaze travelled down the table again, clouded, and came to rest. "I sometimes wonder where Fitz gets his odd ways," he remarked with apparent irrelevance.

Eden glanced quickly at her husband, and found his steadying, ironic eyes waiting. Then they both looked away, and Eden changed the subject from Fitz without replying.

Sue's seating arrangements had not permitted Melicent to sit next her brother Cabot, who was many years older than herself, a grown man for her childish worship which had never diminished. After supper when the family settled into groups and clusters in the drawing-room, she slid a possessive hand under his elbow and drew him away to a corner sofa, murmuring, "I want to talk to you."

"Well, of course you do," he agreed obtusely. "How are things, anyway? You look remarkably healthy, it seems to me."

"Really, Cabot, can't you say I look *nice,* or something?"

"It is nice to look healthy," he insisted. "Happy too. We're a lucky pair, you and I."

"Oh, Cabot, what's to become of poor Bracken?"

"He's going to London, as soon as we see McKinley into the White House in March."

"Yes, I know, but — his *life,* Cabot! It's ruined!"

"I hope not," he said briefly.

"Do you think he can get a divorce?"

"Might."

His jaw set grimly, his heavy, carven lips were hard. She could see that his son's trouble had hit him cruelly, but that he did not intend to expound to her his views on the subject. Melicent sighed.

"I'm not so lucky about Fitz, either," she said. "Cabot, will you help me?"

"If I can. Anything special?"

"Yes. I thought — now, don't jump down my throat, will you! — I thought perhaps you would be willing to give him a job on the paper."

"Fitz? Doing what, for heaven's sake?"

"Well, I thought — with Bracken going away, there might be a vacancy somewhere."

"My dear girl, Bracken was brought up in a newspaper office. Fitz never even saw the inside of one."

"Oh, I didn't mean in Bracken's *place,* I only thought — some one will have to move up into Bracken's place, and some one else will move up into *his* place, and so on, and finally there might be room somewhere at the bottom for Fitz."

"Bracken's departure won't mean a sort of General Post in the office, Melicent. And I somehow don't see Fitz as a leg-man, chasing fires and going round the police stations."

"Please, Cabot — I'm so worried."

"What does Sedgwick think about this?"

"I — haven't asked him."

He tried to see her face, for this was

serious. She would not meet his eyes, but sat winding her handkerchief round and round her forefinger and then unwinding it, only to begin again.

"Mean to say you've quarrelled with Sedgwick?" he demanded.

"Oh, *no!*" That brought her eyes up, shocked and limpid. "Sedgwick and I don't quarrel! It's just — we can't seem to talk together about Fitz any more. Sedgwick isn't — isn't *friends* with Fitz any more, Cabot, it's frightening, I've got to think of something. You see — Fitz is so *different.*"

"Yes, I know. He's not cut to the family pattern anywhere, is he!"

"It oughtn't to matter so much, so far as I can see. But it does, Cabot, Sedgwick takes it dreadfully to heart that Fitz doesn't seem to — fit in anywhere, teaching like Dabney, or — practicing law with his father. But I can't get Fitz to see how important it is that he should do something, and — you see, he doesn't earn anything, and looks to me for pocket money, even, and — that seems to make Sedgwick perfectly furious."

"Well, so it should."

"But what can I *do,* Cabot, I love them both so terribly, and I can't help seeing both sides of it. This — estrangement makes things very uncomfortable at home. Even

Phoebe feels it, and — it just can't go on. So I thought —"

"Well, how do we know that Fitz would come to New York if I offered him a job?"

"Sue might help. He listens to her. Sometimes I th-think she knows him better than I do."

"Jealous?"

"N-no. But he's always turned to her in the strangest way."

"Because she's always spoilt him."

"Perhaps. But you will give him a place on the paper, Cabot? To please me?

"Well, I'll think about it, my dear, you've rather sprung it on me, haven't you!"

4

That night in their bedroom Eden, hairbrush in hand, broke a thoughtful silence.

"Cabot, did Melicent speak to you about giving Fitz a job?"

"She did."

"Well, are you going to?"

"Don't know. What do *you* think?"

"I think it would be rather a responsibility, having him with us in New York. He's not like Bracken."

"He's not like anybody around here, either. That seems to be his trouble."

"Ought we to tell, Cabot?"

"What good would that do?" They gazed at each other, Cabot sitting on the edge of the bed with one shoe off, Eden brushing out her reddish hair with long, regular strokes. "Well, we can if you like," he said after a moment. "But it's going to come as rather a shock to everybody. And just how should we go about it? Shall I take Sedgwick aside and say, By the way, old man, nobody saw fit to mention it at the time of your marriage to her, but the fact is, my sister is not my father's child." Cabot shook his head. "He'll think I'm breaking up in my mind. Or shall I begin at the other end, with something like this: Once upon a time when I was about fourteen, my mother eloped with a vagabond violinist, and Melicent is the innocent fruit of their sin; my poor father found a sort of demented revenge in bringing her up as his own child after our mother died. It sounds, even to me, as though I were having hallucinations."

"It might help them to understand Fitz, though."

"In the circumstances, wouldn't they rather not?"

"Probably. I suppose it is too late now," Eden ruminated.

"Too late to change what's in Fitz's blood, certainly. Melicent had a touch of the same thing, before she fell in love with Sedgwick. As a child she always had a passion for music. A happy marriage seems to have more or less replaced it. Shall we try to get Fitz married, then?"

"Oh, Cabot, you are a chump! Anyway,

we made our decision years ago. Only you and I and Grandmother Day knew — and of course your father. Gran said not to tell. And Gran was always right. Now we're the only two people left in the world who know that you and Melicent didn't have the same father. Let's not say a word. But let's take Fitz under our wing. I think perhaps we owe him something.''

''It's Bracken I keep thinking of. What do we owe him?'' Cabot rose from the bed and came to her where she sat at the dressing-table, the brush in her hand. He knelt beside her and put his arms around her waist and buried his face in her neck and spoke from there, muffled and unhappy. ''Sweetheart, the Murray curse has come upon us. I have some idea of what he's going through, I was old enough to see what it did to my father when his wife left him for another man.''

''But your father loved his wife.''

''True. And until it happened, she was sweet and virtuous, unlike the Austrian. But the net result is the same. My father and my son, both deserted by their wives. What's wrong with us Murrays, Eden?''

''Don't be morbid, my dear. And anyway, *you're* safe enough, didn't you know?''

His arms tightened. She felt his lips against her throat.

"That doesn't help either of the boys," he said then.

After the light was out, Eden spoke again in the darkness beside him.

"Cabot. Has Lisl gone with another man — too?"

"Oh, Lord, you weren't supposed to know! I can never keep a secret from you, can I?"

"I don't see why I shouldn't know."

"Man's reasons, mostly. To save Bracken's pride."

"I always knew she was a slut."

"Eden!" He gathered her into a mighty hug with affectionate mirth. "I don't know where you learn such words, not from me!"

But Eden lay passive in his arms and nursed her wrath against Lisl.

"Tell me the rest of it now," she said. "Who is he? How did it happen?"

"He's got real money."

"Naturally!"

"Beside him, I'm a pauper. He's got half a dozen gold mines in California — came with a letter of introduction to me from that fellow Friedman in Chicago. Wanted to buy the paper out from under me and play politics with it. I managed to convince him that I wasn't for sale, but meanwhile Lisl's price-tag was showing and he took up with her."

"Where?"

"Oh, I got awfully tired of him very soon and passed him on to the Bennett crowd. It was at one of their parties that he met Lisl. After that, all I had to do was duck."

"Cabot, you mean you saw this thing coming and did nothing to —"

"I might have warned Bracken, I suppose, but they would only have had another row. All right, I confess I lay low and tried to set a trap for Lisl. And it went wrong. She got away. She was too quick."

"I don't — quite understand," Eden murmured.

"Eden, darling, I thought I foresaw that Lisl would betray Bracken with this Californian, yes, but I meant to catch her at it, and put her through the divorce court. Don't you see, if I could have got proof of her adultery Bracken was free. I preferred a scandal, if necessary, to what he was enduring from her, and I was pretty sure he would prefer it too. She beat me, blast her. She got on that damn' boat without giving me any evidence I could use in court. I think she saw my game, that's what hurts! Of course that fellow Hutchinson went on the same boat. They're made for each other, they're both tramps. She's going to show him Europe, and he's just the fool to enjoy it as long as his money holds out."

After a silence Eden said —

"Won't he want to marry her?"

"He's not quite fool enough for that," Cabot replied.

"Then what about Bracken? Must there still be a scandal?"

"What happens in Europe won't stink too loud over here, I hope. Anyway, she's gone, and Bracken's bank account won't be bled to death any more, and he isn't going to be harried into an early grave by a wife he hasn't been, as we say, living with, for some time. Maybe the boat will sink under the weight of her sins. Maybe Hutchinson will shoot her full of lead before he's through, he all but wore a brace of Colt .45's at Delmonico's! Let him have her, with our blessing. It's better this way, hard as it seems."

"But it still doesn't leave Bracken free."

"No. It only leaves him in peace. We shall have to trace them now, to get divorce evidence. It will be a long, expensive, legal business, I'm afraid, but we shall win in the end and write her off somehow." He shifted cautiously to lay his face against hers. "Oh, my poor dear — tears. Don't cry, sweetheart, he'll weather it. Bracken has the stuff he needs, he won't go under."

Her arm went round his neck, and she held

to him convulsively.

"I feel so *wicked*," she sobbed, "to be so happy and *safe* with you, when everybody else is so *miserable!*"

5

In spite of the extravagant gifts from Sally and the Murrays, it was a meager Christmas nowadays by the standards of Ransom's childhood. Ransom could remember when the family Christmases were spent at the Sprague plantation called Farthingale, which lay up the river near Westover and was burned down after Cold Harbor in '64. Ransom could remember a household of twenty guests and as many more darky servants, not counting the pickaninnies; great feasts which went on for hours, and dancing which lasted till dawn in a big south room with six french windows on to a Virginia garden, and the portraits of Grandfather St. John and Grandmother Regina looking down from the walls.

It was all gone now, and even the exquisite Regina's portrait was ashes. All gone, except these grandchildren of his own, dancing in the Sprague parlor in England Street while Melicent played waltzes for them on Fitz's new grand piano. Ransom's clear, farseeing eyes followed the drifting couples with interest; Miles and Virginia, Bracken and Phoebe, Fitz and Sue, Eden and Sedgwick, Cabot and Charl — odd how they had paired off, with Dabney sitting beside Melicent at the piano. Wasn't Miles going to dance with anybody but Virginia all evening? What would Phoebe think? Virginia wasn't for bookish, bedazzled Miles. . . .

"How long does it take to get presented at Court?" Miles was asking jealously.

"About three minutes. You place your right hand four inches below the Queen's and kiss the air four inches above it, bending very low meanwhile in a Court curtsey — and then you retire backwards, contriving not to trip over your train, and dipping curtseys as quickly and gracefully as possible to all the other members of the Royal Family who happen to be present, as you go. You must on no account touch Her Majesty's hand with your own, or with your lips. She hates that."

"And what then?" asked Miles.

"Then you either go on in dizzy splendor to somebody's train-party — that means one given specially for débutantes after their presentation — or else, if you haven't a strong constitution, you go straight home in a state of total collapse and have a hot bath with ammonia in it and go to bed for the rest of the day to recuperate."

Miles opened his eyes.

"From what?"

"Excitement. Of course I don't expect it to prostrate *me* like that, but Marietta says the tension on the staircase and in the Picture Gallery — that's the last room before the Presence Chamber — is really devastating, particularly if the Queen herself is receiving the presentations. She doesn't always. Usually it's the Princess of Wales or Princess Christian, deputizing. In that case you don't kiss her hand, you only curtsey."

"It sounds very complicated," Miles puzzled. "Why is it so important?"

"Oh, Miles, really, what a heathen you are! It just *is*, that's all! No English girl is anybody at all until she has been presented, and most of them come to it straight from the schoolroom and almost die of stage-fright. Of course it won't be so bad for me," Virginia added a little complacently, "because I've already seen something of the world in New York. At least I don't expect to chuck the bunny in the corridor, like one poor girl the year Marietta made her début."

Miles was horrified.

"You mean —?"

"Right at the feet of a Gentleman-at-arms!"

"B-but what did they do?"

"Well, the girl felt better, of course — pretty shaky, but definitely improved. And everybody sort of made a screen by turning their backs and pretending not to notice, while a tactful footman in powdered hair and white gloves came and tactfully mopped it up with a tactful cloth and tactfully retired. And everybody said it always happens at least once, and drew a breath of relief that now it was over."

"I should think she would have just died in her tracks," said Miles.

"Well, if she had, a powdered footman would have tactfully removed the corpse, and everyone would have moved up one place," said Virginia. "It's the waiting that destroys you. The Diplomatic Circle goes in first, and that keeps the rest of you hanging about for hours with your train over your arm."

"Can't you sit down?"

"Part of the time, if you're lucky."

Miles pondered it, as they danced. It was to him another world. He was beginning to feel as though he held Royalty itself in his own arms.

57

"Will Bracken go too?"

"Oh, Bracken goes to a levée and makes his bow to the Prince of Wales — wearing knee breeches, silk stockings, and a velvet coat at two o'clock in the afternoon! Wouldn't you like to see him do it?"

"I reckon what I really meant to ask was how long will you be away," Miles reflected.

"All summer. Maybe long enough to get some hunting in the autumn. But the Drawing-Room is in May."

"I'd like to go to London, I think," said Miles, though it had never occurred to him before.

"Well, come on, then!"

"Oh, not this spring," he qualified hastily. "I have to finish school first."

"This is the year to go. It's the Jubilee. Victoria has reigned for sixty years, think of that!"

"Heavens, how old is she?"

"Turning seventy-eight."

"Nearly as old as Grandfather Day," he marvelled. *His* grandmother lived to be a hundred and one. Think what you could remember! And now you can tell your grandchildren that you saw Queen Victoria!"

"Oh, Miles, don't let's talk about my grandchildren *yet!*"

"Would you marry an Englishman, if you got the chance?"

"Of *course* I shall get the chance, idiot, I'm going to take London by storm and have dozens of proposals!"

"Well, but would you?" he persisted, and his arm tightened a little.

Virginia looked up at him through her eyelashes and smiled her closed, mysterious smile.

"Would it ruin your life if I did?"

"Well, I — I — I —" Miles heard himself stammering and pulled up desperately. "I'd miss you terribly," he got out.

"Every Christmas!" she nodded.

"We might — see more of each other — after I graduate. That is — if you — I'll never forget you as you are tonight!" he stumbled on, caught in the maze of a new emotion. "That dress — the way you've got your hair — you're the most beautiful thing I ever saw! Please come back — won't you?"

The music stopped, and they stood still, both rather breathless, looking at each other for a moment before they realized that another waltz was not going to begin at once, and they moved away side by side to a sofa against the wall.

Bracken saw Phoebe's eyes follow them and he said —

"Don't worry about Virginia, my dear, she's just practicing."

"She's so lovely," said Phoebe sincerely. "She makes me feel dowdy and plain."

"Didn't that gown you're wearing come from Cousin Sally in Paris?"

"Oh, yes, but we made it over, sort of, because it was so low in the neck, and now it doesn't look quite right, somehow — not like Virginia's."

"Virginia is an awful flirt, but it doesn't mean anything, you know."

"Oh, I don't mind," she assured him stoutly. "Miles and I aren't — we're just friends."

Meanwhile Eden had been saying to Sedgwick as they danced —

"I'm afraid Cabot is going to miss Bracken more than he anticipates, during the coming year. Do you think Fitz might like to take a job on the paper to fill in?"

Sedgwick gave her a surprised glance, and seemed to come to a quick decision.

"It might get him out of the rut," he said. "Would he really be worth anything to Cabot, though?"

"We won't know till we try. He might come for six months, and see how it goes."

"Did Cabot suggest it?"

"We were talking about it last night," she

evaded. "He takes this business of Bracken's very hard. I thought perhaps if he had another boy to train — one of the family — it might help to occupy his mind —"

"I'm at my wits' end about Fitz," Sedgwick confessed. "So I'm willing to try anything now. Shall I have a talk with him about it?"

"Let's leave it to Sue," Eden suggested. "Let's get Sue to put it to him. She knows how to handle Fitz."

"Better than I do, I admit! And about her going abroad with you in the spring — I think it's a fine idea, and I've told her so."

"I'm glad, Sedgwick. You'll miss her here, I know, but it's only for a few months."

"Do you think you can persuade her?"

"I'm going to try. And I've still got an ace up my sleeve."

6

Eden played her ace next morning when she and Sue settled down for a chat in Sue's bedroom after breakfast. The letter, she explained, had only been to break it gently.

"The fact is, Sue, honey, you've just got to go with Virginia in my place this year. Marietta has started a baby and isn't at all well and has become an absolute fraidy-cat and vows she'll die if I'm not near her the whole time. So then Virginia threw a perfect fit for fear she'd have to give up being presented and miss the Jubilee, and I promised her you'd go with her instead of me."

"But I don't know anything about going to Court and all that!" Sue protested. "I'd be paralyzed with fright!"

"You won't have to go to Court. In fact, you can't, the lists will be closed. My dear friend Lady Shadwell has arranged everything and is going to act as Virginia's sponsor, just as she did for Marietta three years ago. But no child of mine is going to travel without a chaperone. All you'll have to do is go with her to balls and house-parties and see that she doesn't go on too much of a spree at the dressmakers'. And you'll play hostess for Bracken too, of course. We've engaged a suite of rooms at Claridge's Hotel, so you won't have the bother of housekeeping.''

Sue was looking utterly bewildered.

''But, *Eden*, I've never stayed at a hotel in my life!''

''And it's high time you did. Virginia has already been abroad half a dozen times, and Bracken knows London as well as he knows New York, it's a second home to both of them, and so you can rely on them for everything. What's more, you'll have the time of your life with them! Bracken gives the most delightful little parties, and he said himself that you'd look very sweet at the other end of the table. You must come to New York a while before sailing, and we'll get you some clothes — just leave all that to me, please, you're not to touch a penny of your own money from the time you leave Williamsburg till you return.''

''B-but Father —'' Sue began feebly.

"Father seems stronger than he was last year, doesn't he? Now, honey, don't be a stick-in-the-mud, *Sedgwick* thinks you ought to go, you know he does!"

"He wants me to see the other Farthingale, down in Gloucestershire."

"Yes, you must do that for him, he asked me to years ago and I've never got round to it, I'm ashamed to say. Bracken can ask Cabot's handyman in London to find out all about it — a Mr. Partridge at the Temple. He'll write the present owner and arrange for you to visit the house when it's convenient. If they're nice people you might accept an invitation to stay, later on. They might allow Bracken to send a man down to photograph the place for Sedgwick, he'd like that. And speaking of Sedgwick — he's willing that Fitz should come up to New York and work for the paper and see how he likes it. It was Melicent's idea. She thought it might help Fitz to find himself. Do you think you could persuade him to come?"

Thus adroitly diverted from her own appalling prospects, Sue agreed to talk to Fitz without delay, and the sisters conferred carefully as to how best to put it to him. While they were still closeted, they heard Sue's piano being played downstairs.

"There's Fitz now," Eden said. "Melicent

said she'd send him over this morning. You'd better go down and deal with it, he always listens to you, and Sedgwick is pretty well distracted with him.''

Sue went down the stairs slowly, feeling as though a strong wind had blown through her. Herself to go to London, Fitz to go to New York — which was going to be worse?

He looked up at her from the piano as she entered the drawing-room, rose and kissed her cheek, and settled back on the bench.

''This thing wants tuning again,'' he muttered, striking chords.

''Yes, dear,'' she agreed absently, and stood beside him, her hand on his shoulder, wondering how to begin.

''Mother said there was something you wanted to see me about,'' he suggested, his hands still moving on the keys.

''Fitz, honey — they want you to go to New York for a while. Bracken's got to be in London — and they want to have one of the family in the office with Cabot, and — Miles is too young.''

''I couldn't leave here now,'' said Fitz unargumentatively. ''My piano has just come.''

''They want you to go next week, with Cabot and Eden.''

''Hm-mm.'' He shook his head. ''Got me a

best girl now, name of Steinway.''

"Fitz. They want me to go to London with Virginia in the spring.''

"Don't you do it. Much too far.''

"I'm afraid I've got to. Eden can't, because Marietta is having a baby.''

"Good for Marietta. Didn't lose any time, did she!''

"Don't you see, Fitz? We're in for it, both of us. But I would have some time in New York before we sail.''

"Mean you've gone and given in to them?'' he asked in surprise.

"Yes. And so must you, this time.''

"Why must I?''

"Sometimes it's best to give in to things, Fitz. Besides — I'd feel better about my part of it if you were going to be in New York too, this spring. I wouldn't feel so strange.''

His hands came to rest in silence. He sat looking up at her thoughtfully.

"You dead serious about this?''

"Yes, Fitz.''

"You *want* me to go to New York?''

"Yes, Fitz.''

"Kind of interferes with my plans,'' he ruminated. "I figured on doin' a little real composin', now that I've got that piano. She sings to me, she does. Want to hear one she sang?''

Sue nodded and he turned back to the keyboard.

"She calls it *Sun Goin' Down on Me*," he said, and almost beneath his breath he began to sing the plaint of an old darky man who feels his days drawing in.

Tears rose to Sue's eyes as she listened; swift, childish, understanding tears, both for the patient dolour of the words and the melancholy beauty of their setting, the invention of this odd, footling lad she loved. . . .

"Ef de sun set red on a weary day,
De skies will clear ef de mornin's grey,
  An' dat's what I hope fo' me.
Ma shadow gettin' longer 'crost de grass,
Cool ob de evenin' done come at las',
  De sun goin' down on me. . . ."

Sue put her arms around his neck from behind and laid her wet cheek against his.

"Oh, Fitz, honey, that's the nicest one you've ever done!"

"Why, look at you, Cousin Sue, if you aren't crying!" He pulled her down on the bench beside him, an arm around her waist. "You get all the dirty jobs around here, don't you. 'Make Fitz see he's got to stop foolin' and take this job in New York,' they said, didn't they! 'You talk Fitz into it, he always listens to you' — was that what they said? All right, honey, Fitz hears you, dry those tears, now. I'll go to New York, or Timbuctoo, whenever they like. And by the time you get there I'll know my way around and we'll paint the town, huh? Yessir, we'll go to all the minstrel shows and eat peanuts and throw the shells on the floor, and — and we'll go to Grand Opera too, that's what we'll do, and I'll blow you to champagne supper at Delmonico's out of my salary — huh? Don't you cry, now, honey, we'll live through this, both of us, and I'll do what you want, and you do what they want, and by this time next year I'll get myself fired and you'll have Virginia married off and we'll both be right back where we are now, and then maybe they'll let us alone again, huh?'' He took out his handkerchief and dried her eyes and then, still holding her in one arm — ''Listen,'' he said, and his right hand began making chords —

" 'Mid pleasures and palaces, though we
      may roam,
Be it ever so humble, there's no place
      like home —''

Sue lay awake a long time that night, in

the room she and Eden had shared as girls. Alone in the dark, she faced her trouble squarely, as she always did. And she knew beyond any doubt that it wasn't the strangeness of buying a wardrobe in New York, or the dread of sea-sickness on the North Atlantic, or the unknown terrors of life in Claridge's Hotel, or shyness of the English family now in possession of the house called Farthingale — it wasn't any of these, half as much as it was the intolerable prospect of those empty days when it would be impossible, for the first time since the war ended, to see Sedgwick or hear his voice for weeks on end. This was what it was to be only his double first cousin after all, and not his wife. She had no right to insist on staying here beside him, he had no right to go with her. They were severed, all over again, by their close blood tie. Sedgwick belonged to Melicent, not to her. And so she must journey alone to the old house in Gloucestershire where Great Grandfather St. John Sprague had been born, and try to bring back to Sedgwick something of what he wanted to see.

Sue pulled the pillow over her head and wept the loneliest, bitterest tears she had shed since her stricken teens. And over the way in England Street, Fitz sat with all the doors shut and one lamp burning and the soft pedal down, playing, playing, playing — taking leave of his lady, his angel, the grand piano.

PART TWO
SIR GRATIAN

London   *Summer, 1897.*

1

It was Sedgwick, though, who accompanied Sue to Washington on the first leg of the journey in March. Bracken was there, reporting the inauguration, but his time was too full for him to make the additional trip to Williamsburg. Though Sue insisted she could perfectly well find her way to Washington alone, at her age, Sedgwick wouldn't hear of such a thing, and Melicent entirely agreed that he should drop everything and deliver Sue into Bracken's care at Willard's Hotel.

It was with a kind of guilty joy that they glanced at each other as the train began to move. Sue's eyes were very bright above her fur collar, Sedgwick's smile had a quirk in it. He dared to voice what was in both their minds.

"I feel as though somebody ought to be throwing rice at us," he said.

"Oh, Sedgie, what a thing to say after all these years!"

"And we're still not old enough for it to be entirely safe."

"You mustn't say that."

"It doesn't do anybody any harm, my dear, for me to admit now and then that I have never stopped loving you." To his horror her shining eyes filled, overflowed, and tears rolled down her cheeks. He had almost forgotten how Sue cried, without any warning, her quivering face quite undistorted, looking like a rain-wet flower. "Honey, *don't!* I never meant to upset you, I only said —"

"It's all right." Her hand pressed his briefly, then put it away from her. "Don't baby me, Sedgie, I'm not quite responsible today. Too much excitement, I reckon —" She turned her head from him, to look out the window. The tears stopped, as if by magic.

He sat beside her in silence, his dread of the separation which was ahead of them growing with every mile. He still believed that it was right for her to go abroad now that the chance had come again. He still held to his lifelong determination never to try to keep her selfishly to what was at best an arid sort of companionship, however precious it was to them both. But he found himself wondering these days how he could ever have made a life for himself without it. Because Sue was there, in the same town, smiling and sweet and cheerful, not crushed, not grieving, not bitter, he had found with innocent, loving Melicent a form of peace and happiness. But already the prospect of even a few months empty of Sue's presence had made him feel drained and frustrated and irritable. And now a cold, stealthy fear was invading his midriff — suppose something happened, suppose she never came back, suppose. . . .

His quick, impatient spirit, disciplined so long, rose insurgent. They were all right as they had been, why must Eden suddenly upset the applecart, creating a situation which dragged to the fore old aches and agonies lulled by custom and routine and security? He and Sue could manage so long as they were left alone to do without each other in their own hard-won way. But now to be wrenched apart like this, jerked back to consciousness of what they really meant to each other, forced to find a new philosophy and a new endurance — and all just because Marietta was having morning-sickness and thought she was going to die!

But even while rebellion seethed within him, the habit of a lifetime prevailed, and he produced a casual remark to restore equilibrium.

"Bet you were journey-proud last night and didn't sleep a wink," he said, and her dimple showed.

"I was. But Eden says she always is, even going back and forth to Washington. On the other hand, she's never seasick. Do you think that runs in the family too?"

"Sure, you won't be seasick. They say champagne is good for it. Apparently if you're drunk enough you just don't care!"

Their bad moment passed. And as the train sped northward through country famous for what had happened there more than thirty years before, he talked on, quietly but vividly, spreading before her his memories of cavalry days with Jeb Stuart. On a road to the right, just after you left Richmond, lay Yellow Tavern where Stuart had got his death wound; from Gordonsville and Orange, Lee and Jackson had led their army to the Wilderness; at Culpeper the same bedraggled army had licked its wounds after Gettysburg; Sedgwick's mother and sister had waited in the baking heat of Bristoe while the cannon at Manassas boomed; and at Manassas itself Sedgwick had first heard gunfire, and there the Federal Army had twice broken and fallen back on Washington. Sue listened enthralled.

He had never been willing to talk about the war right after it ended.

They found Washington gone rather flat after the inauguration but Bracken had got tickets for the theater and that night they saw Mrs. Leslie Carter in *The Heart of Maryland*. Although Sue knew considerably more about the war than Mr. Belasco, who had written the piece, her mood at the theater was as uncritical as a child's and she wept unashamedly over the tangled skein of Mrs. Carter's unhappy love. Only after it was over did she say thoughtfully, "We didn't really behave much like that, did we, down our way." Sedgwick remarked with a grin that he had noticed the villain was a Yankee. To which Bracken replied that he knew at least one true story where the Yankee got the girl. But none of them knew that their Yankee had won his Eden, without any of Mr. Belasco's complicated heroics, in the shadow of the rope which awaits any secret agent in war time.

The play had filled their evening, and had even caused Sue to overlook for a time that tomorrow morning she must say Good-bye to Sedgwick and see him start back to Williamsburg, while she and Bracken waited for the New York train. That moment was upon her all too soon. Sedgwick took her hand and said, "Well, honey, take care of yourself —" and then they both discovered that they didn't know how to say Good-bye to each other for more than a few days. With Bracken looking on, Sedgwick bent and kissed her cheek, and found his throat rather tight. "Don't you get lost," he said, and was gone, before she had found a word to comfort him.

So then it was Bracken sitting beside her in a train, and Washington lay behind them, and Sue began to long childishly for a sight of Eden in a strange world. Bracken, who had his own thoughts, was unusually silent, and she forgot her private misery in contemplation of his. She stole sidelong glances at him — the thick straight hair and long profile, the mobile brows and generous, well-cut mouth — he could have been Sedgwick's son as he sat there. And mine, Sue thought. Sedgwick's son and mine might have been like this. . . .

Bracken turned and caught her looking at him, and his face relaxed into a smile.

"Sorry," he said. "Did you say something?"

Sue smiled back quickly and shook her head.

"Are you tired?" he asked gently.

"Not very."

"It's a beastly long trip," he sympathized. "Mother will tuck you up with a cup of tea and a hot water bottle when we get home."

"Oh, come, Bracken, I'm not senile!"

Bracken laughed.

"Maybe I was feeling a bit senile myself," he said. "I've had a very aging time, Aunt Sue. And I don't mean inaugurating McKinley, either!"

"It will be easier now, won't it?" she ventured.

"Much. I thought for a while I'd have to light out for the Klondike or somewhere, but the London office is a better idea."

"You — like England, don't you?" she queried, seeking reassurance on what was ahead of her. "That is — you all seem to spend a lot of time there."

"You'll like it too," he promised with understanding. "It's easy to feel at home there. I was only seven years old the first time they took me there, and Virginia wasn't even born. I'd had measles and was very peaky, and they were worried about my health. Father took a house in Buckinghamshire and got me a pony and a groom and turned me loose. I'd know that place, foot by foot, if I saw it again now."

"And you got well."

"I flourished to such an extent that I

haven't been ill since then! I suppose England is some sort of ancestral memory, with our family. Our roots are there. Virginia feels the same way about it that I do.''

"It's our Anglo-Saxon stock," said Sue. "Sedgwick is like that too. And when I was very young I used to write stories laid in England, though I really knew nothing about it. The first story I ever sold was about London in the eighteenth century. Cabot bought it for the Trenton paper.''

"I never heard about that," he said, interested. "Have you got a copy of it?"

"Somewhere.''

"Well, now you can do another story about England, first hand. Just where is this house Cousin Sedgwick is so set on your seeing?"

"In the Cotswold Hills. I've got it all written out.''

"It's lovely hunting country," said Bracken. "I had some good days there only two years ago, with the Badminton pack. We'll all go down from London and see it in the spring.''

She felt that he was making an effort to entertain her, and laid her hand on his sleeve.

"Don't talk if you'd rather not. You must have things to — to think about.''

"I have a great many things I'd rather not think about! You needn't be tactful, Aunt

Sue, because my wife has left me. She had already left me, in fact, some time ago.'' His lips twisted. ''I ought to be used to it by now!''

It was difficult to know what to say to that. You couldn't point out that there were lots of other girls, because Bracken was not free to fall in love again. You couldn't say Good Riddance, because that cast reflections on his judgment in the first place. And you couldn't say I'm Sorry, because he so obviously wasn't.

While she hesitated he spoke again.

''But it's going to be dashed inconvenient, losing my amateur status like this,'' he said.

She had got rather well acquainted with Bracken by the time they reached New York. He was quick and gay and charming, but thanks to Lisl he had a biting, defensive quality which reminded Sue of Cabot at the same age when he had first come to Williamsburg before the war. Bracken had been thoroughly trounced by life before he was thirty. He was taking it pretty well. But it seemed to Sue that he would have been better off with less hard discipline.

She found Fitz acclimatizing himself in all directions with surprising ease. His innate serenity was quite unchanged, but the seeming listlessness which grew out of his being a misfit at home and feeling obstinate and defensive about remaining so had vanished. His soft Virginia drawl was if anything even more noticeable than it had been, but a lot of new words and expressions had colored it. Fitz had discovered vaudeville, where people sang songs and danced to them. Already his head was full of ideas for more songs of his own which a man in blackface or a pretty girl in ostrich feathers and flesh-colored tights could sing and dance to. Sue had not been in the house a day before she was sitting beside him again, at Eden's piano now, listening to new tunes he had thought up.

Almost simultaneously all New York had discovered a thing called musical comedy, a theatrical innovation from Daly's, London, imported by Daly's, New York. *The Geisha* was its name, and on Sue's second evening in town they all went to see it. Fitz sat through it silent and absorbed, and Sue herself was so fascinated that she failed for once to be completely aware of his mood. When they got home he sat down at the piano and, beginning with the *finale,* worked his way back through the show, playing by ear each number as he came to it, in reverse order, fumbling sometimes, muttering at his mistakes, and cursing his memory when it lagged.

In the dining-room supper had been laid out — welsh rarebit in a chafing-dish over a spirit-lamp, sandwiches, cakes, a fruit compote, lemonade and grape juice, and on the sideboard whiskey, brandy, and cracked ice. The rest of them listened, drifting about with their plates and glasses in their hands, while Fitz's drink stood untouched beside him. Sue saw that he was quite possessed by the evening's performance, and it occurred to her that Fitz might write a musical comedy of his own some day. It was no more improbable, really, than it had once seemed that she herself would ever publish stories under Harpers' exalted imprint. She wondered about the chorus girls. But it would not be as though Fitz were up there singing and dancing too. He would only write what they sang and danced to. Besides, some of them looked quite nice.

The next night they all went to the new Weber and Fields Music Hall, where the bar was subordinated to the theater as entertainment, and where, contrary to music-hall custom, drinks were not sold while the curtain was up, and a lady need not fear to hear vulgar language. Again Fitz took in the show in almost motionless silence. Again when they returned to the house he reproduced by ear the songs they had heard on the stage.

"That Lottie Gilson," Sue ventured cunningly when he paused. "Isn't she pretty!"

"Who?" said Fitz vaguely, flexing his fingers above the keyboard. "Oh, Gilson. It's a bad lyric. It ought to go like this." And he played Lottie Gilson's song for them, rewriting it as he went, and they all agreed it was much better his way. Bracken said why didn't Fitz send her the new version, she might be grateful, and it might Lead To Something.

"What, me?" said Fitz, and grinned warily. "You tryin' to get me arrested?"

2

Bracken, Sue, and Virginia arrived in London early in April. There was trouble brewing in the Balkans, where Turkey was bullying Greece, and Crete was in a state of bloody rebellion against Turkish rule. The Italians were attempting less successfully to bully the Abyssinians, and Spain was waging ruthless war against the insurgents in Cuba. Germany was holding its imperial centenary in Berlin, and the Kaiser and the Czar were openly siding with the Sultan against Christian Greece. British relations with South Africa were becoming ''strained to a point which might lead to eventualities'' — a diplomatic euphemism which delighted Bracken's journalistic soul — and General Kitchener was leading the Egyptian Army in a successful campaign against the Khalifa and his Dervishes on the Nile.

But England's Queen Victoria had gone for her annual holiday on the French Riviera, and London was preparing for the Jubilee, and the season's débutantes were trying on their Court gowns and rehearsing their Court curtseys.

One of the things which Cabot Murray most firmly believed in, both as editor of the *New York Evening Star* and as a man of wide social influence, was the necessity for solidarity between the English-speaking nations — though he never allowed it to sound as dull as that. Instead of the Britannia-Columbia labels often attached by cartoonists to white-robed goddesses of heroic build, he preferred the John Bull-Uncle Sam conception: two brothers of one house, quite capable of having sharp words together, even of landing the other fellow with a bloody nose, but — it was a big But — instantly standing shoulder to shoulder with their backs to the same wall and hitting out as one man if a third party tried to interfere or make capital out of what was only a family brawl.

Cabot himself had always felt keenly a sense of his own kinship with the land from which his forefathers had come, and his children were as much at home in England as in their mother's native Virginia. He promptly resented the term Anglophile when

84

applied to himself or his policy. It was not Anglophile, he maintained, to recognize and respect the old racial tie, the common stock, the long mutual belief in certain fundamental rights and privileges, some of which had been even more jealously guarded in the island than in America. Uncle Sam had made innovations and improvements. John Bull had obstinately stuck to some things which were better not lost. But basically the link was there, bone-deep, surviving the inevitable dust-ups and misunderstandings any large, career-minded family was heir to.

The *Star* habitually carried a larger percentage of foreign news than most of its competitors. A weekly news letter from London as a Sunday feature was to be one of Bracken's chores when he arrived there. In it he was to chronicle the special doings of this gilt-edged Jubilee Summer designed to pay tribute to the beloved old Queen who had outlived so many of her enemies and redeemed so many of her mistakes, and who was, after all, Victoria.

Bracken and Virginia viewed the familiar murky skies and dismal docks of Liverpool with blind affection, and they kept their faces to the window-pane on the way up to London in the boat-train and in the cab as they drove from Euston Station to Claridge's in Brook

Street. Not more than half of what they said was intelligible to Sue, but she listened eagerly, trying to learn, and looked at everything they pointed out to her, and did not have to pretend to be excited too.

The new American Ambassador, Colonel Hay, was a friend of Cabot's from the days when Hay had been Lincoln's secretary, and he had always kept an interested eye on Bracken's brilliant progress. Mrs. Hay was presenting one of their daughters at a May Drawing-Room too, and it became a point of honor with the girls to achieve an attitude of blasé composure amounting to indifference to the gay social program before them. Sue frankly blinked at the glittering Embassy doings. Her naïveté endeared her to the Ambassador and his wife, and the young Murrays and their Aunt Susannah were made much of in Carlton House Terrace.

The three daughters of Lady Shadwell, Eden's friend, had all been safely married off long since, and she welcomed the opportunity of sponsoring a débutante again. Sitting beside Sue at the dressmaker's in Bond Street while Virginia was having her fittings, she remarked more than once that she would be presenting one of the prettiest girls of the Season, and inquired in affectionate detail after Marietta and Eden. Marietta, Sue gathered, had not been so much fun because she was shy. Lady Shadwell's own girls, she confessed quite cheerfully, had been plain, poor dears. Virginia's insouciance, so amusing to everyone, sprang from a knowledge of her own good looks which she would have been a stupid prig to deny, and the natural confidence in her world with which a happy childhood had endowed her. She was spoilt, maybe, by indulgent parents and a devoted brother. But it gave her a kind of touching buoyancy which caught at the hearts of sadder, wiser people and made them long to cushion her somehow from the disillusionments they felt were bound to come. Lady Shadwell was before long so taken with her that she proposed to give her a train-party at her own house in Park Lane after the presentation — one of those festive occasions when all one's brothers and one's cousins and one's beaux with their female belongings turned up to hear about one's triumph and one's sensations, and everybody ate an enormous high tea, rather in the spirit of a treat after the dentist.

Mr. Partridge, who was Cabot's solicitor, with offices in the Temple, had some Fleet Street quarters ready for inspection. Bracken decided to settle in there at once without looking further and gather his London staff, which was headed by the same agent the *Star* had depended on for years, a sombre, efficient man named Nelson. Meanwhile Bracken contemplated the lovely little war in Crete wistfully — Richard Harding Davis was already there — but Bracken refrained from rushing off to see it too because his father had impressed on him that the establishment of the London office came before anything else. Also he had promised Eden to see that Sue enjoyed herself in England, and that nothing should be spared to make Virginia's presentation summer a success.

The house known as Farthingale, Mr. Partridge was able to report, was now owned by a Major Sir Gratian Forbes-Carpenter, who had recently inherited it from his aunt, now deceased, and who had promptly put it up for sale. By a fortunate coincidence, Mr. Partridge continued, glancing triumphantly over his spectacles at the three attentive faces before him, Major Forbes-Carpenter was now in England on sick leave, having been severely wounded during the battle of Firket on the Nile, in which — Mr. Partridge had been given to understand — he had played a distinguished part. The Major had replied cordially to Mr. Partridge's letter of inquiry — here Mr. Partridge produced the Major's letter and handed it to Bracken with a little flourish — and doubtless it would be convenient, if one so desired, to arrange a meeting with him and discuss a visit to the house in question, which, as they would perceive by the Major's letter, remained exactly as it was at the death of the Major's aforesaid aunt the previous year.

"What sort of house is it, did you find that out?" asked Bracken as soon as he could get a word in edgewise, and Mr. Partridge produced the Estate Agents' sales advertisements with another flourish. " 'Old stone-built residence with gabled, stone-tiled roof,' " Bracken read aloud from it. " 'Near a picturesque Cotswold village. Hunting with the Heythrop. Lounge-hall, oak-panelled dining-room, library, 2 other reception rooms, 7 principal and 5 secondary bedrooms, master's bathroom, servants' hall and servants' bathroom, convenient domestic offices. Gravitation water. Delightful grounds with roses, herbaceous borders, kitchen garden, orchard, roomy stables and paddock, stream which provides good fishing. About 14½ acres. Freehold for sale. Will let furnished. Immediate possession.' " He referred to the letter in his hand. "Writes from the United Service Club," he said. "I might try and get him to come to dinner at Claridge's and we'll talk about going down to see the house." His eyes went back to the advertisement. " 'Will let furnished,' " he reflected, and glanced at Mr. Partridge under a slanted eyebrow. "Heythrop country, eh? Not too far from London for week-ends?"

"Well, of course it's not Surrey," said Mr. Partridge cautiously. "A good deal would depend on the train service."

"You might look into that," said Bracken, and Mr. Partridge made a note of it, and Virginia said, "Oh, Bracken, what a lark! A house of our very own, this summer — *could* we?"

"Well, the place has got a bathroom!" Bracken grinned. "I must be able to get back and forth to Town, of course. Farthingale would have to be your show during the week, if we took it. You and Aunt Sue would have to run it."

"It would be fun," said Virginia without hesitation. "We could have people down to stay. After all those lovely house-parties we've gone to, we could have house-parties of our own!"

Sue looked from one to the other helplessly. House-parties. Without Eden there to tell her what to do.

When Major Forbes-Carpenter came to dine with them he was not, to Virginia's disappointment, wearing the uniform of an officer of Kitchener's Egyptian Army, sword, headdress, boots, spurs, and decorations. Like any British officer on leave, he was in mufti, and at the moment conventional black and white evening dress. But the Major's evening dress had been cut by the best tailor in Savile Row and was worn with a cavalry air; and he walked, of necessity, with a cane which could not disguise a most interesting limp.

Virginia and Sue had spent some time reading up on the Nile campaign in back numbers of the illustrated papers, assimilating as they went that General Kitchener, Sirdar or Commander-in-Chief of the Egyptian Army, had turned it into an excellent fighting force under British officers. The battle of Firket, they learned, was considered a triumph of strategy. ''Rough and difficult was the road by which the river force advanced that dark night,'' they read, ''so dark that foothold among the boulders had to be felt for. Orders were given in whispers, no talking in the ranks, no smoking — thus did Hunter's division advance upon the doomed and sleeping village. Meanwhile Murdoch, commanding the flank attack, made his detour, timing himself so as to strike when Hunter struck. The flanking column, while still on the desert heights, grew apprehensive that they would be late for the battle and covered the last four miles at a gallop. With the first ray of dawn the blow fell. Torn by the fire of the infantry, by shrapnel, and by the hail of Maxim bullets, the surprised Dervishes made a good fight of it as they always do, but what remained of them was overwhelmed and swept away like chaff.''

Bracken said captiously that it was bad dispatch-writing, much too flowery. But he had no fault to find with the facts about their Major Forbes-Carpenter and his brigade of Soudanese Lancers. ''The senior officer was twice wounded,'' they read, ''first by the butt of a rifle which had been fired at him without effect while he was pursuing an Emir, and afterwards by a spear in the upper leg. The effective work done by his brigade in twice breaking through the Dervishes as they were gathering for a charge was of the greatest value.''

Sue and Virginia regarded their guest with round-eyed respect when he arrived at Claridge's. He was a slender man, not as young as he had been, not as tall as Bracken, square-shouldered, lean-hipped, with a moustache more closely clipped than was the Mayfair fashion. In spite of his long illness from wounds, he was tanned bronze by the Egyptian sun. His hair was grizzled round the ears, and his direct grey eyes were hooded like an eagle's, the full upper lid making a straight line across the iris, which gave him a look of frowning severity until he smiled. He was known affectionately to his troops as Carpers, because of his martinet ways — "Button up, chaps, Old Carpers is coming!" the word would run ahead of him through the camp. But he was as watchful of their comfort and their honor as a mother, they would tell you, and the two of them who had risked their lives at Firket to get him out from under his dead horse and bring him back under fire to their own lines could have been matched a dozen times over and to spare.

Virginia of course made eyes at him during dinner, and he gave her his ready smile which showed his small, even teeth, and answered her carefully boned-up questions about the Nile campaign with patient courtesy and invisible amusement. Meanwhile, he wondered about Miss Day. She said so little and she looked so sweet. He had never seen anything like that dimple at the corner of her mouth, and her low voice with its soft Virginia cadence he found quite enchanting. Miss Day. And what on earth were the men in America made of that this delightful creature should be still unmarried?

At this point the Major's own thoughts surprised him. He was anything but a ladies' man, and since the death of his wife in India years before, he had been all soldier, demanding active service with his men rather than cushy staff jobs, existing on a minimum of leave, living for the Army and the service he rendered to it till he had become, he was sure, a very dull dog indeed. The death of his elderly Aunt Sophie had been no grief to him, as he had not seen her for years, and he knew perfectly well that there was no sentiment in the making of the will which left Farthingale to him. She had long been a widow, childless, almost the last of her family. She had no other heirs, except an ancient cousin or two, who had received legacies. As her sister's only child, he was the logical beneficiary. But her income stopped with her death and she had not been able to leave him the money to keep up the estate as she had done in her lifetime. Liking comfort, and always considerate of her aging servants, she had put in the bathrooms and a telephone only a short time before she died. Farthingale was no good to a man who had no family and no intentions or entanglements, only a small income besides his pay, and no prospect of more. The only thing to do was to put the place on the market and perhaps later on invest the money he got for it in a much smaller house into which he would, he supposed, retire and bore himself to death, if he survived his usefulness in the field.

Something of all this he explained to them with engaging frankness, and assured them of his willingness to let Farthingale to them for the summer if it met with their approval when they saw it. He heard with the keenest interest that their ancestor St. John Sprague had been born in the house in 1749, and listened attentively while Bracken diagrammed how it was that neither his own name nor Sue's was Sprague. The Major admitted that he had no idea how his aunt, whose name was Twombley, had acquired the house. So far as he knew, she had always had it. As a boy, he had sometimes been taken there by his mother to stay, at Easter holidays and so on. . . .

He broke off in the middle of a sentence, as though struck by a startling idea. He looked from one to the other of them, his eyes coming last to Sue, who looked back inquiringly.

"I say," he began with sudden diffidence. "Would you care to — well, no, I suppose not, but just in case — that is, we might all go down there for Easter, you know, if you've nothing better to do."

"Oh!" cried Virginia. "Oh, Bracken, *let's!*"

The Major's eyes waited on Sue. He sat leaning a little forward, waiting for her to speak. But Sue, for whom things sometimes began to whirl, was silent, so he said —

"I think you'd be comfortable there, I'm only just back from having a look round myself, and they did me quite well. My aunt's cook stayed on in the house as caretaker, and she could wangle enough maids in the village to look after us. As a matter of fact, I'm afraid the old lady rather goes with the house. I haven't the heart to turn her out, at least until it's sold —"

"*Of course* we'd be comfortable!" said Virginia, and trod on Bracken's foot under the table to indicate to him that she simply had to go to Farthingale for Easter.

"Won't you please say you'll come?" the Major entreated Sue.

"Why, yes — if the children would like to —" she began uncertainly. "I think it would be delightful."

"Are the children willing?" he demanded of Bracken, with his severe eagle's glance.

"Quite willing," Bracken said at once. "If you're sure it will be convenient to you."

"That's settled, then," said the Major with relief. "I'll write Mrs. Poole at once to

96

engage some maids and have things ready for us. My aunt had a very poor opinion of men, and the indoor staff has always been entirely female. By the way, when is Easter this year?''

''Roundabout the nineteenth, I think,'' said Bracken. ''Will that give you enough time?''

''Too much time,'' said the Major with another look at Sue. ''I shan't know what to do with myself till then. I say, couldn't we take in a theater together or something like that in the meanwhile?''

''Aunt Sue would go to the theater every night of her life if she could,'' Virginia said, a little patronizingly.

''Splendid! Let's go and see Mrs. Pat!''

''As Lady Hamilton?'' Bracken raised his eyebrows and flicked a glance at his charges. ''Do you think they're old enough for that sort of thing?''

''Oh, possibly not,'' said the Major, taking him quite seriously. ''Well, then, what would you like to see?'' he inquired of Sue.

''*Rosemary,*'' she replied with a note of defiance.

''But, darling, you saw that last Tuesday evening!'' Virginia objected, and Sue's dimple showed.

''I liked it. I want to see it again.''

''*Rosemary* it is'' said the Major, without

97

asking anyone else's preference. "We'll dine at Gatti's, what, and go on to the play. I'll see about the tickets tomorrow. Which night would suit you best?"

Sue looked appealingly at Bracken. It was one of the times when she felt her inadequacy as Eden's substitute, for she was sure that Eden would have been able to keep all their engagements in her head, whereas she herself had to write them all down in a little book which was never to hand when she needed it. But Bracken took out his own engagement book and consulted it and said not before next Wednesday.

"Wednesday, as ever is!" cried the Major, who apparently had no need to consult his own engagements. And — Five days to go, he thought. Five days too many. Good Lord, what's the matter with me, I'm thinking like a subaltern in love! His hooded, eagle's eyes went back to Sue. In love. But that's impossible. My leave is up in July.

3

Sue, all unconscious, went on serenely if a little bewilderedly through her fascinating days as Virginia's chaperone. On the Wednesday morning at breakfast as they laid their plans for the day, before Bracken set off for Fleet Street, he said —

"Isn't it tonight that Aunt Sue's conquest is taking us to see *Rosemary?*"

Virginia laughed, and Sue looked uncomprehending.

"Why, *Bracken,* what *do* you mean?" Bracken demanded of himself, in exaggerated tones. "Look at her, Ginny! Pretending she doesn't know she has the Major hog-tied!"

"What nonsense," said Sue firmly. "It's Virginia he wants to see, and you know it."

"Virginia, my neck!" said Bracken inelegantly. "Virginia never worked harder in her sweet life and got nowhere! It's you he's after, Aunt Susannah, and I've got my eye on him, I don't trust the Army as far as I can kick it!''

''Now, Bracken, you've made her blush!'' cried Virginia, accepting her own defeat with entire good nature, and at that Sue got really pink.

''I don't think it's nice of you to make fun of an old lady,'' she objected, not quite sure how to take them, even now.

''Fun!'' shouted Bracken. ''I don't call it fun to have *two* giddy enchantresses on my hands at the same time! We brought you along to lend respectability to Virginia, if possible, and what happens? You go and hook the Army!''

''But that's not *true*, Bracken, I —''

''Did he ask *me* what I wanted to see tonight? Did *Virginia* get any say-so? Not at all! You said *Rosemary,* and to *Rosemary* we go!''

''Well, I'm s-sorry, I never meant —''

''Now, Bracken, stop teasing her!'' Virginia went to the rescue. ''It's all right, darling, we don't in the least mind seeing it again. Behave yourself, Bracken, isn't it about time you went to work?''

''By the way, when *is* Easter this year?'' remarked Bracken *sotto voce,* glancing at the clock and picking up his hat. ''Oh, I say, that's *much* too long! Whatever will I *do* with myself till then? Yah, it's a way they have in the Army!''

There was a silence when he had gone. Then Virginia caught Sue's troubled, doubtful eyes and laughed again.

"Honey, you look so *guilty!*" she said. "You mustn't mind Bracken, and anyway, I think it's cute."

"But Virginia, the Major didn't *really* take any notice of me, that is, he was just being kind because I'm not your mother, and he could see that I felt strange here — he's a very kind-hearted man, you can see that," she pointed out earnestly.

"Oh, very! I'm sure the Dervishes would agree with you!" said Virginia solemnly.

He sent them flowers, which arrived while they were dressing for dinner. Camellias for Virginia — and for Sue, red roses. Bracken's left eyebrow flew up when he saw them, and Virginia pinched him, hard, so he said nothing. Sue seemed quite unconscious of the significance of red roses, and only said how well they went with her new evening bodice, and how had he guessed what color she was going to wear. Virginia, choosing a pink silk muslin dress in honor of her camellias, wondered who was going to be chaperoning whom, at this rate.

Sue always shied from décolletage when dining in a restaurant, and her evening bodice, which was of pale blue Russian net over grey glacé silk, had a high blue satin collar-band topped by a lace Toby-frill which framed her face. The long sleeves were tight from the ruffled wrists to above the elbow, where a wide double net ruffle made fullness to the shoulder. The red roses nestled into a blue satin sash above an embroidered silk skirt. Virginia's silk muslin was cut with a low V in front, and her long rucked sleeves and kilted flounces edged with lace were the very latest thing. They both wore short brocade theater jackets banded with fur, and carried fans.

The Major was proud of his handsome party and ordered champagne, which Sue had learned to appreciate, and Bracken alleged that his favorite aunt was rapidly becoming a drunkard. Sue protested hotly that she never had more than one glass, and Bracken agreed that she didn't as a rule have one in each hand, if that was what she meant. The Major laughed delightedly at this rude family wit, and began to feel as though he had known these people all his life and would never part with them again. Their easy, unself-conscious affection for each other, their unfailing tenderness even in their teasing, bewitched his lonely heart into yearnings it had not felt for years. He had not been aware that life could be like this, warm and light and laughing, or that women could be so easy to talk to and to entertain.

His own young wife, bearing and losing her first child in India all those years ago, had become in his memory a rather fretful wraith whom it had not been much fun to live with. These hearty American women with their expensive pretty clothes and their spontaneous gaiety and their cosseted confidence that all was for the best in this best of worlds, were a revelation to him. And Sue, with those white threads in her coppery hair and some mysterious wisdom in her eyes seemed to him a dream come true — a dream he had hardly known he had. Not young enough to be frightening to a man of his years, but still young enough. . . . Now, look here, the Major told himself severely, if you go on like this, old boy, you'll be making a complete ass of yourself.

But before the evening was over, Sue, having had it pointed out to her at breakfast, began to perceive that the Major was perhaps being a little more than kind to her. No one else but Sedgwick had ever listened to her least remark with just that same attentive concern. His lingering gaze, so unlike

Sedgwick's in everything but a sort of wistful adhesiveness, drove her own steady eyes more than once to her plate or to some distant point in the room. She didn't dare look at Bracken or Virginia, for she felt in them an increasing alertness, a sort of suppressed expectancy which embarrassed and confused her. Sue had never been courted before — poor Sedgwick had hardly had time to begin before that terrible day when Ransom had told them it was impossible, and then everything had been over for them. But Sue had the born writer's sixth sense about things which lay outside her personal experience, part intuition, part atavistic memory. She had written love scenes in her books, and apart from Sedgwick she knew, in her cultivated imagination, how a man in love behaves. And the Major, apart from the champagne, was behaving besottedly.

Small as her worldly experience had been, by the time she went to bed that night at Claridge's Sue was forced to recognize that by some freak of male nature, the Major was very much taken with her astonished self. She had done nothing, she was sure, to bring such a thing to pass. She had minded her own business entirely, while Virginia tried her best to flirt with him. Well, then. But the Major, incredibly, was not interested in

Virginia. It was to Virginia's Aunt Susannah that his seeking, telltale eyes returned again and again. And Sue's reactions came in a rather unexpected sequence. But he doesn't know anything *about* me, she thought first. But I must be *years* older than he is, she thought next. And then, belatedly — But no one could ever take Sedgie's place.

Their engagement calendar by then left little room for additions before Easter, but the Major did turn up, looking more than pleased with himself, at several social functions to which they also had been invited. Once, at a tea in Grosvenor Street, he arrived in a group of officers who had been to the Palace for an investiture, wearing full dress uniform and blazing with decorations. He was modesty itself under the smitten stares of Sue and Virginia. But somewhere at the back of his level eyes, in the laughter-wrinkles at their corners, there lurked the look of the cat with canary feathers sticking to its whiskers; he was caught, but the bird was inside — Sue had seen him at his best, wearing the uniform he loved.

They did go again to dinner and the theater with him. He had got tickets to the new Savoy opera this time, where Mr. George Grossmith was behaving characteristically as the highly improbable king of a highly impossible country called Vingolia. Never having seen Gilbert and Sullivan, Sue never missed them from this imitation product, and Virginia had long adored the agile Mr. Grossmith.

On the Thursday before Easter Sunday, Bracken and Sue and Virginia descended from the train at the little station of Upper Briarly on Cotswold — it was the line which ran from London to Oxford to Worcester, and so the service had proved surprisingly good for so remote a place. They found the Major, wearing well-aged tweeds, waiting with a carriage and pair driven by a coachman in his aunt's brown livery. He had left Town a few days before them in order to see that Mrs. Poole had done everything necessary, and he was determined to entertain his guests in style if it took a year's pay.

They drove across the wold at sundown to the village of Upper Briarly, which was a mile and three-quarters from its railway station, in a fold of the hills where the infant river Windrush ran. The road was built of yellowish Cotswold stone, and low stone drywalls bordered it on either side, enclosing green fields where black-faced lambs frisked on match-stick legs. The fruit trees were in bloom — snowy pear and plum, and pink peach blossoms in the sheltered corners of the farmyards. The hedgerows were freshly green, and poplars and chestnuts were leafing, though oak and elm were backward still. Pale primroses starred the roadsides, and wood anemones and daffodils showed under the trees. The weather had been unsettled and cool, with sharp showers, but the sun was setting red and the Major said it would be fine tomorrow.

The far horizon was the vast parapet of the wold, but the village of Upper Briarly lay snug beside the river at the foot of a wooded slope. No Briarly could well be lower, so it was the only one, and the clear cold stream ran right down the middle of the single street, dividing it into two. Low green banks sloped to the water's edge on either side, and a low stone bridge flung its triple arch across just above where the old ford was. Trout lay idle in full view against the clean gravel bottom, their noses upstream. Beyond the bridge four white ducks rode serenely on the water while others preened themselves on the grassy bank. The old grey village houses faced each other across the broad thoroughfare. Vines garlanded their narrow mullioned windows, wall-flowers and forget-me-nots bloomed at their feet. The gables were small and sharp and capriciously placed in the steep slate roofs. A child in a clean white pinafore looked out of a cottage door as the carriage passed, and waved, and they all waved back.

A mile the other side of the village they could see at a distance a great colonnaded Georgian mansion set on a low hillside above the river, with acres of lawns running down to the water. The Major pointed it out as the favorite country seat of Lord Enstone, and said the Earl was in residence with his family. "I had one of the boys with me at Firket," he went on. "The third son, I think he is. Led his wing with great dash and got a spear in the wrist. Lucky not to lose his arm, but it wasn't bad enough even to get him sick leave to England. Lord Enstone is a great old boy himself, one of the very best. They'll come to call while you're here, I shouldn't wonder."

"Jolly," said Virginia. "What is his wife like?"

"She's been dead for years, I can hardly remember her. It's a largish family, rather scattered now. Lord Alwyn, the eldest son, lives here at the Hall, being a bachelor — he's very keen on hunting. And there's a younger boy, down from London for Easter — the one that's reading for the Bar. There is also a remarkably beautiful daughter," he observed for Bracken's benefit.

"Do you know the Earl well?" asked Sue, impressed.

"Oh, rather, he used to command my regiment! Retired now, of course, but still going strong. I dined there last night, as a matter of fact. Always do, when I'm here. He and Aunt Sophie were cronies, so he's interested in what becomes of the house, you know. Just a bit stuffy at the idea of Americans having it, but I fixed that, I think!" He smiled round at them all, amused, and added to Bracken, "You'd find him interesting, if you can get him talking. He's convinced we're for it in South Africa, now that the Balkans have boiled over. Greece hasn't a hope, I'm afraid."

As a journalist, Bracken had been reluctant to leave London even for a day now that news had begun to trickle in from the Thessalian frontier. Turkish ships had touched off the war by firing on Greek ships at Prevesa, and the Turkish Army was advancing through heavy fighting towards Larissa, which was believed to have fallen by now. The Albanian troops around Janina had revolted against their Turkish masters, and the Greek fleet might attack Salonika any day. But the European Concert of Powers, dominated by the Kaiser and the Czar, was blockading Crete in a wrongheaded attempt to let the Balkans fight it out among themselves. There was an uneasy feeling in London that it lacked only an incident now to bring on the general European war which everyone had begun to dread without being able to see why it should seem so inevitable in an enlightened age like the present. It was easy to blame the Balkans, a notoriously contentious region. But people were also inclined to blame the Kaiser, who always fished in troubled waters.

Since the Fleet Street office of the *Star* was still in process of organization and not yet functioning as an independent unit, Bracken had decided that it would be better for him to take a holiday now, leaving Nelson to carry on in the usual way, than later on when his personal routine was more fixed. "I don't care what you do or how you do it," Cabot's parting injunction to him had been. "All I care about is what results we get. I want more news faster. Use money. Use the cables. Use the brains you got from me."

But it was with an envious sigh that Bracken had seen an eager young man named Hilton set out for the Balkan front, where he himself desired to be. Hilton couldn't whip the London office into working order for him, and Hilton couldn't play nursemaid and master of ceremonies to Sue and Virginia. So

Hilton went to Thessaly and Bracken went to Gloucestershire, and that was the way it was meant to be.

Another mile beyond the Hall gates they turned left and entered an avenue of greening chestnut trees which nearly met overhead, and then Farthingale was before them. Grey stone it might be, but Cotswold stone, which weathers so that it has a golden patina as though perpetual sunlight lay across it. The house was irregular in shape, high at one end, for the original Elizabethan manor had been added to as the family prospered, and an L jutted out. But two hundred years had passed over the new part, now, so that it was weathered and vineclad like the rest. While its windows were larger, they marched in the same narrow mullioned rows as in the old façade. The roofs were as steep, the gables as sharp, the chimneys as simple.

Jonquils and forget-me-nots bloomed against the stone foundations. The grass seemed an almost artificial green, with the last molten rays of the setting sun in long stripes across it. The lawn ran smoothly to the edge of a brimming stream, too wide for jumping, which flowed towards its meeting with the Windrush in the woods half a mile away. The far bank was pale with primroses, and great chestnuts overhung the water.

Beyond the house on the other side the lawn was bounded by a long flower border, not yet come into bloom, where in the middle distance a very old gardener in a faded blue smock was working, assisted by a very young boy with a red wheelbarrow.

"Oh, Bracken!" cried Virginia, and squeezed his arm. "It's *ours!* I want it!"

"Looks like a picture postcard," said Bracken, while something inside him, possibly the blood of St. John Sprague, turned warm and quick, and he felt a stinging in his eyelids.

Sue said nothing as they helped her down from the carriage, because her throat was tight with longing for Sedgwick, who should have been there to see it too.

The door was opened by a smiling country girl in a parlormaid's black dress and white apron, and a starched cap with streamers. Tea, she murmured, was in the drawing-room, and did the ladies wish to come up to their rooms first? Virginia said the ladies were dying for their tea, and the rooms could wait. The parlormaid, whose name was Melchett — she had found it hard at first to answer to anything but Lucy — took their coats, lifted one respectful glance to Bracken's face, and vanished. The kitchen was enlivened to hear that the American ladies were both pretty and smelled heavenly, and the American gentleman was young and had smiled at her as kind as could be.

Farthingale was indeed an Elizabethan manor, but not so much so that great bare black rough-hewn beams overhung you everywhere, or bent to crack your head if you were tall. The oak staircase rose broad and uncarpeted from the hall, with a carved griffin on the newelpost. The drawing-room was in the new wing, and was lighted from two sides, one of them a westward bay. Its walls between fluted pilasters were covered with damask in a gentle blue-green. The worn brocade hangings and upholstery were dark gold. A log fire burned on the hearth beneath a carved oak overmantel. The furniture was easy and cushioned, and a long sofa and armchairs were grouped around the fire where the tea-table waited, bright with old silver. The last of the sunset was shining through the stained glass heraldic shields which were let into the upper panes of the bay.

"Welcome home!" cried Virginia, as though the house had spoken. "Sir Gratian, you'll never be rid of us now! It seems to me we've all been here together before!"

"I'm glad," he said simply, and seated Sue behind the tea-urn where a spirit-lamp had been lighted.

Almost in silence she made and poured their tea. She put sugar in the right cups, and left milk out of Bracken's because he preferred it that way — but her mind went on hearing Virginia's light words. *We've all been here together before*. But Sedgwick too, Sue insisted inwardly while she poured their tea. This warmth of heart, this peace, this sense of *return*, were in Sedgwick's blood too, stronger than in any of them. It was Sedgwick who had remembered about this house in England and wanted to see it. Already she was writing in her mind the letter she would begin to Sedgwick as soon as she was alone. And do you remember, she would say to him in the letter, how at sunset the light comes through the stained glass in the drawing-room and makes little rainbows on the carpet all the way across towards the fire. . . .

4

Bracken, for all his good humor and seeming spirits, was sleeping very badly and had times of black depression which he always contrived to keep to himself. He had discovered some time ago, when the trouble with Lisl first began, that work was the thing — work, and good solid human companionship, leaving no time for brooding, no room for despair. The multitude of details connected with the new office came in handy to keep his mind off himself. Sue's childlike enjoyment of everything she saw and did kept him busy devising schemes for her entertainment. But he hankered at the same time for some more violent preoccupation — such as war.

There was always at the back of his mind a submerged conviction that if he could only go to the war in Greece something might happen, something swift and merciful and final, that would save him years of worry and fortitude. He knew that this was morbid, and would not allow himself to contemplate it at any length, but he knew it was there. If only he went out to Greece and got killed in the line of duty, how simple everything would be.

Overtired now from the extra work he had taken upon himself in order to clear the way for this Easter holiday, when he was already beyond normal human endurance, he slept hardly at all the first night at Farthingale. There was no fault to find with the bed in the master's chamber where he lay. It was a fine four-poster hung with India print and recently endowed with a new mattress. They had all jealously inspected each other's quarters when they went up to change before dinner, and all the bedrooms proved to be chintz-hung and cheerful with fireplaces and four-post beds in each one of them. The old moulded timbers still crisscrossed the ceilings upstairs, except in the master's room, where they had been covered by charming Gothic plasterwork.

After the light was out, Bracken lay watching the dying fire and thinking of what Virginia had said when they arrived. *It's ours,* she said, at her first sight of the house.

And then — *we've all been here before*. Well, yes, they had in a way, through St. John Sprague — that gay and gallant man who had gone out to America in 1771 to claim an unknown inheritance. St John had stayed there, sending back for his favorite sister Dorothea to join him, for he preferred what he had found in far-off Virginia to the role of younger son at home. He served as aide to George Washington during the War of American Independence and married a famous Williamsburg beauty and became a lively legend to his descendants. And he must have carried in his heart until he died a memory of this Cotswold house which had given its name to the brick plantation mansion built by his uncle before him, another younger son, who had made a modest fortune in tobacco and willed it to his nephew St. John. Lying there while the firelight faded, in the very bed where St. John might have been born, Bracken wondered. . . .

The house had a tranquil aura which came of the happy, uneventful lives it had sheltered. It was a fortunate house, he was sure, as some houses undoubtedly are, just as others are unhappy and haunted. Even the Major's nebulous Aunt Sophie must have enjoyed herself there, even after she was old and lonely. You wouldn't be altogether lonely there, for the house in its gracious memories of old dreams and old griefs and old joys which had crystallized in wood and stone and silver and worn, enduring fabric would be company in itself. By the end of the summer, Bracken thought drowsily, if they stayed on here, the house would own them too, it would be a part of their lives, they would never be able to go away and forget it and the things they had thought and done and learned within its walls. A house you came to love was like a person, and loved you back, and then you belonged to it forever after. In less than twenty-four hours Farthingale had taken them to its heart, for they were its lost children by the blood of St. John Sprague in their veins. The house had not forgotten him. And when the Sprague line ran out, as it had done in England two generations ago, and strangers moved in, the house had been patient with them, and kind to them, for they were not to last long, the Sprague blood would still bring Spragues to Farthingale, the house had only to wait. . . .

When Bracken roused, the room was full of early sunlight and for a moment he had to think where he was. It had been nearly dawn when at last he dozed off, and his head felt thick and his body seemed glued flat to the bed in an ecstasy of weariness. He turned on the pillow just to see if he really could detach his spine from the sheet, and buried his face in the cool linen with some idea of sleeping till noon in blissful holiday sloth. But his stretched nerves denied him sleep again, beyond the minimum exhaustion demanded. He began to think of the Fleet Street office and its problems and decisions — because if he didn't put his mind on that at once he would be thinking of Lisl and the man from California. He pulled the pillow over his head and swore. Not here. Not in this nice clean house on a holiday in spring. And then he remembered that the Major had mentioned riding horses lent by Lord Enstone's stables for his use during the visit. He rose and shaved and dressed and went in search of them. A ride before breakfast never hurt anybody.

The Farthingale stables, at the back of the old wing and across a wide paved courtyard from the kitchens, were quiet and deserted at that hour, as he had anticipated. He found his way in through the harness room and came upon several sleek hunters in roomy loose boxes who regarded him with friendly interest.

"Hullo," said Bracken aloud. "Do you speak English?"

The horse nearest him breathed heavily in

his direction as though in applause. Bracken accepted the tribute with thanks, saddled, and led the animal outside. It was a glorious morning, even as the Major had prophesied, and the early mists were burning away under a warm sun.

"We shall now go out and hear the first cuckoo and talk about nothing else all day till everybody hates us," said Bracken to his mount and swung into the saddle.

Riding down the chestnut avenue, he looked back at the house just before a bend hid it from sight, and then rode on very thoughtfully. Virginia was right. He had done that before. Strange how a little scatterbrain like Virginia could sometimes without even trying utter profundities. It was all familiar to him — the powerful horse between his knees, the damp smell of the spring day, the pale warmth of the English sun — even the odd little village, which was still half asleep when he came to it, though the ducks gleamed white on the water above the bridge, and a cow ambled down the righthand road followed by a very small smocked child with a long stick. The child smiled bashfully at his greeting, and walked crabwise to watch him pass.

He went on through the village and turned into a grassy lane beyond it, letting the horse take its own pace. Soon they came to a place where the hedge left off and a stone wall had not yet begun and went through it, away from the lane, up a baresided hill towards the sun.

But you can't see a world like this and not be happy, Bracken said within himself. You can't dwell on past idiocies and future dreariness with the sun striking bang into your silly face like a gong. Or can you. Apparently you can. All right, then, suppose you have messed up your life till it can almost be said you haven't got one at all. You knew everything there was to know, didn't you. Nobody could tell *you* anything about women! You knew better then any of them, and Lisl was a misunderstood angel of light, a blasphemed saint, a brand from the burning — and so on. Bosh. You knew better, even then. What you had for Lisl was a plain old-fashioned case of biology. You were too well brought up, that's your trouble. You should have spent more time out on the tiles in your extreme youth. But you were a very self-righteous young man, and instead of coming out in boils you got married to Lisl, and it serves you right. Or does it. No, I don't really think I deserved all this. I don't really think in this case the punishment does fit the crime. I demand commutation of sentence. I shall appeal to a higher court. If I can find one. Hullo, somebody else can't sleep, I wonder who it is.

Coming towards him at an angle to the sun was a small figure on a tall horse. Bracken turned to intercept it, for he always felt the need of company in these dark moods, and rode down the slope. It was a boy about twelve, he judged as they came nearer to each other — a boy wearing tweed knickers and jacket and a shooting cap, with an excellent seat on a spirited bay hunter much too big for him.

"Good morning!" Bracken called as soon as he was within range.

"Good morning, sir," the child replied rather primly. He had a strange, delicate face, with a sharp, clean jaw line and very large, rather distrustful blue eyes.

"What's on *your* conscience?" Bracken inquired easily, out of long confidence in his ability to make friends with any child and set it telling him the story of its life. He was rewarded by a wide smile, as the boy took his meaning and replied —

"Oh, I slept all right! But I have to get up early if I'm to wangle one of my brother's horses. I'm not supposed to ride them."

"Did you saddle that brute yourself?"

"I can, you know. All but getting the girth

in. I made the stable boy give a pull on that.''

''You'll get him sacked if you're not careful,'' said Bracken.

''I hope not. But Edward *would* be cross if he knew I had Thunderbolt out!'' The boy's hand stroked the glossy neck fondly, and his eyes ran over Bracken's horse. ''You must be staying at Farthingale. Are you the American who may take it for the summer?''

''I am. Name of Murray. Who are you?''

The boy hesitated a moment before he said, ''Campion is my name. Lord Enstone is my father.''

''I see.'' Bracken recalled the Major's remarks about the large family at the Hall. ''Then your brother Edward is Lord Alwyn, I suppose.''

''Yes. Didn't you sleep well? I've heard people don't in a strange bed.''

''Well, no, I didn't. I thought a ride might do me some good. Mind if I join you?'' he asked rather wistfully.

''I'd be glad. That's Sunbeam you've got there. She can go like the wind. Shall we let them out?''

The boy was off on the great racking horse, with a glance and a wave over his shoulder. Bracken tightened his knees and Sunbeam followed her stable-mate, her mane streaming. They pounded down the slope and through a wooded patch and came to a low stone wall which Thunderbolt took like a bird with Sunbeam close behind.

"Hi!" yelled Bracken. "Ought you to jump him?"

The only answer was another wave of the boy's hand, and the wild canter went on, across a field, over a brook, into another grassy lane and straight at a five-bar gate. There was some kind of fumble, Thunderbolt pecked badly, hit the top rail hard, and fell on the landing side, throwing his rider clear.

Bracken pulled up, rather cold around the stomach, and leaped out of the saddle, vaulted the gate, and ran towards the small tweed figure on the ground. The cap had fallen off, revealing two plaits of hair, reddish gold, which had been pinned up under it. The child was a girl.

She sat up slowly before he reached her, and her face was white and scared as she glanced round for her horse.

"Are you all right?" Bracken dropped to one knee beside her. "You must have tried to lift him too soon. It was a damn-fool thing to do, anyway. Are you all right?"

"It doesn't matter about me. Get Thunderbolt up and see if he's hurt."

Bracken laid anxious hands on her, feeling

the sharp little bones through the tweed jacket.

"But are you sure —"

"Edward will kill me if I've lamed his horse. Please get him up —"

Bracken went to Thunderbolt and at the second attempt the big horse got to his feet and stood breathing rather hard, with one foreleg bent at the knee.

"Look at his off-fore!" she gasped, still sitting where she had fallen, braced on one arm, watching them. "Oh, what *will* Edward say!"

"Probably only sprained." Bracken ran an expert hand down to the fetlock and the horse nuzzled his shoulder inquiringly.

"He wants to be friends!" she said in surprise. "He doesn't always take to people. You know horses, don't you!"

"A little. He'll be all right in a few days, I think." He came back to her and knelt beside her on the ground. "How about you, now? Lucky you didn't break your neck."

"Edward says I'm bound to some day. They keep saying I'm too young to hunt with them and then they say I'm too old to ride astride, and I don't really know where I am. These are my brother Gerald's shooting clothes. He's quarantined at school with measles and can't come home for Easter. Bad luck, isn't it!''

Bracken sat back on his heels, looking at her. His face was very still, as though he listened to something a long way off. When he spoke his voice was low, as though some one near by was asleep.

"Frightful luck. How old are you?"

"I shall be sixteen soon."

"Do you often do things like this? You're practically a young lady now, you know."

There was not a trace of coquetry or female awareness in the troubled glance she gave him. She was somehow neither child nor maiden, sexless, ageless, and remote in her odd clothes, like a choirboy's voice. He thought he had never seen so unspoilt a creature, as lacking in self-consciousness as a bird. She had thick, upward-curving eyelashes, golden like her hair. Her mouth was perfect, with long, coral-tinted lips, each exactly the same width, closing lightly with a slight droop at the corners — not a merry mouth.

"That's what Miss French thinks. She's my governess," she was saying.

"Miss French is dead right for once in her life. It won't do, you know, you'll have to give it up. Promise?"

"Just for fear I'll break my neck?"

"Let's say — just to please me," he

suggested carefully. "And Miss French, of course." While inside him something raised a deafening shout — Because you're *mine,* because you're what I've been trying to find, because if anything should happen to you now I should truly have nothing to live for, because I want you for my own as I've never wanted anything in my life before —

"You look sort of green around the gills," said the choir-boy's voice. "Did it give you a nasty turn when I went off?"

"It did. I'm frightened out of a year's growth. Look." He held up one hand in mid-air, making no effort to control its visible trembling. His heart labored unbearably in his side, there was a thin singing in his ears. He had received some sort of cosmic shock, which he tried to use for her benefit. "You can't lunge about the countryside scaring people to death like this," he said, still speaking as though he had entered a cathedral during service. Not sixteen yet, you blithering fool, it's against the law, his own thoughts ran — never mind, I can wait — two more years — three, perhaps — Lord, it will take me that long to get into the clear myself — I can wait — but not forever —

"Well, don't take it so hard, I'm all right," she said unsympathetically. "Besides, you never saw me before in your life, why

127

should you care so much?''

''Would *you* like to see anybody, even a perfect stranger, pitch on his head at a gate? Suppose it had been me, no doubt you'd have gone into gales of laughter?''

''No, but I don't think I'd have got the shakes,'' she remarked. ''I've heard my father say that all Americans are a mass of nerves, because they live at such a pace and never stop for tea or week-ends.''

''He's wrong,'' Bracken said defensively. ''I always have tea, and I'm on a week-end this minute. You know, we're sitting in something of a bog and it's all over your jacket. Stand up and I'll brush you off a bit.''

''Well, as a matter of fact,'' she said, making no move to obey him, ''I'm afraid I've hurt my knee, rather.''

''Which? Where? Let's see —'' His hands gently explored the knee-cap and the hard tendon behind. She winced, but he could find nothing wrong. She could bend it, with a painful effort, her mouth set and drawn. She bore it all in silence, without complaint or exclamation.

''We must get you home,'' he decided. ''You can ride Sunbeam and I'll lead your horse. You'll have to show me the way, I'm new here.''

"It's just at the other end of the lane. Do you think you had better come with me?"

"I can't think why not. Can you?"

She sighed.

"Edward will read the riot act," she said.

"Then I'd better be there, to jolly him up a bit."

"It won't do any good. He warned me the last time."

"Not your first offence, eh?" he grinned. "Well, come on, let's get it over with." He opened the gate, led Sunbeam through, and closed it behind them. Then he returned to her, holding out his hands. "I'll lift, and you take your weight on the other foot. Ready?"

She came up very lightly, between his hands. The golden-red hair brushed his chin, soft and cool. Mine — mine from the moment I saw her, else why did I wait to see who it was? — I never knew it could happen like this, with one of you completely unaware — I must be very careful — she mustn't be made to think twice about it — I must try and behave like a rather fatuous uncle or something until she gets used to me — I must go very slowly — God knows I'll need time — do earls allow their daughters to marry divorced men? — this one will — I haven't much to offer, have I — but she's mine, some day she'll see that too — and she doesn't weigh a hundred pounds —

She stood leaning against him, her shoulder on his chest.

"If you'll lend me Sunbeam I can manage quite well by myself," she was saying resolutely. "Only that would leave you stranded, wouldn't it. Come on, then —" She moved towards Bracken's horse, gasped and staggered when her weight came on the injured knee, and he caught her round the waist.

"Take it easy," he said, and lifted her bodily into the saddle. Not a hundred pounds.

"Thank you," she said, gripping the pommel. "I — must have wrenched it."

"Is it pretty bad?" He handed her the cap and stood looking up into her face. Her beautiful lips were a thin line, tears stood in her eyes.

"It's all right. If you'll just — lead her for me."

He took both bridles and led the horses into the lane beyond the gate. They made the short journey in silence, came into the stable yard at the Hall from behind, and found Viscount Alwyn already there. He was wearing riding clothes, and stood knee-deep in dogs, talking to a groom in the morning sunlight. He swung round as they approached — a big, handsome man, well over six feet tall, with massive shoulders and a heavy, obstinate chin. His stone-grey eyes took in everything at a glance, as though he was expecting something of the sort and was not surprised. You got the impression that Lord Alwyn was never surprised.

"Oh, God save us, don't tell me you've had another spill!" he said with more irritation than concern. "Thunderbolt is limping! Dinah, for the last time —"

"This is Mr. Murray, Edward. He's staying at Farthingale."

"How do you do?" Alwyn gave Bracken his hand rather perfunctorily, his mind obviously on Thunderbolt's injury. "It's very good of you to bring my sister in. I suppose you found her in pieces somewhere on the wold. What has she done to my horse?"

"Just a strain, I think. A few days' rest should put him right."

Alwyn bent and ran his hand down Thunderbolt's leg.

"Arthur!" he said over his shoulder to the groom. "Come and see to this at once. Very well, Dinah, I'll attend to you later. Go and change your clothes." He turned his back on her in dismissal — she was still in Sunbeam's saddle — and gave his attention to her companion. "Sir Gratian mentioned that you were coming down, and my sister Clare intends to call. Would you care to look round the stables, now that you're here?''

''I'd like it very much,'' said Bracken politely. ''But your sister Dinah has a bad knee from the fall, and will need some help —''

''Oh, please don't bother, Dinah's always taking headers. Get down at once, Dinah, and go make yourself presentable. Gerald won't thank you for mucking up his jacket like that. You had better have it cleaned and then put it back in his wardrobe and leave it there, do you hear?''

''Yes, Edward.''

Looking very white, Dinah started to slide cautiously from the saddle. Bracken stepped back to steady her as she reached the ground, and she glanced up at him, half in gratitude, half in a sort of warning.

''Did you thank Mr. Murray for coming to the rescue?'' Alwyn inquired. His tone when he spoke to her was always halfway between what he might use to his dogs and to a child of six.

''Thank you, Mr. Murray,'' said Dinah listlessly, and withdrew herself from Bracken's hands. She took three or four uncertain steps and collapsed on the ground without a sound.

Quickly as Bracken moved, the big man

was quicker, and Bracken stood watching while Alwyn stooped above his sister and raised her limp body across his arms.

"Well, I'm damned!" he said. "I thought the little beggar was shamming! Here, Arthur!" The groom looked out of the stable door, where he had led Thunderbolt away to unsaddle. "Take Lady Dinah into the house, will you, and ask the governess to send for a doctor. It's the left knee. Probably wants nothing but hot applications and a bandage, but we'll make sure." With no more ceremony he transferred Dinah, still unconscious, to the groom's outstretched arms and again dismissed her from his mind. "Being from Virginia, as I understand, you probably know all about horses," he resumed to Bracken. "How does Sunbeam suit you? We'll go in this way," he added, starting towards the stables.

Bracken forced himself to follow without remonstrance, and for half an hour listened with appropriate comments to the life stories and virtues of the Viscount's hunters. Dinah. Odd little name, for his darling. But so right, so essentially hers. Governess — groom — doctor — but wasn't there anyone who *cared?* Wasn't there anyone to hold her hand if it hurt, and make a bit of a fuss because she was so brave? There was a sister — the beautiful one the Major had mentioned. There was the Earl. Who loved Dinah around here, who petted her, to whom did she turn for comfort? He thought he knew the answer, after those few minutes in the stable yard. There wasn't anybody. And that was the reason for her pathetic dignity, the reason she held her small shoulders so straight, the reason her eyes were so watchful and grave. Dinah hadn't anybody. But she would have, from now on. She would have Bracken Murray —

"No, really, I couldn't possibly let you start back without some food in you," Alwyn was saying, for Bracken's apparent attention and few knowing remarks had convinced him that here was a very sound man worth cultivating, and pleasant besides. "Breakfast will be going by now, I should think. You must come along in and meet my father." He set a hand under Bracken's elbow and piloted him firmly out of the stables.

Hoping for further news of Dinah, Bracken allowed himself to be persuaded, and accompanied Alwyn across the stable yard to where a wrought-iron gate opened into the walled kitchen garden. Here there was some delay and confusion while the setter who was Alwyn's privileged companion was separated from the rest of the dogs, who were not allowed in the house. But at last the gate closed heartlessly on canine protest in a dozen keys, and the two men and the setter proceeded across the kitchen garden, in which fat green shoots showed in tidy rows, and espaliered fruit trees bloomed. They passed through another iron gate and came out on the garden front, where the long lawns sloped to the river's brim and white peacocks strutted in full display. Still talking horses, they mounted the wide, shallow steps of the terrace which was on two levels, and entered the house by a door between tall Ionic columns.

The dining-room at the Hall was in the baroque style. Bracken, who was not unaccustomed to grandeur, nevertheless received an impression that all of Farthingale could have been set down comfortably within its four walls, which were the color of a duck's egg. The tall mantel-piece repeated the elaborate plasterwork of the coved ceiling, and the heavily scrolled wall panels were picked out with gold. There were statues, nearly life size and rather nude, in deep shell-niches. A crystal chandelier overhung the mahogany table which stood in the middle of the room, miles from the fire on one side and from the sunlight streaming in the long windows on the other. The hangings were of ivory brocade, the carpet was nearly as pale. The temperature of the room seemed entirely unaffected by the blazing fire, and was roughly the same as that of the stable yard.

At the far end of the table, which was laid for four and would have seated twelve with ease, old Lord Enstone sat alone, drinking a last cup of tea behind the *Times,* with an empty plate and toast-rack in front of him. The two fawn-colored great Danes *couchant* beside his chair raised their heads alertly but made no other move as Bracken entered with Alwyn.

''Morning, Edward. Everybody late, as usual,'' was the Earl's greeting.

''Good morning, Father. I persuaded Mr. Murray to come in for a cup of tea before he rides back to Farthingale.''

Lord Enstone took another look around the edge of the *Times* and perceived the stranger. Then he snatched off his pince-nez, which dangled from a black cord, and rose to extend a welcoming hand, proving to be even taller than his burly son.

''My dear fellow, you're abroad early!'' he said cordially. ''Been trying the horses, eh?''

''I've got Sunbeam out, sir. She goes very kindly. I'm most grateful to you for the loan of her while I'm here.''

"Oh, nonsense, horses all eating their heads off with nothing to do! Glad if they can be of some use to you. Sit here, and Edward will bring you something to eat." He pulled out the chair on his right, and resumed his own. "I can recommend the kedgeree this morning."

"Kedge — kidneys — bacon — cold ham — what'll it be?" Alwyn was lifting covers at the sideboard at the end of the room, where spirit-lamps burned under silver dishes beside a humming tea-urn, and a row of boiled eggs stood upended in their china cups with a tiny knitted cosy over each one.

Bracken said he would have kedge, thanks very much, with perhaps a spot of bacon alongside.

"Dinah has been at it again, sir," Alwyn continued over his shoulder, filling a plate for Bracken and one for himself. "Mr. Murray found her down with a twisted knee, and what's more she has gummed up Thunderbolt this time!"

To Bracken's surprise Lord Enstone only wheezed with amusement.

"It's not really funny, Father. Some day she'll smash up a good horse beyond repair. I say she's still not too old for a thorough whacking. Promised it to her the last time." Alwyn set down Bracken's plate on the table before him with some emphasis and took the chair across from him. The setter lay down behind its master with a sigh and rested its head on its paws. The great Danes guarding Lord Enstone went back to sleep. Nash, the elderly butler, came in with hot toast in silver racks which he placed before Bracken and the Viscount, and Alwyn said, without looking up, "Tea, please, Nash." The butler filled two cups from the urn and brought them to the table, stepping delicately around the dogs with an ease born of habit, and then began to lay another place beyond Alwyn. "What happened, anyway?" Alwyn was demanding of Bracken, as Bracken had feared all along that he might. "Did you see her come off?"

"Not very well. I was pretty far behind her. There was some sort of fumble at a gate, and she rolled clear."

"Tried to lift him too soon," Lord Enstone said, nodding. "She always does that. Good hands, though, what? Rides easy. When she was a little tyke Archie used to practice her with the straps of my field-glasses fastened to the back of a chair, till she learnt to use her wrists right."

"Well, are you going to have a word with her, sir, or shall I use my own judgment?" Alwyn attacked his breakfast. "Ask them to make fresh tea, Nash, Lady Clare can't drink this stuff when she comes down.''

''Dinah has wrenched her knee rather badly, I'm afraid,'' Bracken asserted pointedly, to see what would happen. ''I was more concerned about her than about Thunderbolt.''

''Keeled right over in the yard, sir,'' Alwyn remarked to his father. ''Knocked clean out, by Jove! I told them to send for a doctor. He'll fix her up,'' he added imperviously to their guest.

''Well, I'll have her on the carpet again if you say so,'' sighed Lord Enstone, bored. ''Won't do any good, though. She must be wheedling one of the grooms, you know, she could never manage the girth alone.''

''Find out who it is and sack him, that'll stop it!'' Alwyn suggested. ''Or lick the daylights out of Dinah, I don't care which. We never had trouble like this with Clare.''

''Who said Clare?'' cried a girl's voice, and the beautiful one came in — tall, fair, full-bodied like her brother, a young Diana of a girl. She was followed by two tiny Yorkshire terriers, their forelocks done up in bows of pink ribbon.

Bracken rose, and was presented to her. While he was still on his feet a young man entered by the same door. He bore a faint resemblance to Dinah in his sharp jaw line,

139

fine blue eyes, and small-boned frame — her brother Archie. A handsome black and white cocker spaniel trotted at his heels and paused to sniff Bracken politely while its master shook hands. Archie went on to fill a plate for Clare at the sideboard along with his own, and Nash brought more toast and the fresh tea. The places at table were all full now, and Bracken perceived that Dinah was not expected to breakfast. Her escapade was again recounted, and Archie said, "Hurt herself?"

"Wrenched a knee," Alwyn replied indifferently. "Not enough to teach her."

Bracken returned to Farthingale in a state of indignation and described with some bitterness at his second breakfast table that morning the heartlessness of Dinah's family.

"But, darling, that's the way English girls are brought up!" Virginia assured him. "Until you're out, you're absolutely the dust beneath everybody's chariot wheels, especially if you have an older sister! How old do you think this Dinah is?"

"She's fifteen."

"Well, there you are, she's still in the schoolroom! You know perfectly well you wouldn't see her at breakfast with the family. She and the governess have their meals up stairs. You remember how furious I used to

140

get over here when I was that age, being treated like a child and not allowed in the drawing-room except for tea! All Mother's English friends thought I was most frightfully spoilt and forward for my age, and all the girls wanted to go and live in America when I told them how different things were."

"Oh, dear, women's rights again," murmured the Major, slicing the top off his boiled egg with a single stroke. "At what age do young ladies in America begin to take their meals in the dining-room, then?"

"As soon as we stop dribbling, unless there's company!" said Virginia wilfully, and the Major laughed. "And when there is company we sit on the stairs and peek through the banister. But then, of course I'm not an earl's daughter," she added, Bracken thought rather unkindly.

"These big sporting families are rather hard on their young, I suppose," the Major conceded. "The poor little beggars are put up on ponies before they can walk. And then the girls are made to ride side-saddle, which is an invention of the devil. I never can see *how* they stay on!"

"Oh, that's quite simple, really," put in Sue, who had done it all her life. "It's a much safer seat than riding astride. You just hook your knee —"

"So I've been told, my dear, but we have some very nasty accidents all the same," said the Major.

"Would you have us wear *breeches?*" inquired Virginia, fluttering her eyelashes.

"No, but I'd have you not hunt, I think."

"But think of the fun we'd never have!" she objected.

"And the broken collar-bones! You mustn't take Alwyn amiss," he added to Bracken. "He's no end of a fine fellow, I believe, and very popular with the tenantry. They like a good firm hand, you know, and he won't stand any nonsense from anybody. He's devoted to Clare, too, and very choosy about who comes courting her."

"Yes, tell us about the beautiful Clare," Virginia teased. "You're only going on about this Dinah to throw us off the scent. What's Clare like?"

"Taller than you are — fair — lovely skin — good teeth —"

"You needn't sound as though she was a horse, darling! Is she nice to know?"

"Well, give me time," he hedged cautiously. "You can't tell much at breakfast." He considered this, with a quizzical eyebrow. "Or *can* you?"

"A woman who attracts you at breakfast is surely good for the other twenty-three hours!'' the Major remarked with a giveaway glance at Sue.

''He's just pretending,'' said Virginia, eyeing Bracken shrewdly. ''He can't *wait* to see her again, and he hopes we won't notice! I can tell!''

Bracken made an effort to meet her halfway.

''*How* can you tell?'' he demanded, allowing a certain crafty embarrassment to show.

''You look sort of dazed,'' said Virginia, who often came uncomfortably close to reading his mind. ''And your appetite is gone.''

''Nonsense,'' he replied, not very convincingly. ''I'm full of Lord Enstone's kedge.''

And so Alwyn was devoted to Clare, he thought. Who is devoted to Dinah, then? I am. They can have their Clare, Dinah is mine. I'll get her out of there as soon as possible, and give her a good time. Andromeda in Gloucestershire. What ho, dragons, here I come! — But with a broken lance, he thought ruefully. We'll have to get on with that divorce business as fast as possible now. I'll talk to Partridge. I'll write to Father. Maybe also I'd better pray to God.

5

The ensuing day was a long, bemused interval of time which must be got through before he could do anything about seeing Dinah again. To a household as casual and callous as the one at the Hall, any inquiry about her injury within twenty-four hours was bound to seem officious or else stark mad.

In the afternoon he went up to his room and began a letter to Cabot, tore it up and began another. They had been all over it so many times before, but until now only as it were theoretically. There had been no particular rush or reason for a divorce, except to put Lisl and all she stood for behind him. But now there was Dinah. Now there was a reason.

He had grounds for divorce, certainly, but his own knowledge that Lisl had left him to live abroad with Hutchinson was not sufficient to secure his freedom in a court of law. He must produce evidence, and witnesses who could swear to having seen his wife living with the California millionaire in some European domicile. There would have to be detectives to trace them and make written statements. There would have to be red tape and wire-pulling and a lot of legal advice.

Perhaps, he thought, it could be done more quietly here in England where the name of Murray was not so well known. The English divorce laws were notoriously complex and inflexible. But if he was going to marry Dinah some day — for a moment he sat contemplating the idea with a growing excitement and determination — *because* he was going to marry Dinah, it would be better (if not in fact necessary) to get his divorce in England. Partridge would know. Partridge knew everything. They would have to call off proceedings in New York, which had not made much progress, and begin again here. English detectives. None better in the world. Things might go faster that way, these fellows would know the ground, they would be on the scent in no time.

Meanwhile it was rather difficult to explain, at this distance, to his father. Not even Cabot could be expected to understand

145

the sudden, revolutionary thing that had happened to Bracken when he knelt on the boggy ground beside Dinah in the sunrise. He didn't understand it himself. He only knew that when he woke that morning he had been lost and rudderless and *finished,* an emotional husk, the merest sorry vestigial remnants of a man, his innermost honor soiled, his pride in tatters, his soul tasting of wormwood, his future not worth a bone button to him — and then Thunderbolt had foozled a gate and there was Dinah and he was alive again.

But he couldn't say to Cabot, She is the daughter of the Earl of Enstone, because that would conjure up somebody like Lady Clare. And he couldn't say, She will be sixteen soon, because Cabot was bound to reply that they would have the law on him. And he couldn't say, She was wearing her brother's shooting suit, because that made her sound like a tomboy. And he couldn't tell about Alwyn and the groom and the governess, because that descended to bathos and put her in a class with the Little Match Girl, shivering on the doorstep.

After an hour's struggle he gave up trying to get Dinah on paper — a man who was supposed to make his living by his pen, and he couldn't describe to his father the girl he wanted to marry! — and drifted down stairs to the drawing-room, where he found Sue dispensing tea and the rector come to call.

The rector was expounding happily to his audience on how Farthingale was a good hundred and fifty years older than the Hall, which had been built by the third earl about the time that St. John Sprague had left England for the colonies. St. John could never have seen the Hall in its finished state, the rector was saying, though he must have known that it was in process of building.

"He wouldn't have thought much of it," Bracken said. "Farthingale is much nicer."

"Much," nodded the rector. "I don't care for the Palladian style, myself. This sort of thing is cosier."

When they separated to change for dinner, Bracken tapped on Virginia's door and went in to ask if she and Sue had decided that they wanted to take the house on for the summer. Virginia looked surprised.

"But I thought it was all settled!" she cried. "Besides — I think he'd be glad of the money."

"Well, I only wanted to be sure," he said vaguely, and Virginia came to him and laid a cool little hand on the line between his eyes.

"Does your head ache again?" she asked gently.

"No. I don't think so. Why?"

She put her arms around him like a mother.

"Darling, I wish there was something I could do! I wish Lisl was *dead!*"

All his defences sprang up, and a new, unfamiliar apprehension as well — because naturally no one must suspect how he felt about Dinah. Not for years.

"What made you think of Lisl now?" he asked.

"Because you're worrying. And when you're unhappy it's always Lisl. There's nothing new, is there?"

"No, just the same old things, I guess."

"You haven't heard from her?"

"No. Why should I?"

"I thought you seemed so tired."

"I am tired. I worked pretty hard in order to get away, and the first night in a strange place, you know —"

"Bracken, you do like it here, don't you?"

"Very much indeed," he said guardedly.

"You aren't just taking the house to please me? That is, you'll get pleasure out of it too?"

"Bound to. Be very good for me, I should think — quiet — relaxing — good air — horses —"

"That's what Aunt Sue thought. She said you needed to get away from the office sometimes, right away like this, or you'd work yourself to death before our eyes.''

''I'm pretty tough. You tell her not to worry.''

''We promised Mother we'd take good care of you, you know.''

''Did you, Ginny? That's funny, I promised her the same thing about you!''

''Bracken — is she *very* beautiful?''

''Who? Mother?'' he asked perversely.

''Lady Clare, idiot!''

Virginia was much too clever, sensing already some new preoccupation on his part. Without compunction he threw Lady Clare to the wolves.

''Devastating,'' he said.

That night he went to bed with a stack of books as usual and a bedside lamp, prepared to read himself slowly into insensibility — and awoke with sunlight streaming into the room to find that he had slept like a baby for eight solid hours. Convalescents did that, he knew. People who had nearly died and then suddenly taken a turn for the better. Apparently he was going to get well now.

Sue gazed up at him from the breakfast table in astonishment.

''Bracken, you look like a new man already! I told Virginia this place would be good for you. It's the air. Did you sleep?''

''I did.''

"Are you going for a ride?"

"I am."

"I'll go with you," said Virginia, and —

"No, you won't," he told her rudely. "Solitude is what I need. No offense, Ginny, but down here I can suddenly hear myself think. It's a new sensation."

"Unh-hunh!" said Virginia just as rudely, and he knew she suspected a rendezvous with Lady Clare, or at least a desire on his part to moon over her by himself, and he allowed another opportunity to correct a false impression to go by.

He rode firmly in the opposite direction from the Hall and the village, determined not to succumb until after lunch, when he meant to ride again on the pretext of trying a different horse. Returning about eleven, he found that a note had arrived from the Hall inviting them all to lunch on Monday, and offering the shortness of their present visit at Farthingale as an excuse for the informality. Sir Gratian was artlessly pleased that Lord Enstone was after all disposed to be neighborly with his American friends, and Virginia gave Bracken an extremely knowing look and murmured, "You *did* make a hit, didn't you, darling! Do you think the Viscount will react to me the same way?" "Why not try for the Earl?" he countered brazenly.

About three o'clock that afternoon he entered the stable yard of the Hall by the same back route through the lane, turned his horse over to the smiling Arthur, and walked round to the garden front as he had done with Alwyn. The servants' grapevine functioned perfectly, and just as he was discovering that there was no bell on that side, the door was opened to him by Nash, who looked concerned, and said the family had all gone out to lunch and not come back yet.

"I wasn't expected," Bracken reassured him. "I only came to inquire about Lady Dinah."

"She's confined to her room, I'm afraid, sir. The doctor said she ought to keep off it for several days."

"Very sensible. Do you think I could see her?"

This caused Nash to look surprised, and he said with his head a little on one side, "Well, I'm afraid the governess isn't in either, sir. She had an errand in the village."

"Sounds awfully dull for a youngster with a game leg," said Bracken cunningly. "Might cheer her up a bit if I looked in for a few minutes, don't you think? You see, I was there when she took the toss, so we're quite chums now —"

Nash smiled indulgently, for Bracken was one of those fabulous people who have a way with children, servants, and dogs.

"If you care to step into the tapestry room and wait, sir, I'll go up and inquire," he said, and opened wide the door.

The tapestry room was a small parlor — small, anyway, by the standards of the Hall, which is to say that it was not large enough to house a good echo — on the right of the terrace door. Its long windows looked south across the lawns to the river. It had no pictures, only Gobelins, on its walls, and the furniture was lavish Louis Quatorze, much gilded. But Bracken was not really aware of his surroundings.

He paced the floor, nervous as a boy before his first dance. He was thinking that he ought to have brought her something — chocolates or flowers. He noticed a dozen pink rosebuds, freshly gathered in the greenhouse, still with a dewy look, gracefully arranged in a blue Sèvres vase on a cabinet. They looked defenceless and shy in the regal room. Lonely too, he thought. He removed them from the vase and dried the stems on his handkerchief, just as Nash opened the door again and said, "I think it will be all right for you to go up, sir. Will you come this way?"

Carrying the bouquet of pink roses,

Bracken followed the old butler up the grand staircase and through a long gallery lined with portraits, up a less grand staircase, along a narrower passage apparently running between bedrooms, around a corner into another wing, up a third staircase with no pretensions at all, and into a gaunt, somehow dreary room where Dinah lay on a sofa under an eiderdown.

Still looking a little dubious about the whole thing, Nash left them. He had not, of course, failed to notice the abduction of the pink roses, which was just the cheeky sort of thing a young American gentleman would do, and it rather tickled Nash. He was partial to Dinah and privately disapproved of the way she was snubbed and dragooned by her sister and the Viscount. Besides, when he told her Mr. Murray was downstairs asking to see her Dinah had said, "Oh, *please* let him come up, Nash!" And it wasn't as though they had kept her in bed today. And Miss French was sure to return at any minute, now. . . .

"Good afternoon," Dinah greeted Bracken correctly, but her eyes were bright with pleasure. "It's most awfully good of you to come. What's the matter, you look — surprised."

"It's all those stairs, I expect," he evaded. "I'm out of breath." Now that he saw her as presumably she should be dressed, she looked even more pitiably young than she had the day before. Her hair waved loosely on her shoulders, tied back on the top of her head with a blue ribbon, with a soft fringe across her forehead. She was wearing some sort of shapeless blue flannelette garment which had a ruffle at the neck and long sleeves gathered into ruffles at the wrists. Schoolroom, Virginia had said. More like a nursery. "Are you sure you're nearly sixteen?" he inquired anxiously.

"In September."

"Well, in the meantime, I brought you these." He presented the roses. "They made me think of you, somehow. They need some one to keep them company."

She took them in both her hands.

"Did you *really* mean them for me?"

"Who else?"

"It's always Clare who gets the flowers."

"Now, you don't actually think I'd bring Clare roses and then chuck them at you because she isn't here!"

"Well, but — nobody ever brought me flowers before."

"Then it's begun," he said. "As a matter of fact, I stole those. I don't know whose they were, but they're yours now. Shan't we ask somebody to put them in water?"

"There isn't anybody, unless you want to ring — and they only come up here if they happen to feel like it, anyway. Miss French has gone into the village on her bicycle to get some knitting wool."

"Mean to say you've been left all alone at the top of the house like this? Suppose you wanted something!"

"I'd have to wait," she told him philosophically. "There's a mug in the other room on the wash-handstand. You could put them in that if you like till Miss French gets back."

He crossed the room and entered Dinah's bedroom. It too had a kind of dreariness, as though furnished with cast-offs, and the bed was a narrow white iron affair like a hospital. It was his first adult experience of the Spartan cheerlessness of the English nursery floor, and it chilled him to the bone. He poured water from the white china ewer into the mug and returned to place the roses in it where she could see them from the sofa.

"How long are you going to be laid up like this?" he asked, drawing up a chair. "What did the doctor say?"

"Oh, doctors never really *say* anything, do they? He bandaged it up and told me to keep off it. Miss French thought I ought to stay in bed, but I managed to hobble out here just for a change."

"Does it hurt much?"

"It's not comfortable. The bandage seems too tight."

"Bet you didn't sleep much. Did they give you anything to send you off?"

"Miss French made me a tisane, but it didn't do much good."

"What did you think about?" he ventured to ask.

"Oh, I don't know. How soon I could ride again, and what Edward will say when he gets round to it —"

"Couldn't you find anything more cheerful than that to dwell on?"

She looked back at him candidly, with no thought of any possible allusion to his own possible presence in her thoughts. Once more the choir-boy simile occurred to him — she was utterly without guile or coquetry. She accepted his roses and his call at their face value, schooled to her own unimportance in the grown-up world. Clare wasn't in, so he had come up to be polite to Clare's little sister. She took no more to herself than that. After Virginia, who had begun to flirt in her cradle, he found Dinah very touching because of such simplicity.

"Well, I was wondering about the Major too," she confessed, almost unwillingly. "It seems such a pity he has to give up his house just because he hasn't got money enough to run it properly. The Army is badly paid, you know, it really isn't fair. My brother Oliver is a captain now and even with his allowance from home he has a dreadful time to make ends meet.''

''Has to come down on Father now and then, does he?''

''Yes, and poor Father is as hard up as anybody!'' she assured him carelessly. ''That's why we live down here in the country so much of the time, instead of in the house in Town. Of course I like it, and so do the boys, but it bores Clare.''

''We'll have to try and liven it up for her. My sister likes living in the country, and she's planning a lot of house-parties and what-not.''

''Clare will be glad of that,'' Dinah said. ''Of course I suppose it is rather hard, if you're beautiful and clever like Clare, not to have a lot of money and make a splash in London. Clare says she's got to marry money, and how do they expect her to do it if they keep her bottled up in Gloucestershire! How old is your sister?''

''Eighteen. I'll bring her to see you, may I?''

''She'd rather see Clare, I expect. They'll

have things to talk about.''

''And what do you do with yourself, Dinah, when you aren't riding Thunderbolt?'' It was the first time he had called her by her funny little name. He felt it in his heartbeats.

''Oh, lessons, mostly, and music. Only it isn't often I can get the good piano down stairs.'' She sighed and glanced disdainfully at the old upright in the corner of the room. ''It's not much fun practicing on that thing.''

''What do you play?''

''Etudes.'' She made a face. ''And now as a special treat, I'm learning *The Harmonious Blacksmith*. The name of it is enough to put you off, isn't it!''

''And you live up here, all by yourself?'' he said, trying to visualize her daily existence. ''Don't you get lonesome?''

''It is a bit bleak since Gerald started to school and they let Nanny go. But I have Miss French, and she's awfully nice, not like most governesses. After I come out I shall have a bedroom down stairs and take my meals in the dining-room. I'm hoping for the yellow room, it looks over the sunken garden, but Clare says it's for guests. I shall probably get something dull at the back.''

''What's the yellow room like?'' he asked, sitting very still, speaking very low, for now he was learning, now she was talking to him like an old friend, now he was getting some idea of what went on behind her unchildlike self-possession. It was too soon to say to her, When you are mine you shall have any sort of room you like, and do it up to suit yourself and spend all the money you please on it — when I have the right to give you things, all sorts of things, everything you ever wanted, Dinah, you only have to name it — oh, much too soon to say that. But he could learn, he could encourage confidences, and then some day he could wave his check-book like a wand —

"It's Chinese Chippendale," she was saying. "Chairbacks like mahogany lace, and the wall-paper has lovely long-tailed birds on a pale yellow ground, and the hangings are yellow silk. The sun always seems to be shining there even when it rains, because of the yellow walls. There's the most enormous bed with a canopy, you could simply lie crosswise in it if you liked —"

"Any books there?"

"It has one of those circular bookcases in tiers. Of course my own books aren't bound in fancy leather, I'd have to keep them out of sight!"

"What do you like to read?"

"That's all my library." She pointed at a shelf not far from his chair and he leaned to squint at the titles. "It's sort of handed down, some of Edward's and John's and all of Clare's. Archie's got lots of books in his room, and he gave me the Kipling for Christmas last year. Archie is my favorite brother, he's studying Law up in London. He says he saw you at breakfast yesterday."

"Yes, I liked him." (Archie was the only one who had asked if she had hurt herself.) "Going to be a Q.C., is he?"

"Well, Oliver chose the Army, and John stood for Parliament, and that left the Navy and the Church and the Bar for Archie. He says he'd never be able to take himself seriously in Holy Orders, and judging by the way he feels on the Calais crossing the Navy would never do! Archie is awfully nice, he used to come and read to Gerald and me when we were little and got ill."

"And do you like to go to plays?" Bracken asked, groping happily among revelations.

"I've never seen any, except once when Edward took us all to the pantomime at Christmas."

"Next time you're in London we'll go to a play, shall we?"

"Mr. Murray, why do you —" She hesitated, her grave eyes upon him impersonally, her beautiful lips parted. For the first time she seemed a little embarrassed, a little uncertain of her next words.

"Why do I what?" he asked alertly.

"Well, why are you so kind to me?"

"Why should you expect me to be beastly to you?" he parried.

"Oh, not beastly, I didn't mean that, but — you talk to me almost as though I was grown up."

"How else would I talk to you? You're nearly sixteen."

"That isn't considered grown up in our family. Are things different in America?"

"They seem to be," he said, thinking of their spoilt, precocious Virginia. "My sister considered herself quite a débutante at your age, and was allowed at all informal parties till ten o'clock, if I remember rightly." And what's more, he added to himself, she wouldn't have been caught dead wearing that thing you've got on. Couldn't I send something pretty for Dinah to be ill in, he wondered. No, I suppose not. Must go slowly. Must behave like an uncle. Has she got uncles? Well, I'm the American uncle, and entitled to be a little peculiar. She'd look so pretty in Virginia's clothes. How long must I wait? How careful must I be? What *can* I give her? Chocolates — books — but what does she want? — how can I find out what she wants — "What would you like for your birthday present?" he asked suddenly, and Dinah looked surprised.

"It's not till September."

"But it's your sixteenth. That's important. Got to start thinking."

"Will you be at Farthingale in September?" she inquired.

"Might. In London, anyway. Will you invite me to your birthday party? I suppose you'll have a party?"

She shook her head.

"I never have had. Not till after I come out."

"Then *I'll* give you a party! Virginia always has parties on her birthday, or we'd hear about it! We'll get her to help."

"Are you going to stay in England long, Mr. Murray?"

It was the first flicker of personal interest she had shown in him, and the question was more puzzled than personal even now. Nevertheless Bracken seized it.

"Yes, you see, my father runs a newspaper in New York and I've come over here to start a London office. I shall be here for some time — unless I pop off to report a war now and then."

"You mean you *write* newspapers?" Dinah was plainly startled.

"Well, not more than one. And not the whole thing. I'm a Special Correspondent. My present job is the Jubilee, in which all America takes a friendly interest."

"But I think that's wonderful!" said Dinah, and now her intense regard made him almost uncomfortable. "I never thought I'd know some one who wrote things that were *printed*. Could I see something you wrote some time?"

"Almost any time. But I'm no Kipling, you know, just a run-of-the-mill journalist."

The idea of a man who did anything so incomprehensible as journalism caught her eager, open mind. And now it was she who asked the questions, for she had never thought before how newspapers came into being, having accepted the *Times* rather as she accepted the sunrise, as a natural phenomenon. Literature was an esoteric subject at the Hall, where books were encountered as lessons, or else shut up in the library as ornaments. Miss French had her favorites, of course, and Dinah had read *Evelina* and some early Victorian novelists. And Archie read, other things besides Law, but Archie was different from the rest of them, he was the brainy one, and had chambers in London, and meant to become a barrister. In Archie's bedroom at the Hall books lay about everywhere on the chairs and tables and were constantly used. Archie could quote from things besides Surtees and *Horse and Hound,* and Archie had tried, not very successfully so far, to instill into the young minds of Dinah and Gerald some idea of the solace and entertainment to be derived from just sitting down with a book. Here was another man who attached importance to them, and who not only habitually read the printed word but actually wrote it.

"Did you ever write a *book?*" she inquired finally, for anything was possible to him now.

"Not yet. I probably will, though, most of us do. My Aunt Susannah is quite a well-known authoress at home — though you'd never guess it to look at her, bless her little heart!" He scrutinized more closely the titles of Dinah's nondescript library. "A lot of things are missing here," he complained. "Archie must pull himself together. Didn't they give you Miss Alcott when you were younger?"

Dinah had plainly never heard of Miss Alcott.

"Not too late now, perhaps," said Bracken. "I'll go into this with Virginia. And I'll send you a thing called *The Prisoner of Zenda,* with my compliments."

"I'll read anything you want me to," she promised devoutly.

Heavy footsteps crossed the passage outside and Alwyn swung into the room, puffing a little from the last flight of stairs.

"My dear fellow," he greeted Bracken with outstretched hand, "it's no end good of you to come up and entertain Dinah like this! I'm sorry we were so long, but it's a goodish drive from the Towers."

"I've been quite happy, thank you," said Bracken firmly. "Dinah and I have been getting acquainted."

"Yes, well, come along down and have some tea, it's just coming in."

"No, really, I had no intention —"

"But of course you will, old boy, Clare is expecting you in the drawing-room this minute! Where's Miss French, Dinah?" His stone-grey gaze ran swiftly over the room and to the doorway of the empty one beyond.

"Gone to the village for some knitting wool," said Dinah tonelessly.

"Oh. Well, I daresay your tray will be along soon. Say Good-bye to Mr. Murray now, and thank him for sitting with you."

"Good-bye, Mr. Murray. Thank you for sitting with me," said Dinah obediently. Her eyes as they met Bracken's ironical glance were empty of any expression except a studious politeness. It was impossible to tell if she resented being treated by her brother like a negligible child who was not quite bright, or whether she was so accustomed to that attitude from her elders that she was unaware of it.

Bracken held out his right hand and waited till hers came into it.

"Good-bye," he said. "And thank *you* for letting me come up."

He followed Alwyn down all those stairs in what was becoming a chronic state of exasperation. It had been on the tip of his tongue to demand a nursery tea from Dinah's tray, out of sheer perversity at being bundled off to Clare so high-handedly, but he was doubtful if the repercussions would be advisable. He was prepared to dislike Clare by now. And at the back of his mind there stirred a suspicion that he had been already looked into, and the Murray money brought to light, and that Clare was going to be thrown at his head.

When they reached the drawing-room floor, Alwyn turned left and threw open the door of a room with blue damask walls and a mirrored rococo mantelpiece that was like woven icicles. No one was there, and the hearth was cold.

"Oh," said Alwyn, backing out again.

"You never know, do you! Thought they said tea was in the blue drawing-room, but it must be the white one. Can't think why, the wind is from that side today." He led the way to open another door. "This looks more like it, what?"

The white drawing-room was about the best the Hall could do. It faced west and south above the sunken garden. It had an Adam ceiling and crystal chandeliers. It was so long it required two mantelpieces, each of them supported by classic busts on tapering pedestals, each with a roaring fire. Gainsborough had done the mantelpiece portraits, and the large family group at the end of the room was Hoppner. The furniture was in Adam's airiest design, and the brocades and needlepoints were cream and rose.

It was the perfect setting for blonde Lady Clare, who presided over the tea-table set in front of the nearest fire. She still wore her hat, a delightful affair trimmed with pale blue ostrich-tips and a white veil which she had rolled up so that it formed a misty frame for her face. Her cheeks were pink from the wind, and she welcomed Bracken like an old friend.

"Forgive me for not being changed since the drive," she said as she gave him her

167

hand. "But Edward is such a tyrant, he said there wasn't time before tea. I do think it's charming of you to come and inquire about that naughty girl, don't you, Archie?"

"Rath*er*. Must have bucked her up no end. How's the poor little soul managing?"

"Well, it's tough, having to keep your leg up," Bracken said cautiously.

"Oh, damn' dull, I quite agree!" old Lord Enstone said heartily from a sofa by the fire. "I broke an ankle once, out with the Heythrop. Almost went out of my mind before it mended!"

"Don't I remember!" said Clare, turning up her eyes. "We *all* nearly went out of our minds!"

"I'm a bad invalid, I admit," her father conceded complacently. "Had so damn' little practice, for one thing! You were out with us that day, Edward, it was on that Meon Hill run. Very fast sixty minutes, but heavy going after a rain."

"That was the time you came to grief at a wall, wasn't it, sir? A very bad peck. It was that damn' horse you would ride — too long in the leg for this country. I told you. We got rid of him soon after. Good thing too, might have killed you the next time!"

"Oh, rot, no horse can kill me. Not for years yet," said Lord Enstone cheerfully.

"Ever hunt in wall country, Mr. Murray?"

Bracken said yes, as a matter of fact, he had had a rattling good day with the Duke of Beaufort's bitch pack two years ago. His stock shot up at once.

"Did you really, what day was that?" asked Alwyn keenly. He had a fantastic memory for such things and carried in his head every meet and every run and every covert he had ever heard about.

Bracken said it was early in November, so far as he could recall, and the whole place was hopping with foxes after a dry, bad-scenting spell. They accounted for a brace and a half before noon, he said, and the very first run was a four-mile point after a quick find in Bailey's Wood.

"I heard about that run!" said Alwyn. "Racing pace the whole way, what? Killed handsomely roundabout Jackament's Bottom, what? Heard about it from Michael Trent. He was staying with the Duke at the time. You know Trent, by any chance?"

Bracken knew him quite well.

"Extraordinary," said Lord Enstone. "Small world, what, what?"

"I like a bitch pack, myself," Archie remarked. "Just that little bit more drive and dash and that makes all the difference on a poor scent."

"I say," said Lord Enstone. "These automobiles. They'll be the ruin of good scent, what?"

The Danes and the setter had finished their polite inspection of Bracken's riding boots and retired to their respective masters' heels. Archie was handing round the cups for Clare, so his spaniel was unable to settle, and camped beside Bracken's chair. Bracken scratched its neck with a knowing fingertip, just in the spot no dog can reach, while the talk ran on over the hunting season just past, which had been full of rough weather with too much frost and hard ground. Archie had gone out with the Tiverton, which was a Devonshire hunt, last Boxing Day. "It's terrible country," he said, with a reminiscent shudder. "Banks. With *trees* planted on top! And *bogs!* Only eight of us saw the finish, besides the Hunt staff. And only sixteen out of twenty-one and a half couples, mixed pack. Stout foxes, though. One of them scrambled right up the ivy to the roof of a brew-house — nobody believes this, but I was there! — he lay up on the roof-tree with his nose between his paws and giggled at us. And what did the Master do? Whipped 'em off, of course! That fox deserved another day."

Lord Enstone then inquired, because he

couldn't stand it any longer not to, if Bracken had ever ridden point-to-point. Well, yes, he had, said Bracken, the last time being two years ago at the Pytchley course, which had nasty big gorse-faced fences.

"Lord, yes, I know that course!" said Alwyn. "Wait a minute, I was there!" He snapped his fingers at his obedient memory. "Wasn't that the day an American won a cup? Was that *you?*"

Bracken admitted that it was.

"Well, I'm damned!" said Alwyn, and they all stared at their guest with steadily increasing respect. "I remember now! I saw you win it! But I say, old boy, you do ride short for jumping, you know! I thought you were one of those Newport johnnies, what?"

Bracken said he had learned to ride in Virginia, but managed to get in a season in England now and then.

"Well, I must say I like an old-fashioned hunting seat myself," insisted Alwyn, who was very heavy in the shoulders. "I remember saying at the time, 'That fellow's riding damn' short,' I said."

"I'm long-legged," Bracken pointed out defensively.

"Oh, jolly good leg for a boot!" Alwyn agreed generously. "But do let 'em out a couple of holes, old boy, you can't possibly

171

stay on like that, you know!"

"But he did stay on!" Clare reminded him amusedly, running a shameless glance over Bracken's legs.

"Only just," said Bracken, and grinned. "I was all over the saddle at the first water-jump, I don't deny! Thought I was a goner. Had a good horse, though, he saved me. One of the Master's."

They all said what a pity it was that he was too late for Cheltenham this year, and how he must be sure to come out with them when cubbing began, and the conversation ran on about local coverts and recent runs, and the new Whipper-in, and the merits of coffee as a remedy for distemper, and the idiocy of the foot-people and the chaps who only thought of getting home to their tea, and Alwyn said he had been perfectly sure that Bracken was a useful man on a horse when he first walked into the stable yard leading Thunderbolt.

Dinah was not mentioned again, and it became ever plainer to Bracken that any further efforts by him on her behalf today would be regarded with honest bewilderment by her family. He had never before encountered obtuseness on such a scale, too genuine to be resented. Except for Archie. Archie had asked how she was managing.

Archie's dog had stayed by Bracken's chair, and while he drank his scalding tea Bracken rubbed the spaniel's back gently with the toe of his boot.

6

Sir Gratian Forbes-Carpenter, meanwhile, was not making progress. He vacillated between a horrified realization of his own enslavement and a reckless abandonment to his madness. Poor Sue, who had been made self-conscious by having her attention called to her conquest, resisted the cowardly impulse to avoid her host, and treated him forgivingly, almost pityingly, which he could not account for and which only made him worse off because she was so sweet, and he attributed her attitude to a possible sympathy about his leg, which had finally begun to do nicely, though he was still limping and still unable to ride.

Sue was determined that he should have no opportunity to come to the point, in case he had any idea of such a thing, and ask her to marry him, because she couldn't bear to hurt his feelings by refusing him. She was very sure that she would refuse him. And it seemed particularly unkind to take his house away from him and turn him down in the same breath, as it were.

The Major, who had never cared two pins about the house, now suddenly found it very attractive, adorned as it was by two charming women who actually came down to breakfast in delightful tea-gowns and consulted him as to his plans for the day, his preferences in food, and his wishes and whims in general. It was a considerable novelty to a fellow whose only household equipment for years had consisted of a dour Scottish batman and a military kit. He was becoming quite fascinated with the picture of himself as a family man.

They went to the village church on Easter Sunday, and found it decorated entirely in yellow, with primroses and daffodils, and they all said what a good idea it was, because one had white flowers for a funeral and Easter was just the opposite. The sunlight was yellow too, on the golden stone, and the effect was so singularly gay as to be almost unorthodox, some people thought, though goodness knows the sermon was dull enough to suit anybody — it didn't last long, as Lord Enstone had years ago given the rector firmly to understand that fifteen minutes was the absolute limit.

The Farthingale party sat in Aunt Sophie's pew, and Sir Gratian's secretly religious soldier's heart was immensely touched by having Sue beside him, sharing the same prayer-book and singing hymns. It was a mild, sunny day, and after lunch Sue found herself strolling down the yew walk with the Major. Bracken and Virginia, who had certainly left the house just behind them, had disappeared, and a bend in the grassy path hid the lawn and west front from view. Sue found herself making conversation rather fast.

"We shall never be able to thank you enough for letting us have this lovely house to live in this summer, Sir Gratian," she heard herself saying. "You've no idea how large and oppressive London seems to some one like me, who isn't used to living in the city. Down here I feel I can breathe again. In church this morning I really began to feel quite at home."

"I wish," he said, pacing thoughtfully beside her, so slowly that his limp was hardly noticeable, "I wish I could prevail on you on such short acquaintance to use my Christian name."

Sue did not quite follow, for they had all been calling him Sir Gratian for days now.

"You've no idea, he went on after a pause, "how lonely it is to have almost no one in the world who addresses you informally. And I'm just a little bit tired of being called Carpers, I might add!"

"I can understand your being lonely," Sue said gently. "I grew up in a large family myself, and we feel very hard done by if we can't collect more than a dozen for holidays and anniversaries. I'm very sorry indeed for anyone who hasn't got heaps of sisters and cousins and aunts."

"I wonder if you could be sorry enough to take me in," he said, and then, as Sue was speechless —"You haven't known me long enough, I realize that, but we soldiers are always in a hurry. I am asking you to marry me, my dear."

Sue was enveloped by a wave of hot and then of cold, which left her knees weak and her hands unsteady. He had done it. Oh, how stupid of her not to have seen it coming and headed him off! Now he had done it, and she would have to say No.

"We couldn't have this house, I'm afraid, much as I should like to offer it to you," he was saying, limping along beside her. "But we might be able to find a smaller one, not so expensive to keep up, somewhere near by. And once this show in Egypt is over, I could think of retiring from the Army and raising dahlias, or something. Do you think you could bear to live with me like that, Susannah?''

And one couldn't say a flat No to that, she thought, one had to — to find some way of — breaking it gently —

''Perhaps,'' said Sir Gratian, keeping a tight rein on himself while a vein beat in his temple and his eyes looked very fierce, ''Perhaps you would like to think it over and tell me tomorrow.''

''Oh, *no!*'' cried Sue involuntarily, for a day and a night of suspense would never do. ''No, I — I'm afraid it's impossible.''

''I was afraid so too,'' he said gravely after a moment. ''It was asking too much, of course. You have your life, your friends and your family, on the other side of the water. It was just a little idea I had — thought I might as well mention it.'' He glanced sidewise at her with his squinting, boyish smile. ''Don't let it depress you, my dear. It can't be the first time you've sent some poor fellow packing. Nor it won't be the last, if I'm any judge.''

''Oh, *please* —!'' Sue entreated, her eyes full of tears. ''It's not like that at all, you see, I —'' She stopped. She couldn't tell Sir Gratian right out about Sedgwick all those years ago, she didn't know him very well. Besides, nobody but Eden and Dabney knew about Sedgwick any more, and of course her father. She had begun to hope they might all have forgotten it. Besides — she had no right to speak of it without Sedgwick's permission. And after all, would Sir Gratian feel any better if he knew? She hated to have him think she went about refusing people right and left, though. "You see, my father is very old," she faltered. "I — it was a risk for me to leave him even for this summer, but it was a sort of family emergency. You see, he counts on me, because all the others are either married or — or dead. I couldn't possibly leave him."

"I see." And in spite of him his heart lifted a little. Elderly fathers die. Sometimes a whole lifetime of sacrifice is not required of even the most devoted daughter. Sometimes, too, some other arrangements can be made, if one is determined enough. If Susannah really wanted to stay in England, some solution might be found for her father's care. And more than two months' leave remained. He had until July, to make her want to stay. . . . "But at least you will call me Gratian," he stipulated, and Sue, so grateful to him for taking it so nicely, promised.

When the four of them set out in the

carriage for the Hall on Monday at lunch time, the Major looked round complacently at his ready-made family and said, "I feel like somebody in Jane Austen's books."

"Not enough daughters," said Bracken, and Sue, who knew exactly what Sir Gratian meant, smiled at him in a way to make his heart turn clean over.

The carriage swept in at the tall wrought iron gates and drove through acres of park where fallow deer lifted their heads to see it pass.

"Golly!" said Virginia irreverently as the colonnaded front of the Hall came into view through the trees. "What *is* this place, one of Vanbrugh's off days?"

The Major snorted with laughter, and Bracken said, "The terrace is nice, in a big way, and there is some good Adam inside. They get lost in it, of course, and wander about looking for meals!"

"I was lost for hours at Knole, once," Virginia recalled. "Mother got really frightened before they found me again, and all I'd done was take the wring turning on the way to my room. I saw a lot of things they don't usually show."

"This isn't as bad as Knole," said Bracken as they drew up under the portico. "I think you'd always be heard here if you hollered."

"Not with that row going on!" said Virginia, for the peacocks on the terrace were just then having a screaming match which was clearly audible at the front of the house.

The door opened into a high white-pillared entrance hall from which the grand staircase rose past a riot of rococo plasterwork on the walls. They were shown into the white drawing-room where the family was sitting. Bracken had been in to the village and bought a large gaudy box of chocolates for Dinah and he asked Lord Enstone if he might take Virginia up to say Hello before lunch. The Earl looked surprised, and then said Yes, yes, of course, why not, and rang for a footman to show them the way.

Bracken and Virginia followed their guide along the endless-seeming upper corridors to the nursery floor. They found Dinah dressed in an unbecoming brown blouse and skirt, still lying on the sofa with her legs up. Miss French sat near by with a book, reading aloud, and Bracken inspected her carefully as Dinah introduced them — a thin, gentle-faced woman, no longer young, with soft grey hair above level blue eyes, and a grave smile. It was with Miss French that Dinah spent her meager schoolgirl days and to her that she must look for affection and companionship. Not like most governesses, Dinah had said, and Bracken thought not, for he liked what he saw. And so did Miss French.

Virginia and Dinah shook hands, and Bracken bestowed the chocolates with something less than his usual ease of manner. Dinah was even more surprised than Lord Enstone had been.

''Are these all for me?'' she inquired, gazing at the box he had laid in her lap, and Bracken's left eyebrow rose alarmingly.

''Dinah, when will you learn that I do not bring you second-hand gifts? I bought those chocolates for you, I've brought them to you, and I expect you to eat them all, even if it makes you sick!''

Dinah pulled off the ribbon and lifted the lid, and the top layer was revealed — nice fat shiny black chocolates, with a liberal sprinkling of the kind that are wrapped in colored tinfoil.

''I've always wondered how it would be to choose the very first one,'' she murmured.

''But surely you've had chocolates before,'' he said, watching her.

''This is the first box I've ever had all to myself,'' she explained. ''Sounds greedy, doesn't it! Clare doesn't like the hard ones, so she leaves those for me. Aren't they beautiful?'' she said seriously to Miss French. ''It seems a pity to spoil it.''

"Not before lunch, Dinah," said Miss French, and Dinah offered the box heroically to her guests, who quickly said No, thanks, not before lunch.

"Don't they *smell* good!" she said then, inhaling. "Thank you so much, Mr. Murray. I shall make them last ever so long."

"That might be a nuisance," he said. "There are lots more in the shop. How's the knee? Feel any better?"

"Not much better. I feel as though I'd never walk again!"

"Well, that won't do, because you've got to come to Farthingale for tea some day," said Virginia, and Dinah brightened.

"And see the house? Did Father say I could?"

"I haven't asked him yet, but I will. We're going back to Town next week because I've got the Drawing-Room on the eleventh, but we'll be down again soon after."

"Clare is being presented on the eleventh too!" cried Dinah. "How lovely for you both to go together! Are you nervous?"

"No, is Clare?"

"She says not. I'm going to die of fright when my time comes, I know I am!" Dinah's shoulders hunched in a childish shudder.

"If only I don't trip!" said Virginia lightheartedly. "I'll let you know the minute we come down again, and you'll be seeing a lot of us this summer. Bracken has to rest, he's had too much hard work and worry. We ought to go now, Bracken, they'll be waiting. Good-bye, Dinah — don't forget about coming to tea!'' Virginia swept him away and down the stairs.

''Do you really suppose she's never had a box of chocolates before?'' he said in a daze, as they reached the lower gallery.

''I've told you, Bracken, it's the system over here! A girl is an absolute *Cinderella* till all of a sudden she comes out and is expected to hold up her end and make a good marriage! Of course it's worse for Dinah because her mother is dead and Clare probably bullies her, and the men would never think. She *is* lovely, Bracken!''

''Who, Dinah?''

''*Clare,* stupid! I don't wonder you've been absent-minded ever since you had breakfast here! Clare is rather a change from Lisl, isn't she! Shall you tell them about Lisl!''

''Or shall I just wear a sign around my neck that says CANCELLED?'' he asked bitterly.

''Oh, darling, I only meant —''

''You only meant Be Careful. I will.''

When they reached the drawing-room Clare

and Sue were making conversation on the sofa by the fire and the men were just returning from the gun-room where they had stolen a quick whiskey before lunch, to keep the chill out. Lord Enstone was saying cheerfully —

"Well, Carpers, my boy — where's the next war? South Africa, what?"

"Or Germany, which?" asked the Major, gravitating to Sue's side.

"War with *Germany?* Oh, how *grim!*" Clare objected gaily, and Virginia gave it as her opinion that Sir Gratian was an awful pessimist.

"We got rather the impression at home that Germany's next quarrel was going to be with Austria," Bracken said, pricking up his ears as always when somebody said War.

"It won't stop there. Germany is ruled by a half-cracked buffoon," said Lord Enstone flatly. "He's got his eye on China, I don't mind telling you. He's chucking his weight about in the Balkans. He's egging Kruger on in South Africa. He hates us like poison because we've got a Fleet. Once his grandmother is gone, we'll have him to deal with sooner or later. And Victoria can't live forever, poor soul. But I think," he said, gazing into the fire like a seer, "I think South Africa will come first."

"I never can see how the Kaiser comes into South Africa," Clare said, in pretty confusion.

"He doesn't, by rights," her father replied. "But he is a megalomaniac. Got to watch out for him. Isn't that right, Carpers? Think we can stay out of this Balkan mess, what?"

"If we let Greece go under."

"Got to." Lord Enstone sighed. "Nasty business, though, in Crete." He turned on Bracken, his shaggy eyebrows down. "You've got something on your own doorstep, too. Cuba. What are you going to do about that, eh?"

"I'm afraid we'll have to kick them out," said Bracken quietly. "Spain, I mean."

"Good for you!"

"We oughtn't to have that kind of goings-on in the New World — concentration camps, starving women and children, ruthless killing of non-combatants and hostages — they even got a War Correspondent!" Bracken winced elaborately. "That's got to stop!"

"You think America will intervene, eh?" the Earl asked keenly.

"We may have to, if it keeps on."

"How about this fellow McKinley, then? Good man?"

"Very good. But slow to anger."

"Luncheon is served, my lord," said a voice at the door.

Luncheon was a very gay meal, with no more talk of wars. Virginia flirted outrageously with Alwyn, who responded somewhat in the manner of a St. Bernard dog chasing a rubber ball, and even with Lord Enstone, who twirled his mustache and visibly warmed towards her. Sue sat next to the shy Archie, and succeeded in making him talk about his sister Dinah. Bracken, upon whom Clare turned the full battery of her robust charm, heard Archie saying in his clear Cambridge accents, "And it isn't as though Dinah were a tremendously reckless or even brave person when she does these things. It's as though she were afraid of being afraid, really, and dared herself to punish her own courage. I know, because I'm somewhat the same way myself. Now, you take Edward, on the other hand —" Bracken had lost the thread of Clare's talk, and had to apologize.

"What a *handsome* gang of men those Campions are!" exclaimed Virginia on the way home. "And just think, there are two more brothers — Oliver in the Army and John at Westminster! You had the best one, Aunt Sue, what did you and

Archie talk about?''

''Ah, but you ought to see Oliver!'' Sir Gratian teased her. ''He's the pick of the lot! Not married yet, either. You'd better be quick, though!''

''I'd hate to marry a soldier of the Queen,'' said Virginia thoughtlessly. ''India — Singapore — Egypt — Malta — the West Indies — besides, you'd never see anything of him!''

''Yes, it's a ghastly life for a woman,'' Sir Gratian agreed, and brooded all the rest of the way back to Farthingale, while Bracken contemplated his sister with new respect for being such a clever judge of men. It took a great deal of common or horse sense, he felt, to notice Archie at all in the dynamic presence of the showy Viscount and his impressive father.

7

Lord Enstone had consented, after some financial hemming and hawing, a good deal of filial pressure by Clare, to open and staff the house in St. James's Square for the month of May. His sister, Lady Davenant, was to act as Clare's chaperone and as her sponsor at the Drawing-Room, and Viscount Alwyn took the opportunity to do some entertaining on a suitable scale, even though the Earl refused to come up to Town and participate. The blue and yellow Enstone livery appeared again, and the footmen were powdered and breeched, a matched pair of them to open the door and serve the wines. Champagne was sent up from the Hall, and the silver came out of the vault under Nash's supervision and was cleaned by the underbutler for use at dinner parties where twenty guests sat down to seven courses and five wines. Clare would drive to the Palace in the family brougham, which also had to come up from the country, together with the coachmen and the tiger.

For days no one had troubled to hand down a decision as to whether Dinah and Miss French should be left behind at the Hall or accompany Clare and Alwyn to London. At the last minute Miss French, who was human enough to long for a sight of Town now and then, convinced Lord Enstone that Dinah should visit the dentist and go to the Academy and hear some concerts, and that her injured knee was quite equal to the journey.

Dinah had been at St. James's Square for nearly a week before Virginia, practicing Court curtseys night and day with a portière fastened to her shoulders as a train, happened to mention that Dinah had had a horrid time with the dentist that morning and she did think they might find a better man who wouldn't hurt so much.

Bracken, who was now keeping regular office hours in Fleet Street and saw very little of his womenfolk, stared at his sister in surprise.

"Did you say Dinah was in London?" he demanded.

"Yes, didn't you know? They're all at St. James's Square for the rest of the month."

Bracken swallowed, counted ten. Easy, now, Virginia is sharp. Must keep her on the false scent of Clare as long as possible.

"I'm sorry for that kid," he said, trying to sound offhand. "I promised her a theater next time she came up to Town. Don't let me forget, will you. She seems never to have had any fun."

"You're quite right, she hasn't," agreed Virginia. "Why don't you take her to the Savoy? They're reviewing *Yeomen of the Guard* now, and the music is delicious."

"A very good idea. Let's see — Thursday — Friday — Friday night would do."

"It will have to be a matinée and you'll have to take the governess," Virginia told him.

"Oh, good Lord, Dinah isn't *jeune fille,* she's still a schoolgirl, you said so yourself! Why does she have to have a chaperone to a matinée with an elderly married man like me?"

"She's *jeune fille* enough not to go to the theater with any man who is practically a stranger and hasn't got a long white beard," Virginia insisted. "Besides, they don't know you're married, do they?"

"Well, no, it hasn't seemed to come up. I suppose I couldn't take you along in place of the governess?"

"Why, yes, thanks for the cordial invitation, I'll be delighted to go!"

"I'll blow you both to luncheon at Gunter's first and on to the matinée," he said. "Will you tell her or — no, I'll write a note. Do the whole thing in style."

He wondered as he sat down to write to Dinah if he had been wise to exchange the somewhat damping Miss French for the more observant Virginia. However, he was safer than he knew, as Virginia was accustomed to her brother's fondness for children, and had made up her mind anyway that he was dazzled by Clare.

Dear Dinah — [Bracken wrote after several false starts]

I have just learned that you are in Town and having dentist trouble. Just to take your mind off it, how about that theater I promised you? They are playing Gilbert and Sullivan at the Savoy now, and I propose to take you and Virginia to the matinée on Saturday. We'll have lunch at Gunter's first, to sort of get into a silly mood. If this is all right let me know and we shall call for you with the carriage about one o'clock.

Very truly yours,
BRACKEN MURRAY

Dear Mr. Murray — [Dinah wrote at Miss French's dictation]

It is very kind of you and Virginia to ask me to go to the matinée with you, and Saturday will be quite convenient. I am looking forward to seeing you both again.

Sincerely,
DINAH CAMPION

Bracken read it carefully for the second time and put it away in a drawer in his desk. Well, it's a beginning, he sighed. Would everybody think it *very* odd if I asked her to call me Bracken? *Uncle* Bracken. He shuddered. No. Better leave it alone. I suppose I can't do anything about the way they dress her, either. Certainly not till after they have got Clare's Court dress paid for. And he sat revolving in his mind abortive schemes for getting Dinah to himself as he had had her that day at the Hall when she told him about the yellow bedroom.

He was grateful to Virginia for entering into the spirit of the thing as she did on Saturday. No one could be sorrier for Dinah in her astringent existence as Clare's schoolgirl sister than Virginia, to whom

193

Gunter's and a matinée were no longer a novelty. Dinah was dressed in her best, he supposed, and beside Virginia's flowered foulard from Worth and her smart theater toque Dinah's best was pretty bad. She was wearing a white pongee frock with a pink moiré sash. The gathered skirt came nearly to her ankles and because she was thin the bodice was made with a bertha and a high collar. Her hair was as usual tied back on top of her head and hung down her back under a wide straw hat overloaded with artificial roses.

Virginia helped him to break through Dinah's first reserve and get her to talking about herself and her brothers. Edward was the king and could do no wrong, Oliver was the gilded hero, John was the clever one who on his visits home always gave her spending money, and Archie was the one she loved.

"He'll look wonderful in a barrister's wig and gown," said Virginia, willing to hear more about Archie.

"Oh, won't he!" agreed Dinah fervently. "Wouldn't you like to see him in Court! And he speaks so well, he was born to be a Q.C."

"He's shy, though," said Virginia slyly. "Is he afraid of *all* women, or did I do something to scare him?"

194

"Was he scared?" Dinah laughed. "When I asked him what it was like at luncheon that day, he said, 'American women are always so pretty. I wonder how that happens.' "

"And with Clare right under his nose!" But Virginia was flattered.

"Oh, but you're different from Clare, you're —" Dinah broke off in the middle of her sentence and her eyes returned to her plate.

"I'm what?" Virginia insisted, with a glance at Bracken.

"I don't know quite how to say it," said Dinah uncomfortably.

"I'll say it!" Bracken put in. "Virginia is a spoilt brat, which makes her amusing but very different, as you point out, from Clare. You *are* a brat, aren't you, Ginny," he added affectionately, "but we all love you just the same, I can't think why!"

"Then I shan't bother to change!" Virginia grinned at him good-naturedly. "It's nice to be loved for one's faults and not one's virtues!"

"Oh, it must be!" said Dinah unexpectedly. "I do believe that's the difference I mean. Knowing that whatever you do or however badly you behave, he still feels the way he said just now."

"But if people really love each other their

faults don't matter," said Bracken, sounding rather sententious even to himself, and Dinah regarded him with large, serious eyes.

"I wonder how many people could say that," she murmured.

"Are you by any chance coveting my brother, darling?" asked Virginia kindly, for she understood.

"Yes, I suppose I am, rather," Dinah conceded with unbroken gravity.

"Then I'll share him with you," Virginia offered generously. "He's the only one I've got and you've got five, but if you want to go halves on Bracken I'm willing."

"So is Bracken willing," said Bracken quickly, preferring that role on the whole to the one of uncle. "Virginia, Dinah, and Bracken Murray, Incorporated. I'll have Partridge draw up the papers tomorrow."

He fed them grilled sole, cutlets and new peas, with a glass of Deidesheimer each and finished the bottle himself. And for a sweet they had Gunter's specialty, which was a famous peach ice. After that the Savoy wove its customary spell, and the matinée was to Dinah a time of complete enchantment. Bracken, who knew his Gilbert and Sullivan backwards and forwards, sat a little cornerwise in his chair so that he could see her face in stolen glances, and nearly wept at its rapt enjoyment. But what a privilege would be his, he marvelled, to open doors to this sensitive, half-starved creature, to lay his fortune at her feet like a magic carpet, to watch her unfold and blossom and come into her birthright of love and beauty. It would be, that is, if Lisl could be found and dealt with conclusively.

He had got off a letter to his father after all, and then laid the matter of Lisl before Partridge, who took rather a dim view of it all, but ponderous machinery was being put in motion. It would be necessary first of all for Bracken to give evidence of his intention to settle permanently in England. Partridge had suggested that he leave Claridge's when his womenfolk departed and take rooms in Albany or some such stronghold of respectable bachelorhood. But Bracken was also contemplating another and more fascinating idea. He had mentioned in his letter to Cabot the possibility of their buying Farthingale to use as a country home when Eden and Cabot came to England as they did nearly every year — and as the house to which Dinah would eventually come as his bride.

8

Bracken had already made his bow to the Duke of York at a levée in April, and he was now watching with increasing amusement his sister's gallant *savoir faire* as her own ordeal approached. The gown arrived from the dressmaker's and was put on for his inspection. As described and sketched in *The Queen* the following week, *"Miss Virginia Murray wore white Duchesse satin with an overskirt of white mousseline de soie embroidered in a festoon design in silver and pearls. The close swathed bodice was of the same embroidered mousseline, and the train was apple-blossom pink brocade lined with puffed white chiffon, the edge embroidered in silver. Her ornaments were a pearl necklace, the gift of her father, and a pearl and diamond brooch given by her brother."*

Bracken's proud fraternal eye noticed that

the headdress of three white ostrich feathers with a tulle veil attached to their base suited her heart-shaped minxish face. Her bouquet, which he himself had chosen and arranged for, was pink roses and white orchids. Seated in an armchair, he gravely impersonated Queen Victoria and received innumerable curtseys while Virginia counted her steps and discovered the difference between her brocade train and the portière she had been practicing with, and learned the most comfortable angle at which to hold her head under the Prince of Wales plume and veil. Lady Shadwell assured her that the white-gloved Gentlemen-in-Waiting, the man with the gold stick, and a footman with a little white crook would all assist her in governing the heavy, slippery weight of the train as she made her way into the Throne Room, along the line of Royalties, and out at the further door. But Virginia, looking back over her shoulder at the yards of unruly pink brocade on the carpeted floor of their sitting-room at Claridge's, nursed a growing fear that it would all lump up in an ungainly ball behind her, or become twisted and stringy as she advanced. They will slide it along after you, she was told — they are there just to do that — it will be taken off your arm and spread for you — it will be picked up and given back to you. . . . So then, reassured and reckless, she must try it once more, and that time she caught her heel in the lace and chiffon flounces round her feet and went down, right off balance, in a helpless heap in front of Bracken's chair.

Virginia laughed first, and it wasn't hysterics. While Sue and Lady Shadwell exchanged a quick glance anticipating nervous tears, while Bracken with a mask of concern on his face reached to help her disentangle herself. Virginia leaned against him and hooted with healthy laughter. "You m-mustn't help me!" she gasped, swaying towards the support of his shoulder while she stood on one foot. "The Q-Queen won't help me!"

"She'll do," Lady Shadwell nodded to Sue, and on the theory that you must always get right back on the horse which has thrown you, they began all over again.

No one was giving Clare a train-party. Lady Davenant said she wasn't feeling up to it, but Virginia suspected there wasn't money enough. So Clare and a number of her friends were generously included on Virginia's guest list, with Lady Shadwell's approval. The late Lord Shadwell had owned coal mines, which was a very different thing from depending on rent rolls and land values for an income, as

Lord Enstone did. Lady Shadwell had known Enstone years before when his father was still alive and his sister, now Lady Davenant, was in her first season. It was saddening, she said, to think of him as being in low water financially. The Enstone Town house in St. James's Square had been a very gay place in the old days. You would never believe it now, said Lady Shadwell, but Erminie Campion was once considered a beauty, before her marriage to Davenant took it out of her. But then, Lady Shadwell added with a shrug, she herself was the prettiest of four famous sisters and look at her now. Virginia, who loved to hear stories of the mid-Victorian days, looked as she was bidden, with her candid eyes under winged brows, and said that the least pretty of those four sisters was probably better-looking than anybody was nowadays. Lady Shadwell seemed surprised — her own daughters had no tact — and then her glance softened. It sounded so like Eden.

On the eleventh, Lady Shadwell's carriage with two men on the box drove them to the Palace. The Queen would enter the Throne Room at three o'clock, but long before then the Mall was packed with carriages creeping towards the entrance, full of hungry, dithering girls in white with ostrich feathers in their hair. Few of them had been able to eat anything before they left home, because of nerves, and no refreshments would be served at the Palace. Most of them had been fortified by a cup of hot soup briskly laced with sherry, to which they were not accustomed and which was not sitting well. It was a warm day. They all had cricks in their necks from leaning forward in a special way to keep the veil from dragging backward on the feathers.

Cockney crowds lined the route, making outspoken comments on the occupants of the carriages in voices intended to carry. Careful sponsors, dreading the effect of personal remarks from the curb, especially uncomplimentary ones, kept the carriage windows closed while their charges wilted for lack of air. Lady Shadwell had no fear of the verdict on Virginia and the glass was down. Ribald ''Oo-*ers*'' of admiration floated in, which Virginia bore with great self-possession, though her palms were wet inside the long white gloves, and beads of perspiration showed at the edges of her hair. ''Lucky girl, to have naturally curly hair in this heat!'' Lady Shadwell remarked with a glance at the little rings and tendrils round Virginia's ears, which only became more so with damp. She would never forget how

Maude's crimped fringe had disgraced her mother by going limp and straight before they even reached the Palace gates and Maude had developed a maddening nervous gesture of pushing it up with a gloved hand, which persisted all the way to the Presence.

At the entrance their groom jumped down and presented their cards, and they descended rather stiffly and their trains were arranged over their arms by powdered footmen in the scarlet Royal livery and white gloves. The muggy summer heat of the street followed them into the lower hall, and when they reached the grand staircase the air was heavy with scent and flowers. They ascended slowly and Lady Shadwell had the rail because of her rheumatism. This left Virginia in the middle of the step with no support and dizziness grew upon her as they reached the top. There they paused a moment while Lady Shadwell recovered herself, and she watched with an ironic smile the fragrant, rustling figures which flowed past them. She was thinking that she was not as young as she had been the first time she mounted those stairs — nor the second time, after her marriage — nor even the third, the year Maude had come out. Perhaps, for one reason or another, one always reached the top of those stairs a little breathless. She glanced sidewise again at

Virginia, panting beside her, and Virginia grinned back gamely. "At my age, one longs for a lift," Lady Shadwell admitted, and Virginia answered with her quick, instinctive tact, "And at mine, with my heart coming out the top of my head!"

Court officials were dexterously separating the débutantes and their sponsors from the Diplomatic and the Crown Ministers and their wives, who were diverted down a different corridor as Virginia and Lady Shadwell moved on into a crowded, stuffy, glittering ante-room. They soon encountered Clare, looking as white as her dress, with Lady Davenant, magnificent in mauve satin embroidered with silver and sequins. The sponsors fell into reminiscent conversation, and other people they knew appeared with white-clad girls in tow. Clare agonized because she was convinced that her feathers were working loose, and the smell of so many bouquets and so much perfume out of bottles made her feel very queer. Virginia's pulses were pounding in her ears, and she was conscious for the first time in her life of being laced too tight, and the arm over which the heavy train had been draped ever since she descended from the carriage was beginning to go numb.

Lady Shadwell turned for a last critical inspection of her protégée. Virginia met it bravely, her chin up, while Lady Shadwell patted the shine from her forehead with her own handkerchief — no need to tell Eden's child to straighten her back! Then Lady Shadwell looked to make sure Virginia's right hand was now gloveless, and saw the telltale trembling of the bouquet. What one went through when one was young, she thought with her strangled, ironical smile. Thank God one hadn't got to be young twice. One first season was enough for anybody to have to live through!

As she and Lady Davenant left the girls and moved away to take their own places in the Throne Room, Lady Shadwell was remembering her own girlhood qualms and heartbreaks and blunders with a kind of detached pity. And then you got married. Once was enough for that too, she thought cynically, for she had married well but not very happily, having been given no opportunity to fall in love before the ceremony, so that she drove away on her wedding journey with a man who was little better than a stranger. At least her Maude had been allowed to choose, and the other two as well, when their turn came, though goodness knows they had not had enough offers among them to make it difficult. But she was wondering cynically, even as she performed her own curtsey before the Queen, how much difference it made, really, as you drove away, how well you thought you knew him. All three of her girls had clung to her and cried, before they went. And then, with all that behind you, feeling a thousand years old and doubtless with a baby already on the way, you came back to the Palace and were presented again as a married woman. You weren't so frightened the second time, you'd been through a good deal in the meanwhile. She found herself wondering too if at her age she would still be available when it came time to present this lovely, confident American after her marriage. They said Enstone's eldest boy was madly smitten. . . .

Virginia and Clare stood together, supported by each other's company among the twittering, white-clad throng in the ante-room. At last the doors to the Throne Room swung open, and there was a rustle and a slight press for places. A calm precise voice somewhere up ahead of them began to announce names, it might have been for the guillotine. They inched forward step by step, and reached the Picture Gallery, which was the last ante-room before the Throne Room.

During the wait there the inevitable happened and some poor girl was quietly sick. Everybody turned their heads away and pretended not to notice, and a footman was seen approaching, and Clare whispered, "It's exactly like *mal de mer* crossing the Channel — you're sure to be next!" "Count by three's," said Virginia desperately, through her teeth. "It's very difficult. Try it!" "Edward put sherry in some soup and made me drink it," Clare moaned. "I *told* him it wouldn't stay down, and he *laughed!*"

Virginia felt herself drifting ahead, imperceptibly — there was no way now to go back — the arm which held her train was aching unbearably — Clare was in front of her, Clare would have to go first — at least the weight of the train would soon be lifted from her arm — never take your eyes off the Queen as you advance — don't touch her hand with yours — don't move your lips audibly in the simulated kiss above it — don't forget to curtsey to the other Royalties present — don't turn your back — don't cough or sneeze or move your hands — and for the love of God don't trip — I wouldn't do this again for a million dollars — my arm is going to drop off when he takes the train away — I'm shaking so it shows on the orchids — I *must* hold this bouquet steady —

two more — they say the Prince always smiles if you're pretty enough — I suppose Lady Shadwell has done this so many times it only bores her — I bet the Queen is more bored than anybody — there goes Clare — it's worse for her, being a famous peer's daughter she has to get her cheek down where the Queen can kiss it — there's the man with the gold stick they promised us — he put it where her train had to drag around it and straighten out — clever of him — my arm, my arm — more footmen with white gloves — there, they've taken my train at last — they do handle it nicely — I mustn't look back — oh, golly, *that's me* —

The Queen was seated in an armchair instead of on a dais — it made her so much lower than you expected — a little dumpy lady in black taffeta, with a lace cap and lace lappets, and the broad blue ribbon of the Garter slanting across her breast — so many orders, so many jewels — so many chins — down, down, *down* — she saw me — she *looked* at me, and kindly too — who else is here? — the Princess of Wales — dip — Princess Victoria — dip — Princess Christian — dip — ooh, the Prince! — dip — I'm all right now — the Duke of Connaught — dip — who's that? — dip — I could go on like this all night —

It was over. And the Prince of Wales had smiled.

9

"I never saw anything so pathetic as the way young Dinah enjoyed herself at the Savoy," Bracken remarked at breakfast a few days after the presentation. "It haunts me. I am convinced that her family is a collection of inhuman monsters, yes, including Clare, and that's flat. Ginny, I want you to do something for Dinah."

"Why, of course," said Virginia promptly, wondering if Bracken had some warped idea of courting Clare through Dinah, and unable to see where it would get him.

"I want you and Aunt Sue to borrow her for an afternoon. Go and fetch her here to the hotel in the carriage. And then I want you to turn her over to me for the rest of the time. Don't you think that would work?"

"I think so," said Virginia, interested. "What have you got in mind?"

"Anything she likes," said Bracken vaguely. "A ride on the top of a bus — a trip to the Zoo — the new picture gallery down on the Embankment — some shopping at Hamley's — maybe tea, all of us together, at Rumpelmeyer's — nothing Miss French would take exception to, only I don't want her breathing down our necks."

"That's reasonable enough! When shall I get her?"

"Oh, I dunno — tomorrow, if you like. I'll take the afternoon off."

There were no objections raised to Dinah's spending an afternoon with Virginia and her aunt. Bracken refused the carriage after it had delivered Dinah to Claridge's, and they set off together in a hansom. Sue and Virginia were to shop, and meet them at Rumpelmeyer's at five.

Dinah's cheeks were pink and her eyes shone. She wore the same white pongee dress and ridiculous hat because it was all she had.

"This is fun," she said. "I feel like a real young lady. What are we going to do?"

"Well, first we are going to see about that birthday present. You've got to choose it because I don't know enough about you yet."

"I never chose my own present before," she said. "It seems a very whimsical idea."

"It has only one drawback. You must

211

promise not to think of the price. Just shut your eyes and choose what you want and leave the rest to me. I'm the Bank of England."

"Does that mean you've got lots of money?" she inquired with one of her long, direct looks.

"Well — quite a lot. And I like to give people presents, ask Virginia if I don't."

"She said you gave her that exquisite watch."

"Yes. Would you like a watch?" His voice quickened.

"Oh, *no!* I mean — you mustn't give me one! I — wasn't hinting."

"I never thought you were." He spoke to the driver through the trap. "Asprey's," he said, and —

"No!" cried Dinah in a panic. "You mustn't! Father wouldn't like it!"

"Just a *little* watch!" said Bracken recklessly. "You could wear it underneath, on a chain."

"I can't wear anything underneath that Miss French doesn't see!"

They were still wrangling when the cab stopped outside Asprey's in Bond Street and Dinah refused to budge.

"All right," said Bracken, his left eyebrow a little up. "You wait here. Sit well back so you aren't seen by everybody you know. I shan't be long."

He was back in no time at all, with no visible purchase, and told the driver to go to Hamley's in Oxford Street. Dinah breathed easier. Hamley's was a toy shop.

"As the cab moved on, Bracken put his hand into his coat pocket and then held it in front of her. Lying naked in his palm was an incredibly small ball-shaped watch, with a magnifying crystal and a blue enamel and gold case, attached to a filament of gold chain.

"Just a *little* watch?" he repeated persuasively, and his voice was not quite steady.

Dinah said nothing. While the cab trundled up Bond Street she sat gazing at the watch in Bracken's palm, until suddenly her lips began to tremble and with a gasp she hid her face against the end of his shoulder nearest her.

"Dinah, darling, for heaven's sake —" He sat very still, holding the watch. "I never meant to make you cry —"

"I'm not crying," she said, and her breathing was controlled. "It's just — I can't have it, and I *want* it so, I never wanted anything so badly in my life! Silly, isn't it!"

"Can't have it, eh." Bracken dropped it back in his pocket and locked both hands in front of him. "I'll tell you what. I'll keep it for you. It's yours, you see, even if you can't wear it — yet. Some day I'll find a way to give it to you without there being a row. In the meantime, whatever happens, you'll know it's there, waiting for you."

"In your pocket?" She lifted a smiling face.

"Always in my pocket. It's our first secret. Virginia and I have dozens of secrets."

"What fun she must have had with you all her life!" she sighed enviously.

"Don't forget, now there are three of us," he reminded her. "You're going to have fun too, from now on. Here we are. Don't mind that it's a toy shop, will you, they have lots of things besides dolls and mechanical trains."

For nearly an hour they dawdled about the fascinating shop, warding off helpful assistants, inspecting everything from jackstraws to toy theaters. Gradually Dinah forgot to be afraid of wasting his time, of being a nuisance, of not making up her mind quickly, of spending his money. Gradually it seeped into her humble consciousness that the afternoon was hers and that he was enjoying himself too. Gradually she ceased to try to restrain him every time his hand went towards his wallet, and gradually they accumulated a stereoscope with a large assortment of pictures to go with it, a set of ornamental playing cards for patience, a tiny doll dressed like the Queen at the time of her coronation, a magnet which attracted the oddest things, and a lump of artificial toffee on which an artificial fly was fastened.

Then they came to the music-boxes.

They played them all, and Bracken bantered the young lady shop assistant who was there to demonstrate them till she was dissolved in giggles. Dinah could not help seeing the prices on some of them, and suddenly turned shy about letting him buy her one. There was a handsome mahogany box which played three different tunes, including the Barcarolle from *Tales of Hoffman,* and there was an exquisite small silver-mounted affair which had only one tune — *Du Bist Wie Eine Blume,* with no flatting and no missing notes. Bracken favored the latter, and yet was not sure she might not prefer more variety. Dinah would not choose. Bracken shut his eyes and brought his forefinger down unerringly on *Du Bist Wie Eine Blume.* ''That one,'' he announced, and paid for it without further ado.

When it was wrapped up he handed it to her rather solemnly and said, ''That's your birthday present, Dinah. The rest of this is just trash. Put that away and don't open it till you're sixteen.''

''Thank you,'' said Dinah, awed, and accompanied him out to the cab.

There wasn't time to go to the Zoological Gardens then, so they drove around Hyde Park admiring the flower borders and talking nonsense. Promptly at five they arrived at Rumpelmeyer's and found that Sue and Virginia had been equally prompt. They all entered the restaurant together, which was fortunate, as Lady Davenant was having tea with some friends near the door. When he had given the order, Bracken said, ''Now, listen, children, if anyone should ask you, we all went to Hamley's together and bought Dinah some silly presents because she's having a bad time with the dentist, and a birthday present that she's to put away and not look at till September. The birthday present is a music-box. Is that quite clear?''

They nodded.

''But you might have let us know,'' Virginia grumbled. ''I shall buy her a present myself tomorrow.''

That night when he emptied his pockets on to the chiffonier before going to bed Bracken stood for a long time with the watch in his hand, observing the play of light on the fine jewelled chain and enamel case. Not one of the extravagant things he had given Lisl had ever roused in him the same peculiar possessive joy as the little watch from Asprey's. Some day he would put the chain around Dinah's neck himself, and when that day came he would also be entitled, please God, to collect a kiss as his reward.

Finally he put the watch away in the small flat box which belonged to it, and every day after that it went into his pocket as regularly as his keys and wallet and engagement book, an amulet to keep the powers of evil at bay.

10

It somehow came about quite naturally that Sir Gratian should accompany Sue and Virginia when they returned to Farthingale as his tenants instead of his guests, and take Bracken's place as the man of the house in his absence. It was an arrangement which Sir Gratian himself found highly satisfactory and Bracken was only too glad to have him in charge of them. It pleased the women too, and Sue was heard to remark that any household without a man in it was like an egg without salt.

Virginia found Farthingale a new and fascinating toy, and was inclined to spend more of her time there than in Town. She enjoyed an opportunity to return in kind some of the hospitality the family had received in recent years, and the guest rooms at Farthingale were usually full when she and

Sue were not in London. Her pretty aunt had become a great pet among girls accustomed to more severe chaperonage than Sue was capable of. Even the younger men considered it a privilege to escort Sue in to dinner, seeming as eager for her company as though she were their own age, and they always clustered around to ask her to dance in the evenings when they rolled back the rugs and somebody played waltzes on the piano. Naturally, Sue bloomed under this treatment. She played every game there was going, from croquet to blow-feather and bézique. She took part in their *tableaux vivants* and charades on rainy days. And as Eden had prophesied, she was having the time of her life.

People fell in love with Virginia during that Diamond Jubilee Summer almost as readily and numerously as she had boasted to Miles Day that they would. But she was not satisfied with any of them, and the most fatuous among them could hardly have fooled himself into thinking he was the one. To Bracken, who saw more than anyone gave him credit for and always knew exactly who was which without seeming to keep track of things, it looked almost as though Virginia had something on her mind. Not something to spoil her fun. But something that acted as a balance wheel.

Bracken awaited his father's reply to the letter about Dinah and the proposed purchase of Farthingale with some anxiety. When it came it was in line with his parents' policy of allowing him to make his own decisions as far as possible, and he was grateful for their apparent lack of astonishment or caution. He knew that they could have as yet no clear idea of Dinah Campion, and his request that they keep his letter confidential and not let Sue or Virginia get wind of Dinah's part in his plans was an additional handicap which must have been very irksome to them. He wondered what impression of Dinah they had already got from Sue's and Virginia's letters, and longed for a chance to talk to them face to face — or better yet, to show Dinah to them. He was sure that then they would understand everything and would conspire with him to rescue her from her barren existence at the Hall.

As June came in, the streets of London were full of the sound of hammering, while miles of scaffolding went up for seats along the route of the Procession. Space in these was selling for as much as five pounds per person. Flags flew everywhere, shop windows were decorated, and colorful foreign uniforms appeared, the handsome East Indian troops in their bright turbans the most striking of all the visitors. The Queen's cream-colored Hanoverian horses were exercised in the Mall, and crowds of people gathered daily to watch the changing of the guard at Buckingham Palace. The capital was very crowded, all the great houses were open, and entertaining was on a grand scale. Plague, war, or famine — and all three were abroad in the world — London was *en fête*.

A rumor went round that Victoria would not receive her Kaiser grandson because of her displeasure with his recent behavior regarding South Africa, and therefore no other sovereigns were expected to attend the Jubilee. In most cases the Queen had indicated her choice for their representatives. The Emperor of Germany was no longer a popular toast at even the most sporting dinner parties, and the yachting carnival at Kiel was boycotted by the English amateurs whom Wilhelm had thought to entertain there.

Everyone knew that Greece had intervened to try to save the Cretans from the fate of the Armenians under Turkey's reign of massacre and terror — and on top of sticking in his highly unwelcome oar in South Africa, the Kaiser persisted in joining the Czar in open support of the Sultan, reckless of the opinion of the rest of Europe. *The Prussian policy*

221

under Frederick the Great was not more strictly dictated by the personal whims of an absolute monarch than the policy of Germany has been during the past weeks of the Cretan crisis, Bracken wrote for the New York *Star. It is an unhappy portent of things to come which will surely not be lost on the peaceable and enlightened people of Germany. . . .*

The next American mail brought him that sheet of his dispatch enclosed in a letter from Cabot, who had blue-pencilled it briskly and written across the margin: *Rats. The German people love it. Who told you they were enlightened?* The accompanying letter suggested further that Bracken seemed to have forgotten the salient points of a German tour made in his parents' company a few years before, and advised him to go back to Berlin and learn his lesson again, if necessary. Chagrined, Bracken thought back through a pleasant haze of beer-gardens and Strauss waltzes and magnificent mountain scenery, and remembered the heel-clicking Prussian officers with straight backs to their heads, and their arrogant way of walking down the street four abreast so that mere civilians must step off into the gutter to pass; remembered their meek, mute, mousy wives, and the anxious, abased politeness of lesser Germans in their presence; remembered his mother's tart comment that for all their medals and monocles and bowing from the waist and *Küss-die-Hand,* the Prussian attitude towards women belonged to the dark ages; remembered her disgust at their ways with muddy boots and cigar-ash and tumblers in the drawing-room, which had caused her to remark that as a class they were hardly housebroken; and he decided that he could do without a refresher course in German human nature. He also made a note to look up who it was that had said that nations generally got the Governments they deserved.

The London Season ambled forward, all its familiar landmarks gilded by the Jubilee gaiety — the Queen's birthday, the Royal Academy with its Sargents and Abbeys, the Garden Party, Ascot, Goodwood, polo at Ranelagh enlivened by the picturesque presence of the East Indians, the yachting at Cowes — and in addition that summer the Handel Festival at the Crystal Palace, the Duchess of Devonshire's fancy dress ball, and the birth of the Jubilee Princess to the Duke and Duchess of York at Sandringham.

Lord Enstone's household had returned to Gloucestershire before Jubilee Day, to Clare's and Dinah's disgust, and once re-established there, it did not go racketing back and forth to London as the family at Farthingale did.

Virginia and Sue of course went up to see the Procession, from an expensive window in Pall Mall, and one night Bracken hired a bus, as the fashion was, and took a whole party out to see the Illuminations. The streets of the West End were festooned with colored electric lights and silk draperies; private homes as well as shops were lighted and decorated. Bracken's bus joined the continuous stream of vehicles which included everything from costers' carts full of exhilarated Pearlies, to ducal carriages with two men on the box. Everything had to move at a snail's pace, with frequent blockades, and the police behaved like gods and like angels. There was a constant exchange of witticisms between them and the bus-drivers and the Cockney girls, most of it as good as a music hall turn. During the complete stoppages when progress became impossible, the lower classes turned the pavement into an impromptu ballroom and danced schottisches and reels to concertina music. And poor Dinah had to miss all that.

A few nights later Lady Shadwell took Virginia to a State Ball, which Sir Gratian had also been commanded to attend. Virginia wore white lace with pink ribbons and pearls, and the Prince sent his equerry to request a dance, during which His Royal Highness was more than once seen to roar with laughter, which caused some raised eyebrows at his notorious weakness for Americans, especially the pretty ones. They all went to Ascot, in the Enclosure — Virginia in embroidered white batiste over pink glacé, with a white feather boa and a large straw hat; Sue in pale green muslin with a white toque and sunshade; Bracken and the Major in morning clothes and grey toppers. And the Prince recognized Virginia again right across the Lawn, and laughed again, as though at some private joke between them. Poor Clare would have loved Ascot. Virginia tried to console her by asking her to the parties at Farthingale, and always included Dinah in the picnics and the informal teas.

Meanwhile Bracken reported on it all to the *Star,* and Cabot even cabled his appreciation of the account of the Procession and an article on the Colonial troops in London which reached the New York office at the end of June: *Never better satisfied. Believe you are surmounting personal trouble superbly. Both send love.* That was unprecedented from Cabot, and Bracken, who admired his father both as a man and as a boss, was warm with pride. He wanted to show the cable to Dinah, who was after all responsible for the state of mind in which he was doing his best work again, but the reference to his trouble was awkward. He put the cable away in a drawer with her note and caught a train for Upper Briarly with a feeling that he had earned a long week-end.

There were guests down from London and he found his household in a slight uproar over the fancy dress ball which was being given at the Hall in honor of Clare's début. Bracken had brought down with him his own costume as designed and ordered by Virginia. She had put him into an Elizabethan rig devised solely, he alleged, to advertise his physique. Virginia told him not to be vulgar, and that he went with her Mary Stuart.

"I refuse in any case to behave like the men, if you can call them that, that Mary Stuart always took up with," said Bracken flippantly. "A worse judge of the male character has seldom if ever been known. Now, take that brute Bothwell —"

Virginia advised him to behave like Leicester and be done with it, which made him stare at her with sudden horrified suspicion.

"What sort of dress is Clare wearing?" he demanded.

"The Virgin Queen," grinned Virginia.

Bracken was speechless. Then —

"And Dinah?" he rallied feebly. "What

have you done with her?''

Virginia said they hadn't done anything with Dinah because she wasn't allowed to go to balls yet.

''The hell she isn't!'' Bracken exploded, quite forgetting himself. ''If Dinah isn't invited, *I* won't come!''

Virginia frowned in a perplexed sort of way.

''You know, Bracken, you'll only make trouble for her, spoiling her like this. Her people aren't used to it.''

''It's time she had a little spoiling, if that's what you call it to treat her like a human being,'' he retorted. ''You bung yourself right over to the Hall and tell her ladyship that Dinah is coming to that ball or I stage a one-man boycott!''

''Go and tell her yourself!'' Virginia suggested.

''All right, I will! Get your riding-clothes on and come along.'' He took the stairs two at a time, still boiling.

''But Bracken, Dinah hasn't got a dress,'' Virginia was objecting as she came down stairs in a riding-habit ten minutes later. ''And no one has time now to get her one.''

''I have. And so have you. We'll see to it.''

''But we'd have to go all the way up to

227

London for it!''

''Yes, I expect we will,'' he agreed serenely.

He set off on Sunbeam at such a pace that further conversation was impossible.

By the time they reached the Hall he had got things under control again. When Nash showed them into the tapestry room, where they found Clare writing letters, Bracken was looking bland and lazy, which Virginia recognized as a bad sign and tried to head him off before he could offend Clare.

''Clare, darling, we were thinking — since it's fancy dress and in your own house and all, why not let Dinah come to the ball?'' she began pleasantly before Bracken could speak.

Clare thought it over in her deliberate way.

''She might have, I suppose. But it's too late now to get her something to wear.''

''*Au contraire,*'' said Bracken softly. ''There's something very wrong about my doublet and I have to go back to Town and see about it in the morning. Virginia is going up with me, and we can choose something for Dinah then.''

''*Ready made?* Where could you find anything?''

''At a theatrical costumer's. We'll fit it on Virginia and get it a little snug.''

''Well, it's very good of you to trouble,''

Clare said slowly. "I'm afraid you two will quite turn Dinah's head if you keep on. She's only fifteen, you know."

"It's dull for her," Bracken said easily. "How would *you* like to be shut up with Miss French day in and day out? She'll hear the music and see other people dressing up — I think it's heartless not to let her come and share the fun."

"I don't know what Father will say," Clare remarked doubtfully.

"Tell him your American friends, who pamper their children, insisted."

"Well, if you're sure you want to bother about her dress — but perhaps we could find her something here that would do and save trouble."

"No," said Bracken firmly, for he had been afraid of that. "Since we're going up anyway we'll see about it."

"What's wrong with your doublet?" Clare asked curiously.

"They've bungled it some way since I tried it on." Bracken began to move Virginia towards the door. "Well, we'll see you Saturday night — looking forward to it — good-bye —"

He escaped, holding Virginia by the arm.

As they rode away, Virginia looked at him thoughtfully.

"Bracken," she said, "you're pretty sweet."

"Why, thanks, Ginny, nice of you to say so."

"There's only one thing. You may be putting ideas into Dinah's head."

"What sort of ideas?"

"Romantic ones."

"Oh, stuff and nonsense, to her I'm just a shade younger than Rip Van Winkle," he said carelessly, but his heart beat a little faster.

"Darling, just because you're accustomed to thinking of yourself as being on the shelf because of Lisl, you don't realize that you're an absolute menace. If I weren't your sister I'd be terribly gone on you myself."

"Ginny, dear, spare my blushes! Or are you working up to ask me for money?"

"You may think Dinah's only a child, but when I was fifteen I was in love with the Barlows' coachman."

"I fail to see the connection."

"Well, Dinah's at the *age,* Bracken! She's immature, I grant you, but any time now she'll begin to take notice."

"I trust that in any eventuality I shall behave as well as I hope the Barlows' coachman did!"

"Oh, *idiot,* I never even spoke to him!"

Virginia laughed helplessly.

"Very well, there you are! I'm not just a handsome profile on the box to Dinah — how *is* my profile, by the way?"

"Divine."

"Good. But don't you see, I'm around under foot making an ass of myself all the time. She can't possibly romanticize me, I'm much too commonplace — as the coachman would have been if you had known him intimately."

"I don't think we're getting anywhere with the coachman, I should never have brought him up. Bracken, I want you to be happy and have everything you want and I think it's *beastly* about Lisl — but you do underrate yourself, honestly you do. Clare has an *endless* curiosity about you —"

"Has she, indeed!" he murmured.

"— and somehow I find it rather difficult to — well, to suppress all mention of Lisl, and besides I don't think it's fair to Clare."

"But Ginny, I've never made love to Clare, I've never even —"

"Bracken, you don't have to make love to a girl for her to be most awfully smitten just the same!"

"Oh, don't I?" He seemed much struck by this.

"You just drift around wearing tweeds the

way you do and saying the silly sort of things you do, and that ridiculous eyebrow of yours, and —''

''Which? What's wrong with it?''

''It *slips,* in the most fascinating way, didn't you know? There it goes now. It slips *up.''*

''Does it? I never noticed. And it's your considered opinion that the grand total of these unusual talents of mine is fatal to every woman who sees me? Well, *really,* I had no idea.''

''I'm not fooling, Bracken, honest.''

''No, I don't believe you are. But has it occurred to you, my sweet, that as a sister you might be prejudiced?''

''As a sister I ought to know the worst of you. And if *I'm* crazy about you, what chance have the rest of them got?''

''What *is* the worst of me, Ginny?'' he asked gravely.

''When you're in a black depression as you are now, and try to hide it by being flippant and obtuse.''

For a few minutes they rode slowly in silence. Then Bracken said —

''All right. I'll tell them.''

''That you have a wife?''

''Mm-hm. It may be a trifle difficult to find an opening, of course. Speaking of cutworms, I have been deserted in a most scandalous fashion by my lawfully wedded wife — would that be too abrupt, do you think?''

''Darling, I hope you don't think it's interfering of me, but —''

''No, no, it's all just part of the curse.''

''What's become of her, do you know?'' she asked suddenly.

''Oddly enough, we're trying to find that out. Funny, we no sooner get rid of her than we start in trying to get hold of her again. Partridge has set some sleuth-hounds of his on the trail, but it's all so very hush-hush that it's extra complicated. I don't want a scandal, for your sake.''

''I wouldn't mind, if it got you free.''

''But I would, and so would Father. Come on, we'll be late for tea.''

11

Half the county was coming to the ball.

Both the Hall and Farthingale were jammed with house guests and more people began to arrive in carriages with dress-baskets and band-boxes soon after luncheon. At the Hall a striped marquee had been set up on the lawn below the terraces, and colored lights were hung in the shrubbery, although a full moon was expected. Tubs of azaleas flanked the grand staircase. There was a band down from London to play in the ballroom, which was festooned with Marechal Neil roses, and Gunter's had sent a van full of caterer's assistants who took possession of the dining-room, where the decorations were pink and white peonies in tall silver vases. There would be ices in shapes, and fireworks, and enough champagne to float a battleship.

Lord Enstone and the Viscount had

compromised on wearing Court dress. Archie had adopted the powdered wig, brocade skirted coat, knee breeches and sword of the third Earl's portrait at the time of his marriage in 1745. John and his wife were coming to stay, and were dressing as Romeo and Juliet, which everyone thought rather odd as they had been married several years and didn't get along very well. Mrs. John, whose name was Iris, was a pallid, timorous woman, and John was like Alwyn except that where the Viscount had merely a sort of natural animal arrogance of good looks and superb health, John was domineering and humorless. Sir Gratian was wearing something Wellingtonian with a very high collar, black stock, tail coat and tight pantaloons. Sue had a simple Hogarthian costume that was quite irresistible on her.

At Nathan's in Coventry Street they had found for Dinah a gipsy dress of no particular period — a white cotton blouse with a round gathered neck, quite low, and very short puffed sleeves, and a wide apple-green sash that tied around her slim hips above a flaring, brightly flowered skirt. Heavy bracelets and ropes of gay beads went with it. Virginia reported that she looked adorable in it and was excited completely out of her usual composure. She was still not to come down to dinner, but only after the dancing began.

Bracken endured with resentment the knowing glances brought about by his Elizabethan dress partnered at dinner with Clare's Tudor queen. He realized that Virginia was right and he must somehow convey to them soon that he was — encumbered. What effect that fact might have on Dinah's attitude towards him he could not decide. Meanwhile he observed that Alwyn's rather florid attentions to Virginia were also attracting notice. It was impossible to tell by Virginia's habitual play of eyelashes and smiles whether she was unduly impressed.

After dinner Bracken strolled on the lawn a while with Sue and Sir Gratian, who were as handsome a pair as there was in the whole company, while a tuning of instruments sounded from the open windows of the ballroom.

The Hall had returned for that single night to its past glory, and was full of lights and music and crowds of expensive people behaving in an expensive way. The grand staircase was alive again with silks and velvets and cambric, hooped skirts, powdered hair, and the clink of sword-belts. Just as the music began Bracken went into the entrance hall and saw Dinah peeping over the banister. He motioned her to come down and she shook her head, looking shy and frightened, eyeing his unfamiliar dress critically.

Bracken started impulsively for the stairs, and ran into Lord Alwyn, who caught his arm and said, "Hullo, come along to the ballroom, old boy, that's the first dance."

"Yes, I'm already engaged for it," Bracken replied.

"Clare just went in. Probably looking for you."

"I'm dancing this one with Dinah," said Bracken.

"With *Dinah!* Oh, come, now, you'll have her poor little head completely turned. She's only supposed to look on, you know, at her age."

Bracken felt one of his rare furies rising within him. He had drunk only a little champagne at dinner, and except for that sudden surge of rage he was entirely responsible as he said quietly —

"Alwyn, it will doubtless surprise you to hear that I intend to marry Dinah as soon as she's old enough."

The Viscount stared at him, still holding fast to his arm with one heavy hand. The idea passed plainly across his mind that one or the other of them was drunk, or that Bracken was joking. Reluctantly he abandoned both those surmises.

"Well, uh — have you told her so?"

"Of course not. And I would be grateful if you'd leave me to do it in my own good time."

"But she's — let me see, not sixteen yet!"

"I can wait. In fact, that's not the only difficulty. I have a wife, though we haven't lived together for several years. Her religion makes it convenient for her to refuse divorce, but I hope to get round that before long."

"I see," said Alwyn, obviously not seeing at all.

"I am speaking in strictest confidence, naturally."

"Oh, naturally."

"But I thought it would help you to understand my interest in Dinah."

"Quite. Quite."

Alwyn let go of his arm and Bracken ran up the stairs to where Dinah still stood watching.

"What on earth did you say to Edward?" she greeted him. "He looks simply floored."

"I only let him know that I always choose my own partners for dancing. Come along."

"Me?"

"Please."

"No wonder he was surprised!"

"You can waltz, can't you? If not, I'll teach you."

"At dancing school. But never with a real partner." At the door of the ballroom she shrank back against him with wide, apprehensive eyes on the whirling couples. "I can't do that."

"Yes, you can." His arm went round her waist. "Just relax and listen to the music."

After only a minute their steps matched perfectly.

"It's like floating," said Dinah.

"You're wonderful," he said. "There's nothing you can't do when you try. How much do you weigh?"

"About seven stone. Why?"

"I just wondered." Not a hundred pounds, he thought. And in that slim body he held so lightly was all his hope of happiness. Her throat and breast in the low-cut blouse showed that they were losing their childish thinness, her upper arms had still that heart-catching frailty of the very young. God forgive me for a cradle-snatcher, Bracken thought. If I were Alwyn I'd call me out. But I will be very careful of her. And I promise to wait patiently. Well — I'll wait.

"It was kind of you to make them let me come tonight," she was saying. "Oh, Virginia too, but I'm sure it was you in the beginning, wasn't it?"

"It was, as a matter of fact. But Virginia agreed with me that you had a right to come."

"You're the kindest man in the world, I think. I do appreciate it."

Bracken winced.

"Can't you think of another word?" he asked.

"What did I say?"

"*Kind*. It makes me sound like a very old gentleman who keeps up his charities."

"How old are you?" she asked directly, as though it had occurred to her for the first time.

"Twenty-seven — nearly twenty-eight." It sounded awful as he said it. "Lord help us, that's almost twice your age!"

"It's the same as my brother John," she said unconcernedly. "I don't think that's bad at all."

"Of course when you're twenty, I shall be only thirty-two instead of nearly forty," he reminded himself.

"I wonder where we'll be then."

"I wonder." His arm tightened involuntarily.

"Have you got a birthday coming too?" she suggested.

"November third. I'll give a party. Will you come?"

She nodded. Her eyes were gay and confident.

"I'll beat you, though. I shall be sixteen before you're twenty-eight," she boasted.

"That's a comfort!"

"I have the strangest feeling with you sometimes," she said after a minute.

"What sort of feeling?" he asked hopefully, all attention.

"I can't describe it. It's as though I *mattered* to you a great deal, the way Virginia does. I expect it's just because you're so k —"

"*Kind!*" he said bitterly. "Will you stop it, Dinah?"

She laughed.

"Well, it's a very flattering feeling, all the same. Miss French says I mustn't presume on it. I'll try not to."

"I'll tell you how it is," he said, choosing his words. "I like to see people have a good time. There's so much unhappiness in the world we can do nothing about, and when the expenditure of a little thought or money does give somebody something pleasant to remember — I like to do it, that's all. I sound like a parson, don't I, preaching sweetness and light. Maybe what it all comes to is that I happen to like you rather a lot, ever since that first morning on the hill."

"I like you too," Dinah said frankly. "I'd be crazy not to, after all you've done for me!"

"Then will you do me a favor?" he asked, feeling his way.

"Yes, of course." No *arrière pensées* for Dinah.

"If ever there's anything I can do to — brighten things up a bit for you — promise to let me know, hm?"

"Why, yes — I will." She looked a little puzzled.

"I'll be around, you know. You can always reach me at the office if I'm not at Farthingale. By the way, I've decided to buy it."

"*Buy* Farthingale? Oh, how lovely! That means the Major won't be so poor."

"It also means I can keep an eye on you," he said, piqued that her first thought had been of some one else. "That may be a silly thing to say to a girl with a lot of brothers, but sometimes an outsider can be more useful than one of the family. Don't you agree?"

"I suppose so. I never thought about it."

"And after Virginia and Aunt Sue have gone back to America you'll have to keep an eye on me, how's that?"

"Do you — really think I'm old enough to be your friend?"

"Don't see why not."

"I'd be proud. Not that I could ever *do* anything for you, I know that, but sometimes one wishes there was somebody one could just talk to. At least I do."

"So do I. We'll talk to each other, shall we?"

She nodded gravely, and then the music stopped.

"Now I *will* have to dance with Clare," he said. "Come and see my aunt's dress. Isn't she sweet?" He took her to where Sue and the Major were seating themselves on a sofa and left her with them.

Later, while he was dancing with Virginia he suggested a supper party of six — himself and Dinah, Sue and Sir Gratian, and whatever partner Virginia already had.

She made a face.

"Ed-ward!" she said.

"Oh, dear, that won't do! Can't you swap him for Archie?"

"Too late. And Archie hasn't even asked me to dance."

"What's the matter with him? Nobody can be as shy as all that."

"I begin to think he just doesn't *like* me." Her eyes were hurt, and it occurred to Bracken that he might have to take notice of Archie.

"Is there some other girl he's after?" Bracken gave a quick glance around.

"Oh, no, he seems mostly to be making himself agreeable to the chaperones and wall-flowers."

"The man's a fool."

"Or a saint."

"I hope not! They're very uncomfortable people to have around!"

"I think it would be fun," said Virginia reflectively, "to make Edward dance with Dinah. It would sort of establish her prestige for the evening."

"He's pretty busy, I expect."

"He'll do what I tell him to," Virginia said darkly.

"Oh, that's how it is, is it!" her brother remarked uneasily.

And sure enough, before very long the Viscount led out his younger sister. The triumph was Virginia's. She had been engaged to him for that dance and she contrived at the last moment to catch hold of the elusive Archie and persuade Alwyn that she would be well taken care of while he made Dinah's evening by conferring himself upon her for one waltz. Alwyn had observed that Dinah did herself credit on the dance floor, with Archie as well as Bracken, and he consented graciously enough. Dinah's face was a study, and being nervous she did not do as well as with her other partners.

"Well, are you enjoying yourself, eh?" he inquired in the half bullying, half-patronizing tone he had always used towards her ever since she had first been able to make intelligible sounds in reply.

"Yes, thank you, Edward."

"Don't thank me, thank your friend Murray. It was his idea." Alwyn turned it over in his mind and decided to be clever. Cleverer, anyway, than Bracken Murray. "Queer chap," he went on loftily. "Americans are all dashed queer, of course, one expects that. This fellow's wife seems to have left him"

"Why, I didn't know he was married!" cried Dinah in quite natural surprise.

"To a Catholic, apparently. That rather rules out divorce, you know. Seems a pity, what?"

"Yes, doesn't it."

But Alwyn had not been quite as clever as he thought. Dinah, who had never before thought of Bracken Murray as much but a pleasant phenomenon in her monotonous existence, now suddenly began to think of him as a man with a broken heart, who was being so brave and cheerful you would never guess.

In attempting to block off supposititious romantic yearnings on Dinah's part, Alwyn had instead brought Bracken into focus for the first time and roused her compassion for him. She remembered that Virginia said he had had a lot of worry and was working too hard and needed rest. And this evening while they danced, he had asked her, Dinah, to be friends with him, after his womenfolk went back to America. Even with all that money to spend, even in spite of his jokes and carefree ways and thoughtfulness for other people, and his lighthearted enjoyment of life as it came, there was some kind of tragedy behind him, and he must often be lonely and sad inside, and too proud to show it. Dinah could appreciate that. No matter how badly your feelings were hurt, or how blue you got, or how sick you felt about the way somebody treated you, you mustn't ever show it. You had to keep your chin up and look people straight in the eye and not let them know your inside felt like a mass of screaming jelly. Bracken Murray had had to learn this too. Bracken Murray was better than anybody at looking people straight in the eye as though nothing was wrong with his inside. And he had asked her to be his friend . . .

Womanhood stirred in Dinah. She wondered what sort of creature could have failed to be happy with so kind and lovable a man as Bracken Murray. And she was sure, passionately sure, that whatever had happened, he was not to blame.

12

"One would think I had leprosy at least!" Virginia remarked when she and Archie had danced in silence for a full minute, and he glanced down at her in amazement, holding her off a little farther to see her face better under the becoming Stuart cap.

"I beg your pardon?" he said automatically, for surely she had not said what he thought she had said.

"Well, so you should. I'm not accustomed to have to wangle the privilege of dancing with some one I happen to like."

"Meaning me?" He still looked somewhat stupefied.

"Meaning you."

"I thought you were booked."

"Well, you could have un-booked me! *I* did!"

"Should I apologize, or something?"

"You certainly should!"

"Then I do."

She stole an upward look at him, through her lashes. Seen close in the dance, he was almost too handsome, his lean, fine jaw and brilliant blue eyes framed by the white wig and lace jabot. His mouth was like Dinah's, with long lips evenly divided. Virginia yielded herself a bit more to his arms, and his response was involuntary and quick. She smiled beneath his chin. Human, after all.

"Why do you avoid me so?" she murmured.

"But I —"

"Yes, you do, too!" she insisted crossly. "I can tell!"

"Well, if you must know, you're too attractive."

"Are you practicing to be a monk or something?"

"No. Only a barrister."

"That seems to be the next thing to it."

"Yes, doesn't it!" His encircling arm was once more impersonal, his face with its clean, sculptured lines was inscrutable.

Thwarted, Virginia danced in silence again to the end of the waltz. He thanked her formally and moved with her towards some chairs.

"Aunt Sue was here a moment ago. She

must have gone outside. Oh, don't bother about me if I bore you so!'' she cried, rounding on him fiercely. ''I've got lots of other partners — *willing* ones!''

He looked as though she had hit him.

''Please, Miss Murray, I —''

''Ah, here you are, Virginia,'' said Alwyn's arrogant drawl just behind them. ''All right, Dinah — now you can take on Archie again, what? This is the supper dance, I believe.''

Virginia took his arm, leaving Dinah beside Archie, who stood looking after them.

''Archie, what *is* it, did she hurt your feelings?'' Dinah asked.

''She had a right,'' he said after a moment. ''It's the only thing I can do, though.''

''Are you going to let Edward marry her?''

''*Let* him!'' he repeated with irony. ''Edward never waits to be let, does he? Besides —'' He stopped.

''Well, of course, Edward has got the title and all,'' she agreed understandingly. ''But people do make money at the Bar, don't they?''

''Sometimes. By the time they're ninety. Would you like an ice?''

''Mr. Murray says I'm to have supper with him. Won't you join us?'' She laid her hand on his sleeve urgently. She was suddenly shy

250

of Bracken now that she knew about his wife.

He came up just then, dodging through the dancers at the edge of the floor, and said, "Hullo, Archie, may I borrow her till supper? Join us then, won't you?"

"Thanks, I will."

Archie watched them dance away. Dinah thought he looked rather forlorn, standing there alone, and much too thin. He must be studying too hard.

"You're very silent," said Bracken. "Aren't you having a good time?"

"Oh, yes, lovely," she answered absently. "I think Archie and Virginia have had a quarrel."

"Oh, that. He missed his cue. Didn't ask her to dance. She'll get over it."

"Do you think she's in love with Edward?"

"I don't know." He had nearly said, I hope not. "Do you?"

"I hope not," said Dinah. "Archie is much nicer. For marrying, I mean."

"Just what are your requirements for marrying, Dinah?"

"I've never thought much about it. Except —"

"Yes?" he encouraged her.

"I'd never marry a man I was afraid of."

"Naturally not."

"People do, though. Iris did. I'm sure she's terrified of John sometimes. It sends cold shivers down my spine, the way she looks at him when he starts bullying her. Perhaps I shall never marry," said Dinah, quailing suddenly before immensities.

"That's a strange thing to say at your age," he remarked lightly.

Dinah felt the subject might be painful to him and ought to be changed. Already the idea of his mysterious wife was clouding their relationship, which had been so uncomplicated and serene. She glanced up to find him looking down, and his eyes were just the same as before Edward had spoken. She considered that Edward had betrayed him to mention his private affairs even to her, and a quickening, protective affection for him ran through her. She would do everything she could to spare his pride, and would never let him know that she knew. Perhaps some day he would speak of it to her himself, if he really thought of her as a friend. How could he smile like that, with a droll, slanting eyebrow, after what he must have been through? She smiled back, hesitantly, and Bracken, conscious of a new warmth in her steady regard, which he took to be gratitude for a happy evening, caught her closer in an exultant pirouette.

"Glad you came to the party?" he whispered, his lips near her hair.

"Oh, yes! And it was a good idea to ask Archie to have supper with us. Let's be very gay so he doesn't miss Virginia."

"Let's," said Bracken, and once more he wondered if Archie was going to have to be seriously reckoned with, and his eyes fell on Virginia who appeared to be sulking in Alwyn's arms as they danced. "There will be you and me and Aunt Sue and Sir Gratian and Archie — and lots of champagne."

"Do you think I could have some?"

"Champagne? Certainly."

She looked up at him again, gratefully.

"You make everything seem so *simple!*" she marvelled.

"A little champagne never hurt anybody."

"Have you ever been very, very drunk?" Dinah asked seriously.

"Will this be used against me?"

"No. I just wondered."

"Well, then, I have," he confessed. "But don't you try it. It's not worth the hangover. I'm warning you."

"I do like the things you say!" she laughed.

"And have I said that I like the way you look tonight?"

"Am I really all right?" she queried anxiously.

"You're sweet, Dinah. You're a credit to me."

"I'm glad."

Still no coquetry or self-consciousness, no apparent awareness of him as a male. Virginia at fifteen would have bridled and made eyes. He didn't want that from Dinah, but at the same time he found the total lack of it discouraging.

Sue was being, in her quiet way, one of the belles of the ball. Sir Gratian had managed to secure her for the supper dance, and before it began they went out on the terrace under the moon and among the colored lights, and he allowed the talk to run on freely, enjoying her confidence that he was going to make no more embarrassing proposals. It wouldn't do to chivvy her, but his time was running out.

Sue had, it was true, regained a feeling of security with him, and decided that he had accepted her refusal with resignation. She was so without conceit or experience that it did not occur to her that she might be worth a little caution and maneuvering and then another try. She convinced herself that he had proposed to her on an impulse and that by now he was glad that she had not taken him up on it. The strong attraction between them was still there, in his lingering gaze, in her own heightened pleasure in his company. But she had been through all that with Sedgwick, and it had never come to anything more. So she was caught off guard when he said, quite casually —

"My orders came today, Susannah."

"Oh, does that mean you must go?"

"The end of this month."

"Back to Egypt?"

"And on up the Nile towards Omdurman, dragging the railroad with us." He sighed. "I dread to think of your leaving England, even though I shan't be here to see you go."

"It will be sad, in a way, for me to go. I've come to feel very much at home."

"Perhaps if I could have given you Farthingale along with my worthless self I might have kept you here," he suggested, ruefully.

"Oh, Gratian, I won't allow you to say such a thing, even in fun! Farthingale has nothing to do with it!"

"Susannah — they say the British never know when they are beaten, which is why they usually win. I'm afraid I haven't been able to give up hoping —"

Sue rose hastily.

"Sh! There's Archie, looking for us, I

think. The music has stopped. It must be supper.''

Sir Gratian said something under his breath, and then Archie was upon them.

''They sent me to find you, sir,'' he said. ''Bracken and Dinah are saving places for us with them.''

There was no opportunity for Sir Gratian to speak to her alone again during the rest of the evening, but she knew now that she was in for it. They reached Farthingale in the carriage in the early summer dawn, sleepy and silent and Virginia a little cross, and separated to their rooms with brief good-nights.

But Sue, over-stimulated and over-tired, could not go to sleep. Soon after the sun was up she got out of bed and sat at her window in a dressing-gown, apprehensive and unhappy over what was before her with Sir Gratian. Phrases formed themselves neatly in her mind — but suppose he said something quite different from what she expected and the phrases wouldn't fit. She wasn't writing him in a book.

Then for a time she tried, deliberately and in cold blood, to picture what her life as his wife would be — how it would feel to see Virginia start home without her, with Bracken as travelling companion while she herself stayed on in England — how it would seem to own allegiance only to a man who a few weeks before had not entered her life — how it would be to have to write a letter to Sedgwick to tell him she wasn't coming back. . . . It was there that panic set in, and all she could think of was Sedgwick's face at the station in Washington when he said, "Don't get lost —" and turned and walked away from her.

Finally she went to her desk and took a sheet of notepaper.

Dear, dear Gratian —[she wrote]

Please don't ask me again, I dread saying No to you, and I must, I *must* go back to Williamsburg. Forgive me if I have made you unhappy, I thought you had got over it, and I do treasure your friendship and always shall.

Sincerely,
SUSANNAH

Without even reading it over she put it in an envelope, sealed it, and leaving herself no time for indecision tiptoed down the passage and slid it under his door.

As she reached the door of her own room again she heard his door open behind her and faced about with a little gasp. He stood there, the envelope in his hand, fully dressed in his country tweeds for an early walk. Like herself, he had not slept.

For a moment they gazed silently at each other, the passage between them. Then she went into her room and closed the door.

Leaning against the inside of it, she heard his footsteps go past, with a heart-stopping pause opposite her threshold, and on down the passage towards the stairs. When she moved away from the door at last her cheeks were wet.

Bracken slept, for Dinah had given him back his rest along with his zest for life. But he woke quite early and lay congratulating himself on a successful evening all round. He had, he felt, made some progress with Dinah, even though she did not blush and stammer when he paid her a compliment. She seemed to be getting used to him, that was the thing. And she had seemed to absorb the idea that they might keep an eye on each other in a friendly way. Also, he reflected with some satisfaction as he rang for his shaving-water, he had settled Alwyn's hash.

Finding himself the first one down, he went out into the yew walk to admire the bright new morning, and there he came suddenly around a corner on to a bench where Sir Gratian sat with his head in his hands. It was too late to retreat unseen, and as Bracken hesitated the Major looked up, his face drawn and tired in the revealing light.

"Morning," he said drily, and rose from the bench with a weary slowness.

"Bit of a hangover?" asked Bracken sympathetically, hoping that would do.

"No. Crossed in love," said Sir Gratian grimly, and turned to pace along beside him. "I don't have to tell you more, do I."

"There is a legend in our family," Bracken began in a light, impersonal tone, and slid a hand through Sir Gratian's elbow, matching his step, "which I had from my father, who got it from my mother, who was present at the time, that Aunt Sue fell in love at a tender age with a boy who was her double first cousin, plus. They weren't allowed to marry, and he went away to join the cavalry. But now they still live in the same town, see each other every day, and — seem to keep quite cheerful on it. This is the first time she has ever left him. I suppose she feels that no matter what has happened to her, he's still waiting."

"I didn't know," said Sir Gratian, after a moment. "She mentioned her father —"

"Her father was just an excuse. It's Cousin Sedgwick that takes her back. I'm supposed to be very like him, so you can see what bad taste she has.''

''She might do worse, at that,'' said Sir Gratian. ''Thank you for telling me.''

When they entered the dining-room arm in arm ten minutes later, chatting of this and that, Bracken felt entirely justified in having suppressed the fact of Sedgwick's happy marriage to Melicent.

13

The purchase of Farthingale was completed in Mr. Partridge's office in London before Sir Gratian departed for Egypt, and Bracken felt a new contentment, an end-of-the-journey peace, as though St. John Sprague had stretched out a friendly hand across the generations to guide him home. Now his roots could go down into the soil of England where Dinah's were, and their lives even now could run parallel until they became one. It gave him the right to be in Gloucestershire as much as he liked, to be casual and neighborly and underfoot, and gradually she would learn to count on him.

The Graeco-Turkish war had come to a disastrous end for the Greeks, and the Powers were negotiating a laborious peace. The news from the Northwest Indian Frontier became increasingly grave, and young Hilton was ordered on to Calcutta. Kitchener, who abhorred correspondents, was conducting his campaign towards Omdurman in Egyptian darkess so far as the Press was concerned. He kept the men from the London dailies boxed up in a fortified village a hundred miles behind the end of the railway, and remained impervious, unlike the British Indian régime, to blandishment or prayers. The Kaiser visited the Czar in August, with a full program of maneuvers, fireworks, illuminations, processions, and State banquets. The two absolute monarchs pledged each other publicly as gentlemen, emperors, and friends, to keep the peace of Europe — and the next day witnessed together the most impressive military review of their respective reigns.

Suddenly it was August. You knew the summer was nearly gone because the sweet, melancholy cry of the lavender-women was heard in dusty Mayfair. The West End of London emptied itself into the country houses, the clubs closed for cleaning, the streets came up for repairs, and the City dozed. August was the Silly Season in the journalistic world, which as usual abandoned itself to stories about sea serpents, prize marrows, lost causes, and weather superstitions, so Bracken allowed himself a few days in the country.

He had subscribed three hundred pounds to the Hunt, and had bought Sunbeam from Lord Alwyn for sentimental reasons, with the provision that she was to return to her home stables to board during his necessary absences from England. They all went out for a day's cubbing, though the scent was catchy owing to drought and the ground was hard enough to lame a carelessly ridden horse. "The thing about cubbing," said Alwyn, though not in any spirit of real complaint, "is that you have to get up so bloody early in the morning, what?" He was at first inclined to pamper Virginia, and held back to see her over the walls. This got her dander up, and Bracken's heart was in his mouth more than once while she demonstrated to Alwyn that she was as good a horsewoman at least as his sister Clare. Even Sue did a bit of larking over a locked gate for the honor of the family. Bracken found it good to hear hound-music again, and the lovely heart-shaking double notes of the horn blowing them out, and the stout Hunt-servant noises in the coverts. And next year, he promised himself, he would have Dinah at his side on a good horse of her very own.

Her sixteenth birthday was celebrated by a luncheon party at Farthingale early in September which Archie came all the way down from London to attend. But the presence of Alwyn and her father lay heavy on the meal, which never achieved either the dignity of a real anniversary nor the spontaneous gaiety of a children's party. Because the music-box gift was already in her possession, Bracken had brought the largest and most assorted box of sweets Fortnum and Mason could supply, and was not aware that it passed for his only present to her in the eyes of her family. Some cautious instinct had prompted Dinah not to exhibit the music-box, which she regarded as their secret.

Sue had chosen for her a pink coral pin set with pearls — the Queen of Italy was said to have brought coral back into fashion. Virginia gave Dinah a tiny live Indian tortoise, its shell studded with jewels. These were worn on the shoulder with a gold chain, watch-fashion, by prankish *elégantes* in Town, but everyone agreed that it would be best for Dinah's to live in a basin with a bit of sand and greenery, where it would be much happier, and it was plied with tidbits from her plate which it would have none of. Virginia explained at some length that the man in the shop had said it would eat bits of raw meat chopped up fine, and had shown her how to tickle it under the chin to make it open its mouth. Lord Enstone at that point decreed that the tortoise could wait for its lunch until after they had left the table.

By September Sue had got thoroughly homesick, and Bracken promised her that just as soon as things let up a little more and he felt that the London office could run on its own feet for a few weeks he would leave Nelson in charge there and accompany them home to spend Christmas as usual in Williamsburg, returning to London in January. Virginia heard him without enthusiasm. Archie had pelted back to Town the day after the birthday luncheon, and there he stuck, eating his dinners for the Bar and reading Law day and night in his chambers in Half Moon Street. Lord Alwyn, meanwhile, was becoming a bit tiresome. But all the same, to give up and go home, to turn her back on the man who by his seeming indifference had caught her butterfly heart, was a very difficult dose to take.

Bracken pestered Partridge for news and there was none, until a letter arrived from Eden in New York.

My dear People —[Eden wrote to all of them]
You must be wondering about things here, but I have been kept very busy.

You will have had Cabot's cable about Marietta's baby, a pretty eight-pound girl, and all is well in that direction, and I can breathe again.

I can, that is, theoretically, but there always seems to be something in our family to work up a good worry about if we try. There is no sense in keeping from Bracken the enclosed letter from Sally, who says that Lisl has been at Cannes with her diamond merchant, cutting a wide swath. She is using her maiden name of Oleszi, which is a blessing as even the French *demi-monde* seems to have been a little scandalized at her goings-on. I can find it in my heart to hope that Lisl will come to her bad end quickly, but I am haunted by a foolish fear that if she did die abroad somewhere we might never know that Bracken was free. Cabot says they have taken precautions against that very thing, but when I am low in my mind it always seems to me a most likely thing to happen, and after all, they had lost track of her, hadn't they, until this news of Sally's!

My other fret is Fitz, who I am positive has fallen in love, but short of asking him outright we are unable to

266

learn anything definite. Oddly enough, he is doing well at the tasks assigned to him, and what's more he has sold two of his songs to a music publisher, which pleased him any amount and actually brought him in a little extra cash. A few weeks ago he announced suddenly that he wanted to live according to the money he earned and not under our gilded roof any longer, and has taken a cheap room in a respectable house — he says!— on West Twenty-ninth Street. Cabot is convinced that it is a case of *cherchez la femme,* and talks darkly of detectives, but I hate to think of starting *that* again, what with Lisl too! And yet if the girl he has taken up with is all she ought to be, why hasn't he brought her to see me?

You had probably better not write anything to Sedgwick about this. I haven't, and it may resolve itself any day. I have decided anyway to leave Fitz alone till Sue gets back to New York and see if he won't confide in her, he always does.

And if you don't all come home soon I shall have to come and fetch you. I am glad Bracken has decided to keep the house, and am laying plans to see it myself in the spring.

Love to you all from all of us,

EDEN

Sue was for sailing at once to attend to Fitz, but Bracken, reading Sally's letter, had gone rather white and didn't seem to hear. The next day he left for the Continent and was gone nearly a week, and returned looking sleepless and depressed without having accomplished anything.

Whether or not she had got wind of his coming and wished to avoid him and the small, smooth-shaven man Partridge had sent with him, Lisl had vanished from the gaming tables, taking the man Hutchinson with her. Bracken had gone to see Sally at Cannes, while Partridge's representative joined up with the sleuth-hound already on the job and they went poking about on their own, as they said, turning over stones.

It was the first time Sally and her cousin Eden's son had ever met, and they formed a strange, immediate friendship. There was much in her fantastic household which revolted him — the little yapping dogs, the soft-footed, knowing servants, the unexplained presence of a handsome, sullen French youth she called Paul — but Sally herself, with paint on her face and henna on

268

her hair and a French *r* on her tongue when she spoke English, was somehow still kin, and their blood bond spoke as soon as they touched hands.

From her he received further unsavory details of Lisl's career. Lisl passed openly as Hutchinson's mistress, but apparently took satisfaction in considering him beneath her, and treated him with flagrant contempt, while he on his side was subject to wild, jealous rages when he even threatened her life, and their quarrels could be heard half way to Paris. Sally thought Lisl was acting like a fool, for if she drove Hutchinson away from her, at least unless she had found another wealthy protector, where would she be? Sally was full of impractical suggestions for hurrying on the divorce, most of them requiring some highly improbable coincidence as a starting point, and Bracken tried rather wearily to explain Partridge's course of legal procedure. In the end he had to come back to London with nothing to show for his journey but Sally's faithful promise to keep a sharp eye and ear, and let him know the minute Lisl showed her nose again.

"Let's go home for Christmas, then," said Virginia listlessly, laying her arm around his shoulders the evening he arrived in London and told them how it was. "I don't care if I never see England again!''

Bracken patted her hand sympathetically. Once he had suspected that her perverse interest in Archie Campion arose mainly from the fact that Archie was the only man she had ever looked twice at who had not instantly grovelled. Now he had begun to fear that it went deeper than that. He was glad that she had had the good sense to prefer a younger son to the heir, since Archie was so patently preferable to Alwyn, as Dinah had said, for marrying. No title went with Archie except the mere Honorable. It was pretty obvious that no money went with him either. Lots of money would go with Virginia when she married. Bracken wondered if possibly that was what was biting Archie, and at the same time he surmised that Virginia's money was no drawback in Alwyn's estimation. . . .

14

Their earliest possible sailing date fell so near
to Bracken's birthday that he talked them into
waiting over so that he might have the day at
Farthingale. The house was taking on the
Murray imprint now. Some needed repairs to
the roof and the drains were under way.
Wire gauze was fitted to the windows to
keep the flies out. The sparrows' nests had
been cleaned out of the gutterpipes, and
the jackdaws' nests were gone from the
chimneys. An extra maid was being trained.
The coachman had been put into the claret-
colored livery of Eden's men-servants in New
York, and a smart dog-cart with red wheels
and a high-stepping two-year-old had been
purchased for station work in place of Aunt
Sophie's stately barouche and matched bays.
The cellar was being stocked by a London
wine-merchant — it would take the hocks

two years to settle after the move. And Bracken was looking into the matter of installing a small dynamo for electric light and getting in another bathroom next spring before his parents arrived.

A note from Dinah was waiting for him at Farthingale.

Dear Mr. Murray —[it said]
Could you ride out to our hill quite early on the morning of the third? I should hate to have to give you your birthday present before everybody at luncheon, and besides, it isn't much.
DINAH

This left Bracken feeling distinctly cheerful. Our hill. The one where she had first ridden towards him in the sunrise. He had not known she thought of it as their hill.

It was a very different sort of morning, though, from the one which saw their first meeting. A frosty night had given way to a threat of drizzle, and wisps of mist clung to the hollows. The sky was low and grey. Even the swallows had gone, and the leafless trees were silent and empty. In London they would be eating breakfast by gaslight and setting forth into a real pea-souper. Here in the Hills, Sunbeam's feet rustled through brown fallen leaves, and the bare patches were studded with toadstools.

Dinah was riding side-saddle on a respectable little mare this time, obviously with the benediction of the grooms. Dewdrop was getting old and was considered safe. Clare had learned on her. It was not the first time he had seen Dinah mounted and dressed as it was considered proper she should be. But he noticed that her face was childish and aglow between the severe white stock and the hard bowler hat of her habit, and she was genuinely glad to see him.

"Many happy returns," she recited punctiliously as she rode up to him, and held out a small square parcel wrapped in white paper. "It isn't anything, really, I only have a shilling a week pocket money, and you can't do much with that."

It was a music-box; not one of the best ones, but he saw that she must have begun to save almost the whole of her allowance as soon as she knew that his birthday was coming.

"Oh, Dinah, that's very clever of you, we'll start a collection," he said, much moved. "I'll bring you back one from New York."

"It plays something called *L'Elisir d'Amour*," she said without embarrassment.

273

"But I'm not responsible for that, I had to write and send them the money and let them choose."

"That's funny," he said. "Aunt Sue has one that plays the same thing." He pressed the catch and the music-box tinkled its tiny tune in the morning stillness. "I'll take it home with me when I go, for company."

"Are you *sure* to come back?" she asked, and the words were anxious.

"Very sure." The music-box had gone silent with a little click, and his eyes held hers solemnly. "I swear to come back, Dinah," he said. "You can count on that."

"I do. I do count on you. It's a very cosy feeling. You don't make half-promises like other people and then forget all about them. When you say you'll do a thing I feel as though nothing can stop you."

"Under Providence," he said. "You'll never be rid of me now. How do you like the prospect?"

"I shall bear up under it, I think," she said, with her rare, wide smile, and it was only by the greatest effort that he removed his gaze from her face and forbore to pursue the subject further.

Their horses moved on slowly down the slope while they laid confident plans for things to happen after his return early in the year. He would be back in time for the best of the hunting in February when the big dog-foxes were travelling — Dinah told him how last year they had killed one in the Friday country up near Stow-in-the-Wold which had weighed close to sixty pounds. She pointed out to him, a little farther on, what Archie always said was the prettiest find in England, where the Field gathered on a hill above the covert so they saw the fox leave and hounds gather on his line. By now they had ridden behind a spinney which hid them from view on all sides, and Dinah glanced round and broke off in the middle of a sentence.

"If you don't mind, I'd like to say Good-bye now instead of this afternoon with everyone looking," she said, and drew off her glove and offered him her hand across the saddle. As he took it he saw with dismay that her eyes were full of tears.

"Here, *Dinah,* hold up, it's not for long, only a couple of months, possibly three — and I'll write to you every week, will that help?"

Her lips quivered. She couldn't speak, but sat looking at him helplessly, her hand in his. He slid from the saddle and lifted her down against him and she buried her face in his coat and clung to him, sobbing. But it was a child's grief only, at parting from a friend, and he held her like a child, patting her shoulder and murmuring nothings, while his heart sang because she cared so much, no matter how, and there was lots of time. On a sudden inspiration he put his hand into his breast pocket and brought out the flat box where the watch lived and flipped it open.

"Look!" he said, as though she was about two. "See the pretty toy!"

"*Oh!* You brought it!" Her tears stopped. Her hands cupped the box lovingly, holding his between them.

"I always bring it. It never leaves me. It's our luck, Dinah, whichever of us has it."

"It's the loveliest watch in the world. I'm glad it's going with you because if it's mine that means you'll have to come back to give it to me, won't you."

"My darling, it *is* yours, and you'll see it again in January, at the latest."

Her tear-wet face was raised to his incredulously, while her eyes spilled over again.

"You called me —" With an arm thrown round his neck, she tiptoed quickly to kiss his cheek. "Good-bye till January," she whispered.

"Thank you," he managed to say quietly. "I'll take the twin to that the day I get back."

The farewell luncheon party that day was for Bracken something of an anti-climax. Archie was missing from the circle and Virginia's spirits visibly drooped. Clare's eyes were cool and reproachful because Bracken seemed to have nothing whatever on his mind with regard to her own valuable self, and Alwyn was aggressively cheerful to cover the shock of Virginia's having refused to become the future and eighth Countess of Enstone.

Only Sue was entirely composed and happy, for soon she would be able to see Fitz again, and come at the matter of his hypothetical love affair. She felt as though she had narrowly missed the edge of a precipice, for suppose, oh, just *suppose* she had allowed herself to be bewitched by poor Gratian's good looks and gold braid and sweet ways, and then Fitz had got into trouble and they wanted her at home!

PART THREE
GWEN

Williamsburg.   *Spring, 1898.*

1

Fitz, with his soft drawl and slouching, graceful carriage, professed to have become a sure-'nough Yankee after nearly a year in New York. He was waiting on the dock with Cabot and Eden to welcome his cousins home.

A little in the background there hovered a fourth figure which Fitz dragged forward affectionately, saying, ''You remember Johnny Malone, Cousin Sue,'' and Sue said she did and gave her hand to a young man in a soft hat who seized it gratefully, mangled it in his, and murmured something embarrassed and complimentary. She then recalled having seen him about now and then during the flurried days before they had sailed in the spring, and supposed that he worked on Cabot's newspaper too.

''*Well, Johnny!''* Virginia was crying in

an astonishment too well done to be quite convincing. "Whatever are *you* doing here?"

Johnny Malone blushed, swallowed, and started to explain that he had just happened to come down to the docks to see about a fire —

"That's a lie, Ginny," said Fitz gently. "He's been meeting this boat ever since she sailed from Liverpool. All I could do to keep him from swimming down to Sandy Hook. And will you all please note his alarming state of sobriety at this time of day?"

Virginia laughed happily and patted Johnny's sleeve with light gloved fingertips.

"Never you mind him, Johnny, I appreciate your coming down here no end," she said, and her long eyelashes lifted intimately to Johnny's enraptured gaze. "My, it's good to see some dyed-in-the-wool New Yorkers again, after what I've been through!" she added, and cast herself devotedly on Cabot's chest.

There were two carriages waiting. But somehow when they rolled away from the dock Johnny Malone, after being tirelessly helpful about the luggage, was not in either one of them.

"It must be pretty tough to be in love with the Boss's daughter," Fitz remarked thoughtfully when Johnny's tactful absence was discovered. "If it ever happened to me I'd just cut my throat and rest in peace."

"Johnny will live through it, I think," said Eden kindly. "He's a very impressionable young man."

Eden knew that no young man, however impressionable, but with the good reporter's capacity and affection for hard liquor which Johnny had, stood a ghost of a chance of marrying any daughter of hers. Cabot was not a snob, and Johnny was a good news hound who had manfully served his stiff apprenticeship in the police courts, with the fire department, and among obituaries, several years before Fitz started to work in the same office. Johnny had risen to forty a week now, on the gaudy Tenderloin beat which he loved best, among the theaters and all-night restaurants, where the chorus girls and the crooks and the politicians were as likely to make him their *confidant* as to resent his vocation, and where he had learned more than enough professional secrets to get him shot any day, except for his cast-iron discretion, drunk or sober. Johnny had Cabot's promise — they called it a threat — of a by-line before long if he behaved himself. But he would never make the City Editor's desk at the rate he was drinking.

Johnny drank whiskey the way a baby guzzles milk, with an artless joy and the most harmless results. Johnny was in fact very funny when he was drunk. It didn't make him quarrelsome, he seldom picked fights, and he was never disgusting or demoralized. He simply got delightfully, blissfully soused and he stayed that way for hours, sometimes it seemed for days. It rarely interfered with his work, and he remained quite coherent even on the telephone if it became necessary to dictate a story back to the office. But it did not recommend him as a possible suitor for the Boss's daughter.

Cabot had viewed with approval the firm friendship which grew up between the neophyte Fitz and Johnny Malone, particularly as Fitz showed no inclination to try to keep up with Johnny's drinking. (Fitz stuck mostly to beer.) Johnny knew the ropes around the City Room, knew the map of New York like the palm of his hand, knew all the most useful policemen on the best beats, knew the barkeeps by name from the Bowery to the Forty-second Street Reservoir, and — it came first for Fitz — Johnny was always ready to go to a music hall show.

In Johnny's company Fitz saw them all — the Atlantic Gardens on the Bowery, which had a female baritone and a ladies' orchestra in white dresses who drank beer between times with the customers; Prospect Gardens on Fourteenth Street where the prima donna was the wife of the proprietor and must be treated as such; the Winter Garden whose female patrons were not exactly ladies, though its owner called it a family resort, and it often sheltered on its big-hearted bill some hard-luck act which otherwise would have been laid off and which gratefully drew a maximum fifteen dollars a week; Tony Pastor's which was respectable, and the Alhambra just across the way which was barely so, and the Haymarket on Sixth Avenue which was far, far otherwise and had gambling rooms and other more private apartments up stairs; and many more unsavory holes-in-the-wall where the beer was good and the company quite bad and the music so-so, and where there was seldom a dull moment.

Johnny called most of the soubrettes by their first names and they addressed him in even more intimate terms. From Johnny Fitz learned the rules and customs of each house, and sat night after night under the dim, smoky lights drinking cool dark Münchner while the band played Viennese waltzes and modern ragtime and two-steps; learned to josh the waiters, buy drinks for the musicians, and pay lurid compliments to the specialty ladies in flesh-colored tights and brief spangled costumes with a discreet fringe which came half way down the thigh. From Johnny he learned that the girls got cold tea when you bought them a drink, and that most of them would give you their eyeteeth for a pair of silk stockings; and that if you could get a popular soubrette to plug your song and it caught on and the audiences took up the choruses with her and went away whistling it, you might get it published with *Introduced by* — on the cover, and then if it went into the bill at Pastor's or Koster and Bial's the royalties started rolling in, and first thing you knew you had money, and then those who had looked askance on song-writing as an occupation were confounded and you could afford to be magnanimous and buy them presents with your earnings. . . .

Johnny had been impressed when he discovered that Fitz wrote songs. Anybody could hold down a forty-a-week newspaper job, but only talented people could read music, much less write it. Such an accomplishment ensured that Fitz would never have to live and die a rum-soaked reporter, said Johnny with awe, and added that he trusted when Fitz's tunes had become as well known as *Daisy Bell* and *The Little*

Lost Child and were being sung every week by Lottie Gilson and Della Fox, and maybe with slides, too, he trusted that then, Johnny would repeat, raising the slow, emphatic forefinger which assisted his utterance as his sentences became more and more involved, trusted that *then* the wealthy composer would remember who his old friends were, even when his sales had reached fabulous figures in the piano trade. . . .

Thus, over Fitz's Münchner and Johnny's perpetual rock and rye, they would map out Fitz's profitable future. Fitz also had a responsibility during those tours of the lesser music halls and beer gardens. For whereas Johnny could take care of himself with the soubrettes and the ladies' orchestras, who never seemed to expect from him anything but the most casual amenities, Fitz must never by any chance allow his friend to stray up stairs to where the gambling rooms were. Because if ever this did happen, the results were dire and went on all night, leaving Johnny with nothing to pay his rent or even buy his lunch with the next day.

Fitz was seeing life with Johnny. At first his contacts with the New York underworld had been purely in the line of business and he had considered them quite revolting. His gentle breeding and rural background had not prepared Fitz for the metropolitan night courts, where the human soul sometimes appears at its nakedest, or the morgue, whose sights are not for the squeamish, but both were included in the regular beat of a cub reporter on a New York daily. Fitz set his teeth and schooled himself to Johnny's philosophical acceptance of the baser aspects of humanity. Gradually Fitz grew his own calluses, so that the sight of a nameless man done violently to death no longer made him retch, and he could view the aging, painted, hopeless faces of streetwalkers picked up on minor charges of thievery and vagrancy with only an impersonal compassion, and could refrain from giving away his last dollar to hideous beggars who displayed their deformities as their chief stock in trade.

Finally he ceased to feel strange and apprehensive in the sinister backwaters west of Fifth Avenue, and accustomed himself to Johnny's catholic acquaintance with characters the police were looking for — or should have been looking for, if it had not been made worth their while to be blind. Theodore Roosevelt had been called to Washington to act as President McKinley's Assistant Secretary of the Navy, and under Tammany rule New York was relaxing again into its old easy ways before he had been

Police Commissioner. The clean-up was over. The town was bulging wide open again. Anything could happen almost unquestioned, and most of it did.

Johnny's friends included gamblers, cab-drivers, firemen, beer hall proprietors, vaudeville actors, cheap politicians, barflies in general, strong-arm men who carried guns and felt free to use them, women who lived precariously and died young — Johnny mingled with them all, and in his company Fitz witnessed as bad or worse in his leisure hours as on his routine newspaper assignments. But they were not required to write it up, except that Johnny sometimes used it under the guise of fiction, as Richard Harding Davis did. Fitz no longer winced at language, nor blushed when shameless women made jocular love to him. He held his tongue when it wasn't his quarrel or Johnny's, and he ducked automatically when a gun went off in the middle distance. But he had never learned to control the pit of his stomach. He never quite lost the impulse and the desire to be somewhere else when a ruckus began. Which only went to show, Johnny would point out sadly, that he was not a born reporter.

It was a Cinderella-like existence Fitz lived anyway. Each day he left Cabot's brownstone mansion on Madison Avenue for the grubby environs of Park Row, spent his working hours recording the sordid aftermath of everything from pocket-picking to Chinatown murder, and returned again — often with the most heartfelt relief — to the sane and usual world presided over by his beautiful Aunt Eden, where one dressed for dinner and occupied a box at the theater, and people's more private and violent emotions were kept decently hidden.

''The Shop'' over which Cabot Murray presided as owner and editor of the *New York Evening Star* was not the picturesque madhouse which was becoming fashionable with some rival newspaper offices which considered themselves more live and up-and-coming. There were almost no office politics at the *Star,* or personal feuds and jealousies. There was no visible excitement as the time for going to press drew near, and no frantic last-minute endeavor. The greater the pressure and the higher the tension over a big story, the quieter and more efficient the City Room became.

The *Star* had one of the finest newspaper plants in the world, modestly housed in the basement whence the throb of the presses and the smell of printer's ink rose comfortably to the effective serenity of the editorial floor.

Cabot did not believe in beating the big drum for himself or his plant, but he was one of the first to install speaking-tubes in order to eliminate shouting, and typewriters in order to eliminate bad handwriting, just as he had been one of the first to utilize telephones, and the cables while they were still expensive, to eliminate delay, and to run a leased wire straight from Washington into the office. He hated noise and confusion, even as he hated sloppy writing. He read every line of his paper every day and knew who had written it, and bestowed praise as generously for a bright three inches about a lost child as for a breakneck scoop on a crime case. His pitiless blue pencil developed in *Star* men a trenchant, hard-hitting style all their own which was studied all over the country. Whenever a reporter lifted his eyes from his desk they encountered a sign which carried in large letters the only slogan the *Star* ever employed: DON'T BORE THEM.

Cabot usually wrote the leader himself, and every other editorial line had to pass his inspection. It was an era when most of the big newspapers reflected the personalities of the men who owned and edited them — magnetic, colorful, fearless personalities with the gift of words, who said what they chose and stood by it, and could make and unmake legislators and even Cabinets by the weight and passion of their opinions. He wielded a brilliant and astringent pen, himself. People who bought the paper seldom said, "What's in the *Star?*" but rather, "What's Murray got today?" He could always cover a big assignment better than his star reporters and they knew it.

Cabot had bought the New York paper after the death of his father who during the '60's had owned a contentious, froth-at-the-mouth Republican organ in Trenton. The *Star* was then a prosy sheet devoid of interest or policy. Within a remarkably short time Cabot had turned it into a vital, newsy, highly profitable property which bore the imprint of his own powerful personality on every page. He had a genius for hiring the right subordinates and a profound conviction that a newspaper's first business was news, and not professional crusading nor circulation stunts. His word in the Shop was law, his policy the only one, and his wrath when something went wrong was swift and terrible. Yet he was accessible all day long to anybody from the Managing Editor to the office boy with a toothache, and you were likely at any minute to be called into his private office and praised for something you hardly knew you had done, or fired for something you hoped

nobody had noticed. But if you made good at
the *Star,* and behaved yourself, and tried
always to do better still, you had a job for
life if you wanted it.

Cabot's splendid height and rugged good
looks made him recognized wherever he
went, to say nothing of the trademark he
possessed in a beautiful red-haired wife who
knew how to dress. His hospitality was
famous, and celebrities from all over the
world came to his dinner table in Madison
Avenue. It was rumored that he had been
urged to run for Congress but preferred his
job at the *Star,* and that he had refused the
Ambassadorship to the Court of St. James for
the same reason. His children were much
travelled at an early age, yet were singularly
unspoiled by their father's wealth, although
their precocity had caused raised eyebrows all
over Europe for years.

Unlike the *Tribune,* the *Star* under
Murray ownership had no aversion to college
men as cub reporters. The Boss's son had
graduated from Princeton full of Greek and
Latin at twenty, the youngest in his class,
and had gone to work as a leg-man the same
summer, learning from the beginning. Two
years later a mining disaster in Tennessee
gave him his chance, and his story of the
families waiting at the pithead, the touching

colloquial vignettes gathered in sympathetic conversation with weeping women and frightened children who broke down and willingly told him all, established him as a first-class reporter.

The *Star* believed that a reporter with a clean collar and good manners not only upheld the dignity of the paper but was also likely to get into places where the traditional break-in newspaper man would have got thrown out, especially in crime cases. It also believed that reporters were born and not made, and that a nose for news and a story sense could not be begged, bought, borrowed, or stolen, but had to arrive mysteriously along with your milk-teeth; that the best reporters had a sixth sense which always told them when they were being lied to; and that part of the job was cajoling facts out of people unwilling to talk, instead of trying to bully or bribe them out.

This was the atmosphere which was Bracken's birthright, and it was here that Fitz had quietly, without presumption or push, made a place for himself. He may have lacked something of Johnny Malone's single-minded genius for chasing the fire-engines. But he had tact, and an unobtrusive way of asking the most embarrassing questions, and a shy-seeming good will which disarmed the most reluctant interviewee, and — somehow — he brought back the story.

2

On an evening in May along about the time Virginia had been making her curtsey at Buckingham Palace, Fitz and Johnny were attending a low performance at a questionable resort on West Thirty-fourth Street near Sixth Avenue, where a slightly passée specialty lady named Fay Lea had agreed to plug a song Fitz had written. Its title had caught her ear. It seemed to Fay, who was billed as a female baritone, that a song called *Dusk Until Dawn* might have possibilities, but the lyric had not lived up to her expectations. After some prodding by Johnny and a little coaching by Fay, Fitz had written in some new words, to which Fay added a few graphic gestures and expressed herself as satisfied. This was the night.

Fitz and Johnny arrived early and sat with the usual tall glasses on the table in front of them, watching the name-cards at the side of the stage change one by one towards Fay's, which as the star turn was due about ten-thirty. There was an animal act to open, and a ventriloquist, and a family of contortionists — all very boring. They hardly noticed when a new card came on, reading: DON AND GWEN LASALLE, *The Dancing Wonders*.

The music for the new turn was catchy and gay. The patter of the girl's feet was expert as she began the act alone, dressed in blue spangles and tights, with a provocative shining fringe across her slender thighs, high laced shoes, and a curled blue ostrich plume in the pert hat above her dark hair. Her voice was rich and low when she began to sing, without the loud, strident notes that Fay Lea used.

Johnny was nodding peacefully above his glass and Fitz kicked him on the shin and said, "That's a good tune. She can sing, too. I'd rather have that girl plug my songs than Fay. Wake up, Johnny, do you know that girl up there?"

Johnny woke up politely and squinted through the haze at the name-card.

"Don and Gwen LaSalle," he spelled out with some difficulty. "N-never heard of 'em." He buried his face in his glass.

"Now, watch this, Johnny. She's better

than Fay by a damn' sight."

"But she hasn't got the pull," Johnny said sleepily, and shifted himself in his chair and focussed patiently on the blue-spangled figure on the stage. "Mm-hm," he murmured after a minute. "Nice legs too. Not too fat. 'S funny, I don't seem to like 'em fat. N-not any more. I m-must have outgrown that."

"Not a bad chorus, either," said Fitz, listening critically. "I wonder who writes her songs. Could we get an introduction after the show?"

"Sure." Johnny waved a careless hand. "You watch out, though. Mustn't go offending Fay now that she f-feels kindly towards you. She can do a lot to get your songs started." He paused. His sleepy gaze grew more alert. "That's very s-strange," he said. "She's given him his cue twice and he doesn't show up. S-sing it again, kid, we don't care if he *never* comes!"

The girl had begun the chorus for the third time, still dancing alone. But now her red-lipped smile was a little fixed, and her eyes kept going back anxiously to the left wings from where she had made her entrance and where the other half of the team was overdue. Faintly, above the brassy music, angry voices could be heard back stage where some sort of brawl was going on.

Johnny sat up.

"Trouble," he said, sniffing with his experienced reporter's nose, and a woman screamed in the wings, off left.

The girl in spangles glanced down at the orchestra leader. A signal passed between them. The music wound up with a crash and a blare on the next bar and the curtain came down.

"Let's go see what happened," said Johnny, rising.

"None of our business, maybe," said Fitz, sitting still.

"When will you learn that you are a reporter and not a gentleman?" Johnny inquired severely. "Come on."

With that well-known queasy feeling in the pit of his stomach, Fitz followed Johnny through the pass-door and out on to the stage behind the curtain. Another canvas drop bumped down beside them — Fay's — as they crossed the platform towards the white-faced stage-manager who was saying curtly, "Clear the stage, please — next number, please — orchestra, Jim — all right, Fay, get out there and sing — clear the stage, everybody — let 'em have it, Fay — curtain up, Jim —"

"What went wrong?" Johnny asked casually, easing off into the wings after the stage-manager.

"Fellow shot himself. Busted up the act."

"May we talk to the girl?" asked Johnny.

"Seen you before, haven't I? You from the papers or the police?"

"The *Star*. Tell Jake Malone is here."

"Oh, all right, so long as you aren't flatfoots. Jake's been sent for a'ready." The stage-manager gestured impatiently towards the end of the stage, where the dressing-rooms were, and Johnny moved on with Fitz at his heels.

A knot of frightened-looking performers in various stages of undress and make-up huddled round the open door of one of the rooms, avoiding each other's eyes or whispering among themselves. Johnny and Fitz filtered through and Fitz leaned against the door-casing, watching a man in a shabby, ill-fitting suit who knelt beside the body of a man on the floor, his hands busy with its clothing. The girl in blue spangles stood over him, silent and motionless, waiting.

"Are You Mrs. LaSalle?" Johnny asked her gently, getting out his note-book and pencil in an unnoticeable sort of way. "I was out front and noticed that something was wrong. Can you suggest any reason for your husband's shooting himself in the middle of a performance?"

"He's my brother," said the girl without raising her eyes. "And the name is Murphy. Won't somebody please find a doctor?"

"There's no need for a doctor now," said the man who bent above the thing on the floor, and as he looked round at them Fitz saw that he wore false whiskers and a funny nose, as part of a comic Dutch turn still to go on. He rose, brushed off his knees, and added kindly as the girl only stood watching him with a look of dazed, terrified disbelief —"He's dead, Gwen. It didn't hurt — he's dead."

Her face quivered. Her eyes filled with tears, and the heavy mascara beading on her lashes began to dissolve and smear. Her crimsoned lips twisted, but she made no sound, and still stood looking at the whiskered man in the false nose. Fitz saw that she was shaking from head to foot so that the spangles winked in the gaslight, and the bright fringe rippled and shone against her thighs. He reached for the chair at the dressing-table behind her, turned it round, and holding her by the shoulders guided her into it. Her knees gave way and she sank limply on to the seat. Slowly her eyes travelled back to the body which lay almost at her feet. She stared at it, the tears running down her face, while no sound escaped her.

Fay's strident singing came in strongly through the open door from the stage, borne on the brassy music, and the thump of the drum was like a big heart beating, as the show went on. They were playing *Dusk Until Dawn*. Fay was plugging his song. But the spangled, weeping girl in the chair had the right voice for the song, not Fay. It was her brother, dead on the floor. Name of Murphy. Fitz glanced round for Johnny, who was in a corner with the stage-manager. Johnny was making occasional notes in the little dog-eared book he carried — getting the story for the paper. That meant it must be a good one, this time.

The woman from the contortionist act, wearing a dirty kimono which gaped to show her dirty white tights, slipped into the room and bent to lay a towel smeared with grease-paint across the dead man's face. One by one the rest of them drifted away from the door, and the music went on.

Fitz was still standing close to the chair, but Gwen remained unaware of him. She sat with her hands locked together on her knees, her eyes fixed on the smeary towel while the endless tears slid down her cheeks, making black rivulets of mascara through the powder. Fitz couldn't bear it. He took out his clean white handkerchief and knelt down beside the chair and began to wipe the girl's cheeks, rather gingerly because of the way the stuff ran, and he began talking to her soothingly, as he used to talk to his sister Phoebe when she was little and cried.

"There, now, don't you cry like this, honey, you'll drown sure 'nough unless you can swim," he began in his softest drawl whence all his final *r*'s had fled. "Nothin' I say can help much, I know — but is there anything I can do to make things easier for you tonight, have you got some parents, maybe, you've got to break the news to, and you want me to do it for you? I've got the rest of the evenin', you know, if I can be any use to you. My name's Sprague, I saw your act as far as it went, you're new here, aren't you? You sure got a lovely voice, maybe I could get you to plug one of my songs some time, huh? Now, don't you cry like that, you'll be sick — you just count on us for anything you need done, Johnny, there, he knows the ropes — you got friends, honey, hear what I say?"

Her eyes had come round slowly to inspect him with a sort of wondering curiosity. As he knelt beside her chair his face was almost on a level with hers, and for a long moment they looked at each other straightly while she took stock. Even with the smeared mascara and the hard line of the rouge on her mouth she was beautiful, with a fresh young beauty the gas-glare and make-up could not dim.

"Where did you come from?" she asked finally.

"I was out front, like I said just now."

"You're not from the police?"

"Who, me?" He grinned apologetically. "I just write songs," he said.

"Why did you come here? What do you want?"

"Well, we saw something was wrong, and we — thought we might help out some way." He glanced again around the small room, which was empty now except for the two of them and the still figure on the floor. Johnny had moved outside the door with the stage-manager and was listening to another man, the one known as Jake, who wore a dress suit and gesticulated as he talked. Beyond them the music shrilled to a climax and there was applause. The curtain fell with a bump and rose again with a rustle. The music was resumed. "Your other friends around here don't seem to be very — friendly," he murmured, puzzled.

"Friends? I haven't any. *He* saw to that." Her eyes went back to the towel.

"How do you mean?"

"We had to stick together. I knew he was

wrong, but I had to stand by him. Nobody else dared to, finally.''

''Why not?''

She looked at him, a slow, searching look.

''It's a long story,'' she said, and her lips closed on it.

He laid one warm, strong hand on hers where they rested, locked together, on her knees, and he realized again that she was trembling throughout all her body, as though she was very cold, or as though —

''What are you scared of?'' he demanded, and the question was surprised out of him before his natural tact could operate.

''I'm not.''

''You've got nothin' to be afraid of, honey, we'll look after you.''

''I wish you'd go,'' she said.

''Sure, we'll all go.'' He rose, still holding her hands. ''You get dressed, Johnny and I are going to see that you get home all right.''

''No, I — I'd rather you didn't get mixed up in this.''

''But we are mixed up in it. You don't think we're going to just walk out now and forget all about it, do you?''

''It would be better if you did.''

There was more applause and the curtain swished down again and Fay Lea swung masterfully into the little room, bringing with her an aura of musk and orris.

"Hey, you Dixie, get out there and call off your news hound," she commanded briskly.

"Johnny? He's getting a story."

"Not tonight, Dixie. Some other time. Don't come back here, either, for a while. Take your songs somewhere else, hear me? Go on, scat."

"Scat yourself, Fay, we're seein' Miss Murphy home."

Johnny put his head in at the door.

"Come on, Dixie," he said quietly. "Time for us to get a move on."

"You go ahead if you like," Fitz said. "I'm goin' to see Miss Murphy home."

Johnny caught Fay's eyes and shook his head sadly.

"He's from Ole Virginny," he explained. "Sometimes it takes him this way. Doesn't mean any real harm. The fact is, Dixie, we aren't wanted around here."

"Thought you had a story."

"Reporters, eh?" Gwen spoke suddenly from behind Fitz. "I might have known! Well, none of your sob stuff about my brother, see? Outside, the both of you!"

"Now, wait a minute," Fitz began, rather hurt. "Johnny, here, writes for the papers, I don't deny. But I'm —"

"Yeh, you told me, you write songs!" Her red mouth was scornful. "Well, I'm out of a job now, so you can find somebody else to sing 'em. I'm no use to you, see? Don and I worked together. I'm no good as a single, they won't hire me that way."

"Well — what are you goin' to do for a livin', then?"

"That's my worry. Will you two get out of here or would you rather be thrown out?"

Fitz gazed at her, aggrieved and incredulous. He hadn't done anything but dry her eyes and offer her his protection on the way home, and she had turned on him as though he was prying into her personal affairs.

"No need to get sore about it, Miss Murphy, I was only trying to —" he began with dignity, and Fay laid a heavy hand on his shoulder and turned him towards the door where Johnny waited.

"Yeh, we know — helpful Harry! You can't teach that kid anything, Dixie, she can look after herself."

"I wasn't trying to teach her anything, I just —"

Fay straightened her arm without apparent effort and he reeled against the door-casing, and Johnny held him up and led him away through a maze of ropes and stacked-up wings and the gaudy painted furniture of the animal act, to a narrow dark doorway through which they emerged into a narrow dark alley and eventually into West Thirty-fourth Street.

"Look, Johnny, why should they kick us out like that, I only wanted to —"

"Keep walking, Dixie. It was for your own good."

Fitz gave him a surprised glance in the ill-lighted street.

"What's it got to do with me?" he asked.

"I got the whole dirty story from Jake. It wasn't a healthy place to be tonight, all hell was popping. That boy Don was a very unwholesome piece of work, his pretty sister notwithstanding. It seems he gambled, Dixie, my son — with money that didn't belong to him, mind you. And then, as though playing with dynamite wasn't enough, he grabbed off a girl that didn't belong to him either. And then, just to make sure it wouldn't go unnoticed, he talked back to the rightful owner of both properties and tried to blackmail him. But he wasn't quite smart enough to take on Fagan's gang single-handed. And the girl he stole got cold feet and went back on him. One of Fagan's boys came to the dressing-room tonight and told Don Murphy what he could do. He probably gave him the gun to do it with.''

''You mean they forced him to —''

''Well, he saw the jig was up. There wasn't much else he could do, and his girl had ratted. He should have picked on somebody his size. And that's not all, either. It's hands off the sister, Dixie. Fagan's orders.''

''I see.'' They had come to Sixth Avenue and turned down town. After a thoughtful silence Fitz said, ''What becomes of the sister now?''

''I don't think,'' said Johnny carefully, ''that that is a thing which need concern you and me.''

There was more silence while they kept step together down Sixth Avenue.

''So that's why she was so scared,'' Fitz said at last.

''It's not our funeral, Dixie. Not, that is, if we mind our own business from now on.''

Fitz thought it over for another block.

''I've got kind of a funny idea she doesn't like Fagan,'' he said then, and his pace slackened. ''She's an honest girl, Johnny — did you see her eyes? And she was scared out of her skin.'' He drifted to a standstill. ''I'm going back there and see that she gets home all right.''

"Now, Dixie, will you listen to reason —"
"You comin' with me or not?" said Fitz, and Johnny sighed, and they turned around and began to retrace their steps towards Thirty-fourth Street.

3

As they approached the mouth of the alley which led to the stage door, Johnny put out a detaining hand and drew Fitz into an unlighted doorway. Peering down the street, they could see the glowing end of a cigar patrolling the sidewalk in front of the alley. They waited. The shadowy figure with the cigar moved back and forth deliberately, as though waiting for somebody. Fitz's heart beat a little faster.

''Do you think —'' he whispered, and Johnny's tightened fingers hushed him.

They stood in the added darkness of the doorway for what seemed like hours, while the cigar was thrown away and a new one was lighted. Then figures began to emerge from the alley. First came the man and the two children from the contortionist act. They passed close to the pair in the doorway without noticing them. Then came a couple who might have been the trainer of the animal act and his girl assistant. They turned in the opposite direction. Fitz and Johnny left the doorway and edged closer to the alley. Two women came next — Gwen and the lady contortionist, a bulky figure beside the girl's slight one. The cigar made a lighted arc into the gutter, and the man who threw it moved purposefully to intercept them.

"Leave her alone, can't you?" Fitz heard the woman saying. "Wait till tomorrow anyway, for God's sake." And the man replied brusquely. "I got orders from Fagan," as Fitz and Johnny eased in on them.

"Where is he?" Gwen asked tonelessly.

"That's what I'm here to show you."

"No. If you won't tell me where I'm going, I won't go with you."

"Won't, eh?" said the man softly, and —

"Good evening," Fitz remarked, removing his hat. "It is Miss LaSalle, isn't it? I'd know that voice, even in the dark. I'm the fellow that spoke to you about my songs, remember?"

"Not tonight, please," Gwen said rather breathlessly.

"Well, I don't want to butt in, of course, if you have a previous engagement, but I brought my friend along, he's very musical, and he's going to be kind of disappointed if you turn us down. Thursday after the show, you said, and I promised we'd wait for you, and here we are.''

''Well, I — I don't think I —''

''It's might good of you to take the trouble,'' Fitz went on in his gentle voice, and he took her arm on one side and Johnny closed in on the other and they moved off towards Sixth Avenue with Gwen between them, Fitz talking smoothly as they went, while his heart beat a tattoo against his unaccustomed ribs and he anticipated tautly an angry roar of protest or a physical assault from the man they left standing, strangely silent, at the mouth of the alley. ''Of course I haven't had anything published yet, but there has to be a first time for everything, and I thought *Introduced by Gwen LaSalle* would look kind of pretty on the cover. As soon as I heard you sing I said, 'That's the girl I want to plug my songs,' I said, didn't I, Johnny, and by the way who wrote that number you open with, it's not bad.''

''Don wrote all our stuff.''

''That leaves you kind of high and dry, doesn't it! Well, anything I've got that you want you can use to get a new act worked up —''

By now they had reached Sixth Avenue where the lights were brighter and Johnny decided with relief that they were not going to be followed. Once more they turned down town, with Gwen between them now, and Fitz, with his hand under her elbow, felt her trembling still. As they came to the Thirty-third Street curb she gasped and stumbled, and Johnny caught her on the other side. A moment she hung on their hands, till the weakness passed and she raised her head resolutely.

"I'm all right. I — never faint."

"Sure, you're all right," Johnny said encouragingly. "Just keep walking, you'll get your wind, we'll hold you up."

"I don't know why you bother," she murmured. "I tried to tip you off to let me alone, it's only a question of time anyway, with Don out of the way. They'll tell you wrong about Don. You mustn't believe what you hear. Oh, well, that was true too. He did use Fagan's money and lose it, and he did take Fagan's girl. But Fagan and Madge were about through anyway. The real reason he hated Don was me. Don always said Fagan would get at me over his dead body —" Her teeth were chattering now. "If Don hadn't said that —"

"He'd still be dead," Johnny said grimly.

"Get that into your head, Gwen. He was a goner before you ever came into it, don't make any mistake about that."

"But I'll never be sure —"

"You can be sure. You must."

"I f-feel like a murderess —"

"Now, stop it — stop it!" Johnny gave her a little shake. "You couldn't have saved Don from what was coming to him if you'd gone to Fagan on your knees, and you know it."

"I g-guess you're right."

"You know damn' well I'm right."

"They took him to the morgue. There wasn't any place else."

"No, there wasn't any place else," Johnny agreed kindly. "That's all over now, see? You must try and let it go and forget it."

"There's the funeral —"

"You aren't going to any funeral."

"But I'm the only —"

"The only mourner, sure, I know, but he'll have to do without. You're going to disappear, Gwen."

"Ah, Johnny, what a boy!" cried Fitz from her other side. "You leave it to us, Gwen, we'll see you through. The hell with Fagan, I told you!"

"I don't want you boys to get into any trouble on my account —"

"Fiddlesticks!" said Johnny clearly, for he

was sober as a judge now. "They don't know us. He couldn't see our faces, it was too dark back there. He'll wait for you to — Do they know where you live?"

"Of course."

"Then you aren't going back there. Not for a while, anyway. You've just walked off into limbo, Gwen, with a couple of nut songwriters, that's all they know. Let's see, now, you can sleep at my place tonight, and tomorrow we'll think this out. I live down this way," and he swung them eastward in the Twenties. "Are you hungry?" he demanded. "I'm frightfully hungry. Dixie, here's my key, you and Gwen go along to my room and light up. I know where I can get some sandwiches and beer. Be with you in about ten minutes."

Dazedly Gwen allowed Fitz to lead her up the steps of the house where Johnny had a large room at the back with some old easy chairs, a dilapidated typewriter on which he wrote his short stories in the Richard Harding Davis manner, a gas-ring on which when he was broke he cooked the messes he called meals, and a bed and wash-stand in the alcove behind a chintz curtain. She stood passively, like a shy child in strange surroundings, while Fitz lit the gas and her eyes went gravely round the shabby, comfortable place. There was no way of telling by her face that to Gwen it looked like a palace.

"How do you like being kidnapped?" Fitz asked anxiously as he blew out the match. "Better us than Fagan, huh? Johnny's a great guy. Always knows what to do. Give you the shirt off his back. They don't come any finer than Johnny. You'll be all right here, safe as houses. You stopped shakin' now?"

She nodded, and stood looking at him, her eyes wide and dark in her white face.

"Bet you'd rather have coffee than beer, huh?"

She nodded again, and Fitz burrowed in a cupboard, emerging with a coffee-pot and a paper bag of ground coffee.

"Here's the makin's," he said. "You probably know more about throwin' 'em together than I do."

With the faintest of smiles Gwen laid down her hand-bag on the bureau and took charge of the coffee while Fitz looked on with interest.

"The woman's touch," he marvelled, as she lighted the gas-ring under the pot. "There's nothing like it, I've always heard."

"You boys bach' it here together?"

"No, I live with my uncle over the other side of Fifth." He forbore to mention that it was on Madison Avenue in the expensive East Thirties.

"From the South, aren't you?"

"Now, how on earth did you guess that?" he drawled, and they grinned at each other and the tension in the room relaxed appreciably.

When Johnny came in with the refreshments in two paper bags he viewed the bubbling coffee-pot with horror.

"At *night?*" he said. "I wouldn't sleep a wink!" And he set out large fat bottles of beer, still sweating from the ice-chest at Reilly's on the corner, and thick well-buttered sandwiches with pink ham slices showing round the edges. Gwen brought plates and glasses and cups from a shelf as though she had done it before, and Johnny stood back to gaze at her, entranced. "Look," he said to Fitz. "Look at Gwen being motherly already! That's what we need around here, Dixie — a mother!"

Gwen, who was accustomed to wait on her menfolk hand and foot, gave them her small, one-sided smile and turned away to get the coffee-pot.

"She'd look more at home if she took her hat off," Fitz suggested, and they stood punctiliously behind their chairs waiting while she paused in front of the mirror on the bureau and removed her hat before joining them at the table.

"And of course her hair ought to be grey," Johnny remarked captiously as they sat down. "To give the best effect, it ought."

"That depends on whose mother she is," Fitz told him. "Mine has brown hair — hardly a bit of grey in it. Your mother's hair probably turned white in a night long ago."

"I haven't got a mother," said Johnny pathetically, staring at his ham sandwich. "I'm an orphan."

"Why, that's terrible, Johnny, when did it happen? You never told me you were an orphan." Fitz was deeply concerned.

"I'm getting sort of used to it. They died when I was three."

"Who raised you?"

"Aunt Irma."

"Maiden lady?"

Johnny nodded. Fitz nodded too.

"Now I see everything," he said.

"My Aunt Irma always used to say —" Johnny began expansively while Gwen sat before her untasted food, waiting patiently for them to begin.

She was a little uncertain whether she had fallen into the company of high class wits or just plain downright clowns. Humor was one of the many things which her brother Don had lacked, and laughter was to Gwen a serious business because she was unfamiliar with it. Sheer idiocy for its own sake was something she had never encountered either, and the solemn foolery which passed for conversation between her two knights errant was outside her experience. She trusted them, for she had taught herself long since to judge men by their eyes and the shape of their mouths and hands, rather than by the things they said, but she did not understand these two, not yet. She was hungry, desperately so, and the smell of the coffee curled tantalizingly around her nostrils while she waited.

"Did your Aunt Irma ever tell you to shut up and start eatin'?" Fitz asked pointedly of their host, and at last her teeth met gratefully on the pink ham, which was the kind that melts in your mouth.

She tried not to wolf it, but they were talking and she was not, and her sandwich was gone completely before they had well begun. Fitz laid the untouched half of his on her plate. Without pausing in the flow of his colorful reminiscences of life with Aunt Irma, Johnny did the same. Gwen looked from one to the other of them piteously. It was a little thing, but just that much too much. Tears welled up, spilled over.

"Ah, now, don't do that, honey, that ham is salt enough already —"

But Gwen put her head down on her arm on the corner of the table and cried. And cried. And cried.

Neither of them had ever heard anybody cry like that before — great racking sobs that came up by the roots, long aching pauses while she fought for breath. Neither of them tried to stop her, though. Nobody patted her on the back and talked optimistic nonsense, nobody even gave her a handkerchief. They simply let her howl. When it was over, Johnny was gazing thoughtfully into his beer, and Fitz stood at the dark window, his back to the room.

Gwen rose, moving feebly and with caution, as though she had had a long illness, and went to the bureau and got her handkerchief out of her bag and blew her nose. Still nobody said anything. Johnny roused himself, opened the top drawer, and gave her a clean handkerchief of his own, big enough to do some good. He returned at once to his chair and his beer and they waited tactfully while she got herself together again.

"I never did that before," she said. "I guess I owe you an apology."

"I guess it was time you did it, then," said Johnny. "Maybe you'd like us to go now, so you can get some rest. You can find everything here you need — except a toothbrush. I'll buy you one of those tomorrow.'' And he began to collect his own toothbrush and shaving things, dropping them into his coat pockets.

''It's — awfully kind of you,'' Gwen said, with a helpless, inarticulate gesture. ''I'm making a lot of trouble, I — I'd be willing to try to repay you —''

''You're going to be a mother to us, aren't you?'' said Johnny. ''Here's Dixie, dying of homesickness for Williamsburg, Virginia, and I've been an orphan all my life — what more do you want? I don't know how we've got along all this time without you.''

She looked at them doubtfully, still at sea except that she knew she liked them and felt safe with them. But why? What was there in it for them? What did they expect of her in return?

For Gwen, life had a terrible simplicity. A man did you a favor. He expected something back. Sooner or later you had to pay up. There had been nothing in her experience so far to indicate any exceptions to this rule. She could only regard all this talk of mothers and orphans as some kind of elaborate blind, or a new kind of fancy approach she wasn't wise to. Which one of them would it be, then? The one whose room they were in was ready to leave. Her eyes went to the other one. He had picked up his hat. Were they being considerate, tonight, because her brother was dead? Fagan hadn't shown any such delicacy, though the woman from the contortionist act had seemed to expect him to.

What was their game? How did it end? Was it her move? Perhaps they were leaving it to her, in some subtle fashion, to choose. Nothing they said or did made any sense than that. Was she supposed to say, some time, All right, I'll take that one —? The room rocked under her feet, and she put up a hand before her face. Either one. Any time. She was too tired to care. And maybe it wouldn't be so bad, so long as it wasn't Fagan — so long as she could stay here in this comfortable room, in the midst of this strange, carefree society — so long as she needn't ever go back again. . . .

"I don't know what you boys want from me for this," she said drearily behind her hand. "I don't understand half you say. Please don't make fun of me any more, just tell me what it is and I'll do it." She took her hand away and looked at them straightly, braced against the bureau, with her small, one-sided smile. "You don't have to be polite with me. I like to know where I am, that's all.''

For the first time, she saw embarrassment on their faces. Johnny recovered first.

"Ah, now, Gwen, for the love of God, did you think there were strings to it? The place is yours, girl, such as it is. Neither of us goes with it, now or later, if that's what's biting you. You've had too much Fagan, I can see that, but my name is Malone, didn't I tell you?''

"You mean you're just — *giving* me this room —?''

Johnny and Fitz exchanged glances. Fitz was still speechless. Johnny tried again.

"Look, now, Gwen — the rent here is paid till next Saturday. Friday night it will be paid again for another week. And so on. The milk comes every morning, right on the doorstep. And two morning papers, compliments of the management. There's food of one kind and another — enough to keep you. But you have to promise us one thing.'' His slow, impressive forefinger rose. "Never show your little nose outside this door till we give the word. We'll be back and take you to dinner about seven o'clock. G'night.'' He offered a large, open hand and she put hers into it.

" 'Night, honey,'' said Fitz, and touched

her shoulder lightly as he passed.

The door closed behind them, and opened again to admit Johnny's head.

"There's the key," he said, pointing to the inside keyhole. "Lemme hear you turn it."

They stood outside the closed door, listening. The lock clicked. As they reached the street —

"You come along home with me," said Fitz. "Lots of room. We can say you have lent your place to a friend who is temporarily down on his luck."

"Will the Boss stand for it, do you think?"

"Who're we workin' for? Fagan?"

4

The following day happened to be a slack one at the Shop. Fitz's thoughts reverted more than once to the girl they had so precipitately taken under their wing. He perceived that it was not going to be easy to conceal for an indefinite period of time a person who made her living by singing and dancing on the stage. To spirit her away from the music hall of West Thirty-fourth Street and lodge her secretly, and then pitch her into the bill at Tony Pastor's or Koster and Bial's, even if he and Johnny had the influence to do so, would not solve anything. Fagan or his henchmen would spot her in no time and that was bound to mean unpleasantness all around.

He began to wonder what else Gwen could do besides sing and dance. If only she were a boy it would be so simple. Then you could lug her along to Cabot and ask him to give her a job. If she had been a boy she could have learned typewriting and been somebody's secretary. Nobody wanted a girl for a secretary, though — girls hadn't the right kind of brains. Besides, she was too pretty. In fact, she was too pretty to do much of anything but sing and dance.

The idea of consulting Eden about Gwen did not appeal to him. If Gwen had been the sort of girl to take a job as housemaid it would have been different, or if she had been ill he would not have hesitated to call on Eden for help. But things weren't as bad as that. And he felt a singular delicacy about revealing to anybody for whom life had cut as near the bone as it had for Gwen that he was the nephew of Cabot Murray, who owned the *Star,* and lived with him in a Madison Avenue mansion instead of getting along on his reporter's salary the way Johnny had to. Johnny didn't mind the relationship, being used to it, but Gwen might think he was just slumming. Perhaps it would be better if he took a cheap room somewhere, like Johnny. But at this point in Fitz's meandering thoughts the practical side of the matter cropped up. Gwen might cost them money, if she couldn't work, and Johnny needed all he had each week. Fitz decided to let Cabot feed and house him a little longer. Cabot could afford it. He had just turned over his Trenton steel interests to the new United States Steel Company for a hunk of preferred stock which hoisted his personal fortune into the six cypher class.

She had not answered his question about parents, he realized, nor had she entered into the discussion of Johnny's orphanship with any revelations of her own. There was apparently no one to whom the news of Don's death must be broken, and no one to worry if she spent the night away from her usual lodging. That was tough. He wondered how old she was. Less than twenty, he felt certain. She ought to have somebody to look after her. The best thing would be for her to marry somebody who was capable of protecting her. Johnny, for instance. Fitz contemplated the idea in the light of inspiration. It would be just the thing, if Johnny gave up his hopeless passion for Virginia and fell in love with Gwen, and married her. That would settle Fagan and his gang.

Johnny stopped beside the desk as quitting time drew near.

"You'll have to take Gwen to dinner," he said. "I'm going to Brooklyn for a story. Is it all right if I sleep at your place again tonight? I may be late.''

''Sure. Can't you join us somewhere? We could go to Martin's and sit around till you come.''

''Oh, no! You'll go to Frieda's downstairs, and sit 'way at the back. And then you'll go straight back to my room and stay there till I come. You're trying to hide this girl, Dixie, not advertise her.''

''Just as you say,'' Fitz agreed meekly.

''And be sure to buy her a toothbrush,'' said Johnny as he departed.

Frieda's was a little eating-place next door to the house where Johnny lived. The German food was plentiful, savory, and cheap. Fitz and Gwen sat at a small corner table in the rear, and gradually he charmed out of her some personal history.

She was worrying about a job already, and Fitz said they had enough for three until things blew over. Reluctantly then she admitted that it wasn't just herself. There was always Pa to think of.

''Pa is in a home,'' she said, avoiding his sympathetic eyes. ''A — mental home. We — I have to send money every week for his keep. I have to send it tomorrow.''

''How much?''

''We've got a little behind. We were out of

work a while and — we owe them nineteen dollars.''

''Well, I guess Johnny and I can manage to carry that.''

''I've got seven, and Don had some, but we can't get that now, I suppose. The point is, I have to keep working and not let the payments pile up.''

''Would they put him out?''

''They never have yet, but once you get behind on a thing like that you never catch up again. Don and I had to do all sorts of things towards the end of the week when we didn't have enough.'' Her eyes were shadowed with the things they had done, and Fitz saw for the first time how shabby and cheap her street clothes were. You didn't really notice how badly Gwen was dressed at first because her hair shone with brushing and the lace at her throat was clean and she carried herself as though she wore sables.

''How long has this been going on?'' he asked.

''Since I was a kid. I don't want you to think we've got real insanity in our family, it isn't that. Pa had a fall — from the trapeze. We used to be with an aerial act when Don and I were children.''

''I see,'' said Fitz, trying to.

''He struck his head when he fell. We

thought he was dead, but when he came to in the hospital he'd — well, forgotten everything. And ever since then he's been kind of simple.''

''I see.''

''Mom left the act, they didn't want us without him. We went on the kerosene circuit with *The Black Crook,* but that didn't last. Then Don and I played dime museums and county fairs for a while. We had a paper-tearing act, and sang and danced at the same time. It was cute while we were small, but it ran out when we stopped being children. Don was a born dancer, and we worked out a new grown-up routine while Mom scrubbed floors and cleaned up in a place down on the Bowery to get the money for Pa. Mom stayed respectable — I think.'' She sat a moment, looking back. ''Mom was a real lady. She always made us speak right and taught us manners. I think Mom could have been another Lillian Russell if she'd had the chance, and she always thought I could be. It broke her heart I couldn't have regular singing lessons and learn good music, but we never could afford it. It seems as though as long as I can remember, we always had to get that money by Saturday night for Pa. There's only me to do it now. But tomorrow is Saturday, the same as always.''

"Well, now, wait a minute, I live with my uncle, remember, and don't have to pay rent, so I never need all my salary. You just leave your Pa to me for a while. I've got the nineteen dollars right on me tonight, as it happens. We'll pay it all off and start even for next Saturday."

"I only need twelve, I've got —"

"I know, you've got seven, but you keep that, you'll want it."

"You're very kind, but I really couldn't —"

"Now, Gwen, listen," Fitz said firmly. "Johnny and I hauled you out of that dump last night and we're going to see you through, but you've got to do as we say. If you're going to dodge Fagan you can't go round the halls looking for a job right away. Anyway, your act is gone. Have you thought what you could do alone?"

She shook her head. Her eyes were heavy and haunted.

"I've never worked as a single. Besides, it doesn't pay enough. I haven't even got a costume. It's in my dressing-room."

"How much do they cost?"

"I made it."

"Can you make another?"

"If I could get the stuff."

"We'll get the stuff. And we'll work up a

single act that will make Lottie Gilson look like dime museum left-overs. Your brother Don wrote you some good music, but so can I, if it comes to that, and it won't cost you a cent. When you're ready we'll get you a road job — Philadelphia — Providence — Pittsburgh — so on. Maybe you'd better use another name for a while.''

''But you don't understand,'' she said obstinately. ''I can't wait to work up a new act now, and a single at that. I have to *earn,* beginning tomorrow. I got a job at Macy's once, when we were laid off, but it didn't pay enough either, without what Don could put in.''

Fitz laid his hand on hers, which held a fork tensely.

''Honey, it's you that doesn't understand,'' he said gently. ''Your Pa isn't going to get thrown out, whether you earn or not. You got friends, honey, hear what I say?''

But she regarded him distrustfully.

''Why should you do that for me? You never saw me till last night.''

''Well, I dunno, I reckon Johnny and I have adopted you. How old are you?''

''None of your business. Eighteen.''

''My Aunt Eden is willing Johnny should bunk in with me for a while, so it isn't costin' us anything extra for you to have his room, see? We'd take it very kindly if you'd make it a habit to have dinner with us, it adds a little something to the end of the day, if you don't mind my sayin' so.''

''B-but if you pay for Pa then I'm in debt to you, and how do you know you'll ever get your money back?''

''Well, if you use my songs in the new act, that gets 'em sung in public and they have a chance to catch on, and that brings us out even.''

''Suppose they don't catch on.''

''That won't be your fault.''

Almost against her will she began to believe that Fitz was real, and the wariness left her eyes a little. She had never seen anything like him before, but she told herself perhaps that was because he was from Virginia. Friendliness for its own sake was as new to her as the nonsense he talked with Johnny. But unless all the signs she had laboriously learned were worthless Fitz was all right. His grey eyes were level and honest, his firm, sweet-tempered mouth smiled easily, and his hands — she remembered the feel of his fingers on hers — his hands were beautiful, warm and dry and well-kept around the nails. He was the kind of man they put in books, and the heroine married him and lived happily ever after.

Until now, Gwen had never believed the books.

Johnny turned up in time to join them over their last cup of coffee, and he had got her a job. It wasn't much, he assured them hastily, but it was safe. It was in the chorus of the Weber and Fields show, where she would be known as Fanny Maguire, and if she made good she could go on with the new show when it opened in the autumn.

"So you had to go to Brooklyn," said Fitz accusingly, and Johnny looked sheepish.

"Well, I didn't want to get anybody's hopes up till I was sure about this," he admitted. "I had to think up a yarn, and then I had to get Weber to swallow it. This Fanny Maguire girl I told you about got fired from her last job because she said No to her boss on account of being in love with a reporter friend of mine who is going to marry her as soon as he gets a raise. But she has a sick mother to support, and they have to wait. Weber's a good little guy, he fell for it. One of their girls is in the family way and wants to lay off. Gwen goes on next week, for the rest of the run."

"So you won't need my songs after all," said Fitz rather ruefully, and this time it was Gwen who reached a quick, comforting hand.

"But I will some day," she said in her warm voice. "I'll sing them for you some day, and they *will* catch on, you'll see!"

5

The next day was Johnny's day off and he went along as bodyguard while Gwen used some of her seven dollars to buy the things she had to leave behind and needed, besides a toothbrush. There was a little room on the top floor of the house where Johnny lived, and they took that for Gwen. Then they sent off Fitz's nineteen dollars to pay up in full for Pa, and all wound up at the Imperial Theater to see the Weber and Fields show. Johnny pretended a great weakness for Lottie Gilson, and just for the sake of argument Fitz developed a violent preference for Truly Shattuck, who was famous as the prettiest woman ever to come from the Pacific Coast. Sam Bernard, the best of low German comedians, was in the bill, along with thirteen chorus girls, an orchestra of eight, and a very funny burlesque on *The Geisha*.

After the final curtain, they took Gwen round to meet Weber, who expressed himself as more than satisfied, and called in Fields to be satisfied too, and both asked kindly after her sick mother. The following Monday Gwen went to work in the best-paid, best-treated chorus in New York.

Fay Lea, meanwhile, had gone on plugging *Dusk Until Dawn,* not for love of Fitz, but because the customers liked it. And before a month had passed Fitz received a communication from one of the smaller and grubbier music publishers on Fourteenth Street near Second Avenue, offering him twenty-five dollars for it, outright, no royalties. This wasn't exactly the piano-trade sales Johnny had envisioned, but Fitz rushed round to the address on the letter and collected, feeling like a millionaire. They had a party in Johnny's room that night to celebrate, with a bottle of champagne.

Gwen was shocked about the champagne. "It's a week's rent," she said. But she liked it, and it made her eyes very bright, and she laughed at their jokes now. The ones she understood. Fitz thought how cosy it was, the three of them, and Gwen laughing, and he looked anxiously for signs of love on Johnny's part and found none, and dratted Virginia who just kept Johnny dangling for the fun of it and treated him like dirt half the time. If Johnny's father had not gone to Princeton with Cabot, back before the war, Johnny might never have set eyes on Virginia, and that would have been much better for everybody.

Gwen went back to Macy's for the summer, between shows, and Fitz and Johnny made up the difference when she ran short for Pa. She kept track of what she owed them in a little book. Sometimes, shut up in the room at the top of the house where the roof sloped so sharply you were likely to crack your head getting into bed, she cried over the rising total of her debt to them. But she knew now, for sure, that they weren't going to try to collect in any of the usual ways. And she nursed the hope that some day, when she went back to the halls as a single, she would sing Fitz's songs so well that they would sll to the best publishing house there was, and on royalties too, and then he would be fixed for life, and all because he had bothered to be kind to her.

Meanwhile she mended Johnny's clothes and sewed on his buttons and cooked them delicious meals on the gas-ring and gave them unstintedly of her motherly devotion. She was always ready to listen, always willing to laugh if she saw why, always cheerful and self-contained. They had no idea of what went on behind her little one-sided smile and her shining dark eyes — no idea at all that sometimes when things were gayest she was saying to herself, I must remember this, it won't last forever — I must keep it to think about later when he's gone. . . . For even without knowing about Cabot Murray and the house on Madison Avenue, it was plain to Gwen that Fitz was not really a thirty-dollar-a-week reporter with nothing better to do than loaf around with her and Johnny. Some day Fitz would go back to where he came from, to the sort of woman his mother was, who had never, it was plain, scrubbed floors and played the dime museums. Gwen knew that Fitz was only lent to them, by circumstances she could not inquire into, and the time she spent in his company was doubly precious for it was bound to end. I must remember this, she would tell herself — I must never forget that line in his cheek when he smiles — the way his hair dips in front — the way he drawls his words — oh, God help me, why can't I love the other one, I might have stood a chance. . . .

There was something else she didn't know about Fitz, and that was his musical comedy. He was working hard at it now — which was something new for him. He used the piano in Eden's ballroom, which could be closed off so that he wasn't heard in the rest of the house. After Gwen started with the new Weber and Fields show in September he felt safe to take a room on his own just down the street from the house where Johnny and Gwen lived. When he had moved in there he seemed more like them, to himself at least. But he still went back to Eden's piano, working out his score, laboring at his lyrics.

The musical comedy was to incorporate some of his darky music, and the nostalgic setting was in Virginia before the war. He could not remember those days, of course, but it was a time whose serene beauty was in his blood and bones and in all the traditions of his childhood. He was doing a daring thing, to ask New York audiences to accept darky characters who sang and yet were not minstrel men, whose dialect did not tell smutty jokes, and whose devotion to their white folks was not on the syrupy Uncle Tom plane, but was jovial and cheeky and matter-of-fact. It was a simple enough tale he told, with music, of a Virginia girl who loved a Yankee, and an old darky coachman whose loyalty to his Confederate master conflicted with his desire for his young missy's happiness with the man she had chosen. Fitz worked at it lovingly, and thought nothing of the fact that all his Arabella's songs were written for a voice like Gwen's. Long before Christmas time he was looking forward to playing it for his Cousin Sue when she came back from England.

But to Sue's dismay, in all the companionable hours they spent together after she landed, whether at the piano in the empty ballroom, or shopping for Christmas presents at Altman's and Constable's, or doing the sights of New York, Fitz said nothing about a girl or about being in love. Eden raised her eyebrows at this continued frustration, and in desperation they asked Bracken's opinion on the state of Fitz's affections. Bracken only grinned at them and advised them to mind their own business. Then, because he saw that Sue was really worried, he assured them that he saw no indications whatever that Fitz was in love unless you could call making good at his job a bad sign.

Eden was giving a ball for Virginia before they all left to spend Christmas at Williamsburg, and the question of entertainment for the guests arose one evening when Fitz was dining at the house on Madison Avenue. Victor Herbert's orchestra had been engaged to play for the dancing, and Eden thought it would be nice if they introduced something of Fitz's. They could get a tenor in to sing, she suggested. Mr. Herbert could doubtless provide somebody.

"What would Mr. Herbert be charging you for his tenor?" Fitz asked casually, and Eden looked surprised.

"Why, I don't know — a hundred and fifty or two hundred, I suppose. Of course if you want de Reszke —!"

"For two hundred," said Fitz, "I can get you one of the best singers in town."

"Very well, we'll try him. Who is he?"

"It's a girl named — Fanny Maguire. Johnny knows her. She's got just the voice for my stuff, and I happen to know she needs the money."

"Well, of course," said Eden promptly, exchanging a quick, triumphant glance with Sue which said At Last! "Will you make the arrangements with her, or shall I see her?"

Fitz thought it over a minute, remembering that with Gwen he sailed under false colors.

"She'll have to come here to rehearse, because there's no piano where she lives, so you'll see her then. She doesn't know any of my songs, but she'll pick 'em up in an afternoon, with me playing them for her. Would you like her to sing something else too? Something with a little more class to it?"

"I'll leave all that to you, Fitz. You talk it over with her and when you've got a program made out let me see it."

"Mm-hm. There's just one thing." His grey eyes met Eden's squarely. "I'm kind of ashamed of Uncle Cabot, here, and I haven't mentioned him down on Twenty-ninth Street where I live now. She thinks I'm a real reporter, like Johnny."

"Well, aren't you?"

Fitz looked embarrassed.

"Sometimes I feel like a sure-'nough impostor," he confessed. "Coming here like this to a dressed-up dinner with the family while she and Johnny eat at Frieda's. Johnny doesn't give me away, so I was wondering if I could count on you all to do the same if I bring her here."

"You mean you want us to disown you?" said Virginia. "Oh, I think that's sweet, Fitz, the fairy prince in disguise!"

"Nothing of the sort," he said testily, and Bracken kicked his sister under the table, and Eden's eyes met Sue's again with an I-told-you look. "It's simply that I'd like her to think I'm on the same footing here that she is, if she comes to sing," Fitz was saying. "Otherwise I'd feel sort of embarrassed. See what I mean?"

"Well, I suppose I do, Fitz, but it's going

341

to be rather difficult for us,'' Eden remarked. ''Are you sure it's necessary?''

''I'd feel better that way,'' he insisted gently. ''Otherwise she might wonder why I hadn't said anything before and — I tell you what, though, if I play her accompaniment maybe she won't think anything more about it.''

''If you want it that way,'' said Eden, baffled and amused. ''Has the girl got a suitable evening dress?''

''Well, no, I don't suppose she has, now that you mention it. She lost a lot of things,'' he improvised hastily. ''In a fire, I think it was. Maybe you'd better let us have half the money in advance.''

''It might be still better if I furnished the dress,'' Eden said decidedly, for the Lord only knew what this unknown girl would turn up wearing.

''Besides the two hundred?'' Fitz bargained cautiously, and Eden laughed.

''All right, Fitz, I won't take the dress out of her check! Bring her along to see me, then, when she comes to rehearse the songs.''

''Yes, ma'am. I don't want you all to get any wrong ideas about this,'' he added, and his eyes sought Cabot's. ''She's just a nice kid Johnny and I have been sort of mothering since her brother died and threw her out of a job. It's hard for girls like that in this town. She's pretty and she's decent, and so the cards are stacked against her to start with. I don't say she's any Lillian Russell, but she can sing and she'd look nice in the right kind of clothes. If she came here it might lead to other jobs, too. Some of your friends might want a singer sometimes, mightn't they?''

''Often,'' Eden assured him, carefully casual, for he must not think they took too much interest now that they were on the track at last. ''We'll see what we can do for her if she needs jobs.''

''Thanks,'' said Fitz simply. ''I think you'll be satisfied.''

He explained the situation to Johnny the next day and Johnny agreed that it was best for Fitz to remain incognito with Gwen. ''Else she might have stage-fright,'' Johnny said sagaciously, and he listened with owlish approval while Fitz broke the news to Gwen at dinner that he had got her a bang-up job to sing at a society ball, where there was no danger that any of Fagan's gang would spot her, *and* — he paused for his effect — the fee was two hundred dollars.

''*For one night?*'' Gwen stared at him. ''But that's as though I was from Pastor's or somewhere like that. Do they know nobody ever heard of me?''

"There's one catch in it," Fitz said gravely. "You have to sing my songs."

Gwen thought she saw.

"Oh, you mean they're friends of yours, giving your music a hearing," she said. "Why, I'd have done that for nothing, you know I would."

"They're able to buy music," said Fitz coolly. "Somebody's going to sell it to 'em, and it might as well be us!"

"What do you get? The same?"

"Sure, I get the same," he said without blinking.

6

Gwen shied a little when he turned her up the steps of Cabot's house a few afternoons later.

"Are you sure this is the place?" she asked nervously.

"Yep, this is the place. People named Murray. Friends of my mother's when she used to live up North," he added, improvising again, as the door was opened by Eden's English butler, who greeted Fitz with visible pleasure. "Afternoon, Benson, we want to use the ballroom piano. You might tell Mrs. Murray we're here."

Gwen looked curiously around the dust-sheeted, gilded spaces of the ballroom with its shining waxed floor. There was a small platform at one end in front of a velvet curtain, and a piano and music-racks and gilt chairs were grouped at its foot.

"How many people does this hold?"

she wanted to know.

" 'Bout a hundred couples, at a pinch."

"Have you ever seen it full?"

"Once or twice."

"What's this Mrs. Murray like?"

"Nice. You scared?"

"It's not what I'm used to," she admitted with her half smile. "I can see now why the dress went with the job. She knows I wouldn't know what to wear here."

"It'll be just a dress, I reckon, like the rest of 'em," he said unconcernedly, and opened the lid of the piano. His fingers melted lovingly into the keys, the way he had, and harmony stole out into the room.

"Say, you can play! Where did you learn?"

"Dunno. Just came by it naturally or somethin'. Did you think I was one of those one-finger song-writers? Let's try this one here on the rack first — thing called *Tidewater Rose*. I'll run through it once, and then you come in, huh?"

Gwen stood by the piano looking over his shoulder and sang obediently, giving the best she had. For an hour or so they worked absorbedly, while he interpolated low-voiced, diffident suggestions —"Take it easy, honey, these customers will be fairly sober," he would say. "Hey, hey, don't plug that line, it won't stand it — here we go, now, let it out big —''

Then the door opened behind them and Eden and Sue came in. Fitz rose from the piano bench and made the introductions blandly. Eden was wearing her hat.

"I'm sorry to interrupt," she said, "but I'm going round to my dressmaker's and I thought if I had some idea of your size and your preference in colors —'' Her eyes, friendly but searching, rested on Fitz's girl.

Gwen said the right thing, leaving it all to Eden, who observed that she and Virginia were almost of a size, which was convenient as the dressmaker could use Virginia's patterns to start with. They made an appointment for a fitting, and Fitz said —

"Since you're going out, Mrs. Murray, perhaps Miss Day would like to sit down and hear what we've decided on.'' His eyelid farthest from Gwen drooped briefly at Sue as he spoke. He could never resist showing off for Sue, and he was proud of Gwen and the way she sang his songs. So when Eden had rustled away, Sue settled into an armchair drawn up to the piano and listened while Gwen went on with her singing lesson.

"Now do the one I always liked best," Sue said when they seemed to have finished. "Sing *Sun Goin' Down On Me.*''

Gwen said she didn't know that one.

"It's in his musical comedy. Hasn't he sung it for you?"

Gwen said she didn't know there was a musical comedy.

"Well, there is, but he's bashful about it. Play *Sun Goin' Down* before you stop, won't you?" she pleaded, refraining carefully from using Fitz's name when she spoke to him.

Without any visible embarrassment, but not altogether willingly, Fitz began the song. He didn't think much of his own singing voice, especially after bossing Gwen around the way he had been doing all afternoon. He hummed along to himself at first, crooned a phrase or two, and finally let out his fine, clear baritone. Gwen stood there beside the piano, wide-eyed and silent. His playing was good, but his voice took her completely by surprise.

Sue watched them thoughtfully, trying to see with Sedgwick's eyes and not her own blindly prejudiced ones. This was the opportunity she and Eden had been hoping for, as Eden freely admitted she had only accepted Fitz's singer in order to get a look at her. So far as Sue could tell, Fitz was just the same as always — casual, relaxed, serene. But the girl was in love. Her gaze rested on him revealingly while he played. Her dark, shadowed eyes seemed to be memorizing him, from the deeply waved forelock to his thin, strong hands on the keyboard. There was no possessiveness in that look, and not much happiness either. It was as though she took leave of him as she stood there, Sue thought; as though she might never see him again, and wanted to remember him as he looked now, playing the piano to them in the empty ballroom.

She's breaking her heart for him, Sue thought, with a feeling almost of eavesdropping, so defenceless and young the girl's face had become — so *resigned*. Fitz doesn't know, Sue thought. It hasn't occurred to him. Will it ever? What would Sedgie think of her? What's she like, I wonder, to know? Decent, he said. I think she is, but there's red on her mouth. Awfully pretty. Awfully pathetic. Fitz ought not to go round breaking people's hearts like this, but nobody could help loving him, I reckon. She looks at him like — well, not like a dog, no, dogs haven't got souls, they say. I know how she feels. I must have looked at Sedgie that way, hundreds of times, when I thought nobody would notice. Oh, Lordy, yes, I know how she feels! Would she make him a good wife, I wonder? Perhaps he won't ask her. She's not — not quite our kind. I wonder who her people were. . . .

The song came to an end and Gwen only stood there, looking at him with her heart in her eyes.

"What's the matter? No good?" he asked, glancing up.

"I'm surprised, that's all."

"Didn't think I could write songs, huh? I'll show you yet."

"B-but your voice —" she stammered. "You could do anything you liked on the stage, singing like that!"

"Oh, shucks, honey, I'm no he-actor," he said easily. "Me, I write the stuff. Somebody else has got to sing it."

"Could I use that song, instead of one of the others?"

"Sure, anything I've got you can sing if you want to." He struck a few questioning chords. "What key do you want?"

"Lower."

He slid down one. Gwen's rich voice took up the song, and Sue sat listening with an ache in her throat. It didn't matter, she decided, who the girl was or where Fitz had found her. All that mattered was the way she felt about him. But would Eden see that? Or Sedgie? Provided, of course, that Fitz himself ever saw it. . . .

Gwen suffered acutely from nerves the night

of the ball. Not even the beautiful dress Eden
had provided nor the knowledge that the
songs she was going to sing were good
comforted her much while she changed in an
upstairs room and waited for Fitz's knock on
the door. She had never dreamed of such a
dress. It was made of black sequined net over
rose-colored satin, with a swathed low bodice
and large puffed elbow sleeves of stiffened
net glittering with sequins. Long white gloves
and a sequin fan went with it. Eden's maid
had dressed Gwen's hair high, with an
ornament. The effect was subtly sophisticated
and theatrical, and yet the girl's fresh beauty
enlivened by her carmined lips was *ingénue*.
She stood before a long mirror and gazed at
her reflection with impersonal delight. He
wouldn't be ashamed of her, anyway.

Hired performers were not supposed to
mingle with the guests so she and Fitz were
to sit in the library until it was time for them
to appear. When he came for her they looked
at each other in frank admiration, for evening
dress became him too.

"My, my, they have sure turned you out
handsome," he murmured.

"You're turned out kind of handsome
yourself," she replied with her little half
smile.

"Oh, me, I'm just one of the waiters. But

you sure dazzle the eye, Gwen, I wish Johnny was here!''

A footman came to say would they please go down now. With a nasty sickening flutter in her heart, she walked at Fitz's side down the staircase to the ballroom floor. The dancing had stopped. As they were crossing the hall outside the ballroom door they were intercepted by an ample matron hung with ropes of pearls, who cried in a penetrating voice, ''Ah, there you are, Fitz, my dear boy! Eden says we are going to hear some of your own music tonight at last!''

Gwen felt as though some one had kicked her in the stomach. *Eden says. My Aunt Eden.* It wasn't a name you could forget. These were his people, then, and this was where he had lived — over the other side of Fifth.

''Well, yes, thanks to Miss Maguire, here, she's found a couple she's willing to take a chance on singing,'' Fitz was saying with his imperturbable courtesy.

''How do you do, Miss Maguire, can you sing Tosti's *Good-bye,* by any chance?''

''Why, yes, I — think so — I haven't got the music —''

''Oh, not tonight, my dear, I wouldn't dream of upsetting your program at the last minute! But I wondered if you'd come and sing it at my house two weeks from Saturday, we're having a little party — it's my husband's favorite song, and I'm sure you'd sing it beautifully. You have your own accompanist, of course?''

''Well, no, I —''

''I am Miss Maguire's accompanist tonight, Mrs. Palmer,'' Fitz interposed quietly. ''Maybe you'd give me a job too, if I can learn to play *Good-bye* during the next two weeks.''

Mrs. Palmer shook with laughter and slapped him with her fan.

''Darling Fitz, if you can, you may consider yourself hired!'' she said, and turned away to find Eden and tell her what her ridiculous nephew had said now.

With Fitz's hand at her elbow Gwen threaded the crowded room and arrived at the platform. Mr. Herbert's pianist surrendered the instrument to Fitz with a little bow, and there was a continuous murmur and rustle as people found their places and settled into them. Fitz was improvising in soft, insistent, soothing chords to get them quiet, while Gwen stood with every painful heartbeat zigzagging up behind her eyes; her knees were water, the roof of her mouth was dry, her tongue was stiff and cold, her fingertips were numb — *Eden says* — *my Aunt Eden* —

well, what difference does it make, you knew you never had a chance — he's used to this, he *belongs* here, this is his home — if only we hadn't met that awful woman till *afterwards* — but you knew he wasn't yours, it's no different, really — Johnny should have warned me — I can't sing like this, I can't sing a note — pretending to be my accompanist so I wouldn't feel the only outsider — oh, my dear, my dear, I know it's no use, but why must you try to be *kind*. . . .

The room had gone silent, waiting. Gwen's feet carried her to the front of the platform, she glanced down towards the piano where Fitz was looking up, serene, smiling, confident, proud of her. His hands moved again on the keyboard. She heard her own voice, strong and sure and sweet, obeying his hands. . . .

When it was over, and they had taken bow after bow, and Mr. Herbert had resumed his baton, they found themselves back in the library, where a wood fire burned and a tray awaited them with sandwiches and a bottle of champagne.

Gwen sat down on the sofa near the hearth and Fitz popped the cork in a silence stretched tight over the waltz music across the hall. He came to the sofa, a glass in each hand.

"Well," he said gently as she accepted one of them, and he raised his own, "here's to Tosti two weeks from Saturday!"

"Good-bye," said Gwen, and drank.

"You aren't sore, are you?" he asked anxiously, and when she did not reply he sat down on the sofa beside her, holding his glass. "About Mrs. Palmer, I mean. You meet all sorts of people at places like this."

"Do you think your Aunt Eden will let me use this dress at Mrs. Palmer's?" Gwen asked carefully.

"Oh, sure, you're to keep the dress, she wouldn't —" He paused, looking trapped. "Who said she was my aunt?"

"Too late, Fitz. It doesn't matter, anyway. Why did you think it would?"

"Well, I dunno, reckon I wanted you to think I could earn my own living like other people," he said humbly. "All the same, Uncle Cabot is tough. I don't think he'd keep me on the payroll now if I was too much of a drawback. Of course anybody can do what I do down at the Shop, I don't give myself any airs about that!"

"You can give yourself airs about your music, though, from now on."

"Well, if it comes to that, so can you!"

And he sang in a false tenor with a horrible burlesque tremolo —*"Good-BYE, for-ev-er, Good-BYE for-ev-er, Good-byee, Good-bye, Goo-hood-buh-hyeeee!"*

In spite of her preoccupation, Gwen was amused.

"Maybe we'd better call that off."

"Not on your life! We're hired, she said so! Why shouldn't we take her money, somebody else will!"

"The same as tonight?"

"The same!"

"Own up, Fitz. You don't get paid for tonight, you only said that to make me feel good."

"I get paid two weeks from Saturday, though!"

"Oh, Fitz, you *couldn't!*"

"Watch me! She has practically bet me I can't learn the accompaniment to *Good-bye* in two weeks. That's castin' aspersions on my manhood. Got to demonstrate."

"But she's your aunt's *friend!*" Gwen reminded him, horrified.

"Well, s'posin' she is, I'm all the accompanist you've got, aren't I? I discovered you, didn't I? All right, then! From now on, you don't sing without me at the piano, see? It's nice work. I like it." He drank some champagne. "We've got a whole bottle of that stuff here, you'd better drink up.''

Cabot put his head in at the door. He looked very handsome in his evening tail coat and white tie, his crisp dark hair gone grey at the edges, his tall body held as straight as when it wore a Federal uniform more than thirty years before.

''What is this, the children's table?'' he inquired with a grin. ''Fitz, that man Herbert is having a quiet fit over your music. Go out and talk to him, he wants to see the score of your operetta or whatever it is.''

''He *does?*'' Fitz was impressed, and turned to Gwen. ''Mind if I —?''

She shook her head, and he went off to the ballroom, leaving Cabot by the door.

''We're getting a lot of compliments on your singing,'' Cabot said, advancing to the table to choose a sandwich. ''Fitz said you might be willing to take some other engagements, is that right?''

''I'd be glad to, but I haven't got an accompanist. Fitz told Mrs. Palmer that he'd play for me at her house, but that can't go on indefinitely.''

''Why not?''

They looked at each other, Cabot munching his sandwich, Gwen with her glass at her lips. In that instant, while his hard, hooded eyes bored into her, they understood and liked each other.

"You needn't worry about him, Mr. Murray," she said. "He won't come to any harm through me."

"D'you take me for a fool, my dear?" he said, and went to lean on the mantelpiece, looking down at her. The firelight threw sharp shadows upward on his rugged face. "So you've tumbled to it," he added, smiling. "How?"

"He mentioned his Aunt Eden once. Then Mrs. Palmer called your wife by her given name, and I knew. It wasn't really news to me, though. That is — I knew he didn't belong in West Twenty-ninth Street. You see, Mr. Murray, I'm no fool either."

"Would it be any use to you to know," he remarked, watching her from the hearthrug, "that when I first went to Virginia, where I found my wife, I felt as though I had stepped into another world where I had no right to be?"

Gwen sat motionless, looking down into her glass. Was it written all over her that she loved Fitz and couldn't have him? She wouldn't admit it, though, much as she liked this knowing, outspoken uncle of his. He wasn't going to hypnotize her into giving herself away.

"Well, I just thought I'd mention it," Cabot was saying.

Still she made no answer, obstinately.

"Who are you?" he demanded gently. "How did you first meet him?"

"At a third-rate music hall." She let it sound just as bad as it could.

"Mm-hm. I said How."

Slowly her eyes came up to him. Then they went to the door. There was no sign of Fitz to rescue her. When she looked back Cabot was still waiting.

"I worked there with my brother as a dancing team. He got into trouble with the Fagan crowd. They called his hand and he shot himself — during a performance. Fitz and Johnny were there that night. It was their own idea to protect me from Fagan — I needed it, too. They walked me right out from under Gyp O'Connor's nose and hid me in Johnny's room. They loaned me money, they fed me, they got me another job where I'd be safe. With the money I get here tonight I can pay back what I owe them. And that's all. I didn't know there were people like them. I kept waiting for the catch in it. There wasn't one. But you know them better than I do, you're not surprised."

"Fagan — O'Connor —?" he said, and his eyes glinted. "For the love of God, *those* small-time crooks! If you have any more trouble with them, let me know.''

''Are you — with the police?''

''No, I'm Murray of the *Star*. We know those fellows, every one of them — that's our business. Part of it. We helped clean up the Piotti gang last year. That was safe-cracking. Your Fagan is a gambler, and that's harder. All the same, we're always interested in him.''

''He's a killer. You want to look out.''

''You've got friends from now on, Miss Maguire. Remember that.''

''Funny. That's what Fitz always says.''

''Don't you believe it?''

Gwen rose and set her glass back on the tray.

''Mr. Murray, if you have any idea that I — that Fitz and I — well, it's like I told you, he wants nothing of me, nor I of him. When I give him back the money I owe him we're all square. I could walk out tomorrow and there's no harm done.''

''I sort of hope you won't, though.'' He had not moved from his position against the mantel. ''You're good for Fitz, I think. But don't be too easy on him. He wants shaking up.''

She faced him, the light full on her troubled, honest eyes and curving red mouth.

"I hope you aren't putting ideas into my head, Mr. Murray," she remarked with dignity, and Cabot grinned, strolling towards her with one hand in his pocket.

"Well, it suddenly occurred to me that you might have some idea of paying back your debt and then going out into the night and closing the door behind you with a dull, Ibsenesque thud. And I just wanted to say, while there is still time — Don't." He patted her shoulder briefly on his way to the door. At the threshold he turned and caught her eyes across the room. "Don't do it," he said firmly, and went.

Gwen stared after him a moment. Then she poured herself another glass of champagne.

"Hullo, Mr. Tosti," she murmured, and drank to him gravely.

7

The entire Murray family and Fitz escorted
Sue from New York to Williamsburg and
spent Christmas there, as usual. Plans were
already being made for Dabney's son Miles's
coming-of-age in April. Coming-of-age
parties were even more regarded in the
family than Christmas. They occurred less
frequently. There was always a special wine
which had been laid down at the time of the
christening with the date on it, and there
were certain table traditions and ceremonies.
Only the worst kind of personal disaster
or emergency prevented any member of the
family from attending, no matter how far he
might have to travel. Although Eden's son
Bracken had been born and reared in New
York, he had come of age in Williamsburg,
with all the fixings and everybody there
to drink his health. And now it would

be Miles's turn.

In order not to miss Miles's party, Eden and Virginia had set their sailing for England for the first week in May. Cabot's plans for going abroad with them were provisional, for he had now become deeply interested in the situation in Cuba, where Spanish brutality was receiving a good deal of publicity through the reports of adventurous Special Correspondents from the American Press.

The ubiquitous Richard Harding Davis had been sent there by Hearst, and had witnessed the dawn execution of a young Cuban patriot, his account of which had wrung the hearts of his readers. Scovel of the *World,* Flint of the *Journal,* among others, had been risking their lives under fire with the insurgent forces — dodging Spanish spies, burning up with fever, sometimes landing in jail, and somehow getting their dispatches smuggled out. Most of them were wanted by Spanish firing squads. Ralph Paine had gone pirating with a filibustering ship running arms to the insurgents and nearly lost his life in a running fight at sea. Frederick Remington, Stephen Crane, Ernest McCready — only a few years earlier the name of Cabot Murray would have joined the distinguished list. But in that climate it was a job for a young man, as he well knew; a man moreover who had not for thirty years been subject to recurrent bouts of malaria which laid him low, put severe strain on his heart, and then departed abruptly till next time. He now perceived with incredulous surprise that Bracken was not going to demand Cuba as his next assignment instead of returning to the Fleet Street office, which in his absence Nelson was running creditably. It was inconceivable to Cabot that any son of his should so neglect a spectacular opportunity for news gathering.

Bracken for the first time in his life was not completely alive to his father's wishes. His mind dwelt obstinately on getting back to England, to Farthingale, to Dinah. Her letters, written spontaneously now without Miss French's supervision, were full of Edward's hunting talk and news of the weather. But always somewhere in their schoolgirl content he could find a line to comfort him which showed her need of him and her sustaining confidence in his quick return. Since it was impossible yet for him to write as he felt, he tried to bring her closer to his life by telling about the parties Eden gave, the plays they saw, the endless variety and stimulation of a newspaper shop. And at the end of each letter he promised again to come back soon — by the end of January, anyway.

Just before they all left New York for Williamsburg in December Cabot came to a decision and Bracken got his orders — on to Tampa right after Christmas, and thence to Key West and Havana, where he was to report to the American Consul, General Fitzhugh Lee, under whom Sedgwick had served as a cavalryman during the War Between the States. With General Lee's approval Bracken would make his manners to the Spanish Captain-General and take all the safe-conducts and introductions Blanco would part with, as Davis had done the year before with his predecessor. Then, with other credentials supplied by the Cuban *junta* in New York, Bracken was to get out at night between the lines, talk to the insurgents, learn both sides, never take notes, never go near the cable office, and bring back the story in his head to be written on uncensored American soil.

As an assignment it was a Special Correspondent's dream, and Bracken knew that a year ago he would have been blissfully happy at the prospect. He was nearly as aghast as his father would have been to discover that he only wanted to go back to England instead. He found it hard to talk to Cabot about Dinah, when at one time he had longed for the chance. It was still too soon.

The best parents on earth could never understand this cobweb romance which nevertheless held him fast with the strength of steel. And so he had said very little after all, and left them wondering, which was not his way. He told himself it would be much simpler once they saw her, when they came to Farthingale in the spring. He had given up without even trying to describe to them his own fatalistic belief that he and Dinah were meant to be, and that obstacles were only put in their way to be overcome, and that the more unlikely it seemed that he would ever be free to take her the surer he became, inside, that she was his.

And now there was this Cuba business. It never occurred to Bracken to question his assignment, or try to beg off from it. It was a nuisance, qualified by many emphatic adjectives, but he would see it through, although it meant that now he would be lucky to arrive in England before the first of March. But he told himself firmly that Dinah must learn to wait for him, and could not begin too soon, and he sat down to write and explain. This was rather difficult to do, for it must on no account be a love letter and yet on the other hand he must not sound like just another careless adult who found it inconvenient to keep a promise. He wrote the letter more than once and was not satisfied with the final version. But he sent it off along with the best music-box New York could produce for her Christmas present — in a gold case, with a tinkling minuet tune and a French miniature on the lid.

Fitz, happily exempt from family tradition and obligation, returned to New York with Cabot and Eden after Christmas and settled down to finish his musical comedy. Victor Herbert had backed up his own enthusiasm with an introduction to a manager he thought would be interested in producing it, and from him Fitz had received substantial encouragement in the form of an option. No one had ever seen Fitz so busy.

"It must be that girl," Eden said to Cabot one evening towards the end of January. "I do believe Fitz is going to find himself at last. She believes in him. He needed something like that."

"She needs a job," Cabot said. "Fitz will always go out of his way to help somebody else. That's why he wants to sell this operetta of his — so she can sing in it."

"Do you think he —?"

"I think he's too near-sighted. But maybe he'll come to, eventually."

"*Marry* her?"

"You married me," he reminded her, and

they smiled at each other.

"Still, it's not quite the same thing," Eden said then.

"Not quite. I had a great deal more on my soul than this little waif of Fitz's ever dreamed of."

"But do you think she's —"

"Virtuous? Oh, *women!* She's not nineteen yet, he says, so she's not had much time for sin!"

"She's got red on her mouth, Cabot. I'm only thinking of the family, if he should ever take her home to Williamsburg as his wife."

"And how much did you think of the family, beloved, when you fell in love with your rough Yankee journalist?"

"I wish I could feel sure she wasn't just feathering her nest," Eden said wilfully.

"You are a cat, Eden. All women are cats. That girl can't see straight for being in love with Fitz. She'd feel the same if he was nothing but a leg-man and couldn't play a note. I thought you might be more charitable in your old age and in the light of your own experience. Or did you marry me for my money?"

"And why else do you think I married you?" They were safe to joke like that, after thirty years together.

"It's Bracken I don't like the look of," he

added after a moment, playing with her rings as they sat hand in hand before the fire. "He wasn't keen to go to Cuba. He went in the line of duty and he won't spare himself, but he *wasn't keen*. Must we take that girl in England seriously, d'you think?"

Eden brooded at the fire.

"He's been very silent about her. But he's different from what he was last spring, he's more — lighthearted. As though Lisl was wearing off. We should be grateful for that, in any case."

"He didn't say so — but I know he would rather have gone back to London than to Cuba," Cabot ruminated unhappily. "That in itself is a terrible state of affairs, at his age!"

"Perhaps it's just the delay on the divorce that upset him. He says they can't get on with that until he is back there living in London. Sally wants to rush right over and swear before the Queen's Proctor or whoever it is that she saw Lisl and the Hutchinson person living together at Cannes. But Bracken says that isn't the way it's done."

"The mills of the English legal gods grind slowly," Cabot said. "But he seems to think an English divorce, if he can get one, will have weight with the Earl. *Must* we have a ladyship for a daughter-in-law next, I wonder? Why can't he fall in love with an

American? I did!''

''At least she sounds very different from Lisl,'' Eden murmured.

''Oh, anything but Lisl!'' he agreed, yawning, and somehow comforted, they put out the lights and went to bed.

8

When Bracken reached New York again the second week in February, he was the complete correspondent with nothing on his mind but a story. He had written feverishly all the way up in the train from Tampa and was sleepless and unshaven. He handed over a thick sheaf of manuscript in his neat longhand with the request that Cabot have it typewritten at once, fell into a hot bath with groans of joy, dropped into bed and slept all day till nearly dinner time.

Around seven o'clock Cabot couldn't bear it any longer and invaded the room, the typed story in his hand.

"Wake up, you young son-of-a-gun, and tell me more!" he shouted, landing heavily on the edge of the bed. "How did you get this stuff about the shooting of bound men? Where have you been? What else did you see? Wake up, I say, and go on from here!''

Bracken, who was a light sleeper and always woke up all there, opened one eye, grinned, and burrowed deeper into the pillow.

"Got a cup of coffee on you?'' he wanted to know.

Cabot stripped back the covers with a ruthless hand and then, lest his favorite Special catch pneumonia, went to close the window and toss a dressing-gown at the bed.

"Come out of that,'' he said. "Who was the man in the café? Did you ever find out?''

"Mm-hm. He'd been jailed for photographing Morro Castle, and escaped, and was hiding. He was in cahoots with the A.P. man, whose real name *nobody* knows. Except me. I saw him. It's Hilgert. But don't tell. He didn't see me. Mind if I have another bath?'' He drifted away towards the bathroom, Cabot at his heels.

By the time Bracken had shaved and dressed for dinner, at which there were several guests, Cabot's curiosity had been a little appeased. Yes, said Bracken, the insurgents *had* shot a Spanish colonel under flag of truce. Women and children *were* starving by the hundreds because the Spanish did burn down whole villages of homes in order to drive the population into the concentration camps where they could be

372

exterminated by hunger and disease. Yes, there had been a riot in Havana while he was there. But it was a strictly Spanish riot against the native advocates of autonomy, and there was no particular anti-American feeling in it, except that all the Havanese blamed the American newspapers — with cause — for fanning the flame of rebellion. During the rioting the American Consul, a not very even-tempered man, had gone right off the handle and started cabling the State Department for battleships. Yet Bracken himself had accompanied General Lee through the streets of Havana unmolested that same evening, and had seen him dining publicly at his usual table in a window at the Hotel Inglaterra. The old gentleman put up a magnificent front, and the Spaniards were impressed. Things cooled off. Ten days later the *Maine* had arrived from Key West and dropped anchor in Havana harbor. Her presence there was intended to suggest to the Spanish Captain-General that it would be well in the interests of American life and property to keep order in the city. There was no demonstration against her as she passed sedately in under the guns of Morro Castle, but there was no denying she wasn't welcome. Looks can't kill, though, said Bracken, and when Captain Sigsbee of the

Maine came ashore to render his compliments to the Captain-General the manners of the Spanish officers, as well as their Spanish caution, had been impeccable.

The Spanish army in Cuba, Bracken went on, had pretty light blue and white uniforms made out of bed-ticking, with red and yellow cockades. Their personal habits and condition were a disgrace to any so-called civilized nation, and none of them had ever heard of sanitation in any form. "Forgive me for sounding like a Hearst man," Bracken said gravely, sitting in the tub soaping himself while his father leaned against the wash-basin firing questions at him every time he paused for breath, "but it's got to stop, down there. I'm convinced, even though it means lining up alongside the yellow-kid press and screaming our heads off for intervention. Not because I have any shining belief in the holy democratic destiny of Cuba. But the place is a garbage-heap on our doorstep, breeding future ills. We've got to go in and clean it up. What we will do with it then remains to be seen. Somebody said once that only the Anglo-Saxon nations were capable of governing themselves democratically. I must look up who that was."

Cabot nodded in encouraging silence, waiting for more. Richard was himself again, he thought, and then groped ruefully for the rest of the quotation, which was something about the shrill trumpet sounding, to horse, away, my soul's in arms and eager for the fray. Whatever hold that girl in England might have over him, Bracken was first and last his father's son, and had been weaned, the story went, on printer's ink.

Long after midnight, when the guests had gone, the family was still sitting around the drawing-room fire listening to Bracken's stories. Johnny was there too, drinking whiskey and pumping Bracken enviously. Fitz was thinking how nice it would have been if only Johnny could have brought Gwen along with him, to make one more in the comfortable family circle.

"You don't have to believe more than half you hear down there to be converted," Bracken was saying. "I heard what were apparently the muffled volleys of execution squads in the Cabañas fortress from where I sat drinking coffee at a table on the Prado. But I *saw* the bodies of forty unarmed villagers who had been dragged out and shot at the roadside without trial because one of them was supposed to have given shelter to insurgents. The local Spanish military commander had drawn up a formal report of a 'skirmish' with an estimate of 'enemy dead.' That night a Cuban patriot took me out there, at some risk to both of us, and we went to work with spades by lantern light. It wasn't a pretty sight we uncovered, and the men had been killed with their hands tied behind them. The whole island is a slaughter-house and pest-hole. The churches are fortresses with barricades at the doorways and hammocks hung from the altars. Many of the Cuban patriot soldiers are children hardly taller than the Mausers they are almost too weak to carry. The babies are wizened skeletons that never stop mewing. They haven't strength to cry. Non-combatants are herded into filthy stockades with no shelter and no sanitation and left there to rot.''

''Then our worthy New York competitors don't make up the atrocity stories,'' Johnny said, still a little unbelieving. ''You saw just as good or better. Is that right?''

''There's no need to make up atrocity stories. They happen all the time, better than Hearst's gang can invent 'em,'' Bracken said impatiently. ''But don't let's forget, either, that it was their precious Gomez who devised the idea of burning the food and the cane-fields and the industries in order to force the Cuban patriots to join him in the fight for their own freedom from Spanish misrule. Well, naturally the Spanish caught on. It works both ways. And so now the island is devastated by both sides. Don't let's overlook that most of these so-called American citizens whose wrongs must be avenged, bear Spanish names and have always lived in Cuba. On top of that, let's remember that the patriot agitation, and the funds, *and* the ammunition, originate in the good old U.S.A. That's largely furnished by professional enthusiasts for liberty who never go near Cuba themselves. They take it out in attending meetings in New York and Jacksonville. From there they egg on professional guerrilla fighters like Gomez. Everybody has forgotten that he comes from San Domingo!''

''Well, then what are we all crying about?'' Fitz wanted to know. ''What's all this fudge about the-same-fine-old-American-war-against-European-tyranny?''

''The Spanish *are* tyrants, particularly nasty ones,'' Bracken told him seriously. ''The *insurrectos,* no doubt, are mostly brigands. But the Spanish are behaving like medieval barbarians, and they've got to learn that we have outgrown their way of thinking, over here. If they can't administrate their colonies decently, with a minimum of bloodshed, as the British do, they must get out — at least out of the Western Hemisphere. And that, my dears, is how

377

much I give for the sacred cause of Cuba Libre! Taken by and large, it's about as bogus as Hearst and Pulitzer put together!''

"But still we do back the Cubans against the Spanish," Cabot said keenly.

"I do, from now on," Bracken nodded. "For one thing, I just don't like the Spaniards. They seem to stand for all the things we have got rid of on this side of the world. Besides, a Spanish officer calmly told me across a dinner table at the Hotel Inglaterra in Havana that if we should declare war on Spain because of Cuba they would invade us."

"Oh, they would, would they!" said Johnny.

"They are convinced their navy can lick ours, and they have more than twice as many men in Cuba right now as we have in our whole regular army scattered all over the United States. They have a solemn, carefully considered plan to land at Charleston, cut us in two, and take New York in no time at all!"

"Well, of all the gall!" cried Johnny angrily.

"Well, they have got a fleet, damn it all," said Bracken. "And they've got colossal nerve and impudence. Of course they couldn't take New York, but they might try.

Even as it is, they are playing hell with our West Indian trade and prestige. There is going to be no place in the twentieth century," he wound up firmly, "for the pompous militaristic nonsense Spain believes in. All this parade of fleets and armies and big guns and two-for-a-nickel officers in fancy uniforms rattling sabres is out of date. Spain has got to learn that it's a civilized world we live in nowadays. If we have to beat her up to prove it, that, by a species of Irish logic, is what we've got to do!"

"Listen," said Cabot suddenly, lifting one hand. Faintly through the quiet house came the persistent shrilling of the telephone on his desk in the library. He rose and streaked out of the room, Bracken just behind him.

It was the briefest kind of message that came down the wire before he was yelling, "*What?* Say that again!" and reaching for a pad and pencil. "Go on — *go on,* what happened? — yes — how? — *I said How?* —" And meanwhile the pencil in his fingers wrote excitedly for Bracken, hanging over his shoulder: *The* Maine *has blown up in Havana harbor. . . .*

9

The *Maine* sank within a few minutes of the explosion, with the loss of two hundred and fifty-three lives. It seemed only logical to assume that she had not blown herself up, but a cautious administration in Washington refused to be stampeded into a declaration of war until it received evidence that the Spanish authorities were guilty of her death. The White House sent out word that there were no grounds (as yet) for suspecting any kind of Spanish plot. Captain Sigsbee, who survived, had included in his first cable a levelheaded sentence which read: *Public opinion should be suspended until further report.*

But the column of flame which shot up from the *Maine* that night sparked a slow fuse which ran all the way to Washington and New York and westward, to touch off the sentimentalists and the idealists and the jingoes, along with the honest patriots — the politicians in opposition to the administration policy and the people who wanted to sell more newspapers — the professional intriguers and fire-eaters — all America, according to its lights, was swept by a wave of belligerency. The *New York Journal* offered a reward of $50,000 to any man who, presumably for a much smaller sum, had been involved in the supposed conspiracy at Havana and would now come forward, confess, and implicate his colleagues. The circulation of the *Journal* promptly passed the million mark, and a flood of "war extras" poured from rival publications with great black type running all the way across the front page like a banner.

While Washington tried to stress the idea of an accident on board the *Maine*, the Navy was naturally reluctant to countenance a theory which convicted itself of carelessness, to say the least. A Naval Board of Inquiry was immediately appointed and sent to Havana to interview the survivors and hand down an official opinion, while the country seethed with righteous anger.

Bracken was off again at once for Havana, his return to London indefinitely postponed. What might prove to be the biggest story of his lifetime was breaking now in Cuba. It seemed apparent to Cabot that as it was the *insurrectos* who stood to gain by American intervention, they were much more likely to hold the key to the tragedy than the Spanish, who could not seriously have desired to provoke a war. This was for Bracken to prove if he could. He had a natural gift for languages, and Spanish was one of the three he had spoken adequately even before he began an intensive brushing up. By mingling with the shadier characters of Havana around the waterfront and encouraging them to tipple he hoped to come at the truth.

Between censorship and native hostility it had been as much as an American correspondent's life was worth to enter the Havana cable office for some time past. Hilgert of the A.P. after skulking about for weeks in his cherished anonymity had dared to flash the news of the *Maine* from there the night she sank. But after that the office was closed to American newspapermen. The Spanish Government in Havana had been gravely disturbed by the presence of the *Maine* in the harbor to begin with, and they now resented being suspected by the entire nation of laying the mine which was said to have sunk her.

The correspondents who reported on Cuban

affairs during the secret sessions of the Board therefore had to use the Key West cable, which meant that they spent their lives on chartered dispatch boats running to and fro across the hundred miles of choppy water in the Florida Straits. Bracken, who was a good sailor, got tired of trying to wedge himself into a bunk with a pad of paper on his knee, and took to writing his copy lying flat on his stomach on the floor, from where it was impossible to fall when the trampy little boat shipped it green over the bow.

Meanwhile Fitz in New York was pursuing his customary unruffled course against the tide of public opinion. No fault could be found with his efficient routine on any assignment given to him by the City Editor, but neither was there any evidence that the news from Cuba gave him the slightest personal concern. Johnny had taken to making fiery speeches, and was threatening to join the army himself and personally kick Spain out of the Western Hemisphere. Fitz heard him patiently, almost without comment, revising lyrics meanwhile in his head, or working out a new chorus in the nearly finished score of the piece which was to make Gwen LaSalle a star with Victor Herbert's blessing.

Thus March passed and April came, and the Board at Havana decided that the *Maine* had been destroyed by the explosion of a submarine mine, which had caused the partial explosion of two or more of the forward magazines. The findings added that the court had been unable to obtain evidence fixing the responsibility for the destruction of the *Maine* upon any person or persons.

"There, you see?" said Fitz. "It will all blow over."

But Johnny was so mad he went out and enlisted. That was sobering.

With Bracken rolling about the Florida Straits in his tin can of a dispatch boat, and Cabot spending most of his time mysteriously closeted in Washington, with Johnny missing from all the usual places, and Park Row an hysterical beehive of rumor and patriotism, the world in which Fitz lived was all askew. Gwen, of course, was just the same. She had taught herself to use Johnny's typewriter and with his help had got odd jobs of copying to do. It was tedious work and paid only a few cents a page, but money was money to Gwen, and for the first time in her life, what with the chorus job and an occasional engagement to sing at the houses of Eden's friends, she had a little money laid up ahead, so that the regular Saturday night payments for Pa were less of a bogey than she could ever remember. When Johnny left for the army she moved down into his room and set up housekeeping there with the typewriter.

Fitz would drop in sometimes in the old way and she would cook a meal for the two of them on the gas-ring. They missed Johnny on those evenings. Fitz hired an old upright piano and when it was fitted in alongside the typewriter his work on the musical comedy went faster, because Gwen was right at hand to sing the songs in her own way and make her diffident suggestions. Cabot had good-naturedly bought a chunk of the show to insure Gwen's place as Arabella against better-known singers, and she had given in her notice to Weber and Fields.

Miles's birthday was the twenty-third of April and Eden had set the morning of Monday the eighteenth for their departure to Williamsburg. Cabot was in Washington and would join them there on the way down. Bracken would try to come up from Key West for the day.

Gwen and Fitz spent Sunday afternoon going over the completed score from the beginning for the last improvements before sending it in to the impatient manager, who was waiting for it to start rehearsals. Almost before they knew it, the day was fading and there was still one more act to go. Fitz said reluctantly that they'd better go and eat at Frieda's and finish afterwards.

"Unless you'd rather I got us something here," Gwen offered. "Then you could go right on. Let's see, there's coffee and bacon — four fresh eggs — and some cookies and milk. Would that do?"

Fitz nodded, his fingers never leaving the keys, and she sang along with him as she lighted the gas and drew the shades and put on an apron. Pretty soon the smell of coffee was in the air, and then the sizzle of bacon. Fitz's hands slid off the keyboard and he sat watching her from the piano stool, his shoulders drooping. She set the well-filled plates on the table and turned to say that dinner was ready and met his eyes. But only for a moment. She looked away quickly, untying the apron.

"You'd better come and eat," she said. "It will go better after you've had some food."

"It's goin' all right," he said, not moving.

"Well, come *on,* Fitz, things will get cold!" She took her place at the table, still not looking at him, and began to pour out the coffee.

He followed slowly, sitting down opposite to her.

"I was thinking about the first night you came here," he said at last.

"Seems a long time ago, doesn't it."

"It's a year — almost."

"It will be queer without Johnny, won't it — as time goes on," she suggested rather at random, making conversation against a preoccupation on his part which she found vaguely alarming.

"Gwen — I've got no right to ask you this, but —"

"You've got a right to ask me anything you like, Fitz. But maybe you'd better not," she added gently as he seemed unable to go on. "Eat your eggs while they're hot, why don't you?"

"Gwen — are you in love with Johnny?"

Gwen took time to swallow.

"No," she said evenly.

"You sure about that?"

"Sure I'm sure. Johnny and I are just friends, that's all. Whatever made you think of that?"

"Oh, I dunno, Johnny does the right thing at the right time. Thought maybe you might be grievin' for him, now that he's gone into the army."

"There's no war yet, Fitz. He's perfectly safe in the army. It might even sober him up."

"Yeah, that's how I figured it. There's no war. Not yet, anyway."

For a while they ate in silence.

"Now, take me, I'm always out of step," he brooded finally, thinking out loud. "At home I was supposed to go into my father's law business. In our family one of the sons always does what his father did, and I'm the only one. Take my cousin Miles, his father teaches at Charlottesville and *his* father ran a school there in Williamsburg — so now Miles is studying to teach when he gets out of college. And then there's Bracken, givin' up goin' back to England, where he's bought a house and all, just to go into the field as a Special because that's what Uncle Cabot did back in the War Between the States. And even Johnny, his father was a Yankee captain of artillery at Gettysburg — so now Johnny rushes off and joins the army at the first sign of a fight. Accordin' to all that, I oughtn't to just go on sitting around writin' songs."

"I wouldn't worry about it, Fitz." She poured him another cup of coffee. "People need songs to sing, even if there is a war. People can't get along without songs."

But he was not comforted, and accepted the coffee absently, gazing past her at the piano while he drank. Unintrospective Fitz had become aware, with growing dismay, that he didn't want to go home to Williamsburg tomorrow. Having achieved that revelation, he went further to discover why. Cabot would be there, fresh from Washington and his confidential sessions with Theodore Roosevelt, who as Assistant Secretary of the Navy was known to have no patience with the administration's policy of cautious neutrality in Cuba. Bracken would be there, strong in his conviction that now United States intervention had to come, trailing glory from his active and useful career as correspondent while tension rose. And he, Fitz, still had nothing to show for himself but a few songs, as usual. They were good songs. The best he had ever done. But it suddenly seemed to Fitz as though he couldn't face it, down at Williamsburg.

He rose with his lazy, easy movement, and drifted to the piano, his one sure solace no matter what happened. Moodily he began to play again, random chords at first, merging into Arabella's third act solo, *Moonlight on the Floor*.

After a few bars of it Gwen followed him and stood leaning against the corner of the piano singing softly, compassionately, watching his face. Her desire was all to lay her arms around his shoulders and beg him not to mind anything; to mother him, cosset him, comfort him with all she had of love and devotion. Gwen too could remember that first night she had entered this room of Johnny's, and how she had looked from one to the other of them, wondering which would expect to claim the fee for their protection. And even then, she was hoping dimly that it might be this one.

She had come a long way since that night. The debt, which he had never recognized, was anyway squared between them. She had paid back what they lent her, and she had been a help with Arabella, she knew. She was friends with Johnny as she had never supposed it was possible to be friends with a man. But for easy-going, absent-minded Fitz she had learned a passion deep and still and hopeless, so that she no longer cared what might become of her if only he always had what he wanted and did as he pleased and had no problems and no responsibilities and no cares.

She was in his hands now, in a selfless ecstasy of love, and whatever he asked of her she knew she would give freely as long as he wanted it, and no regrets when it ended — as even this association between them was bound to end some day, to leave her with nothing but what she could remember of times like these. She had already grown greedy and jealous of the memories she gathered up and stored away against the lean times without him which were sure to come. And she wanted more to remember. It seemed to her that Cabot Murray had given her the right to it, that night in the library. She wasn't to leave Fitz, Cabot Murray had said, for his own good. It was for Fitz's good that she should be there when he wanted her, Cabot Murray had implied, tacitly recognizing her own state of mind, realistically condoning what she felt people like his wife Eden might have condemned — handing her over to Fitz, that night in the library, as though on a silver platter with his compliments — possibly buying her Arabella as a reward. Arabella had worried her a little. She had even thought of confronting Cabot Murray again and making it clear to him that she didn't have to be bribed to be Fitz's girl, but that anyway Fitz wasn't thinking along those lines, and apparently wasn't ever going to. All Fitz wanted of her was her voice. It would have come hard to confess that to Cabot Murray, she thought, now that they understood each other. — And so after nearly a year Gwen still had much to learn about this different breed of men who had entered her destiny.

Fitz, brooding above the keyboard while

she sang, was thinking how dull life had been before the night when he and Johnny happened to go to that little dump on West Thirty-fourth Street to get Fay Lea to sing his song — and how because of a sordid small-time gambling suicide, out of violence and poverty and terror Gwen had come to stand here singing his tunes. And he remembered how that first night she had thought they would expect to collect for having saved her from Fagan, which was a thing he had never been able to bring himself to contemplate fully — what could her life have been, for eighteen years, to make such a thing seem to her natural and inevitable? As always when something brought him face to face with Gwen's dark background of fear and crime and beastliness, his soft heart recoiled in embarrassment, and he fell to thinking how she had insisted on paying back out of her poor little earnings every cent he and Johnny had ever lent her — and how she had stuck to them, no matter how late it got or how tired she must have been, always patient and kind with Johnny when he was drunk, always ready to sing or make coffee or go to a show — and he thought, Johnny won't be here to help me look after her now — and he thought, Funny, she didn't fall in love with Johnny — and he thought —

His hands lay idle on the keys. His eyes as they rose to her face were full of an innocent surprise. And then slowly, as though he had been lifted by marionette strings, Fitz came up off the piano stool and put his arms around her where she stood, and his lips took hers. She was soft and willing in his hold, and so much smaller than you'd think, because she always held herself so straight — and her wild, triumphant joy ran through him in the kiss and he was quite sure now that it wasn't Johnny she loved. . . .

"Gwen," he marvelled, when he could breathe again. "Oh, Gwen, why didn't you tell me, I've been wastin' time —!" And he felt her smiling as he kissed her again as though he could never bear to stop — felt her arms slide up around his neck, felt her slim body give with laughter, and tried to see her face, which she hid against his chest, *laughing* at him, in that solemn moment when he felt so shaken and profound. But it was a nice way to start, wasn't it, with laughter, and her arms locked tight behind his head. It was all right with him, so long as she was happy, only what had he done that was wrong? And then, with his cheek against hers, he felt tears —"Hey, *honey,* what's the matter, here, I thought you were *laughing* —"

"I am." She showed him, but her eyes were wet. "Oh, Fitz, I *am,* but how could I tell you, it wasn't my place to let you know until you — w-wanted it —"

Fitz turned this over in his mind, while he cradled her closer jealously.

"How long has it been goin' on, then?" he asked. "How long have I lost, bein' so thickheaded?"

"You haven't lost anything," she whispered. "I'll make it up to you, somehow. You'll have all there is, Fitz, I promise."

"Honest? From now on?"

Her eyes were shining and steady. From this minute on, with never a backward glance. She nodded, wondering if anybody had ever had so unpredictable a lover as hers.

"Blast Miles, anyway," he said thoughtfully, trying to plan ahead. "I tell you what, I'll just miss that train tomorrow morning and we'll go down to City Hall and get married, so I can take you with me to Miles's party."

Gwen stood perfectly still, her lovely mouth ajar.

"M-married?"

"Too soon for you?" he asked ruefully. "Well, it was just an idea. I kind of hate to let you out of my sight now. Of course Aunt

394

Eden will fix you up a grand church wedding with all the trimmings if we give her time, but I thought it would be kind of fun if you could come to Miles's party on Saturday.''

''But, Fitz, I never meant I — I don't expect you to — it wouldn't do for you to *marry* me,'' she got out desperately, for she was quite sure that a grand church wedding was not quite what Cabot Murray had had in mind.

Fitz held her off to look at her. His brows were very straight, his chin stuck out.

''What's that you said?'' he demanded quietly.

''Don't you see, Fitz, you feel like this now, but I'm from the wrong side of the tracks and you're nice people — they wouldn't — your family would never — well, don't look at me like that, I'm not going back on anything I said, I can't help loving you, but I don't belong as your wife, Fitz, I — I'm not — not —''

''Are you tryin' to tell me that you'll go to bed with me tonight, but you won't go to Williamsburg tomorrow as my wife?''

Gwen put her hand up in front of her face. It was the same gesture she had used that first night before she said, ''You don't have to be polite with me.'' It was as though she had been struck, and was waiting for her head to clear.

"I didn't mean to make you angry," she said faintly. "If you — just take time to think you'll see how right I am."

Now that she mentioned it, he supposed that the thing he felt was anger, an emotion he was fairly unfamiliar with. Something was pounding in his temples, there was a constriction in his throat, and his heart was hurrying uncomfortably. His hands dropped from her shoulders and went into his pockets, and he took a turn around the room, trying to assemble himself into his usual state of inner law and order. At last he spoke from the other side of the room, and his voice was as slow and gentle as it ever was.

"What I'm trying to figure out," he said, "is what the hell kind of a fellow did you think you were in love with?" And when she did not answer, her face hidden by her shielding hand, compassion overtook him and he went to her, lifted her off her feet in one swift compelling movement, and sat down with her on his lap in Johnny's capacious old Boston rocker. Patiently and in silence he coaxed and wheedled and was firm, until she relaxed against him, obedient and content. "Now, don't think I'm not sore at you, because I am," he said then, while his thin, strong fingers cupped her chin. "But I've got the habit now, so I'm askin' you again. I know that crowd down at City Hall and they'll marry us tomorrow. Will you come quiet, or must I drag you?"

10

Sue hurried through the April sunshine towards Sedgwick's office, the telegram in her hand-bag and chaos in her mind. But there was one clear, recurrent idea: Thank goodness I came home from England. Thank goodness I'm here now to — well, to *what?* What was she going to say to Sedgie to resign him to this new wrongheadedness of Fitz's, marrying a girl nobody in Williamsburg had ever heard of, a girl they weren't going to understand at first, a girl who had red on her mouth? How could she now explain her own failure to mention Gwen when she returned from New York at Christmas time, which had arisen mainly out of her uncertainty what to say and Eden's hope that there was nothing in it anyway? And how could Fitz have done such an inconsiderate thing, without warning, behind everybody's back, as though — as though he was *afraid* to let them know in time?

Weddings were sacred in the family, like coming-of-age parties. Everybody had to be there, everybody had to toast the bride, there had to be presents, and speeches, and all your friends at the church, and her father had to come and give her away — Who *was* Gwen's father?

Married Gwen yesterday. Bringing her with me arriving Friday. Counting on you to break it gently. You know how lovely she is.

Love.
FITZ.

But he shouldn't have done it like that, with a telegram. He should have taken her to Eden, she should have come down to Williamsburg for a visit with his people. Fitz knew better than to marry anyone that way, no matter how much they were in love. . . .

For all her deep affection and her obstinate pride in him, Sue had no inkling this time of why Fitz had done what he did. She did not guess the sudden near panic which had possessed him at the idea of coming home to Miles's party with war in the air and nothing but a musical comedy in his hands — even though it had got as far as going into rehearsal next week and might make him thousands of dollars. The miracle of Gwen seemed to Fitz the answer to all his deficiencies in the eyes of the family. With Gwen beside him he could face anything. They none of them would have anything like Gwen to show, at Miles's party. Gwen was his own, she had chosen to love him instead of Johnny, and so he had a wife now, and they were partners in his music and were going to be famous and make money.

He had no doubts at all that she had only to smile at them with her honest, shining eyes and maybe sing one song to his new piano in the drawing-room in England Street, and they would all take her to their hearts at once, for this was no Lisl Oleszi, fair and cool and haughty, speaking with a German accent and looking down her high nose at her husband's country cousins. This was Gwen, who had never had the right sort of family life, and who needed piteously to feel that she was safe and cherished and didn't have to worry any more about people like Fagan or about finding money for Pa. To Fitz, who had always been a little off the beat in his relationships and had never done quite the way he was expected to, and had always kept his own diffident counsel, it was a new and intoxicating experience to share his life with some one who was so passionately sure he was right as Gwen was, so completely uncritical, so warm and quick and worshiping. Fitz had been lonely all his life, and was only just beginning to discover what he had lacked. Gwen had become for him the answer to everything, the sum of all delight. Fitz was headlong in love.

But Sue, mounting the dingy stairs to Sedgwick's office over the bank, knew only that poor Fitz had done it again, and again it was up to her to smooth his way for him somehow and make them all see that his judgment was always fundamentally sound and that he had never been a fool about women, whatever else they might say, and she had seen the girl herself and noticed that she was pathetically in love with him. . . . But as Eden said when the telegram came, why, oh, why had they neglected to mention the little singer Fitz had brought to Cabot's house last December? It was as though they had all *avoided* the subject, and that made it ever so much worse now, as though they had deliberately conspired with Fitz against his parents —

And then Sedgie was so glad to see her, as he always was, and as always she felt herself a traitor to be on Fitz's side, and found it hard to begin.

"Brace yourself, Sedgie. Fitz has got married."

"*Fitz!*"

"Now, wait, it's not as bad as you think, honey, I saw her when I was there, and she was in love with him then fit to break your heart. I didn't mention it to you all because Fitz didn't seem to notice how she felt, and I — well, I thought it might not come to anything —"

"When did he marry her? How did you hear? *Who is she?*" They were lawyer's questions, sharp, crackling, to the point.

"He married her yesterday, and sent me a telegram. She's coming with him on Friday."

"Who is she?" he repeated, for she had skipped that one.

"She is a singer, Sedgie — an awfully pretty girl. She's a Yankee, of course, but that doesn't matter any more, does it! He brought her to the house in New York while I was there, and she sang some of his songs at a ball and made a great hit. Eden says she is going to sing the leading role when Fitz's musical comedy is produced next month."

"Did Eden know he was going to marry her?"

"Oh, *no*, Sedgie, you see — now, honey, Eden feels terrible about this, that's why I came here to talk to you alone. You mustn't *blame* Eden, when you see her. Fitz isn't living at their house any more, you know, he took a room because he wanted to be like the other reporters and live on his salary. Cabot's raised him, too, did he tell you? He gets thirty-five a week now, and if the show is a success it will make him lots of money.''

''But — do you mean to say this girl he has married is an *actress?*''

''Well, yes, dear, in a way. That is — she *sings.*''

''How did he meet her in the beginning? Has she got people? Were her parents at the wedding we weren't invited to?''

''I don't know.''

Sedgwick stared at her hopelessly. There seemed to be so much that she didn't know.

''Does she earn her own living? What sort of home does she come from?'' he asked then.

''Well, I did hear something about a brother who had died, and so Fitz and Johnny Malone helped her along till she got another job. She — maybe she lived alone, she's been earning her living as a chorus girl with the Weber and Fields show.''

''Oh, my God!'' Sedgwick threw himself into his chair with a groan and put his head in his hands.

"Now, you're not to take it like that, Sedgie, she's not — not at all the way you might think. She's only eighteen anyway, and Eden says Cabot said she's not had much time for sin."

Sedgwick raised his head.

"What does Cabot think of her?"

"I just told you, Eden says Cabot seemed quite taken with her and thought she might be the making of Fitz."

"Mm-hm. But does Cabot know Fitz has *married* her?"

"N-no, you see, Cabot was in Washington."

"Quite so!" said Sedgwick with irony.

"Eden is afraid you may feel she should have been more watchful. But after all, Fitz is a grown man and when he telephoned from the office on Monday morning to say he would have to take a later train, she thought nothing of it, because she's so used to Cabot and Bracken always being detained."

"What did he say in the telegram? Did you bring it with you?"

She handed it to him silently, and he tossed it down on the desk when he had read it.

"Poor Melicent!" he said. "He's hiding behind your skirts, as usual!"

"You mustn't say that, Sedgie, it was natural for him to tell me first because I had seen her, and he thought I could explain right away so you wouldn't — wouldn't feel —''

''What is there to explain, except that Fitz has been hooked? And serve him right at his age!''

''Sedgie, wait till you see her, please! She's a nice girl, I'm sure she is, and you mustn't make her feel unwelcome when she comes.''

''But heavens above, Sue, an *actress!* She doesn't belong here at a family party! What about the girls?''

''I think you are being very stuffy and old-fashioned,'' Sue said firmly. ''Gwen is only a girl herself, and not half as impudent and worldly wise as Virginia, if you ask me! I intend to do everything I can to make her feel at home here and see that she has a good time, and I sincerely hope that you and Melicent will do the same. Fitz has married her, they're in love, and I can't believe you will be so stupid and silly as to make them unhappy by being angry about it. And anyway, it's too late!''

Sedgwick sighed, and looked at her across the desk with a rueful smile.

''You're right, as usual! I'll kiss the bride if she's painted an inch thick. It's no use expecting Fitz to do anything the right way, but I can't seem to learn that. If you say she'll do we must make the best of it, I suppose. But it's hard on his mother.''

''Sedgie. There's one thing more I want to say.''

''Yes, my dear? What's that?''

''Don't for one minute think he — well, *had* to marry her.'' Sue's hazel eyes met his levelly, but her cheeks got rather pink. ''I know your son, if you don't, and Fitz isn't that kind of person. I don't think she is either. It's an honest marriage, Sedgie, because they want to be together. You must believe that.''

Somewhere at the back of Sedgwick's consciousness a weight was lifted. He came around the desk and took one of her hands and turned it palm up in his and kissed it.

''I'm glad you said that,'' he said. ''I don't know what I'd do without you, Sue.''

11

But it was Melicent's place and not **Sue's** to welcome Fitz's bride when he brought her home. So Gwen faced a stranger when Fitz said, "Mother, this is Gwen," and then, when Melicent had kissed her dutifully and in silence, Fitz added with noticeable pride, "And this is my father."

Gwen knew by now that Fitz idolized his father, who was all the things a Sprague should be, and the face she raised to Sedgwick was full of childish appeal with terror at the back of it. Gwen was quite literally frightened stiff. No amount of kindness from Eden or bluff encouragement from Cabot while she was just Fitz's protégée could give her confidence now to confront this large, impressive, surprised unit known as the Family. She expected that they would be hostile and unfriendly, considering her an interloper, which she undoubtedly was, and it was agony to her to anticipate that through her Fitz might be hurt by the people he loved. She felt instinctively that they were too well-bred to snub her outright, or to disown Fitz, or make any sort of scene. But she had no hope of being accepted as one of them, and all her defences were braced against condescension or coldness or sarcasm of just plain despisement, any one of which would boomerang Fitz and make him an outsider henceforth, like herself, to his own flesh and blood.

Therefore the look she gave Sedgwick was truly piteous and he thought with astonishment, "Why, she's scared to death of me," and his kind heart acted before his head and he took her by the shoulders — she held herself like a princess, anyway — and said, "Well, my dear — it's not a den of lions you've come to." And while he kissed her cheek he heard her whisper, "Thank you, sir." Then it was Phoebe's turn, and Phoebe said, "Oh, Fitz, she's *beautiful!*" and they could all laugh at that, and presently Gwen found herself alone with Fitz in the room he had slept in all his life, and he was saying, "There, it wasn't so bad, was it!"

She turned in his arms to look at the late afternoon sun streaming in the double window above the April garden — white curtains, chintz-covered armchairs, rich old rugs on a dark polished floor, gay flowered wall-paper, a spacious four-poster bed with a frilled tester and hand-made counterpane — Fitz's bedroom seemed to emphasize and epitomize more than anything else the gulf between his secure, dignified background and the sordid surroundings of her own scant nineteen years.

"Fitz, I don't belong here. I had no idea it was so beautiful. I'm sure to do something to make you ashamed. How long do we have to stay?"

"Why, honey, what on earth ails you like this? You belong where I am. We'll go back to New York the first of the week, but I — sort of wanted you to like it here."

"Oh, I *do,* it isn't that, but —"

"Well, then," he said matter-of-factly. "How about takin' off your hat and hangin' up a few things and makin' yourself at home? Last time I slept here I didn't know there was any such person as you in the world. Gives me a kind of funny feeling."

The hard clasp of his arms reassured her again, and she raised her face to his kiss. Maybe she was from the wrong part of town, maybe she had slept in bureau drawers and trunk tills in the corner of cheap railway boarding-house rooms on tour with her parents who snored exhaustedly in the one bed, and meanwhile Fitz was growing up in this elegant serenity. Maybe she wasn't what the family wanted for him, but she was what *he* wanted, and she loved him more than anyone possibly could who had always been accustomed to his gentle ways, and when they were alone together she never had any doubts at all. . . .

"Mm-hm," he murmured, as though she had spoken, holding her. "That's the way I feel too, but I reckon we've got to start thinking about changin' for dinner pretty soon."

She sighed. More family, and dinner at the Day house across the way. Cabot Murray was arriving from Washington this evening, with his discerning eyes that looked right into her and his embarrassing familiarity with all the things no one else knew about her — for sure. He had told her to stick by Fitz because she would be good for him, but now he would think she had taken advantage of that conversation in the library. And she knew that one did not take advantage of Cabot Murray with impunity.

"Fitz, do you think my dress will be all right tonight?"

"Sure. Aunt Eden bought it, didn't she?"

"Yes, but — for me to sing in."

"You're goin' to sing to 'em tonight, honey, after dinner."

Gwen gave it up. It was still hard for her to understand that families dining alone together at home should put on their best for each other.

"And now," Fitz was saying as he rang a bell by the mantelpiece, "you'll have to get a going-over by Mammy. She raised me, and she owns me, so you mustn't mind anything she says. She'll help you unpack and change your dress, and if there's anything you want just say so and she'll fix it."

Gwen stood still in the middle of the room staring while Fitz was enfolded and exclaimed over by a small wizened colored woman in a starched white turban. She saw that he bent and kissed the withered black cheek, and that he submitted patiently, even gaily, to being patted and stroked by the gnarled black hands, seeming almost as happy at the reunion as his old nurse was. Past surprise, docile and smiling and silent, Gwen allowed herself to be hugged in her turn and gave her cheek to be kissed, noticing that Mammy smelled only of soap and that real tears shone in the wrinkles round her eyes.

Then the old woman stood holding both her

411

hands and peering up at her with wise, twinkling eyes that queried her inmost feelings until Gwen felt naked in her conscience and thanked her stars that it was clean, and her love for Fitz flamed up into her face in a scarlet blush, denying that she had married him for any other reason. Mammy nodded, and patted the hands she held, and her smile was a benediction.

"Dat's good," she nodded. "Dat's mah lamb. He be all right now he got you."

Fitz came and put an arm around each of them, linking them to himself.

"She's a Yankee gal, Mammy. Makes her feel kind of strange down here. We've got to find ways to show her she's come home."

"She know dat," said Mammy, holding Gwen's hands. "In her heart, reckon she know, fast enough. She get used to our ways in no time. Dark hair an' a red mouth — dat's de kin' ob wife foh mah boy. He safe wid you, missy, I kin tell!"

It was the thing Gwen so wanted them all to know — that Fitz would be safe, that she would love him always. This old black witch had seen it, and perhaps the others would too, in time.

"I'll do my best, Mammy," she said, as solemnly as she had spoken her marriage vows.

Later they all walked through the warm April dusk to Ransom Day's house, which shone with lights, and there was Fitz's cousin Sue saying, "Welcome to Williamsburg, honey," with both hands outstretched. Then Gwen was presented to a very old gentleman who, with an apology, did not rise from his easy chair by the fire; and this was Grandfather Day who, Fitz had told her, had been on General Lee's staff during the war. Gwen, having a deep, unself-conscious reverence for old age, said rather breathlessly, "I never knew a grandfather before. I have been looking forward to you, sir." And she bent swiftly and kissed the fragile hand he held out to her.

The family was touched, but at the same time her impulsive words raised new questions in their minds. No grandfathers? No *people?* But what sort of upbringing had she had?

Fitz's Aunt Eden came next, with a warm kiss, and his cousin Virginia, whose merry brown eyes were curious but friendly, and her sister Marietta who had married the Princeton professor; Cousin Dabney Day was next, the one who had lost a leg in '64, but you'd never know — a great handsome man still, bringing forward his wife Charlotte, who was as pretty as could be; and their

413

daughter Belle, with two babies and a husband, and her brother Miles, whose birthday it would be tomorrow, a tall, grave, charming boy — all kissing kin, they told her, gallantly exercising the privilege, while Fitz never let go her hand for fear she was nervous, as he led her from one to another and spoke their names so that she could fit them into the family pattern he had painstakingly explained to her on the train coming down. And he noticed as the ordeal went on that her fingers were cold and damp in his, and clung convulsively, and he thought, Stage-fright — like when she sings — I suppose it does look like rather a mob when you're not used to it. And the Family in its collective mind was thinking, She's dressed all right, anyway, nothing flashy — Fitz has got himself a beauty, at least — I do believe she's got red on her mouth — lovely eyes — she's shy, poor thing, I never thought an actress would be shy — well, it could have been much worse — wait till Cabot comes, he knows more about her — what will Cabot say, when he finds her here as Fitz's wife. . . .

They were all unconsciously reserving judgment until after Cabot gave them their cue, quite forgetting that once Cabot himself had been an outsider, viewed with dismay and apprehension when Eden had insisted on adding him to the family, back in the days of the war. Now they counted on Eden's Yankee husband to resolve most of their problems and difficulties — a virile, knowledgeable, up-to-date man he was, with worldly experience where they, in this timeless backwater, had none — a hard man to hoodwink, unlike simple-minded Fitz, a man who must have formed his own opinion of this actress girl, and who would have strong views on her place among them. She had, of course, gone to his house in New York, but only, they understood from Eden, as a paid entertainer, not as a guest. They were sure they could tell by Cabot's attitude when he arrived exactly what sort of person she was. And Bracken's too, in a lesser degree. Bracken knew what was what.

They had finished dinner before Cabot came, and Gwen had sung them some of Fitz's songs, standing straight and slender and brave against the piano while he played. The family watched and listened wonderingly. She was actually going to sing these songs on the stage, in a theater, within a few weeks' time. Marrying Fitz had not stopped her being an actress. She was going to go right on singing for money, as his wife. They had somehow supposed that she would retire from the stage. And what about Fitz's home, what about his babies? Had he thought about that? Didn't he *mind* having an actress wife, who would have to spend all her evenings away from home, in the theater, being stared at and admired by thousands of people who had paid to see her? And could he keep other men from — well, from making advances, to a woman who was on the stage? And yet — even the least perceptive of them had noticed by the time dinner was over that Fitz was different, and not one of them but recognized the change as an improvement. Where he had been listless and lazy and indifferent, remote, on guard, defensive, uncommunicative, and exasperating, now he was lively, confident, mature, one of them as he had never been before, with some of the true Sprague sparkle and dash. Fitz had found himself, up North.

Melicent, who knew that his music was better than it had ever been, and Sedgwick, who liked his new air of authority and peace of mind, exchanged glances more than once. Whatever it was, it had done him good. She had been right, to suggest that Fitz should go to New York with Cabot. She had saved him from himself, when nobody else knew what to do. But it was Sue who had talked him into going. Sedgwick's eyes sought her out across the room while Gwen sang, and she looked back at him, the dimple showing at the corner of her mouth, and nodded. Fitz was going to be all right now.

It was late evening before Cabot came, and they had almost given him up. They all converged on him, laughing and crowding for their turn to be kissed, until at last with Eden in one arm and Virginia in the other he turned and saw Gwen by the piano. She, like the rest of them, had been awaiting his verdict, and she stood looking back at him tensely, her head a little down, her red mouth tightly closed, her brows drawn level. There was an instant's pause, for his surprise. Then he left his womenfolk and came towards her across the carpet.

''Now, don't tell me, let me guess,'' he said quietly as he came. ''My crazy loon of a nephew has had the luck to marry you!''

His towering height and broad shoulders hid her from the rest of the room and only Fitz saw the way both her hands went out to him, the way her eyes filled with grateful tears as she whispered, ''You aren't angry? I was afraid —'' But they all saw Cabot take her into his bear's hug and heard him say, ''God bless you, my dear, I'm delighted! Maybe now he'll amount to something!''

They all breathed easier after that. Until

they heard Cabot's news, that is.

He had apparently been stopping at telegraph offices all the way down, and he told them quite simply, with no flourishes, that war with Spain was now only a matter of hours. Earlier in the week Congress had passed resolutions demanding that Spain's rule in Cuba must cease, with noon of Saturday the twenty-third as the deadline for Spain's acceptance of the ultimatum. The document had been sent to President McKinley, who had deliberated a whole day and finally signed it and sent a copy to the Spanish Minister in Washington. That evening Señor Polo y Bernabé had asked for his passports.

Eden was the first to speak in the silence that followed Cabot's words.

"Oh, Lordy, not *again!*" she sighed. "It makes me feel lost and lonely and childish, the way I felt last time, after they fired on Fort Sumter!"

And Sue asked timidly, with a glance at Sedgwick, who surely wouldn't have to go this time —

"Will we send an army to Cuba, Cabot?"

"If they don't clear out peacably, and they probably won't. There will be a call for volunteers, of course. We haven't enough regulars even if we called them all in from the West. Roosevelt talks of a regiment of volunteer cavalry, the pick of the country. If only I were ten years younger —!''

''Where's Bracken, Cabot?'' Eden asked quietly.

''Coming up by way of Hampton Roads. I expected to find him already here. He'll show up any minute now, I should think. What I'd give to be in his shoes! He'll see all the fun, I'll put him ashore with the first troops to land in Cuba, he's had about enough of that dispatch boat, I gather!''

''I suppose it's better than having him in the army,'' Eden reflected, and Cabot glanced at her uneasily, well aware that bullets make no distinction between a Special Correspondent and a soldier.

A big tray of coffee, hot chocolate, and whiskey was brought in by Pharaoh, and the maids followed with another of cheeses and a third of sweets. Belle's babies and Grandfather Day had long since gone to bed and Virginia and Phoebe had begun to yawn when Bracken arrived, wearing riding clothes and a broad hat, with a yellow silk handkerchief knotted around the open throat of his dark blue flannel shirt. They all fell upon him, the warmth and excitement of their welcome complicated by their desire for more news. Bracken had it. But first he must kiss

Gwen resoundingly and remark that Fitz had certainly not lowered the family standard of good looks when he chose a wife. Then he relaxed his long, weary body into a chair and waited for the hot coffee his mother prepared with loving care.

"Well, children, the balloon is going up," he told them, his eyes very brilliant in his tanned face, and his gaze locked intimately with his father's. "The Fleet is on its way from Key West this very minute to blockade Havana. A flying squadron will base at Hampton Roads to patrol the Atlantic Coast and head off the Spanish Fleet if they try to come at us up here."

"Do you mean they think Spain will attack *us?*" cried Virginia, and her brother glanced at her under a slanting brow.

"Spain is supposed to have a nice little fleet," he said noncommittally. "Run by a man named Cervera. Until we know exactly where it is and what he plans to do with it, this is going to be a very naval war." Again he looked at his father. "I would like to get aboard one of those battleships off Havana," he said, and Cabot nodded.

"I'll see what I can do about it," he said.

"Somebody else can have the damn' dispatch boat for a while, begging everybody's pardon for language," Bracken announced. "I've done my time on her. Hang Johnny for enlisting, he's just the man I want to take her over. Young Wendell has her now while I'm away, but he's only a cub, he can't do it all alone for long. Tampa is going to be Army headquarters, as you probably know," he added to Cabot. "Why don't you come down there and see the fun?"

"I might," said Cabot, and his eyes glinted.

"That volunteer cavalry regiment you mentioned, Uncle Cabot," Miles said in his unemphatic way. "Could I maybe get into that?"

"Oh, *no!*" cried his mother quickly. "You're too young!"

But, "I'll see what I can do about it," said Cabot again, and Dabney nodded at him gratefully.

"I'll take your little old dispatch boat," somebody said, and they all realized incredulously that it was Fitz. "I'll never be as good as Johnny would, but I reckon I can stay afloat."

There was a thundering silence. Bracken broke it, sipping his coffee.

"Nice to keep it in the family," he observed. "You're hired, Fitz. As of Sunday morning, when I start south again."

12

Together in their room that night, Fitz said apologetically —

"Maybe I shouldn't have spoken up like that, without talkin' it over first with you —"

"Oh, but I was proud!" Gwen assured him, and she didn't look hurt or sad, but only rather excited. "It was the right thing to do, Fitz, the other boys will be in it and I'm glad you're going to run the boat, it's better than enlisting."

It occurred to Fitz that some girls might have cried, or reproached him for volunteering to risk his neck like that after only a week of marriage. But not his girl. Whatever he did, his girl would always back him up.

"Supposin' I hadn't offered to take over the boat," he said, pursuing this idea.

"Would you have been disappointed?"

"Well, it would have to be up to you, Fitz. I don't suppose the boat is going to be any picnic, with a real war on. It's hard to go back to New York without you and start the show, but — I still think it was the right thing to do."

"And if I'd done the wrong thing," he insisted, "would you have told me?"

She looked at him gravely, pausing in her undressing with a petticoat in one hand. Her hair was a little loosened, her eyes were sleepy.

"I'll never have to tell you what's right," she said then, after considering the remote possibility he had mentioned. "It's something you'll always know better than I do, I guess."

"Well, I dunno, seems like most of the time I'm gropin' round in the dark," he ruminated. "For instance, I hate having you go back to New York alone. Would you any rather let the show go hang and stay here with the family while I'm away?"

"Stay *here?* Oh, I couldn't do that, Fitz, I've signed a contract! If I walked out on them now up there I'd never get another job in show business as long as I lived."

" 'Tisn't absolutely necessary you should, you know. You've got a husband to support you now, remember?''

She shook her head.

''I've got to think of Pa,'' she reminded him. ''With what I earn in this show if it's a success I can lay up a year's keep for Pa if I'm careful.''

''Now, look, honey, when I married you I took on your Pa too, see? You can have all my salary while I'm gone, and if you lived here —''

Gwen was still shaking her head.

''He's not your responsibility. I wouldn't feel right for him to cost you money. Besides, the show will keep me busy and I won't have so much time to eat my heart out for you.''

''Well, if you want it that way —'' he murmured, reflecting that she would be bound to find Williamsburg dull anyway, after New York. She'd have more fun in New York doing the show and earning good money. He could never expect her to give up the stage, especially if this show of theirs was a hit.

Some time later, lying very still in the dark beside him, Gwen spoke again.

''Fitz.''

''Mm?''

''Will the family have to know about Pa? Couldn't we just say I had to go back on

424

account of having signed a contract and wanting to help out with your show? They might not understand — they might think Pa was a real loony, and he's not, it was just that fall. I mean, it's nothing that might come out in our children, I wouldn't want anybody to think it was hereditary —''

''Sure, we can just say the show can't go on without you,'' he agreed. ''The only question that's botherin' me is, how am I goin' to get along myself?''

Bracken sought out his parents in private the next day and handed Eden a folded piece of note-paper.

''I don't want to sound melodramatic,'' he began rather gravely for him. ''But I've written down there the address of Dinah's brother Archie, and if anything should happen to me in this silly war we're starting I want you to write him just how it was, and ask him to tell her the best way he can. Not that I expect it to be necessary. But Scovel damn' near got shot against a wall when they caught him, and from now on it's going to be open season on American journalists in Cuba. They blame the American Press for starting the war, and they consider every correspondent a spy, and they're not far wrong, at that. Your own dispatches are your death warrant if you're caught with 'em on you.''

"Then I hope you'll be very careful to swallow yours, my dear, the minute you're caught," Eden said with a brave smile, to show him she knew there was nothing for her to be anxious about. And Cabot said that swallowing Bracken's dispatches would be certain death for anybody, which wasn't really a very good joke, as he knew very well, and then there was a little silence.

"You wouldn't care to tell us about your Dinah?" Cabot suggested delicately, for they knew only that she was the still unconscious cause of the shift in divorce proceedings to the English courts, that she was very young and an Earl's daughter, lived in an enormous Georgian house near Farthingale, and had hair almost the same color as Eden's. Beyond that Bracken had never gone, and they had as usual respected his silences and promised themselves that Eden would get a look at her during the summer and then things would be clearer. But now Eden's sailing would be indefinitely postponed on account of the war, and Dinah remained a mystery.

Bracken walked over to the window and stood looking out into the garden, his long, picturesquely clad body sagging a little as he realized anew that he was not spending Easter in Gloucestershire this year, but far otherwise. Easter had become a sort of anniversary in his mind, with associations as important and personal as birthdays.

The disinclination to speak of Dinah which had plagued him so long was still there. But now, with so much uncertainty before him, the yearning to see her again and the need to share with some one his intense preoccupation with her rose up and choked him. Standing at the window with his back to the room, choosing his words, controlling his voice to an unemotional monotone, he began.

"It is very important, I think, that Dinah shouldn't know just yet how I feel about her," he said carefully. "Especially in case I don't come back from Cuba in condition to — carry out my plans for her. She was sixteen last September and compared to Virginia is young for her age. If she should never see me again she will forget me and, presumably, make a good marriage and have some sort of life of her own. That is why I am not leaving a letter for her. I won't have her saddened by the loss of anything but a strange, brief friendship. Archie would be the one to handle that."

"Yes, dear, but there won't be any need for Archie," Eden remarked firmly as he paused. "Go on about Dinah."

"It's difficult," he admitted after a moment, staring through the window, his hands in his pockets. "I don't know why, but it is. I have been in love before, more or less, I don't have to tell you, and we've always joked about it in a normal sort of way — except in the case of Lisl, there was never anything very funny about that, was there! This thing with Dinah scares me. I have no choice. I am possessed. I didn't see it coming, there was no beginning, there is no end. Dinah is *mine,* it is impossible to imagine that anything can prevent me from marrying her. That is why I have forced myself to consider the alternative, and provide for it through Archie."

"Does she — has she noticed the same thing?" Eden asked gently.

"I can't tell. It's too soon. Well, yes, I can tell that she's drawn to me, likes to be with me, counts on me as a friend. But you've no idea how circumspect I've been. I let her kiss me good-bye — *let* her, mind you! I stood like a stump and felt her face against mine. It aged me by ten years, but I did it. She was crying —" He struck the window-casing beside him with his closed hand, ricocheted off it back into the room and faced them grimly, one eyebrow askew. "Don't think I'm kicking about this job that's ahead of me, because I'm not. I wouldn't miss it for worlds. If I had got back to England before it started I should have had to leave there at once and go to Cuba, make no mistake about that. I suppose what really gets in amongst me is that I couldn't bring her with me last autumn. Our times are out of joint, hers and mine. I have to wait. I have a long way to go yet, before I can get to Dinah. I'm going to get to her — somehow — some time. It has to be the longest way round, but Dinah is home for me, journey's end, and all the rest of it. You won't need that piece of paper with Archie's address on it, that's just a form of crossing my fingers." He came and bent over his mother's chair and kissed her lightly. "These red-haired women!" he said. "Once they've got you by the heart the devil himself can't save you!"

When he had left the room Eden sat looking down at the paper she held: *The Hon. Archibald Campion, — Half Moon Street, London.*

"Virginia mentioned an Archie Campion," she said thoughtfully. "He was the one she liked better than the Viscount who wanted to marry her."

Cabot had not heard.

"I'm so sorry for Bracken," he said, as though speaking to himself without meeting her eyes. "I ache for him, Eden. And it is singularly little use to remember that I myself had to go the longest way round to get to you."

Eden rose and laid her arms around his big shoulders and her cool cheek against his.

"I begin to think you have to earn it," she said softly. "What comes too easily — remember Lisl — may not be worth having."

Miles's twenty-first birthday took place on Saturday with all the trappings — toasts, speeches, gifts, family jokes and ceremonies — heightened and colored in every instance by the knowledge that the country was at war and that after that one last day together the family would be scattered again, some of it in uncertainty and peril. For Eden and Sue and Charlotte the day held a poignancy almost too sharp to bear without tears, for it roused their memories of other days when Cabot had come to say Good-bye before catching the last northbound train out of Richmond in '61; when Sedgwick rode with Jeb Stuart, and Dabney was brought back from Drewry's Bluff with a shattered leg. Oh, not *again*, they said to each other piteously with white, resigned faces. Not for Bracken and Fitz and Miles. Not every generation, this agony of parting and waiting and picking up the pieces when it was over. Not for their sons, the same ordeal their lovers had miraculously survived. . . .

But already Cabot had promised to lay Miles's application personally before Theodore Roosevelt for the volunteer cavalry regiment. Already Fitz and Bracken were cheerfully accumulating the ominous paraphernalia of the tropics — nux vomica for fever, rhubarb pills for bowel complaint, talcum powder for saddle-chafing, sun cholera drops for diarrhoea, acetate of lead for insect bites, vaseline for sunburn, quinine, calomel, mosquito-nets and abdominal bands — all the feeble, futile safeguards against unknown ills and emergencies. Cabot, an old war-horse smelling powder, was going with them as far as Tampa, that sultry, sandy city which was the bottleneck through which all traffic to and from Key West must pass. Some correspondents had been sweating it out there ever since the *Maine* went down, and more were arriving every day. Now that it had become Army headquarters, everything that happened would happen there, until the Navy had dealt with the missing Cervera and his fleet.

Eden was schooled to journalistic habits and viewed the preoccupation of her men philosophically. Sue thanked God many times a day that Sedgwick's fifty-six years would keep him at home in Williamsburg this time. But Gwen — not even Fitz had any idea what Gwen was living through while the festivities of Miles's birthday swirled around her.

Gwen could not remember another war, from which some men had returned more or less intact so that' life could go on. She had grown up ignorant of the stoicism and heartbreak of the '60's, which were still woven into the everyday fabric of living in Williamsburg. For Gwen the departure of Fitz for the blockade waters between Cuba and Florida was cataclysm, holocaust, and the end of the world. But Gwen was not an actress for nothing, and it was impossible to detect her inner panic and desolation. To Fitz she showed only her pride in him and her faith that he would be back safe in time to see the show in its prime. To the family she was the quiet, self-contained, rather mysterious girl who was going back to New York to sing Fitz's new songs just as though nothing had happened, and they all thought it a little heartless and strange of her, though they might have found it hard to say what else they would have expected her to do.

But Gwen, lying awake while the small hours of Sunday morning ticked away, was waiting in a kind of frozen patience for the end of the world. Somehow she had got through the day with composure. Somehow she had shared without tears the loving tempest of Fitz's farewell when at last they were along together, and now he slept, still holding her in the hard, possessive circle of his left arm. She lay quiet, her head on his shoulder, more aware of the strong, steady beat of his heart than of her own. Desperately she drew even now on her waning self-control, forcing herself not to clasp him convulsively and sob out her grief and terror while he was still there to comfort her. Even more than she needed the reassurance he would give if she woke him, she wanted him to have his rest, the last good sleep in a good bed he would get in nobody knew how long.

She had always fought her battles alone, and now she fought this one the same way, while dawn greyed the edges of the room — fought and fell back drearily into those last ditches of fortitude where there is nothing left but: I've had it — it's mine forever — nothing can take away from me what I've *had* — I can be thankful for that — I must be glad I've got it to lose. . . . And flinching closer to him in her extremity, she felt the instinctive jealous tightening of his arm as she stirred, and held her breath until she was sure he had not roused after all. . . .

PART FOUR
BRACKEN

Cuba.   *Summer, 1898.*

1

When he was very young and somewhat given to hero-worship, Bracken had been inclined to feel hard done by that there was so much peace in the world and hence so little opportunity for him to distinguish himself as an intrepid Special scoring endless scoops as he was sure his father had always done during the war between the North and South. When he happened to mention this state of mind to Cabot, he was taken severely to task and informed that any correspondent during the late hostilities who had thought only of beating the other papers to a good headline was usually guilty of giving information to the enemy and deserved to be shot like a spy. And then Cabot's ears had got red and his oratory had suddenly run down, as he remembered with a shock of real surprise, after all these years, that the word

435

Spy was pretty personal to himself and might be better left out of the discussion.

Now Bracken had got his own war. He viewed it with mixed feelings, where only a short time ago it would have caused him undiluted joy. He and Cabot had so far regarded the Cuban rebellion hardheadedly, without any glorifying mist of the traditional ready-made American sympathy for any life-and-death struggle anywhere for the thing called Liberty. They recognized clearly that, unlike the wars in which their family had taken part in the past, it had been agitated by expatriates, politicians, and financial interests without many altruistic spirits among them. They had beheld with disgust the cheap sensationalism of the American yellow press, and had retreated from it into a perhaps too Olympian detachment.

Bracken's own experience in Cuba had changed that viewpoint. He had seen for himself the most sickening evidence of barbarism on both sides. He had come back convinced that after two years of insurgent activity famine would have been imminent anyway, even without the Spanish reprisals. He resented the success with which the sponsors of the patriot cause had contrived to pin the responsibility for suffering entirely on the Spanish Army. He believed that by pouring food and supplies into the island America might nullify the starvation tactics of both sides and bring about a solution without resorting to armed intervention. There had already been fighting enough, of the sort which he considered a civilized word had now outgrown. But if Spain hindered the distribution of those supplies, or if no autonomous Cuban government proved strong enough to keep order — then America must go in with bigger guns, bigger ships, a more efficient and harder-hitting military force than anything Spain could put into the field. In any case the thing must be cleaned up. At once.

Before the paper could launch its own campaign along these lines, the *Maine* went down.

While the Board of Inquiry sifted evidence in the secret sessions on the revenue cutter *Mangrove* in Havana harbor, the insurgents continued to demonstrate their right to liberty and the pursuit of happiness by burning cane-fields and dynamiting trains within sight of the city. Cabot's opinion that the *insurrectos* had blown up the *Maine* for the sake of the advantages they would reap from American intervention had now been voiced by other reliable sources. The chief question it raised was whether the patriot forces would have had the equipment or the technical knowledge to accomplish such a thing. Bracken bought innumerable drinks for talkative harbor rats and dock workers at Havana, his Spanish improving daily with use as he pursued his investigations into the possibility that the mine had been exploded by a plunger hidden somewhere along the shore and manipulated by one or more insurgents who had then concealed the length of wire which remained and disappeared from the scene. But so far his catch-question, sprung suddenly when the chosen witness was well fuddled and full of bonhomie — What did you do with the wire? — had met only the blank stares of innocence and non-comprehension. Somewhere, Bracken was sure, there was a man who knew what had been done with the wire. And if he said, "We sank it," or "It's in so-and-so's warehouse" — why, then, the *Star* was on the right track.

By the time he attended Miles's birthday party, Bracken was convinced that no matter who had sunk the *Maine,* as a symptom of the unbridled terrorism and disorder in Cuba it called for drastic action. When he returned to Tampa with Cabot and Fitz the blockade of Havana had begun and the first shot had been fired — at an astonished Spanish merchantman, unaware of war, which had been promptly boarded by a prize crew and brought into Key West.

Everybody rushed down from Tampa to see her, and Fitz was introduced to the dispatch boat, which had been left in charge of the excited cub named Wendell when Bracken went to Williamsburg. The kid had cabled a very fair story about the departure of the Fleet on the night of the twenty-second — the ships showed no lights except the Ardois signal lamp flashing red and white on the masts, and there was the scurry of launches to and from the outer anchorage seven miles off shore. He had also seen and recorded the capture of the Spaniard outside Key West. He received Cabot's praise modestly, and would now act as second in command to Fitz, which would leave Bracken free first of all to make a voyage in a torpedo boat as an experience. Davis and Scovel had already snagged the coveted post on the flagship, where they would presumably be completely in the know and see everything.

Fitz's boat, as she was henceforth known in the family, was a none-too-well-found little sea-going towboat with a bold sheer and a speed of ten knots if she was scared. She wore the name of *Daisy* in black letters on her grimy bow. She was a wet boat, and always flooded her galley in a blow, so that you had to subsist on hardtack and sardines. At other times her black cook broiled a very fine pompano, or made turtle soup, and there was guava jelly or some such tropic delicacy.

She was the best Bracken could do in the scramble back in February when all the newspapers at once had begun to charter all available small craft, and he maintained sourly that she was better than a Key West sponging schooner or a degenerate yacht. She had probably been a filibuster boat running arms to the insurgents before she joined the staff of the *Star*. It was convenient for a towboat to carry unknown cargo to unknown destinations — she could always show a wrecking license if questioned, and say that she was going to a rescue and mustn't be detained. When she slipped back into port some days later with her coal bunkers empty and nothing to show for her run it was sometimes awkward for her captain, who in the *Daisy's* case was a battered Swede, subject to opportune attacks of deafness on top of knowing very little English.

Whatever her past, the *Daisy* was now respectable, and was always spoken of without the article. "Take *Daisy* down to the flag-ship today," Bracken would say, during the lull while the Fleet lay ten miles off Havana with nothing much to do but chase blockade-runners and wonder where Cervera had got to. Or — *"Daisy* and I thought we'd tail the Hearst gang today,'' Fitz would remark, and Bracken would jibe at the company they kept.

Fitz was now wearing the correspondent's regulation blue flannel shirt, khaki breeches and leggings, and wide slouch hat, with the yellow silk handkerchief which was the *Star's* badge knotted loosely round his throat. His life with *Daisy* was not monotonous. It was their job to keep in touch with the blockading Fleet, remaining at sea for several days at a time till something happened to write about, and then racing for Key West in any kind of weather to reach the cable office.

Unable to exist for long without some form of music, Fitz had acquired a raffish Spanish guitar on which he accompanied himself with melodious effect during the long idle hours at sea. Young Wendell proved to have a very decent bass, and together they recalled all the songs they had ever heard, teaching each other the ones they did not both know. Wendell heard the whole score of the musical comedy and could soon sing it too, and he listened sympathetically to Fitz's artless talk of Gwen and the surprising fact that she had chosen him, out of all the men she might have married, a pretty girl like that, and hadn't raised a whimper when he left her in the lurch and came down to run Bracken's boat for him.

They were known to all the Fleet by their minstrelsy and were welcomed by the other Press boats where everyone was bitterly bored, and they sang their way in and out of Key West and across the Florida Straits and back to the most spontaneous applause. Sometimes Fitz wondered if it was quite dignified, considering the *Star* and all, but Wendell reminded him that the Boss was not the kind to care about a thing like that so long as they didn't overlook a story and nobody threw things at them.

Meanwhile Dewey took Manila in the far-off Philippines without a casualty. Cervera was known to have sailed eastward from Cape Verde and was due off the Atlantic Coast or the West Indies. A state of alarm existed from New England to Hampton Roads, where the flying squadron waited under Commodore Schley.

The Army was concentrating its thousands at Tampa, which had become the center of interest to the Press after Admiral Sampson steamed out of Key West towards Puerto Rico to look for Cervera there. Tampa had begun to resemble a mammoth county fair, with the tents of the regiments laid out in military streets in the sandy wastes all round the town, and horse dealers from all over the U.S.A. bringing in their wares for sale and parading them before prospective buyers.

It was a crazy place anyhow, a collection of sagging wooden houses built upon sand at the end of a single railway track nine miles inland from its port. Wind-driven sand had worn away the paint from the buildings, sand blew across the sidewalks and buried them, sand seeped in around the doors and windows even when they were shut, sand was in your shoes and in your food and in your eyes.

In a disastrous and half-forgotten real estate enterprise avenues had once been laid out between the scrubby palmettoes and pines festooned with dreary hanging moss, and a large hotel had been built for winter tourists. The tourists never came. But now the Army and the correspondents and the foreign attachés in their colorful uniforms and the rich Havana refugees had come. It was a most incredible hotel, even if it had not stood fantastically in the middle of a desert — a Byzantine palace built of ornamental brick. It was topped by silvered minarets, and fretwork columns supported its vast verandahs which jutted out in front of round, decorated arches above massive brass-studded doors leading to a colossal lobby and rotunda.

Rugs, chairs, stuffed round sofas, potted palms, naked statuary, all strove without success to fill the luxurious void. There were electric lights, and bathrooms, and running water. Richard Harding Davis said it was like a Turkish harem with the occupants left out.

At first, it was true, there had been no women. Everybody gave up white linen and took to flannel shirts and comfortable neckerchiefs and sometimes forgot to shave — everybody but Dick Davis. There was a cheerful conviction that the Army would be moving out within a few days — well, next week at the latest. Time passed, and everybody was still sitting round in the fleet of rocking-chairs on the miles of verandahs, drinking gallons of iced tea and fanning themselves and greeting old colleagues they had not seen since Geronimo or Wounded Knee or Larissa or the Soudan. But now wives and daughters and sisters and aunts were sprinkled in the rocking-chairs behind the flowering vines, drinking iced tea and fanning themselves. That was much pleasanter, but it meant the Army was not going to move just yet. Gloomily the white duck suits and dress clothes were dug out of the trunks again, and razors were used. There was dancing in the grand ballroom in the evenings, with music by a regimental band,

and colored lights were strung along the verandahs. Mr. Davis, a cigar in his teeth and a flower in his bottonhole, was heard to remark that war was certainly hell.

By mid-May General Shafter had arrived, in command of the Army. He weighed almost three hundred pounds, and wore a blue woollen uniform and a wide white sun helmet, and suffered visibly from the heat. Ten thousand men were encamped around the town, ankle-deep in dirty sand. Their water supply was deficient, and there were not enough tents and blankets in good condition. There was a plague of flies and mosquitoes. Tarantulas and centipedes frolicked through the men's belongings with malign impudence. Typhoid fever and typhus-malaria were beginning to appear. Supplies, unlabelled, unsorted, unassigned, lacking invoices, filled droves of box-cars stranded all over Florida. Miss Clara Barton arrived, with her Red Cross nurses. General Fitzhugh Lee was there, reminiscing about Havana. English, French, German, Austrian, Russian, and even Japanese attachés matched stories and recalled old acquaintance over their tall, sweating tumblers. And finally Johnny Malone arrived in his regiment, tanned and elated and completely sober, telling in lively detail what he was going to do to the

Spaniards. Young Miles Day was still at San Antonio with the Rough Riders.

There seemed to be nothing to do in the circumstances, Cabot said, but send for Eden and Virginia, who had remained at Williamsburg waiting to see what would happen. They brought with them suitcases full of frivolous presents and trunks full of beautiful summer clothes, and all the family's love. A New York mail brought Fitz a letter from Gwen. Rehearsals were going well, and everybody said they had a hit. But if it hadn't been for the show, he thought, she could have come to Tampa too. Well, no, there was Pa, who still had to be kept. But a Special Correspondent's salary was big enough. . . .

Then Cervera showed his nose at Martinique, and boats rushed off after Admiral Sampson to hurry him out in time to intercept the Spanish Fleet before it could make port safely in Cuban waters. It was next heard of at Curaçao, where Dutch neutrality made coaling next to impossible. And then it vanished again on the blue tropical waters.

When Admiral Sampson arrived back at Key West Schley had hurried down from Hampton Roads to join him. The very next day Schley was off again toward Cienfuegos, where Cervera might head in. Fitz and Wendell were on duty with *Daisy* at Key

West, and Bracken stayed at Tampa to sail with the Army. *Daisy* was to attach herself to whichever transport carried Bracken when they reached Key West, and become his only link with the cable-head at Jamaica. But the Army still could not move until Cervera was found.

He outwitted Schley, who was unduly preoccupied with his own coaling difficulties, and gained the security of Santiago harbor. By the time Sampson arrived there, fuming, Cervera was snug inside. The U.S. Navy cabled for the U.S. Army to come and take Santiago overland, and began to walk up and down off shore, daring Cervera to come out and fight, which he had no intention of doing.

On May thirtieth General Shafter got his orders from Washington to move. After all those weeks in camp the news still exploded at Tampa with the effect of a bombshell. There had been no staff-work on embarkation plans, and Port Tampa had but one pier at the end of that single railway track nine miles long. The harness was not with the artillery carriages, the small arms ammunition was not with the guns, the food was not labelled, the volunteer regiments were mostly without uniforms, equipment, weapons, tents, or blankets, and there was no transport provided for the cavalry horses. Everything promptly dissolved into profane and perspiring confusion and remained there for another solid week. Late on Monday evening, the sixth of June, a caustic War Department received what proved to be an over-optimistic telegram from General Shafter announcing that the men were being marched on board.

2

Bracken had labored conscientiously at a letter to Dinah after the sailing orders came. Each one he wrote became more difficult now, because Dinah was getting older every day and every day his impatience and uncertainty grew. He had had a couple of narrow squeaks already, with *Daisy,* and going ashore with the troops was not going to be any outing. An attack on Santiago from the hills would hardly go unopposed. The strongest Spanish garrison in Cuba was there, as well as the Fleet. One might as well face facts. There was going to be a fight for Santiago. Several fights. It was known that the Spanish couldn't shoot for sour apples, but if enough of them shut their eyes and fired into the American lines somebody was going to get killed. There were quite a lot of Spaniards ready to do that at Santiago.

Dear Dinah — [he wrote on the third try]

Orders have come for the army to sail for Cuba, and I shall be going with it. From the time we leave here I shall have to depend on the dispatch boat for letters, but will try to send you word as often as I can. I think that once we get started on this job it won't be terribly long until we finish it, and then I can come back to England. Everything here is in an uproar, and I am sure Sir Gratian would be amazed and disgusted at our incompetence.

Mother and Virginia are here with my father —

How dull. How inexcusably, excruciatingly dull his letters must be, as though they were written by a rather feeble-minded undergraduate to a half-wit child. That was what came of bottling up all your feelings, remembering Lisl, considering that Dinah was only sixteen, never forgetting that you weren't free, always trying to sound like a favorite brother — so that if you died or lost an arm in front of Santiago there would be no scar on Dinah's life beyond the childish grief she had shown at the parting in the spinney.

Mother and Virginia are here with my father, and they probably won't sail for England now until we have done this job in Cuba. It is unbelievably hot here, and I often think of cool green Farthingale, and the sun coming up over the hill.

Our luck goes with me, Dinah — on its little gold chain around my neck inside my shirt — and some day I shall bring it back to you. I feel sure that if I wear it under fire I shall be kept safe —

No, perhaps better not. Just like Alwyn or Clare to read Dinah's letters. He tore up the page, which began with the word Farthingale, and wrote more discreetly.

—Farthingale, and the sun coming up over our hill.

The trinket we bought that day we went shopping in London goes with me as my luck. Everyone here seems to have a mascot and that is mine. My best regards to all the family and believe me,

Most sincerely yours,

B.M.

Well, that would have to do. Some day he

451

would make it all up to her. Some day he would write her letters that said what he really felt about her. . . .

On his way to the mail-box in the lobby he met Virginia, all in white with an applegreen sash and a fan and a lace parasol.

"I was looking for you," she said, and tucked her hand under his arm. "Come and have some iced tea, my tongue is hanging out."

She had very little to say until the tall tinkling tumblers were set before them at a table in a corner of the verandah some distance from the main stream which poured incessantly in and out of the doors of the hotel. It was bakingly hot from the sun glare in the street below, and there was everywhere the smell of horse, and coffee, and cooking, and people, and — the just plain *smell* which was Tampa in summer. The flies were myriad. Virginia fanned them off the table automatically and raised the glass to her lips. Her eyes met his over the brim.

"Bracken. Do you ever think of going back to England?"

"Often," he admitted cheerfully.

"So do I. Do you think we ever will?"

"Oh, come, Ginny, we've got the house! I have to see to the London office, too. Nelson is doing very well there, but it's my baby, and I want to get back to it as soon as we settle this Cuban business.''

''Have you heard from Clare lately?''

''No. Had a letter from Dinah, though, in the last mail.''

''From *Dinah!* How cute. Why didn't you tell me? What did she say?''

''Nothing much. It's been raining. She's read *The Prisoner of Zenda* again. Archie has been down for the week-end and looked perfectly splendid.'' They eyed each other silently, over the tall glasses. ''Mother is wondering why on earth you turned down that nice Conover boy who is so devoted to you,'' Bracken said finally.

''You know why.''

''I thought maybe I did. But I didn't say anything about that to Mother.''

''Thanks. I'll do as much for you some day.''

''Good,'' he said, and smiled at her affectionately.

''Bracken. Have you ever been *terribly* in love? I mean, besides Lisl? I mean so you can't sleep at night for thinking about it, and you lie there making up long, lovely conversations where the other person always says just what you want him to and never misunderstands anything you say, and — and —''

"Yes," said Bracken kindly as she paused with very pink cheeks. "I've had it like that. And it wasn't Lisl."

"Did you get over it finally?"

He shook his head.

"Hm-mm."

"Well, what do you do?"

"You wait. Like me."

"Is it Clare?" she demanded curiously.

"Ginny, I'll tell you a secret. I don't care if I never see Clare again!"

Her eyes widened.

"Somebody *else?*"

"Somebody absolutely else."

"Do I know her?"

"No." A bare-faced lie. But she didn't know Dinah. Not really. Not his Dinah.

Virginia returned to her glass, baffled.

"Suppose they marry somebody — and it isn't you — while you're waiting," she suggested.

"You have to take that risk."

"If you can get rid of Lisl before that happens are you going to propose?"

"Mm-hm."

"Does she *know?*"

"Nope."

She gazed at him with increased respect.

"You're awfully *cheerful* about it," she commented.

"Can't afford to mope, Ginny. Nobody can afford to mope. *Sursum cauda*. That means Up with the tail. Not a bad family crest, do you think?"

Virginia stirred her glass, looking down.

"At that last dance we all went to in New York I let the Conover boy kiss me — just so I could pretend it was Archie."

His brows shot up.

"I hate to sound like a brother, but was that wise?"

"No. It wasn't. He thought we were engaged, and I had a terrible time getting out of it."

"I should think so!" said Bracken.

"Besides, it didn't work. He was shaking all over. Archie wouldn't be like that." Her wide, grave eyes reproached the beginnings of a smile on his face. *"Would* he?"

"Probably not," he conceded. "But I wonder how you know that."

"I know a lot about Archie. And I can guess the rest."

"Well, now, Ginny, no more experiments like that, hear me?"

She wrinkled a fastidious nose.

"I'll tell you who would be all right, though, if only I hadn't seen Archie, and that's Johnny Malone," she confessed. "I like Johnny a lot, since he's been in the

Army. It's improved him. *Now* why are you looking like a brother?"

"Well, here goes, I suppose it's my duty," he sighed. "Look, Ginny, it's Archie you want, isn't it. Then why don't you let Johnny go?"

"*Let* him go!" cried Virginia indignantly. "Well, I like that! Johnny simply —"

"I know, I know, Johnny simply loves you to trample on him! But it's not fair, as things are. You'll go off to England and land Archie one of these days and then where will Johnny be? Meanwhile, if you don't dangle him he might find somebody to be happy with."

"What shall I do, then, tell him I'm in love with a man who has forgotten I exist?"

"How do you know he has?" Bracken objected.

She shrugged — a small, pathetic hopeless movement of her slim shoulders.

"He has given me no legal evidence to the contrary. I never thought I'd be like this, but I'm as bad as Phoebe is about Miles. Have you noticed the way she watches him, as though she couldn't even make up her mind to laugh without waiting to see if Miles is amused? It's *abject!* I never meant to fall in love *all the way* — I meant —"

"You meant to cheat, eh?" he accused her grimly. "Well, it serves you right, that's all, and now you know. Most of us do learn sooner or later. You're lucky it's not later. It's your own fault now, if ever you have to make do with second best.''

''If he'll have me,'' she said humbly. ''What do I do that's wrong? *Edward* likes me!''

''Edward has to finance the title, with all due respect to you. Maybe Archie is afraid you'll think he's fortune-hunting.''

''Oh, Bracken, he couldn't be such a chump! As if I cared about the money, I'll get Father to cut me off with a shilling!''

''Now, don't let's do anything hasty,'' Bracken grinned. ''I'll think of something, just give me time. If it's really Archie you want, then Archie's number is up, and I'll stick by you until we get him!'' He reached out a hand to her across the table, and she put hers in it quickly and their fingers gripped.

''Here's luck to you too,'' she said. ''And now I think you ought to go up stairs. Mother is awfully worried.''

''I will. Are they sure yet?''

''Yes. It's the fever again.''

Cabot had gone down that morning under another attack of his old enemy malaria.

3

By the night of the seventh, when everyone was ordered aboard the transports, Cabot was worse and his heart was giving trouble. Bracken left the hotel at the last possible moment and found the railroad a quite indescribable scene, and became at once, in spite of his anxiety, the complete reporter.

Word had gone round the regiments that the transports were sailing from Tampa port at daybreak the next morning for an unknown destination. How the men were to get aboard them had apparently been left to the enterprise of the men themselves for the limited transportation, the American troops turned that night into hilarious pandemonium, with fairly successful results.

The Ninth Infantry stole a wagon train from the Sixth, which had not got itself together fast enough to protect its property.

The Seventy-first New York took possession of a railway train belonging to the Thirteenth Infantry, who in their turn commandeered some cattle cars and a wood-burning locomotive, and thus beat the Twenty-first and the Twenty-fourth to the pier, cheering themselves triumphantly as they pulled in.

The Rough Riders had arrived at Tampa only three days earlier. With the usual idiocy of the Florida railway management, the regiment had been dumped out of the train about eight miles from their camping site, which was a cavalry drill ground not far to the rear of the hotel. They rode through the town in rather loose troop formation, their practical, dust-colored khaki outfits envied by the Regulars, who sweltered in canonical blue wool. It was also reported that their guns were the new Krag-Jorgenson carbines which used smokeless powder.

Miles Day was among them, in K Troop — which consisted mostly of supposed dudes from the universities and eastern cities. He came round to the hotel as soon as he could and they all said how tanned he was and how he had *grown,* and Eden gave him all the gifts from home — Phoebe had sent him a copy of *Soldiers of Fortune* — and he heard with passionate interest all the latest news from Charlottesville and Williamsburg. In return he described the fantastic tangle at the camp, with the railroad unloading their baggage just where it pleased or where the jam made it possible, and how there had been no regular issue of food for days — the officers had had to buy the men's food out of their own pockets, Miles said. And always his wistful, dazzled eyes had kept going back to Virginia, who was wearing pale blue *mousseline de soie*.

Some time before dawn on the eighth, Bracken sought out the Rough Riders at the camp behind the hotel, for Miles had insisted that it was only friendly for him to travel with them to the port and catch a ride to Cuba on the same transport. Cabot when consulted grinned enviously and said it would do no harm to ask Theodore if he might go along, but be sure to duck. Bracken found the ex-Assistant Secretary of the Navy, now a lieutenant-colonel of cavalry, charging about in search of his superior officer, Leonard Wood, who was out hunting for their train, which had not showed up. By this time several other regiments had got aboard their trains, but none of the trains had started. The lieutenant-colonel's language with regard to the whole situation was free and picturesque. Bracken was swept cordially into his sizzling orbit and contrived not to lose sight of him.

At six o'clock the Rough Riders seized some coal cars and in them, with the engine in reverse, backing, they made the journey to the pier, which was now jammed with trains, luggage, troops, and apoplectic officers, all at cross purposes. A K Troop sergeant was heard to remark that hell wouldn't be more crowded on the Last Day than Tampa pier that morning.

The transports lay out in mid-stream and had to come alongside the pier a few at a time for loading. Bracken tagged at Roosevelt's heels, a delighted spectator, while the Colonel ran to earth the swamped depot quartermaster and wrung from him the name of a transport which was not yet occupied. She was the *Yucatan,* and she was still out at anchor, and it soon developed that two other regiments claimed her. Wood nabbed a stray launch and went out to take possession of her, while Roosevelt pelted back to the train at the far end of the quay and brought up the regiment at the double-quick in time to board the *Yucatan* as Wood brought her alongside the pier. The two rival regiments came up just too late, and there was some expostulation — the word was Roosevelt's — to no purpose, for the Rough Riders were firmly embarked. But they weren't cavalry any more. All the horses had to be left behind, except those belonging to the officers, and they were on another boat.

Before nightfall the *Yucatan* had pulled off and was anchored again in midstream, her khaki-clad passengers packed in like sardines. A week's devastating anti-climax followed. Until the thirteenth of June the loaded transports swung at their anchors in the steaming discomfort of Tampa Bay, because of a report that there were Spanish warships at large in the St. Nicholas Channel.

She was not a lovely boat by any standards, being an ancient freighter whose unplaned, built-in bunks were likely to come apart under their occupants. Her capacity was seven hundred and fifty men, and she now carried two hundred more than that. Over her side she wore a waggish sign which read: *Standing Room Only*. The meat contained in the travel rations issued to the troops was not salted or corned beef, but terrible stuff called canned fresh beef — stringy and tasteless at best, nauseating in the murderous heat which turned it smelly a few minutes after it was opened. There were no fresh vegetables, no ice, and the water was already bad. The men slept on the bare decks because the air was so stale below, and the only diversion was cards and bathing over the side. Because he was his father's son, Bracken had the freedom of the bridge.

Their naval convoy was to pick them up at Key West where there was more delay — fourteen mouse-colored warships accompanied by a disreputable flotilla of dispatch boats, among whom Fitz's *Daisy* was not the least presentable, although her deck was piled high with extra coal in sacks. She distinguished herself, among a lot of irresponsible behavior by the other Press boats, by running up and down the straggling lines of transports getting in everybody's way till she found Bracken, whereupon she cuddled in against the *Yucatan's* side and Fitz came up a rope, to the admiration of all beholders.

Fitz had telegraph news from Tampa. Cabot was holding his own, and it was time for the attack to abate soon. The show had opened in New York and was a success, and Gwen was well and happy and proud. Some Marines had left Key West to join Admiral Sampson's patrol off Santiago. This last made everybody more impatient than ever, and hard things were said of the Navy for taking time to coal and provision after the precautionary run into the St. Nicholas Channel, which had netted no Spanish ships.

It was not a very impressive armada when

it finally steamed eastward from Key West, towing its torpedo-boats and landing-scows and a water-schooner. Its speed was necessarily the speed of the slowest ship in the convoy, so the water-boat set the pace at a spanking five knots. Even *Daisy*, loaded to the gunwales with coalbags, had no trouble to keep up. At night they ran with all the lights on and the bands playing ragtime. By day they did the drill in the manual of arms for exercise, watched the flying-fish and the strange things that float on tropical seas, told tall stories, played poker, and were hungry. The scanty water supply tasted like a frogpond and smelled worse. Heat ailments began to appear.

On the following Sunday, when they entered the Windward Passage and encountered the breeze that lives there, everybody lost interest even in flying-fish. But the next morning there were mountains to the north of them, rising almost from the water's edge. Everybody gathered at the rails and cheered the mountains, which were Cuba, and the convoy steamed on past small Navy picket-boats outside Guantanamo Bay where the Marines had already landed, and everybody cheered the Marines. That afternoon they knew by the sight of grey-painted warships ahead that they were off

Santiago Harbor, and everybody cheered the Navy, which fired a salute to General Shafter. Then the engines stopped and the transports began to wallow idly in the seaway.

Daisy bustled over to look at the headquarters ship, which carried Shafter and his staff and all the attachés and Richard Harding Davis, and after hanging about there for a while came snuffling back to report that Admiral Sampson's chief of staff had gone up over the side from the flagship's launch. Soon the headquarters ship was seen pulling away towards a conference, and for two more days the transports waited on a nasty swell.

The water supply on board had diminished to almost nothing, and nobody had had a decent meal since they could remember. Everybody was bored to death and inclined to curse out the Marines, who were cosily encamped on shore with room to move about and a chance to prepare their own food. Fitz unlimbered his Spanish guitar again and drifted melodiously among the transports where they lay, singing songs everybody knew and could join in on, and pennies often rained down on *Daisy's* deck, embarrassing her into flight.

Then orders came for a landing to be made in force at daybreak at Daiquiri, which was a small mining hamlet on the shore about eighteen miles east of Santiago and about the same distance west of Guantanamo. Everybody perked up and forgot to be seasick and began to make plans.

Daisy already knew her part. She was to take Fitz and Bracken ashore with the troops and then stand by for Bracken's first dispatch, ready to rush it off to the nearest cable-head at Jamaica. By the time she returned there would be another dispatch waiting. Fitz was to act as shuttle between Bracken at the front line and *Daisy* at the pier. Wendell complained bitterly that he and *Daisy* had been given the short end of the stick and would miss all the fun.

4

Before daybreak Bracken and young Miles were keeping vigil at the rail of the *Yucatan,* shoulder to shoulder with several dozen excited, cheerful members of the regiment. They were watching fires scattered along the shore where Daiquiri was, and which might be signal lights of the Spanish, but nobody knew.

As dawn came up and Bracken's field-glasses became more helpful, they could see the flock of transports huddled off the indentation of the shore line which was the little mining port. The American firm which owned the iron mines behind the town had built a steel pier, and there was a small rickety wooden dock beside it. These, and the sloping white shingle of the beach were all the landing facilities there were. Out of the landing-craft provided by the Army quartermaster to get the men ashore, one lighter had broken down on the way, one had simply got lost, and a tug had deserted.

The watchers at the transport rails saw the borrowed small boats assembling below them like a regatta — empty Navy steam launches and long-boats, and all the life-boats from all the transports, bouncing on the deep blue water.

On shore there was no sign of life visible to Bracken's glasses. The mining company's machine shop and a string of ore-cars on the pier were ablaze. The rows of native huts thatched with palm leaves appeared to be deserted. Behind them rose the enigmatic jungle-clad Cuban mountains, with a Spanish blockhouse and flag-pole crowning a nearby spur. Bracken noticed with something like awe that the men around him seemed in happy ignorance of the obvious fact that, with a little well-placed gunfire from good positions on the hillside below the blockhouse during the landing operations, the white beach beside the pier could become a shambles. The general atmosphere on board was that just before the kick-off on a football game. Or were they all covering up, as he was, a strange crawling sensation in the midriff? Glancing at Miles's eager, unclouded face beside him, Bracken began to wonder if he himself was going to prove to be — squeamish.

Invasion of a country whose border was a line drawn on a map was comparatively simple. History was full of such things. But sea-borne invasion of a hostile shore was not a venture to be so lightly undertaken. Look at England, Bracken was thinking, gazing at Cuba from the *Yucatan's* rail. For centuries twenty-four miles of water had preserved England from molestation by the continental powers. Even Napoleon had thought twice about it. Even Caesar had failed. A hundred years after that, Augustus had managed it. William the Norman had been the only other one. Landing from boats lengthened the odds to suicide if the land force was ready and competent.

There were very few precedents for this morning's work in Cuba, Bracken thought, leaning on the rail. Very few rules to go by. But surely these open boats packed with troops in no position to return fire from the beaches and with no protection from it were against even commonsense. Where *were* the Spanish? Waiting. Waiting for the range to shorten, of course. Waiting till the invaders were beached and helpless.

The Navy launches towing their long strings of little empty boats were swinging in below the *Iroquois,* and Lawton's brigade had begun to tumble into them — a difficult business, attended by shouts of rude laughter and blasphemous comment as the men, weighted with cartridge-belt, blanket-roll, haversack, and gun, made the tricky descent overside into the heaving open boats, which either fell away beneath them or rose so high that it doubled them up as they landed. If one of them had missed and hit the water instead, he would never have come up again. But that too seemed not to occur to anybody, to spoil the fun.

The Rough Riders were brigaded with Regular cavalry under General Young, and both were under General Wheeler, and third on the list for disembarking. Orders had been so worded as to bar correspondents from the first landing, which had caused considerable friction on the headquarters ship where the journalists attempted to argue with the commanding officer. *Daisy* came alongside the *Yucatan* and Bracken shook Miles's hand and descended to her deck by a sea-ladder, so they would be ready to follow the boats in as soon as possible.

Fitz's grey eyes met his, candid as a child's, but thoughtful. Wendell was in the wheel-house talking to the captain and for a minute the two cousins stood together at

Daisy's coal-blackened rail, while the tug rocked drunkenly beneath them, their field-glasses trained on the abandoned village.

"Well," Fitz drawled at last with a sidewise glance round his glasses at Bracken's silence, "it is sure a nice mornin' for an ambush."

"I'm glad you've thought of that too," Bracken grinned. "I began to think maybe I was getting the creeps."

"Creeps? I'm all over goose-pimples!" Fitz admitted frankly. "All they need is a few Gatling guns up there in the bushes. They'll wait till we hit the beach, if they've got sense, and then — they'll open up on us. Let's you and me go home before it starts, huh?"

Bracken laughed, and felt love for the man beside him surge up through veins where the same blood ran. He knew without even thinking about it that nothing on earth could induce Fitz to leave Daiquiri before it happened. But because he had not been at Manassas and Yellow Tavern, Bracken had no way of knowing that the flicker of pointed light that had appeared in Fitz's eyes under their lazy lids was the same that had lived in Sedgwick's during the war their fathers fought, and it had been in St. John Sprague's at Camden and Yorktown too. All the

Spragues loved a fight. That was history. And this morning at Daiquiri, waiting for the Spanish guns to open up, Fitz was finally and completely a Sprague. Murrays fought grimly, savagely, cool-headed and dangerous. Spragues fought with laughter and insults and a fierce joy — equally dangerous. Their fathers could have told them. Now they would find it out for themselves.

Standing together, feet wide apart on the rolling tug *Daisy,* seasickness long a thing of the amateur past, they felt between them the strange, heartening, inexplicable bond which is kinship, mutual heritage, mutual memory, *blood* — and each knew without words that there was no man anywhere he would rather have at his side than this one, no matter what happened. Somewhere at the back of Bracken's consciousness a last wisp of doubt dissolved and was seen no more; for who had said Fitz was different, who said he had an odd strain, who said he was not quite one of them? Not Bracken, ever again.

The morning wore on and the sun got hot, while the transports wallowed and the small boats bobbing beside them slowly filled with joking, swearing, seasick men, girdled with glistening cartridges, the white blanket rolls gleaming across their shoulders, and their muskets pointing any which way. Delays were caused by over-cautious captains who would not bring their precious vessels close enough in shore to facilitate loading the boats — for the transports were all merchant ships, still owned by commercial companies who would hold their officers responsible for any damage suffered. The Navy steam launches scurried distractedly about after whole battalions marooned on distant decks and wildly apprehensive lest they be forgotten and miss the picnic ashore.

For nearly three hours the loading of the small boats went on in full view of the beach and the blockhouse and the jungle, and nothing stirred on shore. Then Lawton's first brigade signalled that it was ready, and the launches began to marshal their long strings of open boats on tow-lines for an untangled dash to the beach. It was also the signal for the Navy bombardment to begin, and for another twenty minutes the crowded boats were held back while the big guns pounded and the village took fire and bits of beach and jungle were blown into the air. But there was no answering fire.

In a silence which was loud and ominous after the echoing voices of the guns had ceased, the bow-to-bow shoreward race began. The steel pier was too high to be used at all. The first boat touched at the wooden dock and the first men jumped for it, and the rotten planking held under them and they dragged their comrades up beside them, timing the swell the best they could. Other boats grounded some yards out and their occupants took off their shoes and rolled up their trousers and waded in. Two infantrymen fell into the water and were drowned by their equipment. They were the only casualties of a landing which invited holocaust. For some incredible reason of inertia or bad judgment or caution — for they were not cowards — the Spanish had withdrawn from the town to inland defences, throwing away their best chance at turning back the invasion.

Daisy went waltzing in beside the Navy boat which was landing Rough Riders — ahead of their turn because its officer knew the lieutenant-colonel. Bracken and Fitz jumped for the dock and made land dry shod, and *Daisy* backed off to await developments. Fitz stood on the white beach, gazing first at the mountains, then at the little bay, which was black with boats and mean and confused, swimming animals — the only way to land four-legged transport was by opening the side hatches and pushing the unwilling beasts into the water.

''We don't deserve this,'' Fitz said

solemnly. "God is sure good to Shafter. Look — natives."

A ragged band of *insurrectos* was straggling in to meet the Americans. Even a non-military eye could see at a glance that as allies they would be pretty negligible. This was the native force with which the American Army was to co-operate in driving out the Spanish rule.

"Think we'd better send back to Tampa for some reinforcements that wear shoes," Bracken said. "The Colonel seems to be mad about something special. Let's go and see what it is."

The Colonel was mad because one of his horses had been drowned. The pony called Texas stood dripping faithfully beside his master while Roosevelt's colored body-servant recounted almost with tears the fate of the other horse. While they all stood mourning, thunderous cheers broke out from the boats, the beach, and the dock, and all the whistles on all the transports began to blow with banshee glee. The stars-and-stripes had gone up on the cupola of the Spanish blockhouse on the hill.

By the time the swift tropic nightfall struck the Daiquiri beach things had reached the usual high state of American pandemonium, and when the bright, unwinking Navy searchlights were turned on to make it possible to continue the job of unloading men all night, they illumined a most improbable scene of lighthearted inefficiency.

Shrieks of laughter greeted each awkward spill or harmless accident. Cheers went up for all minor accomplishments. The men still awaiting their turn on the transports sang *There'll Be a Hot Time in the Old Town Tonight,* and stamped in unison to pass the dull hours of inaction. The men who had reached shore stripped and went swimming in the surf and danced naked round the bonfires on the beach, yelling like Indians from sheer exuberance, while the ragged Cuban contingent looked on in paralyzed bewilderment, and the officers gave up with helpless mirth the task of curbing the rodeo-football-rally spirits of the men. The sea was full too of anxiously swimming animals, their halters strung together and attached to rowboats, while cheery buglers on the beach tried to guide them in with the musical water-call. The little dock where supplies were coming in lacked some of its planks so that the bare girders, two feet apart, were often the only foothold. These were awash most of the time and very slippery. Many precious articles fell through and were sometimes recovered by diving for them, but most of them stayed there. It never occurred to anybody to repair the dock, and anyway the Engineers were down the coast just then on a job for the Cuban army — Shafter's orders.

Several miles along the jungle trail which ran parallel to the shore to the port of Siboney, Lawton's brigade were already pitching their dog-tents under the royal palms and beating off with some hysteria hordes of large land crabs, varying in color from pale orchid to leprous, which scuttled fearlessly over the blanketed forms of tired, restless men who were trying to catch some sleep their first night in the field. From Siboney the trail turned inland, passing over a gap in the coast range into the rolling country around Santiago.

Lawton's men flushed the Spanish rear guard at Siboney next day, but the enemy slipped away with a final rattle of Mausers from the jungle's edge behind the town. Lawton had no casualties, but now the men had been under fire, and knew the sound of hostile bullets intended to kill. Its effect was not visibly sobering.

Daisy was away for Jamaica with Bracken's story of the landing, and orders to ask Key West for news of Cabot Murray and wait for an answer. With Siboney in American hands, the landing operations were shifted there from Daiquiri, for though it was little more than an open roadstead without even a pier, it was seven miles nearer Santiago.

The Rough Riders had exceeded their orders and pushed forward along the jungle trail from Daiquiri on Lawton's heels, full of curiosity and zeal, disgusted at having missed the first skirmish. If they had had their horses, they could have caught the retreating Spaniards.

That night the Navy searchlights made Siboney as light as a ballroom while the disembarking went on through a roaring surf under a white tropic moon, and the smell of bacon and coffee rose from the camp-fires along the shore. Naked men waded out to catch the painters of the loaded boats that were being pitched on to the beach by headlong combers, and tried to hold them there while the occupants piled out into waist-deep water, howling with triumph at having arrived at last on the soil of Cuba. On either side the black overhanging ridges rose above the pearly gleam of dog-tents and the red glow of fires.

Then it rained. Cuban rain, which comes down in solid sheets of water, extinguishing camp-fires, drenching through water-proofed material. Supper was late.

At the Rough Rider camp there was wakeful excitement among the officers. A Cuban scout had come in to say that the Spanish were intrenched at Las Guasimas five miles inland from Siboney, at the apex of two trails which there joined to lead on to Santiago. While Shafter remained on board the flagship, Wheeler was the senior officer ashore, ranking Lawton. After a reconnaissance in person, Wheeler gave orders for an advance by Wood and Young the following morning. He assigned the valley trail on the right hand to Young's Regulars, and gave the Rough Riders the ridge trail which ran along high ground a mile or so distant from Young's route. Both lines of march were supposed to be infested with sharpshooters and both offered every opportunity for ambush.

Wood and Roosevelt were known hardly to have lain down at all when reveille went at three-fifteen A.M. and they were still prowling about in their yellow slickers. Wood was haggard and hoarse, Roosevelt was lively as a lark and apparently quite unfatigued. Packing the mule train was a terrible business, for the overnight downpour had left the ground the general consistency of a dish of oatmeal, and water had seeped into everything. There was nothing dry enough to burn right, and breakfast was hasty and half-cooked, while Wood went roaring that anyone who was not ready in ten minutes would be left behind.

They moved out at six, with the sun coming over the hills. Half a dozen of the officers were mounted, but the troopers carried full packs, ammunition and carbines like infantry. Colonel Roosevelt rode the pony called Texas with a borrowed saddle — a secondary war having been narrowly averted when his own was discovered to be missing. His dotted blue bandana marked him as soon as daylight came, and the early sunlight flashed on his spectacles as he rode.

Bracken and Fitz were with K Troop, their only field equipment a mackintosh and toothbrush and canteen apiece, their yellow neckerchiefs and field-glasses the badge of their profession. They had spent part of the wet night on the porch of a native shanty but their khaki clothes steamed with dampness as the sun burned down. Richard Harding Davis was stricken with his recurrent curse of sciatica, and rode an Army mule unhappily near the head of the column.

The ridge trail was extremely narrow and the regiment went single file with two Cuban scouts well in advance and a ''point'' of five trained American scouts two hundred yards behind them. Then came Wood and Roosevelt with a group of other officers and some correspondents, and Captain Capron with L Troop, composed largely of cowboys and Indians from the Indian Territory. The first ascent of six hundred feet was gruelling, and protests from exhausted men brought a halt on the summit. From there they looked back on the little bay full of boats, every level piece of ground studded with white tents, and they heard the camp bugle calls like the horns of elfland blowing.

Advancing inland from the brow of the hill with Capron's troop strung out ahead as an advance guard, they passed desolate plantations, burnt out and abandoned to the encroaching jungle — evidence of Cuba's three years of revolution. The trail drew in until twenty-foot vegetation met over the men's heads, a tunnel with whispering green walls, heated like an oven, and bordered on each side by derelict barbed wire fences five strands high. No flankers were possible on either side of the trail. The pace set was severe for troopers carrying accoutrement on foot, and men dropped out and lay gasping in the terrible heat beside the wire. The empty jungle silence around them was broken only by the startled *wha-leep* of the brush cuckoo or the rustle of some small animal escaping from the line of march, and an unkind suspicion was voiced that Lawton's had imagined the Mauser fire at Siboney.

Fitz and Bracken with K Troop were arguing the actual size of tarantulas viewed in cold blood, when the order to halt came from up ahead, and the men lay down where they were in the sour trampled grass. They were glad of another chance to rest, fanning the air with their hats, longing for a smoke or a glass of beer, grumbling because they were forbidden to remove their blanket rolls. An order for silence in the ranks was regarded as an unjust reprimand for complaints and everybody subsided aggrievedly, for it is the soldier's inalienable right to mutter.

On a single mutual impulse Fitz and Bracken raised themselves cautiously and edged along to the head of the column where the officers were. There they found troopers kneeling with their carbines at the ready, peering into the solid green bushes while Wood went forward to reconnoiter. A knot of officers stood together over the body of a not very freshly dead Cuban scout. As Fitz and Bracken arrived unobtrusively on the scene Colonel Roosevelt lunged at them fiercely and bade them be quiet — quieter, anyway, than he was, somebody said.

The orders to unsling rolls and prepare for

action, load chamber and magazine were given in whispers passed along, followed by another order for absolute silence in the ranks. Men were set to cut the barbed wire either side of the trail with nippers. Troops G, K, and A were ordered into the tangle of creepers and bushes on the right to try and make contact with Young's forces coming up the valley trail. D, F, and E were deployed in skirmish line into a natural clearing on the left preparatory to a flanking movement. Before the maneuver could be completed the first Spanish bullet sang over their heads, and then came a full volley. Everyone dived for cover in some astonishment. There were Spaniards in Cuba after all.

Bracken and Fitz side by side stepped over the wire on the right immediately behind Colonel Roosevelt, and plunged into the rank vegetation full of exotic blossoms which had to be torn and beaten apart with hands and carbines and knives before any progress could be made. Somewhere ahead of them across a mile or so of such country was Young's brigade. The intervening jungle was so thick that if you lost touch with the man on either side of you you might never see him again, and would yourself be confused, isolated, and left behind. The Spanish firing was high but they had the range, and men began to go down. A dressing-station was established at the place where the column had first halted, and a couple of surgeons who were members of the regiment went to work. Capron of L Troop got a mortal wound in the first few seconds of fighting. Before very long, Roosevelt's eyes had been filled with dust and splinters when a bullet struck the trunk of a palm tree close beside him.

Nobody had yet seen a Spaniard and their smokeless powder left nothing to shoot at, while singing death poured into the American ranks. It was uncanny. The jungle itself spat fire. Bracken crouched at the foot of a palm tree, his notebook on his knee, and wrote furiously, Fitz lying at his side with field-glasses and calling out things he might miss. They could see Wood now, standing in the front line, waist-deep in tall grass, leaning against his sorrel horse between it and the Spanish firing line ahead. The grass all round him moved as though in a capricious wind, which was the passing of bullets for no air stirred. Indentations in the grass near him showed where men had fallen, or were lying down to fire.

Every now and then bullets struck Bracken's tree trunk with a *chug,* and when they dropped in the grass near by it was with little *zips* like raindrops on a roof. Once a covey of Spanish soldiers who had had enough crossed an open space running like rabbits, and with a whoop the Americans opened a delirious fire on the first enemy to show themselves. Wood ran at his own lines, shouting, *"Don't shoot at retreating men!"* He was not heard, or at least was not obeyed, until he had a trumpeter blow *Cease firing*. It was some time later that Bracken learned that Wood's action came from his grim knowledge that shooting at men already in flight was a waste of precious ammunition which would be more needed later on.

Bracken was pleased to find that he still functioned efficiently as a reporter, and that his hand had steadied after the first few minutes under fire. He was able to record with detached interest that bullets hit human flesh with an audible, rather hollow sound, and bodies went down like wet rags with a jingle of canteen and metal and a thick thud as their weight struck. Mauser bullets in the clear made a thin, shrill song past your ears, he noted coolly; those which struck foliage went *ping*, and there was sometimes a brief eerie silence in which the rustle of bullet-clipped leaves could be heard.

Young's brigade was now in heavy fighting on the right, and always the regiment was working forward, across a shallow valley and towards the ascent on the other side, which was open ground. The noise of firing was so great from both sides that an L Troop lieutenant could not make his voice heard at all with the word of command and ran along the line striking his men with his hat to make them know what he wanted. They had to travel flat on their faces now, through sharp, thorny bushes which tore at their skin and clothes, through suffocating grass so thick and high it cut off what air there was. But they kept on moving forward, driving the Spanish ahead of them. Wood was up and down the line in touch with all his officers, but the growth was so dense that he never saw a whole troop at a time. The wounded lay still where they were, flattened under the hot fire, and the surgeons crawled out to them to put on tourniquets and dressings at the risk of their own lives, sometimes delaying to drag a man into the shade. As Bracken and Fitz followed doggedly the advancing line of fire they heard again and again the death-rattle clank of the big land crabs which gathered to feed on the wounds of bodies which were still warm; and they saw the helpless wounded batting hysterically with their hats at a hideous patient ring of the scavengers who waited, on tiptoe and with protruding eyes, for movement to cease.

The ground they traversed in the immediate wake of the battle was spattered and matted with blood and littered with abandoned equipment and the twisted forms of wounded men. They used up their own first-aid packets and resorted to pocket handkerchiefs and torn strips of clothing and blankets to make tourniquets and dressings, and found ownerless canteens for disabled men in an agony of thirst. Once they turned back to help carry a wounded man to the dressing-station in a blanket, wincing in sympathy when his body bumped on the uneven ground, answering his delirium kindly — ''We must given them hell,'' he kept imploring them all the way. ''They've killed my captain — the damned dirty Mexicans have killed my captain —''Sometimes they knelt to write down names gasped out in pain, receiving keepsakes, promising to deliver messages which became incoherent on the lips of dying men. They had lost track of Miles soon after they left the trail, and they watched for him anxiously. Sweat ran down into their eyes and their clothes were soaked as though they had forded a stream, and both of them were smeared with blood which was not their own.

Somewhere along the way Fitz had picked up a carbine and ammunition belt, and now when they paused for Bracken to bend above a wounded man or scribble something in his notebook, Fitz lay on his stomach and fired busily towards the murderous jungle ahead, taking his direction from the nearest trooper, and cursing softly to himself in words Bracken had no idea he knew.

"Hey," said Bracken once. "You aren't supposed to do that. War Correspondents are non-combatants. That's one of the rules."

"The hell with rules!" Fitz replied, the Krag-Jorgenson cuddled lovingly against his cheek. His mouth was thin and white, his grey eyes flickered with a steely glint. "If I could only get my sights on one of those bastards I'd give 'im rules!" He pulled the trigger again and squinted as the gun kicked his shoulder, and loaded again from his belt. "Come on out and show yourselves, you lousy, crawling, lily-livered sons-o'-bitches, gimme a chance at your backsides, you blue-bottomed baboons, you —"

"We can't print that," said Bracken. "Come and lend a hand with this bandage."

Eventually Young's left wing connected with K Troop in a thin skirmish line, cheering like a grandstand as they sighted each other, their guidons fluttering through the trees like football pennants. After an hour's fighting the Spanish were driven back, foot by foot, some three hundred yards into their third line position which included the building of an old distillery. Towards this Wood's left wing was advancing in quick, stubborn rushes — half a troop racing forward to throw itself flat in the deep grass and go on firing. The fire discipline was excellent, and they fired in volleys at the word of command. The whole regiment was engaged now. There were no reserves.

Marshall of the *Journal* had been shot near the spine and was carried back to the dressing-station in convulsions of pain. The surgeon passed him up as hopeless and worked on men who had a better chance of living. When Bracken left him he was trying to finish his dispatch before he died.

A bullet passed through Bracken's sleeve, burning his arm as it went. Fitz turned his head and saw the rent it had made and the reddened skin beneath. At that moment the order for the final charge came echoing along the line, and Fitz broke cover with a shrill Rebel yell inherited straight from his father.

''Yo-who*eee, here we go!''* he howled, and took off with K Troop, firing as he ran.

Bracken followed instinctively, unaware that he was panting with laughter. The air was full of cheering, and the Spanish, already disconcerted by the unorthodox behavior of soldiers who only knew how to move forward after every volley poured into them, retreated upon Santiago, convinced that the entire American Army was after them.

5

Reinforcements from Siboney arrived just too late to take part in the fight or to overtake the fleeing Spaniards. They were assigned to outpost duty while the tired men who had fought their first battle and won it made camp at the junction of the two trails where the Spanish front lines had been. Supper consisted chiefly of beans taken from the load of a dead Spanish mule. Young Miles Day turned up unhurt, and excessively proud of a bullet hole through the crown of his hat. The wounded and the dead were gathered into the little field dressing-station in the trail. The defenceless bodies had been mangled by vultures and land crabs, which invariably tore at the eyes, lips, and wounds. Over these dead comrades the cow-puncher's brief, philosophical epitaph was more than once spoken: *Many a good horse dies.*

There was no tent at that hospital in the trail, only the branches of a mango tree, and there were not enough blankets to go round, and the regiment hadn't a stretcher to its name. The blood-soaked surgeons cut the sleeves out of their shirts and worked with claret-colored arms, operating on men laid on strips of canvas shelter tents on the ground while they made the worst cases ready to be sent down to Siboney on improvised litters.

Fitz was going with them to carry Bracken's dispatch and make himself useful with the wounded on the way. Until then, he drifted casually among the prostrate forms, dropping a comforting word here, holding a canteen there, raising a laugh where he could from men who were pathetically eager for a joke. Thus he came to a boy shot through the neck and already half delirious, who was trying to beat time with his forefinger to a tune which had run through his head all day. His mouth was open slackly, making dry little sounds which had a sort of rhythm. Fitz knelt down beside him.

"What key are you in?" he asked gently, and the boy's eyes wavered to his face and rested there with recognition. His lips formed words. "Once more," said Fitz, bending closer.

Again the black, parched lips moved.

"I got it, son," said Fitz, and his clear, easy voice floated out on the hot jungle air —

"... Sweet land of liberty,
  Of thee I sing.
Land where our fathers died,
Land of the pilgrims' pride —"

Just beyond them another voice took it up. Behind them a fine cowboy tenor came in. And soon all the wounded were singing, some of them jerkily, stitched with groans, some thickly, for lack of water, some hoarsely, from the cheering. . . .

"Our fathers' God, to Thee,
Author of liberty,
  To Thee I sing.
Long may our land be bright,
With freedom's holy light,
Protect us by Thy might —"

Fitz took them through to the end, and it was a heartening sound to a group of homesick, hurt men, most of them barely come of age, facing death or amputation or long agony, feeling very far from home. Bracken's eyelids stung as he listened, and he added a paragraph to his letter to Cabot which Wendell would post at Jamaica when he filed the cable:

> Anybody who has anything to say henceforth about this fellow Fitz will have to come outside with me [Bracken wrote.] Heroism has been cheap around here all day, but our Fitz so far forgot his duty to the *Star* as to charge the Spanish rifle-pits waving a gun and yelling blue murder. Right now he is singing lullabies to the wounded while sharpshooters fire into the camp. It is a man.

Bracken decided that Fitz was doing more good than he could there, and himself went off before dark with the first lot of wounded, carrying one end of a makeshift litter, his dispatch and letter in his pocket. Those that were left under the mango tree sang the long dark night away, following where Fitz's tireless spirit led them, through *Tenting Tonight, The Girl I Left Behind Me, On the Banks of the Wabash,* and even *Yankee Doodle* — until a certain rivalry arose to think up new ones to try to stump Fitz on a tune he didn't know. There could be no camp-fire because of the sharpshooters, and there could be no sleep because of the groans and ravings of delirious men.

Bracken's party was fired on all the way down by sharpshooters hidden in trees along the trail. When one of these was brought down by a lucky pistol shot he was found to have green branches tied to him for concealment among the leaves. Davis had got a stretcher up from Siboney for Marshall, who was taken aboard the hospital ship *Olivette* anchored off shore on a sickening swell, and there he obstinately refused to die, no matter who gave him up. By midnight on Saturday Siboney was full of suffering men. Yellow fever was beginning along with the wounds, adding its own horrors of vomiting and haemorrhage, besides the scarcely lesser miseries of the chills and fevers attending malaria.

Bracken found Wendell in a state of nerves because of the wild reports which had reached Siboney from stragglers, walking wounded who had left before the fight was over, and mule-packers who had never been near enough the front to see for themselves. These described with what Roosevelt later called minute inaccuracy how the Rough Riders had run headlong into ambush, and both Roosevelt and Wood were rumored dead in action.

"How could we be ambushed when we were expecting to be shot at from the minute we left town?'' Bracken demanded disgustedly. ''How headlong were we with a couple of Cuban scouts ahead of a five-man point ahead of Capron's troop which was practically single file? I have seen both Wood and Roosevelt since the shooting stopped, make that quite clear to everyone. What's the news from Tampa?''

Tampa had reported no change, and Cabot was apparently going to weather the attack as he had done many times before. Bracken saw *Daisy* off for Jamaica and spent the rest of the night firmly setting everyone right about the fight at Las Guasimas.

When he returned along the trail to the Rough Riders' camp on Saturday morning he met more sorry cavalcades of wounded on the way down. He found the regiment established in a marshy spot close to a stream a mile or so ahead of the place where the skirmish had begun. They were now host to two of the attachés — Captain Arthur Lee, the Englishman, whom everybody liked, and the German von Götzen, who seemed very anxious to be popular.

General Young had got fever, and Wheeler was laid up too, so Wood was the brigadier now and Roosevelt was colonel of the regiment. General Shafter, said to be suffering acutely from the heat, remained on board the headquarters ship. Transport was the greatest problem at the camp. The officers' baggage had come up by mule-train, but they possessed few comforts anyway and whatever extras they might have been entitled to in the officers' mess they turned in to the wounded, refusing everything which was different from what the men had.

Thousands of tons of rations were still on the transports in the bay, but the unloading and wagon-train service up the trail were so slow that the Rough Riders were on one-third rations, which consisted of salt pork and hardtack and were more suitable for the Klondike than the tropics. Coffee and sugar were short, and there was no tobacco. Roosevelt went all the way down to the coast with an improvised caravan of officers' horses and a stray mule or two and brought up beans and canned tomatoes for the men, purchased from the commissary with his own money.

Many of the men had lost or thrown away their blanket-rolls and knapsacks and other equipment at Las Guasimas, and it had been appropriated by the Cubans, who then swore that they had had it all their lives. Shelter tents were inadequate against the periodic downpours of rain which started rivulets large enough to float away a mattress unless it was being lain on. Shacks were built and thatched with palm and banana leaves, and these harbored tarantulas and other callers who came out at night. Lights were forbidden, no matter what dropped on you, for the Spanish sharpshooters never slept. They even picked off the unwary by the flashes of solid lightning which accompanied the tropical thunderstorms.

For nearly a week the regiment rested and sorted itself out while reconnaissance went on and maps were made and the Engineers attempted to widen and corduroy the trail from Siboney, in rich loamy soil that went to sticky mud every day during the regular afternoon downpour. The trail ran on to Santiago from the crest whence the Spanish had fled. About three miles ahead as you stood in their deserted trenches you could see where it cut through a series of jungly ridges known collectively as San Juan Hill, commanded by heights either side which were scarred by the lines of freshly dug Spanish earthworks. It involved itself too in the windings of the little Aguadores River, which it sometimes closely resembled, and there were no bridges, only fords. A broken-down wagon could snarl traffic for an hour almost anywhere. A narrower track led into it from El Caney on the right, where there was a stone fort with a strong Spanish garrison.

On the twenty-seventh General Shafter rode up from Siboney and observed the view towards El Caney, which would be the next point of attack. He returned to the headquarters ship the same afternoon. Still nothing happened at the front-line camp. The regiment was blooded now and wanted another go at the Spanish. It was uncomfortable where it was, and wanted to move on. There began also to be a certain feeling that the place for headquarters was in the field and not on a ship eight almost impassable miles from the front.

After two more days Bracken was increasingly anxious about his father and curious about the situation in Siboney. He and Fitz decided to go down to the coast — the journey would have to be made on foot through mud like black glue — give Wendell the story of the dull week in camp, and put themselves in touch with things.

On the way they met General Shafter coming up again, his enormous bulk carried astride a lathered horse, his blue woollen jacket open over an expanse of damp white shirt, his white helmet pulled low. He rode like a bag of meal and the slender, easy figure of Lieutenant Miley, opening and reading a handful of dispatches as he rode beside his General, was not complimentary.

Bracken paused, frowning, when they had squeezed to the side of the trail to let the group of mounted officers pass.

"I'd better go back," he said. "Might miss something at last. You go on down with these." He handed over the dispatch and some letters. "Give them to Wendell and — now, Fitz, don't you lie to papa, don't feel right today, do you?"

Fitz blinked away a persistent haziness which had afflicted his vision all morning and turned an aggressively cheerful countenance on his cousin.

"Who, me? I never felt better!"

"Got a headache?"

"Well, maybe — just a little one. Too many beans, I reckon."

Bracken felt the skin of his forearm.

"Are you kind of chilly?"

"*Chilly!* In this heat? You're crazy!"

"Fitz, do me a favor, won't you? When you get down to Siboney find out if Wendell has any more quinine and start taking it."

"What for?"

"Quinine is usually for malaria."

"But I haven't got malaria. I just feel kind of all-overish, that's all. It's those beans."

"Will you do as I say, Fitz?"

Fitz blinked again, for Bracken's face, not three feet away from him, had a way of weaving in and out of focus when he tried to see it.

"Oh, sure, sure, anything you say," he agreed meekly, and turned away down the trail. "So long. Back in the morning."

"Take a day's rest down there if you need it."

"Think I'm a sissy?" floated back as the green jungle walls closed in on Fitz, walking very straight and rather fast, because things showed a tendency to slip sideways.

By the time he reached Siboney the sun was dropping and he ran down to the beach to signal *Daisy,* who lay off shore plucking peevishly at her anchor chain on the swell. While he stood there, waving the *Star's* yellow scarf to attract the captain's attention, a voice spoke behind him.

"Thought you'd *never* show up," said Wendell. "What's going on up there?"

"Nothing. That's the trouble. Here, before I forget 'em —" Fitz handed him the papers for the cable and the mail. "You seen a cup of coffee anywhere?"

Wendell took another look at him in the fading light.

"Gosh, you've lost *pounds* along that trail! Had anything to eat lately?"

501

"I just want a cup of hot coffee, that's all."

"Come on over to the Engineers, they'll find you something. But first —" Wendell put out a detaining hand. "Fitz, the news is pretty bad."

"Uncle Cabot?"

"He died last Monday."

6

Fitz woke with a jerk and found himself in a cramped position on an improvised mattress on the porch of one of the Cuban shanties at Siboney. It was just before dawn. For a moment he was unable to collect himself at all. Then he remembered everything with sickening clarity. Wendell — who, like everybody else, had run out of quinine — had put him there some hours before, with solicitous care for his night's rest, and then gone to Jamaica with *Daisy*. And it was now his, Fitz's, job to go back up the trail and tell Bracken that his father was dead.

Cautiously he unkinked himself under the rough blanket which smelled strongly of horse. Things seemed to be far from well with him somewhere. He still had the headache — not such a little one now — and an unreasonable desire for hot food and drink. As he sat up a long, shuddering shiver began at the back of his neck and ran in detail down the whole length of his spine. A cup of coffee — that was the stuff. Go wake up the Engineers and get a cup of coffee. . . .

But before he reached the first smoky cook-fires his teeth were chattering and he had begun to shake. The sergeant was helpful and advised going over to the hospital and asking for quinine.

"Hm-mm," said Fitz, and the slight shake of his head set it pounding like a bass drum. "I've got no time for hospitals and they've got no time for me. Must go back up the trail today."

"You won't go up no trail like that," the sergeant told him gloomily. "You got malaria, that's what you got."

"Well, the hell with it," said Fitz, trying to drink coffee without the tin cup clattering against his teeth. "Think I can find anything to ride?"

"Might try and steal a mule," the sergeant suggested. "Can't any more'n get hanged for it if you're caught."

"You got any mules lyin' round loose?"

The sergeant said they hadn't.

"You might try the Artillery," he added as

an afterthought. "They're a mighty careless lot."

For an hour or so while the sun got hot, Fitz pottered about in search of a mule, trying not to attract attention to himself because by now he had the shakes good and proper. Suddenly something fell on him from behind, almost knocking him over and sending out bright red sparks in all directions from his headache, and he looked round to see Johnny Malone.

"Fitz, for the love of God!" Johnny was yelling. "I've asked everywhere for you! Where's Bracken?"

"Up the trail."

"You don't look like much," Johnny accused, squinting at him. "You been sick? Say, you've got the fever!"

"Sh! Not so loud. Find me a mule, can't you, I've got to get out of here."

"You aren't fit to travel like that, you'll keel right over!"

"Got to get to Bracken." Fitz wet his lips nervously, and looked away from Johnny's anxious face. "Johnny, the Boss is dead."

"*Our* Boss? Why, he was good for years yet! What happened?"

"His heart wore out. Bracken's got to know, you see, he'll have to — well, he's in charge now."

"And you've got to tell him?" Johnny shook his head. "Man, you'd better rest up some first!"

"Can't stop now, got to find something to ride. You seen a spare mule?"

"Where's the fellow that runs the boat for you — Wendell, wasn't it? You'd better send him."

"He's gone to Jamaica."

"What for?" Johnny wanted to know. "The cable at Guantanamo is working now, why doesn't he use that?"

"Government supervision. They limit your wordage. Army comes first there. You know what happens when somebody cuts Bracken's copy!"

"When will Wendell be back from Jamaica?" Johnny stuck to his idea.

"I dunno. I can't wait. This is bad news, and it's got to travel fast."

"It's terrible news," said Johnny solemnly, and slid his arm through Fitz's and eased him down on to a pile of feed-sacks near by. "It's the worst news I've ever heard. When did it happen?"

"Last Monday. At Tampa." Fitz put his elbows on his knees and his head in his hands. "And it's got to be me," he moaned. "I've got to be the one to tell Bracken."

"Send Wendell when he comes," Johnny

insisted. "You're all played out."

"Nope. Even if Wendell was right here it's got to be me. Bracken will want — there ought to be somebody from the family there, when he hears — can't just send a message — not that message — not to Bracken —" Fitz slid off the feed-sacks sideways and lay in a heap on the ground. When Johnny bent over him he didn't move.

He came to some time later on a cot in a small white-washed room with a single little window high in the wall which gave a glimpse of the green jungle at the edge of the town. He was very hot now, and his skin felt the way a rhinoceros looks. His thirst was a tangible, corporeal thing, pressing in on him from all sides. He lay for a minute trying to push it away but it was too heavy and would not budge. The cell-like room was empty, but it seemed to him he heard voices outside. With a great effort of his will he summoned strength to make a noise.

"Hey!" he croaked feebly, and a chair scraped back somewhere and a head looked in at the door.

"Hullo," it said. "You've come round. Want something?"

"Water," said Fitz.

The head disappeared and soon its owner returned with a canteen and a quinine pill.

"You're not supposed to drink it all at once," he said kindly. "Wouldn't be good for you. Go easy, now."

"Is this the hospital?" Fitz asked after a few grateful gulps of rather tinny lukewarm water.

"Lord, no, you wouldn't be half as comfortable there! This is the Siboney poker club for newspaper men. A friend of mine started it. My name is Baker, by the way — Philadelphia *Clarion*. Have you heard about Ed Marshall? He's still alive."

"Can you fellows find me a mule?" Fitz asked. "I've got to go up the trail."

"Not right now, you can't. Not till after the sweat has been and gone. That's the way malaria acts. Once you've had the sweat you'll be all right for a few hours before it begins all over again. You might get up to . the front and back again if you're quick, between spells. I don't recommend it, though."

"Got to try," said Fitz, and closed his eyes against the glare from the window. "How long have I got to wait?"

"Twelve hours — fifteen."

"Oh, hell," said Fitz.

"Can't be helped. Could you eat a little something? We've got rice and canned tomatoes."

"Too hot."

Baker said it would break, finally, and meanwhile just to take it easy, and if there was anything they could do, holler.

When he had departed the murmur of voices and the click of chips outside went on. Fine way to write up a war, Fitz thought. Sittin' on the beach playin' poker. He'd get fired from the *Star,* we work for our money! Think of Bracken being Boss now. Maybe he ought to go home. Cuba would be kind of lonesome if Bracken goes home. . . .

For hours he lay in a waking nightmare of flies and heat and fever, dozing, mumbling to himself, trying in wretched lucid intervals to imagine how he was going to tell Bracken the terrible news he brought. Then the sweat started, and the nice clean clothes Wendell had brought him from *Daisy's* lockers were drenched and wringing. Somewhere he had laid down the bundle which was Bracken's clean clothes and lost them. That was stupid, just because he had a headache. . . .

Johnny looked in at nightfall, and sat a little while on a stool beside the cot, and dried Fitz off with a towel and got him to eat some canned tomatoes and drink a cup of coffee. Fitz began to talk about the mule again. Davis had had a mule at Las Guasimas —

"In the morning," said Johnny soothingly, afraid to tell him that they were all moving up for another attack. "You get a night's rest here, and then maybe you can make it. Can't start now, you know, it's dark."

But in the morning Johnny was gone up the trail with the Army. White hospital tents were being put up around the single dingy railway building which had done duty as a hospital for the wounded from Las Guasimas. Clara Barton's Red Cross outfit had arrived and gone to work along with the Army doctors, led by the little Massachusetts spinster who had first begun to bandage and feed wounded soldiers after the battle of Bull Run in '61. Since then she had seen war and disaster all over the world — Strasbourg, Paris, yellow fever in Florida, the flood at Johnstown, famine in Russia, massacre in Armenia — and now, at seventy-seven, she came to Cuba, to find that the Army medical corps seemed to have learned very little since those hot July days when the Federal retreat had swamped Washington with suffering, bewildered men nearly forty years ago.

After a night's exhausted sleep, Fitz was shaky and lightheaded but fairly comfortable. Siboney was emptying itself slowly up the congested trail towards the entrenchments at San Juan. He lost some more time arguing about mules before he finally boarded an ammunition wagon bound for the front and refused to be dislodged from it.

It was a slow way to travel. Every now and then he dropped off and walked ahead and got on another wagon further along the line. When he came at last to Las Guasimas and the camping ground beyond, he found Shafter's headquarters roundabout there and the Rough Riders gone. They had been moved up to El Poso a couple of miles nearer Santiago.

Fitz threw himself down on a horse blanket and slipped into uneasy slumber. His respite from the fever might be running out, with the setting sun. Any time now the chill could come again. He must get on to El Poso first thing in the morning. . . .

7

There was cold water and hardtack for breakfast, and about seven o'clock the guns began on the right. That was Lawton, firing into El Caney, which he was supposed to take within a couple of hours. Then everybody would move in together on the San Juan entrenchments.

Meanwhile there were complete stoppages in the trail, which was barely wide enough anywhere for a column of fours. Fitz gave up the wagons and slithered along at the side, jabbed by chaparral thorns, sworn at by mounted orderlies in a hurry, rudely advised by stalled companies of infantry. This went on till he came to where the track forked left to El Poso, when he learned that the Rough Riders had already been ordered up and were somewhere further ahead. ''Look for the balloon,'' he was told. ''They're just in front of the balloon.''

It didn't seem a very desirable place to be, but Fitz pushed on through the stifling green trough in the jungle. He was now in the firing zone, and met wounded coming back, who said the shrapnel was fierce. Not a breath of air stirred. The balloon was moving along the trail in front of him, and the Spanish were throwing everything they had at it, which was cruel punishment for the men marching below in a rain of shrapnel. Its presence naturally disclosed the line of march and provided an excellent target for guns which had already studied the range. The troops were jammed in column and unable to return the fire, even if they had known just where it was coming from, but the Spaniards' smokeless powder left no trace on the face of the jungle. Also it had begun to occur to them that to retreat would be even more impossible than it had become to advance.

Fitz kept going stubbornly, in pursuit of the Rough Riders. He came to the ford across the Aguadores River, which lay under a nasty dropping fire and was fringed with dead animals. The crossing was at the edge of the jungle where it fell away into a sort of grassy meadow. On its far side the meadow was bordered by the little San Juan River which flowed almost at right angles to the

Aguadores and which had another ford two hundred yards ahead, at a bend in the trail. Beyond the San Juan, with cat's-cradles of barbed-wire across the approaches were the bare, steep slopes of the San Juan ridges and the Spanish rifle-pits and blockhouses near their crests.

At the San Juan ford the balloon had fouled the trees with its anchor ropes and becoming stationary was soon shot down, much to the relief of everybody in the vicinity. A group of wounded Regulars lay neatly on the left, in a magnificent silence of fortitude, where the hospital stewards had assembled them in rows with their feet at the water's edge and their bodies lying up the muddy bank. Surgeons moved calmly among them. Besides the Mauser and shrapnel fire from the front, snipers' bullets came winging in from everywhere, killing the wounded where they lay, picking off the men with the Red Cross brassard on their arms. A mounted aide drove his horse furiously through the water, splashing everything for yards around, and when he reached the opposite bank dropped like a stone, shot behind the eyes. His horse galloped on alone. Fitz coveted it, but knew it could never be caught now.

By the sound of his guns, Lawton was still held up at El Caney, and some one said the last reserves had gone in. The hospital personnel to the rear were swamped with casualties. The Rough Riders had gone off the trail to the right along the bank of the San Juan, where a line of trees provided slight cover before the open meadow began. Immediately in front of them across that meadow was a small round hill crowned with red-tiled ranch buildings which spurted flame.

Fitz turned doggedly to the right, walking sometimes in the water and sometimes along the muddy bank, which slowed his progress still further. You'd think it was good news I'm bringing, he thought, the way I'm hell-bent to tell it. Poor Bracken — in the middle of a battle, too. . . . Confused by the heat and the fever and the deadly, creeping weakness, the din of trumpet calls and stuttering machine guns, the evil whistling of shrapnel and the boom of distant artillery and the noise of howling, cursing, excited men, Fitz's mind held firmly to its one imperative idea — get to Bracken and tell him he has to be the Boss now. Get to Bracken *first,* so he would not have to learn it from a stranger.

The Gatling guns had come up to the ford behind him and began to have some effect on the Spanish trenches on the slopes beyond the meadow. And so Fitz no sooner came to the ground where the Rough Riders had been lying flat on their stomachs while the bullets drove in sheets through the leaves above and around them with a sound like rain, than Roosevelt ordered the charge up the first slope and led the way, riding the little horse Texas, his dotted blue bandana worn as a havelock streaming out behind.

They were men on foot, toiling up a steep slope in the face of bitter fire, under a blistering sun at midday, and they had little breath for cheering now, and none for running up hill. They went quite slowly, bent a little forward, their rifles at the port, slanting across their breasts, taking no notice when comrades dropped near by and lay still. They went in cold-blooded courage, waist-deep in the sharp, hot grass, indomitable, inevitable, and to the watching Spanish inhuman. Only near the top they gathered themselves for a burst of speed, yelling as they swept in on the hacienda whose cellars and walls were speedily vacated by all the Spanish who could still travel. Regulars of the Ninth arrived almost simultaneously from the left, and there was some argument, even then, as to whether or not the red-and-white silk guidons of the Rough Riders had been planted first on the top of Kettle Hill.

Heavy firing continued from the crests beyond, where the squat San Juan blockhouses were. Above it, the drumming of the Gatling guns which had moved forward from the ford could be heard. Infantry was charging the next hill and Roosevelt got his men together again and led them, himself on foot now because of the barbed wire, down across another open grassy meadow and up the slope towards the next line of Spanish entrenchments. Skirmishers from other regiments poured out into the meadow at the same dogged pace, sometimes pausing to fire, with the excited yammer of the Gatling guns as an obbligato to the crashing rifle volleys. Once more near the top there were piercing cowboy yells and a rush, once more the Spanish fled, and San Juan Hill was taken.

All of this ultimate glory was lost on Fitz, whose knees were trembling from fatigue and whose eyes were strained for the flutter of Bracken's yellow neckerchief. He was aware that he must not be quite right in the head when he found himself trying to buttonhole the sweating, breathless men who were ascending Kettle Hill to ask them if they had seen Bracken Murray. Some didn't hear, some brushed him off, some cursed him, but finally, to his dazed surprise, one of them had.

"Go back towards the river," he said. "This side of the ford — right out in the grass below the barbed wire — he had a bandana like yours — I saw him go down — you better get him out of this sun quick —"

Fitz thanked empty air and turned back towards the river. *I saw him go down.* . . .

8

The battle roared on undiminished all around him as he left the slope and started down into the deep grass. Here and there were depressions in it, where wounded or dead men lay. Bullets were whirring and dropping everywhere, but he was too tired to take precautions and plodded on, looking for a man with a yellow scarf, deaf to other men's pleas and warnings.

He came to a place that was matted with fresh blood. From it a small trail led away towards the trees along the river above the ford — the sort of track a big dog makes through ripe hay. Fitz went to his hands and knees from sheer exhaustion and followed it, crawling, and at the end of it was Bracken, many yards short of the shade he had sought — face down in the hot, rank grass, betrayed to a Spanish sharp-shooter by the yellow badge he wore. If the aim had been truer it would have killed him, but the gunsight had wavered to the right. Fitz turned him over and found the wound, bleeding freely, just below the collarbone.

Bracken opened his eyes.

"Hullo," he said. "Thought we'd lost you." Then he fainted.

Patiently, foot by foot, Fitz began to drag him towards the shade at the river bank. It took all the strength he had left, and each effort moved them further from the sight of possible first aid men following the battle. The bullets weren't so thick, though, and finally only a few spent ones came in.

Fitz lay down and panted, long, sobbing breaths in the airless heat. Fever took your wind. It was now well past noon and he wondered how much longer he had before the shakes began again. When he had rested a little he would crawl down to the river for some water — enough to bring Bracken to. After that he must go for a surgeon. Couldn't move Bracken alone, not the way he was.

Lying there beside the unconscious man, Fitz slipped a little too, and lost track of time. When he roused, the sun was much lower and the guns had slackened somewhat. At a little distance in a watchful semicircle the monstrous land crabs waited, on tiptoe, twiddling their beady eyes. Fitz realized with horror what he had never noticed before — that to a man lying down, unable to lift his head, the crabs would be taller than he was. With the same hysteria that he had seen with amused pity in a hundred other men, he waved his hat wildly at them and they withdrew with a rattle and scuttle and a whispering of dry grass. But not far. By the brevity of the sound they made as they went, he knew they were not far away.

He raised himself above the grass but could see nothing of the block-houses on the crest of San Juan from where they were. Bracken stirred and Fitz turned to him anxiously. He should have had a dressing long ago, but everybody had run out of first aid packets. Fitz made a pad of his pocket handkerchief as they had done for other men, to staunch the wound, and began to untie Bracken's neckerchief to bind it in place. As he did so he discovered inside Bracken's shirt a woman's tiny ball-shaped watch, worn around Bracken's neck on a jewelled chain.

For a moment Fitz wondered if it was something of Lisl's, and then dismissed that idea. Bracken had no sentiment about Lisl, it was no keepsake of his marriage. Who then? None of my business, Fitz thought, working at the wound. Must come hard, though, as things are. Must come mighty hard, to wait for that divorce. And he thought of Gwen, and what an obstacle like Lisl would have meant to them once he had tumbled to the fact that Gwen might love him. The time you could lose, over a thing like divorce — time you might have had together — time that would never come again. . . .

Bracken roused under his hands, and cursed him for the pain.

"That's better," said Fitz soothingly. "Want a drink? I'll go down to the river, the canteens are empty."

But Bracken's eyes were bright and blank and could not focus, and he fumbled anxiously for the watch.

"It's there," Fitz told him. "I didn't pinch it." Then he saw that Bracken didn't know him any more.

"Dinah," Bracken said. "It belongs to Dinah — you won't let anyone steal it, will you — I promised her she'd have it — some day —"

"All right, we'll get it to Dinah, don't you worry —"

"My mother has the address," Bracken insisted, as to a stranger. "Will you take the watch to my mother — ask her to send it — tell Dinah — tell Dinah I didn't forget —"

"Tell her yourself," said Fitz. "We're not

done for yet. It's me, Bracken. It's Fitz. Lie still, now, while I get some water. Shan't be long.'' He crawled away with the canteens towards the river bank — going on all fours not because of the bullets, for there were none now, but because it was easier.

When he returned Bracken was thrashing feebly at the land crabs with his hat. Fitz waved his arms and yelled at them and they all vanished into watchful silence.

''Go some place else, you're wastin' your time!'' he yelled. ''We aren't dead enough! *Scat!*''

''Water,'' said Bracken, fingering the watch.

''Can't drink that water. I found you some limes.'' Fitz slid an arm behind Bracken's head and held the cut lime to his lips. ''You know, you were right about that fever,'' he said, while Bracken sucked. ''Remember what you told me when you turned back after Shafter? It's coming down on me again soon, and there's something I've got to tell you first. You listenin'?'' Bracken's head fell back against him, his eyes were closed. Fitz bent over him. ''Bracken, you've got to hear. Uncle Cabot is gone. You're the Boss now.''

''They won't let her wear it,'' Bracken mumbled, feeling for the watch. ''They open her letters, I think — I daren't say how

I feel — not yet —"

"Bracken. Your father is dead."

"What?" said Bracken, lying very still.

"I hate to tell you now, but it's kind of up to us. Uncle Cabot died last Monday."

"It's Fitz," said Bracken, without moving.

"Yeh, it's me. The battle's over. Looks like we won. I've been chasin' you all day, as though it was good news I had."

"You said — Father —?"

"Yes. At Tampa. Wendell told me."

Bracken lay quiet against him, and Fitz could not see his face — so quiet that the land crabs stole out again to see, on tiptoe, twiddling their eyes. Then Bracken tried to sit up, and they all disappeared into the leaves, while he swayed against Fitz's shoulder.

"I've got to get down to the coast," he said.

"Sure, sure, we'll get down, all right. Only, you know that fever you promised me? Well, I got it."

"That's tough. Any first-aid men around?"

"Not a soul. We seem to be sort of on the edge of things here."

"Sun's going down already," Bracken discovered with surprise. "Where's the day gone to? Is that the river there?"

"Yep, we've got to cross it, just for a

starter. Up to our necks right here.''

''Oh, go on, Fitz, it's never more than waist deep.''

''Banks are steep,'' said Fitz. ''Come and see.''

Bracken was trying to feel around on the ground under him.

''My notebook — I had it — I had the whole story up till I got hit — I wrote some with my left hand after that —''

''Here's your notebook.'' Fitz put it in his own pocket. ''Let's get on our way now, Wendell will be having a fit. Can you walk if I hold you up?''

He made a sling of his own yellow scarf for Bracken's right arm, and by lifting and heaving they got Bracken to his feet.

''Gosh, I'm tall,'' he said wonderingly. ''It looks such a long way to the ground. Gimme your shoulder —''

''You got it!''

''Hell, we're off!''

And so they were, with a rather drunken stagger, through the trees and down to the river bank, which was decorated just beyond by a dead mule, his insides running out into the water.

''He's down stream,'' said Fitz. ''Come on.''

''Let's find the ford,'' said Bracken.

"Things were pretty thick there when I came through."

"Probably still are. We can get hold of somebody going down to Siboney and ask him to deliver us to Wendell in case you give out."

"Oh, shucks, I'm good for hours yet," said Fitz, who was momentarily dreading the recurrence of the first chill.

For some minutes they floundered along the bank which was slippery with mud, afraid to lose sight of the water, often throwing themselves down with panting groans to rest.

"*By the rivers of Babylon, there we sat down, yea, we wept when we remembered Zion,*" Fitz chanted unexpectedly. "Remember when we used to go to church? Where *is* Zion? Don't I hear voices?"

Bracken seemed to recall something about an innumerable company of angels in connection with Zion, and said he wasn't ready for that just yet, he had things to do.

By the time they reached the ford a train of empty ammunition and ration wagons returning from the front had already removed the rows of wounded men Fitz had seen there on his way up, taking them to the field hospital established near Shafter's headquarters back of El Poso. Bates's brigade was now coming up the trail from El Caney to reinforce the exhausted troops who were in perilous possession of San Juan heights. There was almost no traffic in the other direction, and not much chance of getting a ride to Siboney just then.

Fitz and Bracken crossed the ford, for the river seemed to be rising, and sat down on the other side where the trail widened for a space, hoping for a stray ambulance or provision wagon going their way. While they sat there the jungle echoed to the *whoop-la!* and the shrill whistles of the mule-packers, the pistol-like snap of their black-snake whips, and the rural tinkle of the cowbell round the lead mule's neck, as a pack-train emerged from the shadows of the trail in the wake of Bates's men. It splashed recklessly through the ford, and disappeared behind the trees which rimmed the meadow, bound for the front.

They said very little as they sat there waiting beside a trail strewn with everything from tin cups and toothbrushes to the wreckage of the balloon. Fitz's head felt twice the size of a football, his clothes were wet to the waist from the ford and had set him shivering again even without the malarial chill which still held off. He had begun to think of Gwen, with a need which gnawed like the hunger he had half forgotten because he was now so accustomed to it. He longed for Gwen till it ached in his bones — for her little half-smile, her quiet voice, her sweet, warm hands — and he began to try to remember everything they had done together, hoarding it against oblivion, building it into a shelter for his weary spirit there beside the trail.

He remembered the first time he had ever seen her, and how she had trembled under his hand for terror of Fagan and his small-time gang — and the night she had sung at Eden's party, wearing the new dress, and he had realized that she was beautiful — and the night he asked her to marry him and she said — what had she said? — *I don't belong as your wife* — a funny idea — well, she knew different now — by the time they had their wedding supper at Delmonico's, maybe, she knew different — and he remembered going to Lord and Taylor's with her to buy a trousseau out of his option money — two new dresses, and three hats — slippers, things to go underneath — Gwen was half shocked at his extravagance, half like a greedy child, holding the froth of silk and lace in both her hands, looking up at him across her treasures, saying, "Are you *sure* it's all right? Can we *really* afford it?" She had had so little all her life — there was so much he wanted to give her of cherishing and good times. She had come a long, hard way but now she was safe, now she had a home, he had seen to that — because if anything happened to him they would always look after Gwen at Williamsburg — had he asked them to? — but Cousin Sue would know — Cousin Sue would always take care of Gwen. . . .

Bracken, lying beside Fitz at the ford that night, covered with a white mist and drenched with dew, was his father's son, and he thought mostly of the man who was dead at Tampa and what that would mean back at the Shop in Park Row — what would they do without the Boss? — Temple, the Managing Editor, was Murray-trained and knew all there was to know about newspapers — but there would never be the feeling about Temple that there was for the Boss — that took a Murray, and the only Murray left was one called Bracken — he wasn't ready for that job yet — he didn't know enough, he hadn't done enough, he wasn't big enough — he had always known dimly that some day he would be expected to sit at his father's mahogany desk and run the *Star* — but that time had always seemed a long way off — his father was still a young man, healthy, except for the malaria, straight as a flag-pole, confident, successful, looked up to, at the height of his powers — and now he was gone, and the mahogany desk was waiting for his son, who felt small and humble and forlorn in the face of his inheritance. Inevitably, the question came: What about Dinah now?

What about the leisurely life he had meant to live in England with week-ends at Farthingale, waiting for Dinah to grow up and marry him? He couldn't very well court Dinah from the New York office in Park Row. Separations like that might not be fatal once you were engaged, once you knew where you were, but Dinah would soon be at the age where she might fall in love with anybody. She might even be pushed into some sort of suitable marriage without ever falling in love at all — some marriage arranged by Alwyn and Clare, no doubt with the best intentions, to better the family fortunes or to get her a comfortable establishment of her own. They would rule him out of their plans for Dinah because of Lisl. Alwyn, at least, knew that he was married. And that was another thing. How was he going to get the divorce now, with Lisl hiding on the Continent with her California millionaire, and himself dependent on the New York courts, where conclusive evidence would be exceedingly hard to produce? And then he reproached himself for thinking of his father's death as an inconvenience in his own affairs, and mourned him bitterly and sincerely, and thought about his mother and Virginia and how he must get back to them as quickly as possible and put things to rights as far as he could. *Daisy* would take him to Jamaica and he could get a steamer to New York from there. Fitz and Wendell would have to run the war in Cuba now. Unless Fitz was through too, because of the fever. He put out his hand in the dark. Fitz had the shakes again.

The first streaks of dawn were showing over the treetops when they were roused from a feverish stupor by the crack of the black-snakes and the language and the bell which accompanied the pack-train returning across the ford. Bracken dragged himself up and hailed the packer who rode the lead mule. The man slid down and called up one of his fellows. Together they hoisted Bracken and Fitz aboard a couple of mules and held them on for the jolting, wretched journey to the field hospital, and there lifted them down and half carried them to the crowded cluster of inadequate dog-tents and canvas flies where the surgeons worked wearily in the morning sunlight.

Wounded men in every degree of misery were waiting in uncomplaining, prostrate groups for attention from the exhausted doctors. Those who had come back from the operating tables, where blood-soaked, sweat-drenched clothing had been cut away, were some of them almost completely naked. There were no spare garments, no cots, practically no blankets. Most of the men lay or sat on the bare ground.

Each regiment of Regulars was supposed to have carried with it three months' hospital supplies, and practically all of this equipment had in each case been left on board the transports. Most of the rest was piled up at Siboney awaiting the trickle of wagons and mule-trains. Many of the ambulances had been left behind at Tampa for lack of shipping space. Each Regular was supposed to have carried on his person a small emergency packet of antiseptic gauze, but most of these had been lost or thrown away along with the blanket-rolls and knapsacks, and the best of them needed replacement.

Fitz was now quite helpless with fever and weakness, and lay where he was dumped by the packers, breathing unevenly, his eyes closed. Bracken retained consciousness by a supreme effort and circulated with difficulty among the driven hospital orderlies, begging for a quinine pill — even just one — which he finally captured and carried back to Fitz. After that they lay side by side in the shifting shade cast by a tent already full. Some one came round with black coffee. It was all the food they saw, though a cook-fire smoked somewhere in the middle distance.

Along about mid-afternoon some one dressed Bracken's wound, which was fortunately open at both ends, the bullet having passed clean through, missing the lung. Soon after that it began to rain, but they lay still where they were for every inch of shelter was occupied. As the night went on they formed little human islands in standing water, for the hospital ground was as level as a floor with no drainage and the rain came down too fast to soak in. Both were half delirious now and they carried on a fantastic dialogue in which neither one really replied to the other or was quite aware of what he himself was saying, but the sound of each other's voices was comforting.

The ghastly night passed in this way, and with the drizzling dawn Fitz began to emerge from the second fever attack, and sat up waveringly, a hand to his head, and gazed about him. The sun came out and began to dry things a little. Apart from everything else, they were now faint with hunger, and he made his way somehow to where the fire burned sulkily with damp green wood, and begged a quinine pill and some coffee. There was a kettle of soup stewing sluggishly, but after one swallow he poured it out on the ground and secured a cup of coffee for Bracken instead. As he was turning away from the fire, he saw approaching it a group of people, among them three women in white nurse's uniforms. The Red Cross had come up from Siboney.

"Miss Barton is here," he told Bracken, patiently pouring the coffee into him. "Give *them* a few hours and this place will be run right! Now that I'm able to wobble around again, I'll see about gettin' us down to Siboney. You stay right here, now, so I can find you again."

Bracken had no intention of moving.

Fitz hovered a while in Miss Barton's vicinity, his subconscious reporter's mind taking notes while he admired the efficient way they got a new fireplace built, much larger and higher, and set their ten-gallon agate kettles going with oatmeal gruel and soup. "I never thought to make gruel over a camp-fire again," he heard her say to one of her helpers. "How it takes one back! Is this Sharpsburg or San Juan? Was it ever as bad as this in the old days?''

The rain began again, and Fitz was one of those who helped, rather fumblingly, to unload the Red Cross supplies from the wagon and raise a tarpaulin over them. Swaying on his feet, he accepted from Miss Barton's own hand a cup of the thick white gruel, rich with condensed milk, and gulped it down and asked for another for his cousin who had been wounded.

''Will there be ambulances going down soon?'' he asked as she ladled it out for him. ''We're able to travel — within reason, that is. Bracken Murray has just learned of his father's death, and I want to get him down to the coast where our dispatch boat is.''

''We're short of ambulances, I'm afraid,'' the little grey-haired woman told him kindly. ''But they're trying to move men out as fast as possible in the wagons. Tell Dr. Egan what you need and where to find you.''

''Thank you, ma'am.''

''What's the matter with you? Malaria?'' She peered up into his drawn, unshaven face.

''Yes, ma'am. I'm sort of between spells right now.''

''Ask the Sister over there for some quinine pills.''

''I sure will. Here's Colonel Roosevelt, ma'am, comin' to talk to you,'' he added as

Roosevelt strode up to them.

"Miss Barton?" he inquired politely, touching his hat-brim. "I would like to buy some of your supplies for my men at San Juan."

"Our supplies are not for sale," she answered, fronting him sturdily, her thin face severe and unsmiling.

The Colonel was nonplussed.

"But you seem to have a lot of things we can't get from the commissary," he explained. "How can I get some dressings and corn meal and dried fruit and quinine pills for my men in the trenches?"

"You just ask for them, Colonel," said Miss Barton gently, and Roosevelt's big grin flashed as he saw the point.

"We're not used to such generosity around here, ma'am! If you can spare me a sack I'll take the stuff with me right now."

They moved away together, towards the tarpaulin-covered dump of Red Cross supplies.

Dr. Egan visited Bracken and said he was fit to be moved, approved their plans to go to Jamaica with *Daisy* and home from there by steamer, and ordered Fitz out of Cuba too. That afternoon they were loaded into one of the springless wagons and made the agonizing descent along a trail which often ran hub-deep with water. Wendell was waiting at the bottom, anxiously searching the faces of the wounded as they were lifted out, for he had somehow learned that Bracken had been hit. The reunion was enthusiastic.

"Have you heard the news?" he cried, pumping their hands excitedly. "Cervera came out and we sank him! The war is over!"

"Go on!" said Fitz unbelievingly.

"It's true! Cervera tried to run for it and we finished him! There *is* no Spanish Fleet! And without it Santiago may as well surrender!"

"When did all this happen?" they asked, dazed.

"Today! It just came in from Guantanamo — eye-witness account from the shore, cabled from Guantanamo everywhere by now! It's true, I tell you! We've won!"

He was more or less right. The white flags of truce were already passing between Santiago and Shafter's headquarters on the hill.

9

Fitz lasted as far as Jamaica and there, before they could get on to a steamer for New York, he collapsed entirely and was only just saved alive by an English doctor at Kingston. Meanwhile, Bracken's wound healed nicely and he was pretty much himself, though still thin and tottery, by the time they sailed at the end of August.

Eden and Virginia and Sue went up to New York in time to meet the steamer, and they took Gwen with them to the dock. Bracken had not known how to prepare them for the change in Fitz, who was barely able to stand and came down the gangplank supported on either side by Bracken and a steward. Sue's face went white when she saw him, but Gwen, the actress, gave them all a lesson in self-control by her gallant gaiety over getting her man back safe from the wars.

Bracken's house had been shuttered and dark since Lisl's departure for Europe, and he had been living with his parents in Madison Avenue. Fitz and Gwen were to stay there too until he was better. While they drove there in one carriage, followed by the others, Gwen answered all his eager questions about the show, which had been much on his mind and which now looked as though it would run forever. And she told him, sitting with his hand held tight in both hers, about singing into a horn-thing which made a gramophone disc of the song and played it back to you. And if he approved, she could get paid quite well to sing other songs into the horn for the new machine. They offered her fifty cents a round and she could make twenty-five rounds in a day, singing into seven grouped horns at once. All the songs Fitz could write the gramophone people would buy, said Gwen, and it would all mount up. And so even after the show stopped they could still be sure of something coming in each week.

To Gwen, singing into the horns, making the little black discs at fifty cents a round, was one more barricade against the old Saturday night nightmare of getting together enough money for the next seven days. Fitz was ill — she could see how ill — and he wouldn't be able to work for a long time, as a reporter. They had money in the bank, yes, but it wouldn't last forever, money never lasted. You had to go on earning, to keep ahead. It was like a treadmill in an animal act; the little dog had to keep on running just to stay in the same place. Now that Fitz wouldn't be able to work for a while, it was very lucky that she had found the gramophone people so that she could earn for both of them — and Pa — after the show closed. It never occurred to Gwen to look to his family for help if their money ran out. Fitz was ill and she would support him. She was young and strong and could sing.

"So you see, I haven't been wasting our time with you away," she added as the carriage rolled up Madison Avenue. "You can just sit with your feet up and the money rolls in!"

" 'Bout all I'm good for now, I reckon," he said.

"You'll get well, Fitz. All you need is a little time."

"Sure, that's all I need."

But when they put him to bed in Cabot's house he was thinking of his old room at Williamsburg, with the sun coming in the window above the garden and Mammy's wrinkled black hands to tend him, and he sighed. He was homesick. He told himself firmly that he'd rather have Gwen, and he couldn't ask her to leave the show and the money she was earning and go down to Williamsburg with a sick husband and nothing to do but put up with him.

Gwen had to leave for the theater after an early dinner, and when she came in after the show Fitz was asleep. No one knew that she locked herself into the bathroom that night and turned on the taps so she couldn't be heard, and cried, and cried, and cried.

In the morning Cabot's doctor came and went over Fitz and said he must stay in bed and rest. Fitz said the hell with that, he was going to see the show, but they persuaded him to leave it for a week or two. Plenty of time to see the show. Fitz subsided, almost too willingly, for he was very tired — tired above everything else, of being ill and unable to do what he liked. Everybody could be as cheerful as they liked, but he knew what they were thinking. He knew how he looked. Worse, he knew how he felt. It would be weeks — months — before he was on his feet again. He kept thinking of Williamsburg, and his mother and Phoebe chattering around the house like birds, and his father coming home from the office — his tall, handsome, vital father, who was everything a Sprague should be, and who was doubly to be cherished now that Bracken's father was gone. Tears of weakness and despair stood in Fitz's eyes. He wanted to go home. But not without Gwen. He lay there, waiting for Gwen, who was playing a matinée, and Sue looked in at the door.

"Sleepy?" she whispered.

"Nope. Just bone-lazy."

Sue came in, and sat down by the bed.

"Fitz, tell me honestly, is there anything you want? I promised Eden I'd ask you if there was anything that money could buy to help you to get well faster. She said Cabot would want a fortune spent if it would make any difference."

"What on earth could I want besides what I've got?" he objected with a glance around the luxurious room. "There's something I could do without, even. That nurse. I'm able to come down to meals, and take my own baths, and the footman shaves me, so what good does she do?"

"Well, with Gwen away so much, we thought —" Sue stopped. There had never before in the history of the family been a wife who left her husband to the care of a trained nurse. Retreating hastily from tactlessness, Sue put her foot into another pitfall. "If only we had you down home at Williamsburg, Mammy could look after you," she said.

"Yeh, I — I've been kind of homesick lately."

They looked at each other levelly, both remembering Gwen, who had to be in the theater every night and two matinées a week.

"Perhaps, by the time you're strong enough to make another journey —" Sue began, and he interrupted her.

"I won't ask Gwen to give up the show," he said firmly. "It's everything to her, Cousin Sue — maybe you don't quite understand, but she grew up in show business, they all want what she's got, a leading part in a success. I'm kind of proud she got it through me, and I meant her to have it. Besides, the money is important to her, she's never had enough." And he told, in strictest confidence, about Pa, who had fallen on his head and so it wasn't hereditary.

While they were still talking, over an extra cup of tea, Gwen returned from the matinée, bringing with her a vibrant, fragrant something that enlivened the stale air of the city-bound room like a window thrown open to spring. Sue slipped away and left them together, Gwen sitting on the edge of the bed with Fitz's hand in hers, making him laugh.

An hour later, when Sue was dressing for dinner, there was a tap on her door and Gwen came in. Sue thought as Gwen crossed the room towards her in the lamplight that the girl got more beautiful every day. Gwen's first words took her by surprise.

"Cousin Sue, do you think Fitz would be better off in Williamsburg for a while?"

"Well — yes, I do," Sue said courageously.

"Then we must try and make him go," Gwen said, looking worried. "We could tell him it was just for a visit —"

"And leave you here?" Sue looked incredulous, and Gwen answered, uncomprehending —

"They think the show will run till spring."

"Does the show mean so much to you?" Sue watched her with troubled, affectionate eyes. "I know it must be everything you've ever dreamed of — to make such a big success while you're so young. But I thought —" Her words died away, on the guilty knowledge that in a minute she would be interfering, and Fitz would hate that.

"You mean you think I ought to give up the show and go with him?" Gwen put the question gravely, without resentment.

"Well — yes —"

"But, Cousin Sue, you surely don't think I put the show before Fitz!" Gwen cried. "It's what I dreamed of, sure, it's what my Mom dreamed of, for me, and I never thought it would happen, and I owe it all to Fitz. But don't get any idea that I'm so stuck on hearing myself sing every night that I wouldn't give in my notice and go south with him — if it wasn't for the money! Of course I've got some saved up, but we don't know how long it will have to last. I wouldn't want Fitz to be a charge on his folks, not while I can earn for him.''

Sue frankly stared. The women of the family nursed their husbands and bore them children, but this girl's Spartan code was different. This girl considered herself a breadwinner. Sue perceived an entirely strange set of values, and realized that she had judged Gwen by the wrong measuring stick. Gwen had her own ideas of a wife's duty — ideas which took no account of the easy, hospitable, family life at Williamsburg. Sue tried in some embarrassment to explain.

''But, Gwen, honey, it's Fitz's *home*. They'd be only too glad if you'd both come and stay there as long as you like!''

''Two more mouths for them to feed?'' Gwen shook her head. ''I couldn't do that, it wouldn't be right, except for a visit. I'm healthy and I've got a job. It's my business to keep Fitz till he can work again. My Mom kept Pa for years, after — And that's another thing. It's not just Fitz and me, I've got Pa to think of.''

And so Sue heard again about Pa, who was queer because of a fall and not because it ran in the family. She said untruthfully that she saw what Gwen meant, and then tried again.

''Fitz's royalties go on as long as the show lasts, don't they, whether you leave or not?'' she suggested, and Gwen's chin came out.

''That's his money,'' she said. ''I don't want Fitz paying for my lame ducks. Pa is my job. I've got to find his keep myself, as long as he lives.''

''That's a very — advanced viewpoint,'' Sue remarked cautiously. ''In my day when a man married he took on his wife's responsibilities.''

''In a family like yours, maybe, where you all know each other,'' Gwen conceded. ''But Fitz has no call to love Pa, he never knew him the way he was. It's been so long I never knew where to find the money for Pa that now I've got it coming in like this, I'm kind of afraid to stop. I'm laying it up for him, I don't spend it on myself,'' she added, with an anxious look, and Sue put her arms around her.

''I know you don't, honey, but I think Fitz would far rather pay your father's expenses, if it came to that, than do without your company while he gets well."

"Well, I don't know, Cousin Sue, it doesn't seem fair that way. If I could be real sure —"

"Ask him."

"You know how he is." Gwen's little half-smile came. "He'd think he had to say Yes or hurt my feelings!"

"But if he's convinced you'd hate to give up the show on his account —"

"Oh, but he knows nothing on earth really matters to me but being with him. He knows it's only —"

"Are you *sure* he knows?"

For a moment Gwen gazed at her in naïve astonishment.

"Well, if he doesn't," she said then, and started for the door, "he's going to now."

Fitz was lying as she had left him, relaxed and listless, a book open on the coverlet which he was not reading. The lamplight from the bedside table threw sharp shadows on his thin face, with its broad cheek-bones and narrow chin. He turned his head towards her as she came in, and the look in his eyes, patient, tethered, expectant, somehow humble, cramped her heart. She went straight over to the bed and put her arms around his shoulders and her cheek against his.

"Fitz, listen. If I didn't have to sing every

night we could go to Williamsburg and you'd get well faster. Would your parents let us stay there — for a while, anyway? I've got money in the bank, we could pay a little something each week.''

''Let us —? What on earth are you talkin' about? It's *home!* Like this is home for Bracken, only I expect you'd like this better. Maybe you should have married Bracken instead of me, have you ever thought of that?''

''Oh, Fitz, *don't,* I'm so tired of pretending!'' And while it was the last thing she had ever meant to do, Gwen began to cry, her face hidden in his neck.

Instantly his arms tightened round her in concern.

''Tired of *what?*'' he demanded. ''Talk sense, honey, what are you gettin' at, anyway?''

So it all came out, between sobs which had got beyond her control at last — how tired she was of singing every night when she could have been with him — how tired she was of show business and the people in it, so if it weren't for keeping Pa she'd never go near a theater again except maybe to buy tickets to watch somebody else work — how tired she was anyway of standing on her own feet and holding up her head and not asking quarter from anybody — and how ever since she had first seen Williamsburg heaven had looked just like that to her, a place to live like other people, in a house with a garden, where your children could grow up right, with grandparents and Christmas and birthdays —

Then her tears stopped suddenly with a wrench, for she was horrified at having broken down before him when he was so ill, and she dreaded that she might have made him worse. But instead she had given him what he needed — a sense of responsibility — a job to do — incentive to get well. Because if Gwen left the show and wasn't earning, it would be up to him. He would have to write some more songs, he would have to start that new musical comedy he had thought of during the long, idle days on the dispatch boat, and they would have to look into this gramophone business. He could write some new songs in Williamsburg, while he was getting well, with Gwen to sing them as he worked. The mere idea of working out a new song with Gwen was a tonic —

"Oh, Fitz, I'm sorry, I don't know what got into me, please don't take any notice —"

"You need a holiday," he said, and his arms held her close where she was when she tried to sit up. "I reckon what you really need is a honeymoon. Shall we go down home and start our honeymoon all over again?''

''You mean — you wouldn't mind if I quit the show?''

''Give 'em your notice tonight. They can find somebody else.''

''Are you *sure* it's all right?'' she asked wistfully, as she had when he bought her the trousseau at Lord and Taylor's. ''Can we *really* afford it?''

''Gwen, honey — will you do something for me from now on? When there's something you want — like going down to Williamsburg to live — will you for the love of God let me in on it? I'm your husband, honey — I'm here to make you happy if I can, but I haven't learned to read your mind yet. I have to have a little help now and then.''

''Well, so long as your folks won't think we're sponging —''

''My folks aren't so hard up as you seem to think. We raise everything we eat, almost, right on the place, in the garden.''

''And you won't think I'm a piker about Pa? I've got quite a lot saved up for him —''

''There'll be more when you need it.''

Gwen drew a long breath, where she lay against him.

"Fitz."

"Mm-hm?"

"For the first time in my life I feel —
I —"

"How do you feel, honey?"

"I feel *free*. And that's funny, because
now I'm married, and before I wasn't."

"You aren't half as married as you're goin'
to be," he promised her serenely.

10

Because Cabot had died suddenly at Tampa, when it had never occurred to anybody that such a thing could happen, the readjustment always necessary at such times was even a little grimmer than usual. His clothes, his papers, his small personal belongings were all where he had left them, awaiting his return to New York with the pathetic confidence and helplessness of inanimate things.

Eden and Virginia had spent the time since his death at Williamsburg, and now with Bracken in New York they set about the heart-breaking business of putting away and tidying up all those possessions which Cabot would never want again. Eden would have been the first to admit that she was a wife before she was a mother and the loss of the man who had been to the end of his life her devoted lover was a stunning blow. She rallied very slowly, and was thin and white and piteous in her soft black gowns. She showed no inclination to cling round Bracken's neck, and if she leaned on anyone it was Sue, for they had always been very close. She spent hours alone in her room, emerging at meal-times calm and unravaged by grief, a little withdrawn and absent-minded, but willing to smile and join in the usual family conversation and quiet diversions. Sparkle and zest were gone from her, and a new passiveness and patience had set in. Nothing mattered to her very much.

During the first day he spent at the Shop, Bracken discovered that his father, at least, had foreseen the thing which had happened and prepared for it in scrupulous detail. His Will and his private papers were in order. There were substantial bequests to each of his children, and the rest went to Eden during her lifetime, after which it would pass in full to Bracken. But there were small, mute evidences everywhere that he had not known he was leaving his office for the last time, and Bracken sat alone at the big desk with his head in his hands, striving for strength to face them, while the portrait of Lincoln above the mantelpiece looked down with the same compassionate eyes which had rested on

Cabot day after day as he sat in the same chair.

The strings of proofs and stacks of marked exchanges and the overflowing wastepaper-basket were naturally tidied away. But the shears and the paste-pot, the pearl push-bells in a row — unmarked because he knew so well whom each would summon — the colored inks and pencils, a pile of new books in bright jackets awaiting review, pipes in a rack, an over-size ash-tray, a full stamp-box — they might all have been still warm from his hand. When Bracken raised his head he looked down through a floor-length window at Park Row and the City Hall. On the wall beside the window was Cabot's framed diploma from Princeton. Should his own come down now to hang beside it. . . .

He returned to Madison Avenue at twilight, white-faced and unnerved, and was pouring himself a stiff whiskey at the sideboard in the dining-room when his mother looked in at the door and smiled at him faintly. Eden had been so happy and so blessed that she was far from looking anything like her fifty-five years, and even now above the sheer black dress her face looked pinched and girlish rather than widowed, and her reddish hair still gleamed in the dusky room.

"Oh, God, you always did look so

beautiful in black," said Bracken ruefully, and gulped half his drink, and came to put an arm around her waist, moving her towards the drawing-room. "Maybe I shouldn't have said that. There doesn't seem to be anything one can say safely at a time like this. Shall we go on talking about the weather?"

"No," she said gravely. "I want to talk about your father, Bracken." She sat down on a sofa, and he followed, the glass still in his hand.

"Yes, I suppose we must," he agreed. "So far, I've been dreading it. There's something wrong about that. He wouldn't have put up with that at all. Tell me."

"It was entirely unexpected," she said steadily. "We all thought he had taken a turn for the better, and everything was quite cheerful the last night. He died without waking. I was sitting by the bed, reading — suddenly the room was empty. That was all."

Bracken drew a long sigh. He had been imagining things, and he felt a great relief.

"We talked a lot about you while he was ill," Eden's low voice went on beside him. "And he left you a message. That was before we thought the worst was over. There were two messages, in fact."

"All right," said Bracken, gripping the tumbler. "Let's have them."

"First, there was something he wanted you to write. He tried to do it himself, but he wasn't strong enough. I have his notes for you. He wanted you to make people see that this war with Spain has made us one nation again, healing the old wounds left from fighting each other. He felt it very deeply — that the army in Cuba is made up of men from nearly every state in the Union, North and South, shoulder to shoulder, all brothers in arms, no matter which side their fathers fought on in the '60's, with officers from both sides too, all under one flag again."

"Yes, I can do that!" Bracken nodded. "Look at Fighting Joe Wheeler, the wildest Rebel of them all, and at Guasimas when the Spanish finally lit out for the rear he clean forgot which war it was and yelled, 'Come on, boys, we've got the damn' Yankees on the run!' "

"Your father would have liked that!" she smiled.

"Well, the first one is easy enough. What next?"

"He said you were to go back to England for Dinah, however long it took."

Everything in Bracken relaxed at once. He had had no idea how he had been braced for the opposite until then. He wanted to cry. He set down the glass and rose and walked about the room, his hands in his pockets, fighting the tightness in his throat. Eden went on talking softly, giving him leeway.

"He said that Temple could run things here for a while and that anyway you would have to go over and put the Fleet Street office under a permanent deputy. He said, 'If I should peg out before he can marry Dinah and bring her back here, I don't want my empty chair to be a millstone round his neck.' And he said, 'Tell him not to rush her — it's asking a good deal of her to leave England with him as she'll have to.' And he said, 'Tell him what you went through with me.' "

Bracken turned to look at her.

"Was it bad?" he said. "I never thought. Was it?"

"I'd do it all over again," she said, and her chin came up.

He went and knelt beside the sofa, his arms around her.

"It *was* worth it, wasn't it?" he entreated her. "It won't be asking too much of her?"

"Your father was worth it," she said. "Tell Dinah that for me."

"Come and tell her yourself," he said urgently. "Come with me to England, Mother, and see the house and get a breath of air, after all this. Do you good, hm?"

"Well, do you think it would appeal to Virginia? Of course we can't go out much now, wherever we are.''

"Leave Virginia to me, I can talk her into it. Anyway, I can't start for a few weeks — months, maybe. There's a lot to do here first, he knew that as well as anybody.''

"Well, perhaps — after Christmas?'' she said doubtfully, and while it seemed like a century to him he saw that she was interested, and it was the first interest she had shown in anything since his father died. But —"We wouldn't have to miss Christmas with Sue, would we?'' she was asking anxiously.

"No, of course we wouldn't,'' he reassured her, thinking of the letter he must write to Dinah. "We could go over early in the year. Think how lovely England is in the spring! There's nothing to keep you here, is there?''

"N-no, if you can persuade Virginia. I'm worried about her, Bracken, I begin to wonder if she's ever going to marry.''

"Are you so anxious to get her off your hands?''

"Heavens, no, but I had quite made up my mind before I was seventeen —''

"Virginia isn't twenty yet!''

"I suppose it's her attitude, more than anything else,'' she said thoughtfully. "She makes fun of everything. She's too bright and flippant and — well, heartless. Do you think it's just a phase?''

''She's a spoilt brat,'' he said affectionately, knowing quite well what was the matter with Virginia. ''She'll grow out of it. A few months in England might improve her manners. Now, look here, if I promise to wait for Christmas in Williamsburg, will you promise to spend Easter in England with me?''

''I promise,'' she said, and there was something live and quickened in her face that had not been there since his return. ''I had almost forgotten about Farthingale. What will you do with it now that you — well, now that you and Dinah will have to think about coming back here to live?''

''I shall hang on to it for a while, at least, because of the divorce. I must show intention of residing in England for that, you see. After all, we'd be spending quite a lot of time in England. Father always did.'' He suppressed the solution which nearly slipped out — Virginia and Archie could have Farthingale as a wedding present. But first, Virginia had to catch Archie.

''Does Dinah know about Lisl?'' Eden asked delicately.

''No. Neither does she know that I'm in

love with her. I'm going to tell her as soon as I get back. Lisl first, of course.''

"Will it take long — the divorce?''

''I don't know. I've written Partridge, but I won't really know anything till I get back there. Anyway, you've taken the most tremendous load off my mind. I was afraid —''

She smiled at him reproachfully.

"After all these years,'' she said, ''don't you know him better than that?''

And so once more he sat down to write to Dinah —

This will come too late for your birthday [he wrote.] It isn't that I forgot, but I have only just returned to New York and am trying to straighten things out here and see where I am. When I wrote you from Jamaica I could tell you nothing but the facts. Since then I have learned that my father wished me to return to England and go on with the job there in Fleet Street, for a while at least. So I shall be coming back, Dinah, perhaps not as soon as I'd like to, but still very early next year.

And now you are seventeen and I suppose completely grown up. By the time I come to England it will be nearly two years since we first met, that morning on our hill, so in spite of all this time when it's been impossible to talk to each other we are really quite old friends. Now that I am back here it won't have to be so long between letters, if only you will write to me and tell me what you're doing. I keep wondering if you have changed much, and I keep hoping you haven't. I know my letters are dull as ditchwater, but I shall try to make up for that by their frequency and by the brilliance of my conversation when I see you again. There was a letter from you waiting for me here when I landed, and I am more grateful for it than I can say. But within a week I shall be convinced I'll never get another, because I always am . . .

He paused and took Dinah's letter out of its envelope and read it again, wondering how much he dared to say in reply to her artless anxiety for his welfare, so freely expressed as soon as she learned that he would be under fire in Cuba. Miss French could not have been looking over her shoulder when she wrote: . . . *and if anything happens to you there it will happen to me too, and if you die I am sure to just die of loneliness myself and*

561

follow you to heaven, like the poor little heathen girl in the legend who followed the Crusader king across the world with only his name as a password. . . .

Did she know what she was saying, and did she mean it the way it sounded? Did she really think of him like that, as a bulwark against her loneliness? Because that might mean that she was beginning to think of him permanently — as a fixture in her life — as a man she might cleave to, forsaking all others —

I like what you say about the Crusader king, [he resumed cautiously.] But that won't be necessary now, I am pleased to say. The wound has healed and I am quite fit again. It does remind me, though, that it would have been very awkward if you had had to ask St. Peter for *Mr. Murray,* and it seems to me that now you are certainly old enough to call me by my Christian name, which, in case you have forgotten, is still Bracken.

I look forward to our rides again, Dinah, more than you have any idea. In the meantime, I have sent off a parcel, which you must regard as a late birthday present and not as an early Christmas present. . . .

PART FIVE
DINAH

Farthingale.   *Summer, 1899.*

1

A week before they were to sail Virginia caught a cold and developed a deep bronchial cough which threatened pneumonia. Bracken suppressed all his impulses, postponed their sailing reservations, and wrote again to Dinah to explain one more delay. He had to write to Partridge too.

As soon as he had returned to New York he communicated with Partridge to inquire the status of his suit for divorce, and had already received a most unsatisfactory reply. The mousy, smooth-shaven man who had accompanied Bracken to Cannes had gone on with his investigations, aided by a photograph of Lisl, and had finally caught up with her at Biarritz. She was living at a hotel there as the travelling companion and *amie,* not of Hutchinson but of a South American named Serrano — which, wrote Partridge philosophically, was a distinction without a difference and would have served their purpose just as well. But Partridge went on to say that it was no good serving the papers until Bracken had established something like a permanent residence in England. And as the date of his return had appeared to be indefinitely delayed by the state of affairs in Cuba, Partridge had not seen fit to keep Lisl under observation at Bracken's expense during all those intervening months. And what that amounted to was that once Bracken returned to England and took up his residence there as planned, she would have to be found all over again and duly served with papers. So except for the evidence they were not really much forwarder, Partridge concluded rather callously, and asked for Bracken's sailing date. When he had read that exasperating letter Bracken walked up and down the room and swore at Partridge. As he cooled off a little he was able to see that Partridge had acted only with his customary prudence and economy. But Lisl might be anywhere by now.

Virginia got better slowly, and in the middle of February she was still coughing, and tired very easily, and Eden worried because she seemed so low in her mind. Bracken went into her room one evening to cheer her up and found her in tears.

"Here, here," he said firmly. "I thought you were getting well."

"Oh, Bracken, please let's go back to England!"

"Well, my dear child, that's what we're trying to do, just as soon as you're able!"

"B-but the doctor says I m-mustn't start for another month!" she quavered.

"*What?* I never heard of such a thing!"

"He says a winter sailing would be too risky for my chest. Oh, Bracken, you don't think I'm going to die of tuberculosis!"

"Good Lord, no, nobody in our family ever does that!" he reassured her.

"He says I'm badly underweight and run down. He says —"

"Oh, damn the doctor, Ginny, what does he mean by scaring you to death like this? Maybe you aren't quite the thing just now, but you'll be all right as soon as the weather warms up. Easter comes early this year, and we're going to be in England for Easter. You tell the doctor that, with my compliments!"

Virginia looked more cheerful.

"I began to think maybe I was going to just pine away," she said doubtfully.

"For love? That doesn't run in our family either!" But he sat down beside her, really fascinated by such constancy. She had not had a word from Archie Campion since she left England, and yet his remembered image still outshone all the pleasant realities with which her life had been filled in the interim. He wondered how many proposals she had passed up, for Archie, who had done little but ignore her from the beginning. "I think it's just stubbornness," he said, to try her.

Virginia began to lay pleats in her damp handkerchief, and looked at him out of the corners of her eyes. He noticed that her long, curving lashes cast pathetic shadows on her pale cheeks, and a wave of tenderness for so pretty and so funny a sister ran through him.

"I dream about him," she was confessing, her slender fingers busy with the handkerchief.

"Good heavens!" Bracken murmured, keeping his face straight.

"And it's a funny thing — in the dreams he's always fond of me."

"*How* fond?"

"Well, he — never quite proposes," she admitted seriously. "But I always wake up feeling as though he *might*. You don't suppose he'll have married somebody else by now?"

"We should have heard about that. Dinah writes to me every now and then, you know. Clare is engaged, but Archie seems to be going on just as usual.''

"Oh, Bracken, you might have told me you'd heard again! Who is Clare going to marry?''

"Whom, darling. I don't know his name, Dinah just said Clare was engaged to a man with pots of money and everyone was very pleased, but she (Dinah) was glad *she* didn't have to marry him.''

"It's all right for Clare to marry some bounder for his money, but Archie is afraid of mine. Does that make any sense?''

"None whatever,'' he assented, knowing exactly how Archie must feel, all the same.

"I thought perhaps if I dressed very plainly and never wore any jewelry —''

"Ginny, as a matter of pardonable curiosity, why are you so set on Archie?''

She thought for a long minute, gazing into the middle distance.

"I thought you were in love too,'' she said then. "What ever became of that?''

"It's waiting on the divorce. Which is waiting on my return to England.''

"Oh, poor Bracken, and here I've made you a month later by being ill!''

"Never mind about that,'' he said. "Just answer my question.''

"Could *you* answer it? Could *you* make out a list of reasons why you want to marry whoever it is?"

"Certainly I could. As long as your arm."

"Well, then, he's good-looking. And he's well-born. And he knows how to behave. But those aren't reasons, I could say that about lots of other people I wouldn't touch with a barge-pole. I just don't want anybody but Archie. I've tried, honestly I have. But he makes them all seem gauche, and stupid, and bumble-footed."

And Bracken, thinking of Dinah's tiny bones and effortless self-possession, which had something to do with race and caste and national atmosphere, nodded gravely.

"Ginny, would you say that I was bumble-footed?" he asked humbly.

"Oh, *you*, if you weren't my brother I'd marry you like a shot!"

"Well, thanks very much," he said in some surprise.

"A girl could always be comfortable with you," she went on frankly. "You've got yourself on the leash. It's the difference between champagne and raw whiskey, I should think. You can get just as tight on champagne, and it's nicer."

Bracken stared.

"But that is the wisdom of the ages, speaking," he said, dazed. "Where did *you* learn it?"

"Oh, I was born knowing that!" she said airily. "And that's why I want Archie. He's champagne too. Very dry."

2

Easter was early that year, but spring was late. They arrived at the station at Upper Briarly in Gloucestershire about teatime on a bleak grey day when the treetops were showing just the faintest film of green, tossing in a shrewd wind.

But Virginia's heart-shaped face was pink-cheeked and sparkling as they drove through the village to Farthingale, and she vied jealously with Bracken in pointing out to Eden all the matters of interest along the way. Eden sat beside her in the barouche, wrapped in sables, enjoying her first sight of England in nearly three years, and determined to ignore the ache in her heart which reminded her that Cabot had meant to come to Gloucestershire too and see Dinah and the house.

Bracken, sitting with his back to the

horses, looked lovingly on the rolling Cotswold Hills, and when he said, "There's the Hall on the left," he felt his heartbeat quicken. Then he caught the warning in Virginia's eyes and thought how complicated it was getting, now that his mother knew about Dinah but wasn't supposed to know about Archie. That wouldn't last, of course. Once Eden saw Virginia in the same room with Archie she would guess.

In the drawing-room at Farthingale a log fire burned and the tea-table stood ready, gleaming with Worcester china and old silver, and there was a big bouquet of *Gloire de Dijon* roses from the greenhouses at the Hall, with Lord Alwyn's card. Virginia sniffed them superciliously, caught Bracken's eye upon her, and grinned.

"Whiskey," she murmured. "Raw enough to choke you." Her eyes went wistfully around the warm, lighted room. But because it held no message from Archie, it was as good as empty to her. "Who is at the Hall now?" she asked Melchett the parlormaid when tea came in.

"They will all be down for Easter, I think, miss. Mr. Archie came yesterday and brought Master Gerald with him, and Mr. John and his wife are expected, and Lady Clare's fiancé too, I believe."

"Everybody well?" Bracken asked casually, and his far eyelid drooped at Virginia.

"Yes, sir, except the Earl had influenza at Christmas time and they all but gave him up. He's out and about again now, though. I was to say they had sent your horse back, sir, and two others for as long as you'd like to keep them."

"Splendid," said Bracken. "That's very kind of them."

Melchett was too well trained to add that Lady Dinah had ridden over with the groom who brought the horses and left a note for Bracken, so it was not until he went up to his room to change that he found it on his mantelpiece.

Dear Bracken —[Dinah had written]

Sunbeam is back in her stall, waiting for you. I have had her out nearly every day since you went away, and she is in excellent form, though I think she missed not hunting. Edward is sending Daybreak and Misty too, in case Virginia and your mother want to ride. They are both very gentle.

This may sound as though I wasn't the least bit excited about your coming home, but I am, it seems as though I can't wait to see you! Can you ride out to our hill in the morning? I shall be there, just in case. I don't think I've changed much, they say I'll never have a figure, but I've put my hair up and my dresses down and that helps. I do hope you won't expect too much after all this time, because I'm just

DINAH

When he had read it twice he sat down and put his head in his hands, which were not quite steady. Coming home, she had written, unconsciously. Nearly two years since he had first seen her, wearing her brother Gerald's Norfolk jacket and breeches, with her hair tucked up under a shooting cap. More than a year since he had seen her at all, and now she was seventeen, and tomorrow he would have her back again, all to himself, on the hill. But he thought, I must tell her about Lisl — and that's what tomorrow comes to.

On his way through London he had conferred with Partridge, and the mousy little man had been sent for and again despatched to the Continent. But no amount of reproachful profanity on Bracken's part could alter the fact that Partridge had allowed the scent to get cold and that now it might take some time to get things under way again.

Bracken censured himself, not for the first time, as he rose wearily and began to change to his dinner clothes. He should have told Dinah about the necessity for a divorce before he left England. He was not to blame for the delay in his return, but he could at this rate be to blame for Dinah's falling in love with a man who had a wife already. I object, he told himself angrily, jerking at his tie, to feeling like a character in a Pinero play. And then, surveying himself in the glass in his immaculate black and white — Good Lord, I even *look* like a leading-man, he thought in disgust and went down to the cheerful American custom of cocktails in the drawing-room.

He woke as the sun came up and lay a moment, savoring his own excitement, which was almost like stage-fright. His riding-clothes were laid out and waiting on a chair. All the time he bathed and shaved and dressed he was telling himself that he must be calm, he must not lose a grip on things, he must remember to tell her about Lisl. That was quite enough to anchor him to earth. He was going to be free, of course, eventually. But he would certainly not be regarded as free now by Dinah's family, and it was time Dinah knew what they were up against.

So at last he rode Sunbeam down the

chestnut avenue in front of the house again, through the sleepy village where there were still ducks on the stream above the bridge, through the gap in the wall and out across the hillside. Backward spring though it was, the air that morning had the first velvety mildness, the sun had that delicate caressing warmth of Eastertide, and the sky curved pale and virginal without a cloud. The pollard willows were feathered with green, but there was no blossom yet on the fruit trees. Rooks were kissing in the elmtops, and lap-wings lamented joyfully in the meadow grass. And there was added to his own secret inner happiness the reckless, heathen exaltation that stirs in the spring of the year.

Dinah was before him at the rendezvous, dismounted, kneeling in the grass at the edge of the spinney to gather primroses, while staid little Dewdrop grazed near by. She waved as he came up over the crest of the hill, and he waved back and half way down the slope he swung out of the saddle. As his feet touched the ground Dinah ran to meet him, straight into his outstretched arms, and before either of them had time to think about it, their lips had met. He let her go at once, partly from sheer astonishment, but the kiss had happened in spite of his good intentions.

"Dinah — darling — I do believe you've

missed me," he said rather shakily, and Dinah with her arms still hard around his neck and her slight body against his, said, "I feel as though I was the one who had come home!"

It took all he had of resolution after that to say lightly, "Let me look at you," and hold her a little away from him, his hands resting on her shoulders.

She submitted with her usual composure, standing docilely before him, her face upturned and defenceless to his searching eyes. He saw again the clear, delicate skin which did not freckle, the direct blue eyes with their thick golden lashes, the long, lovely line of her lips, the resolute chin. She was just as he had remembered her — but with a new, soft, shining something which came of being seventeen in the spring.

"You see," she said after a silent moment, "I told you. There is no improvement whatever."

"Aren't you taller?" he said rather at random, rather short of breath.

"It's this hat." She touched the smart low hunting topper she wore with some pride. "It came from Locke's. They had to buy me new riding clothes, I had clean worn out the old ones. With most of my other things, though, they have just let down the hems or put insertion in, and flounces, now that I'm supposed to have long skirts. I can't have anything new till after Clare is married, but Miss French has bagged two of Clare's prettiest dresses to make over for me because Clare is getting new ones.''

"Your hair has got darker," he added, peering at it under the hat's brim.

"Has it? I wear it up all the time now. Makes me feel lots older."

"Do you want to? I suppose the first thing I know you'll be coming out, and going to dances, and having proposals of marriage, and all that sort of thing."

Dinah made a face.

"I hope not!" she said decidedly. "Besides, nobody will ask me, I'm not like Clare."

He bit off the impulse to say that there was one proposal she might as well make up her mind to, and that was his. Instead, as they strolled on in step along the edge of the spinney, leading the horses which often paused to graze, he locked her arm in his with their palms together and said, "Tell me about Clare. Is this fellow all right?"

"I suppose he is. His name is Mortimer Flood, and he's made a lot of money in hemp, or something, and is giving her the most wonderful house in Belgrave Square. I could never bear him myself even if he offered me Buckingham Palace to live in, but I doubt if I ever get married anyway, so my opinion isn't worth much.''

''That's a very drastic state of mind,'' he objected mildly. ''What's wrong with marriage?''

''The husbands people get, mostly. Bracken, do you mind — about Clare, I mean. Once I thought you were a little in love with her.''

''You know, as a matter of fact, I wasn't. Besides — perhaps I should have mentioned it before — I have a wife, you see, and while we haven't lived together for some time, I am still technically married to her.''

''Oh, I knew that,'' she said easily. ''Edward told me.''

''Well, blast Edward. I would have preferred to do it myself. Of course I had no idea of being away so long, and it seemed a stupid thing to put in a letter. How long have you known about it?''

''Since the fancy dress ball.''

''And you never mentioned it! What tact!''

''Well, I thought perhaps you'd rather not.''

His relief was anti-climax. Whatever she felt about him, it was in spite of Lisl. And she had still run into his arms.

"There will be a divorce eventually, of course," he said. "And then I shall be free to marry again."

"And shall you?"

"I hope so."

"Oh," said Dinah rather flatly. "Then it wasn't — you aren't breaking your heart over her."

"My dear, I am anything but heart-broken. The whole thing was a sorry mistake from the beginning. My fault, of course, and I have paid for it very dearly."

"I don't believe it was your fault," she maintained.

"Mine, anyway, to have married her at all. Nowadays I would know better."

"Edward said — said she had left you." Dinah was looking straight ahead.

"For another man." He shrugged briefly. "Sounds bad, doesn't it!"

"Oh, Bracken, that's not true! Nobody would!" She was as indignant as though a third person had slandered him.

"Why do you say that?" He paused and stood gazing down at her. Their faces were very near.

"Because you're — because any woman would be proud and — and happy with you."

He swallowed all the things he wanted to say, and said anything else.

"I hadn't enough money," he said. "Or perhaps I was stingy. Anyway, she wanted more than I could give her."

"Then you're better off without her."

"I am. Most decidedly."

"And that was why you never proposed to Clare," Dinah reflected. "You knew she wanted a lot of money too."

"Dinah, darling, I never would have proposed to Clare because I never was in love with her. Strange as that may seem." He put his hand to the bulge in his coat pocket and took out a square black leather case. "Here's your music-box from New York," he said.

Inside the case when she opened it was a silver box with a jewelled and embossed design of trees and a stream and a fisherman in an odd hat. He showed her how to press the catch and a tiny feathered bird with an ivory beak came up through a grid in the top and whistled an intricate tune. When you released the catch he popped down out of sight and it was just a box again. Dinah was completely entranced, and held her breath each time lest the bird get caught in his little trap door.

At last she closed it up safe in its case again and they left the horses under some willows and went on, hand in hand and full of gossip, to where Dinah had a surprise for him. He stood silent with delight when he saw it — a carpet of anemones, dancing white stars on stalks, trembling in a wandering breeze on the bank of the stream, spread as far as the eye could travel among small bare tree trunks.

"I've been saving it for you," she said with possessive pride. "If you hadn't come this week it would have been gone. It's all the present I have for you, I'm afraid."

He dared not say that he had had his present when she kissed him. It would take so little now to jar Dinah out of her unawareness, and the time was not yet. They went on, treading delicately, and sat down on a log near the water, and Dinah heard about Virginia's convalescence, and how Eden already loved the village and the house and how anxious she was to know Dinah.

"Clare and Edward will come to call, of course," said Dinah. "Father's not gone out much since he had influenza."

"That will be charming of Clare and Edward, I'm sure. But I want my mother to know you. We must get Archie to bring you to lunch."

"We can try. Archie's rather queer lately. I wouldn't be surprised if he was in love."

"That's new, isn't it?" he asked.

"Archie is always very mysterious.

Perhaps that's why I think so much of him. But it's nothing like you and Virginia, you tell each other everything.''

''Well, not quite everything,'' he qualified hastily.

''She must have been nearly out of her mind when you were shot. Which shoulder was it? Are you quite well again?''

''It was just here.'' He tapped his right collarbone. ''The bullet went clean through so it healed nicely, though it will probably complain of wet weather for the rest of my life.'' Dinah's eyes rested on his tweed-clad shoulder as though she saw the blood and felt the pain, but she said nothing. ''I wouldn't have worried you with it,'' he went on, ''but my handwriting looked so funny for a while you were bound to wonder. Your watch was with me, and I like to think that made a difference.''

''And if prayers do any good, you had those too,'' she nodded. ''Please tell me how it happened. Your letter was just tantalizing.''

''It's not really very interesting. I'd rather hear about you.''

''Oh, *I* haven't done anything! Archie gave me *The Light That Failed*. Was it anything like that in Cuba?''

''Not very much. Though Fitz behaved in a

582

rather Kiplingesque way, I suppose.''

"Tell about Fitz,'' she begged him.

"We all thought Fitz had a screw loose somewhere. We were never so wrong. That just shows you. Can't tell about your own family, even!''

Sitting there on the log, absorbed in each other, they allowed half an hour to slip away while Bracken told about *Daisy,* and the beach at Daiquiri, and the balloon above the Bloody Bend. Dinah listened almost in silence except for a prodding question each time he seemed to slow down or tried to skip. Cuba had taken nearly a year of his life and had nearly killed him. She had to know about Cuba, and Bracken was the only one who could tell her. She kept him at it until she was satisfied, and the sun was high. And finally —

"I'm starving,'' he said suddenly. "Look here, why don't you come back with me to breakfast and say Hullo to Mother now?''

It seemed to her the wildest adventure, all of a sudden like that. Her eyes were round with it.

"Could I?''

"Why not? We'll send Luke over with a message that I met you out riding and kidnapped you.''

"You can telephone now. Father hates it,

but Clare made him put one in."

"All right, come along, we'll telephone!"

Before they left the bank they gathered some anemones to put with the primroses as a bouquet for Eden and strolled back hand in hand to where they had left the horses.

"You always make everything so *simple!*" she marvelled, looking down at him from Dewdrop's saddle when he had tossed her up.

"Why shouldn't it be simple? We're both hungry, and Mother will be delighted."

"It's good to have you back." Impulsively she laid one small warm hand along his cheek as he stood beside Dewdrop looking up. "Please don't ever go away again."

He caught her hand quickly and held its palm against his lips. Then he mounted Sunbeam and they rode almost in silence to Farthingale.

3

They found the breakfast table laid for one, and Melchett said that the ladies were having trays up stairs.

"Just lay another place here and boil another egg," said Bracken. "I've promised Lady Dinah something to eat."

"Perhaps I oughtn't to stay," Dinah suggested anxiously when Melchett had gone. "Your mother might rather I'd wait till I was asked."

"You *are* asked." Bracken drew her into the morning-room which was streaming with sunlight and had a fire. "You wait here and I'll go up and rout them out."

Eden was covered with chagrin when he knocked at her door, for it was not her habit to breakfast in bed, though Virginia had done so since her illness. She explained that she felt perfectly well, and had only asked for a tray because Bracken seemed to have gone out, and the maid was unpacking and she could keep an eye on things —

Bracken kissed her apologies into silence.

"Take all the time you like," he said. "Dinah and I will have breakfast together. Just a sighting shot. She'll have to learn how I like my morning coffee sooner or later!"

Followed by Eden's laughter, he ran down stairs to the telephone, which was in the morning-room, got through to the Hall and asked for Archie.

"Hullo, we've got your sister over here at Farthingale," he announced. "The little one. I went out for an early ride and found her picking primroses. She's having breakfast with us if you don't mind."

"Jolly good idea," said Archie. "Sorry I wasn't out after primroses myself."

"Come and join us. Lots of time."

"Thanks, old boy, I think I will. We're all delighted to have you back, you know."

"Good. As soon as you like, old boy," said Bracken in the vernacular, and hung up, grinning. "He's coming straight over," he said to Dinah. "Excuse me again." And he went up stairs to Virginia's room. "You'd better come out of that!" he yelled through the door. "Dinah's down stairs, and Archie's on the way!"

"What? *Come in!*"

He opened the door and stuck his head around it. Virginia made a very pretty picture propped against the pillows in a pink sacque, drinking tea.

"All right, Camille, get into something with lots of lace on it, the curtain is going up! But he can't come up here, you know, you'll have to use the sofa down stairs."

"Oh, *Bracken,* why didn't you *warn* me! How long have I got? Do take this tray, you chump, and hand me that robe, quick, and *stop grinning at me!* What shall I wear? Ring for Mary, can't you? What did he *say?*"

"Can't stop to gossip now, Dinah's starving in the morning-room. I'd get a move on if I were you."

He ran down stairs again and collected Dinah, who said as they entered the dining-room together, "Maybe *you* can get Archie out of his shell, I can't! He works all the time and never comes down for week-ends, and never has any fun. It's such a *waste.* He's much the nicest of us all and nobody ever sees him!"

Bracken herded her gently away from the sideboard towards the table, where beside his mother's place there was a large silver tray with the tea and coffee things on it.

"You sit down in Mother's chair and pour out my coffee the way she does. She has finished breakfast and will be down soon. What do you like for breakfast?" he went on, peeking under covers at the sideboard. "Isn't it odd how little we really know about each other after all these years? They *have* done us well this morning! Scrambled eggs — kippers — bacon —?"

"I think the eggs, please — and bacon. How do you like your coffee?" she asked.

"Hot milk — quite a lot — and one sugar."

He set the plate in front of her and sat down with his own. Dinah handed him his coffee. Melchett brought in the toast in a silver rack and put it down between them and went out. He watched while Dinah poured tea for herself and put milk and sugar into it. She looked up at his silence, with candid, questioning eyes.

"I like this," said Bracken. "I think this was a very good idea. Let's do it again some time!"

"You know, what I missed most while you were gone is the way you say silly things quite sensibly," Dinah remarked. "Nobody in our family does that. I feel as though I hadn't laughed since the last time you talked nonsense!"

He had to let it go at that, though he knew it wasn't nonsense. He had to go on allowing Dinah's sublime inexperience of the *arrière pensée* to retrieve his own reckless utterances, frustrated and enchanted by the way she accepted without blinking remarks which other girls would have tripped over and taken him up on. Virginia in Dinah's place with, say, Archie instead of himself, would by now have been blushing prettily and behaving like a three-days' bride. But he was grateful that it was so. Dinah went to his head and spring was in his blood and he felt gay and heedless and experimental. He longed perversely for Dinah just once to betray consciousness that he was a man, attractive enough, and that she was a female. His irreverent impulse was to impinge, ever so little, on that touching choir-boy innocence of hers with his own surging emotion. And yet the last thing he wanted was to propose to Dinah in the subjunctive mood. If and when I get my divorce, will you marry me. Oh, no. That wasn't good enough for Dinah. When he was in the clear, then he would ask her and they wouldn't have to wait. Meanwhile, she baffled him. Not that he didn't enjoy that too.

But Dinah, who was so much deeper than even he had any idea, was hearing over and over inside her head those apparently careless words on the hill . . . *then I shall be free to marry again . . . and shall you? . . . I hope so.* . . . And while she had never really thought as far as marrying Bracken herself, those few words seemed to demonstrate once more her own chronic negligible state — too young, too thin, too schoolgirlish and dull to be anything but his faithful friend, for that she would be all her life, while he married some one like Clare, only nicer, who would grace his home as a wife should, a brilliant hostess, a famous beauty — all the things a person with red hair and no figure and a country education couldn't possibly be. . . .

Dinah ate her scrambled eggs and poured his second cup of coffee the way he liked it, and went on talking sensibly, replying to his questions about the past winter, recalling anecdotes for his amusement which she had saved up to tell him — how some one had left the front door at the Hall open early one morning and some deer from the park had come right into the entrance hall and cornered a timid housemaid with her duster till her screams aroused the rest of the household —''You'd have thought she was being murdered at least, and they were only asking for apples, they wouldn't hurt a fly!''— and how a fox, hard-pressed on a six-mile point in the Friday country roundabout Moreton, set his mask straight for Blockley's Farm and went to ground in the kitchen, where he was killed, and it made the most awful mess, because it was a very muddy day, besides the blood and all, but old Blockley only halloo'd them on and said Better the kitchen than his hen-house any day — and how Edward riding Thunderbolt had come down hard at the first water-jump in the point-to-point, and made a terrific splash, and Thunderbolt was found to have damaged himself so badly he had to be shot —

"That must have been just the least little bit in the world satisfactory to you," Bracken suggested, and Dinah after an instant's shocked surprise burst into delighted laughter.

It was the first time, he thought, that he had ever heard her laugh aloud, and Eden entered as she finished. Dinah jumped to her feet and made a schoolgirl curtsey when she was presented to Bracken's mother, who barely refrained from taking her at once into her arms. Eden accepted the rather limp bunch of primroses and anemones with joy and spent some time propping them up in a small glass vase fetched by Melchett, while Dinah diffidently resumed her chair beside the urns. Then Eden said she thought she would have another cup of tea if they could spare it, and Dinah said Oh, there was lots, and poured it with grave dignity. As she did so, Eden noticed with a mother's eye that Dinah's poor little hands were red and chapped because it had not occurred to anyone to give her a lotion, and she thought, If we don't get her out of that tomb of a house she'll be having chilblains too, before she's much older. All that was maternal in Eden rose up to take Dinah to its heart. And the look in Bracken's eyes for his oblivious darling was something his mother had never seen there before.

Then Archie wandered in, clad in his well-worn riding-clothes and polished boots, and more tea was sent for, and another chair drawn up, though he assured them he had already fed, thanks very much.

"Virginia will be down presently," Bracken said, answering Archie's unspoken question at once. "The fact is, we're being rather careful of her and she breakfasts in bed since her illness."

"Was it as bad as that?" asked Archie, surprised into lowering his guard, for Dinah had only told him that Bracken wrote Virginia had a heavy cold.

"It was nearly pneumonia," said Bracken solemnly. "She's had a wretched time, and we're lucky it wasn't worse. You'll notice how thin she is, but don't say anything, we try to keep her cheerful."

Eden turned for a long look at him, as this was not his customary off-hand attitude about his sister. Bracken met her eyes blandly, and offered Archie a cigarette. Eden then had another look at Archie. Brother of the Viscount. Nicer than the Viscount. She liked what she saw.

At that moment there was a scurry of feet in the hall and Virginia arrived on the threshold, obviously under the impression that she was beating Archie to the dining-room. At sight of him she checked neatly and entered with a royal leisure, wearing a cashmere tea-gown the color of heliotrope with flowing sleeves and a foam of lace from throat to hem.

"Dinah, *darling,* it's lovely of you to come over our very first morning!" she cried, enfolding Dinah in a sisterly embrace. "How nice you look — quite grown up! And *Archie,* is that really you? This *is* a surprise Are you all still drinking tea? Would there be another drop for me? Dinah's pouring out — doesn't she look cute in mother's chair?"

Archie insisted that she should take his

cup, which he hadn't yet touched, and still another cup was brought for him, and they all settled down around the table again and nibbled rather cold toast and marmalade while Bracken and Virginia were brought up to date on the news of the countryside. Eden began to see daylight on Virginia, as Bracken had thought she would. Finally, out of consideration for the servants she rose, saying, "Children, we must let them clear away. Come into the morning-room and tell me more."

But Archie said they really must be going, as some people were arriving by the morning train from Town, and anyway perhaps Virginia ought to rest — and she must be sure to drink lots of Bovril, he added earnestly, that was the stuff, it had got the Governor back on his feet in no time after his influenza. Virginia, the picture of health, said she was allowed to go out now on mild days, and Archie told her firmly that the wind still had fangs and she must on no account risk getting chilled.

"But I get so *bored,* staying in all day!" she wailed, and Archie said Oh, well, in that case, would it be any good if he popped back for tea. Bracken assured him warmly that the sight of any new face, even that of Archie Campion, would cheer her up no end, and

Archie said Right-o, he would bring his face back roundabout four-thirty, and departed with Dinah.

The door had barely closed behind them when Virginia hurled herself round her brother's neck so that her feet left the floor, crying, "Bracken, you're *wonderful!*" and danced away to review her wardrobe.

Bracken and his mother were left looking at each other quizzically.

"So that's how it is," said Eden.

"I thought you'd catch on," he agreed.

There seemed still something to be said between them. Eden went and put her arms around him.

"Don't have any doubts about Dinah, my dear. Just have patience."

"But did you ever see anything so *young?*" he asked hopelessly.

"You watch. She'll grow up all of a sudden and start mothering you!" Eden promised.

4

Thus Archie cast his dearly bought discretion to the spring winds and allowed himself to convince himself that it wouldn't hurt just to look at Virginia now and then, and try to cheer her up a bit, because after all, pneumonia was no joke — and at the end of a week's teas and walks and rides and visits to the greenhouses at the Hall he was most wretchedly in love, just as he had known all along he would be.

And Lord Alwyn, who had been carefully cultivating a taste for the rather bovine daughter of a rich stock-broker friend of Clare's fiancé, was put right off the whole idea by the proximity of Virginia's dark-eyed vivacity, which as he pointed out to himself over and over again, was nothing, if you came down to it, but sheer American impudence and would be wholly unsuitable in a peer's wife. But within the month Alwyn proposed to Virginia again, and got the same answer, which was quite incomprehensible to him and made him very snappish for days.

Archie had eaten his dinners and been called to the Bar at the Inner Temple the previous year and was beginning to be very well thought of as an industrious Junior in the Chancery Court. It was steady work, and paid moderately well, and he had chosen it in preference to the Criminal Court, which was showier but less profitable, or the Divorce Court, which was likely to be easier but was considered not quite the thing. By hard work and fond attention to his Leader's whims, he had amassed fees up to nearly two hundred pounds for his first year, which was pretty good going. In another ten years or so he would take silk, if he could afford it, and there was nothing to prevent him, by the time he was fifty, from being made a King's Bench judge at five thousand pounds a year, and, if he lived long enough, from becoming Attorney-General.

Meanwhile he had taken to a single eyeglass, which became him, and when Virginia teased him about it he merely remarked that as only one eye was bad two lenses would have been extravagant. When he had got really tired of hearing about it, he did the trick few single-eyeglass men neglected to at least try to learn — he flicked the glass into the air like a coin and caught it in his eye as it came down. Far from silencing Virginia, however, this feat only roused in her an insatiable desire to see him do it again.

Shortly before they all left the Hall to go up to Town for Clare's wedding, Virginia and Archie were making the usual tour of the greenhouses where the prize-winning roses were grown, and in the warm, scented semi-privacy Virginia suddenly said, ''This Mortimer Flood Clare is marrying — tell me honestly, Archie, isn't he rather a wart?''

''Well, yes, he is, rather,'' Archie admitted unwillingly, for Mr. Flood had sort of stuck out as a foreign body on the informal family gatherings at Farthingale and the Hall during the past month — teas on the lawn, luncheon parties, a carriage picnic or two, in which, at least when they were initiated by the American household, the younger members of the Campion family were included.

Mr. Flood had usually been present at these little functions, in attendance on Clare. It was difficult to put one's finger on the trouble with Mr. Flood. He spoke the hunting and country-house idiom, but one was somehow surprised that he had all his *h's*. His clothes came from the right tailor, but somehow they always looked new. He laughed in the right places and never told the wrong jokes. But the embarrassing fact remained that he did not quite belong. Young Gerald, home for the Easter holidays and aged fourteen, had come the nearest to putting it in a nutshell. "His collar's too tight," he had murmured in a scathing aside to Dinah, just as Mr. Flood was appearing at his picnic-lunch brightest and best. It wasn't, really. But Mr. Flood's neck was too thick.

"Then why do you let Clare marry him?" Virginia insisted, when Archie did not rise to defend him.

"Clare thinks she knows what she's doing. She wants that house in Belgrave Square and fifty thousand a year to spend."

"Archie, why is it all right for a girl to marry for money, but not for a man?"

"Is it? Besides, men do it every day, I thought."

"Would you?" she asked softly.

"Good Lord, no!"

"That's what I mean. Why, would you believe it, there was a man who was terribly in love with me, and — I found out later — he never told me about it because he thought I was an heiress!"

"Well, aren't you?" he put it to her.

"Not really. Not till I'm twenty-one. And then it's only ten thousand a year."

"Pounds?"

"No, dollars. The capital is all tied up, with trustees and things, Father saw to all that, and I just ask Bracken for what I want to spend. Archie — would you think better of me if I didn't have a penny in the world?"

"That would be difficult," he said. "I adore you already."

"Oh, *Archie —!*"

"Now, please don't misunderstand me," he added hastily. "I couldn't possibly ask you to marry me, Virginia, you couldn't even dress on my income, let alone run an establishment."

"I could dress on *my* income. Archie, you wouldn't let a silly prejudice ruin my life?"

"It's not a silly prejudice and I doubt very much if it will damage your life in the least."

Virginia stood still in the fragrant aisle beside the *Gloire de Dijons* and looked up at him, allowing her large brown eyes to fill with tears.

"I can't *think* why I love you so!" she whispered. "You're about the most disagreeable man I ever knew!"

Archie reacted in the only possible way. And when he had kissed her —

"This is completely mad," he said. "It's the one thing I swore would never happen. I simply can't do it, Virginia, have you any idea what my expectations are at the Bar? How could we live, even in the country, on what I earn? With any luck perhaps one day I shall land a sensational case and become famous and my fees will jump. Until then, I shall have to just plod along."

"Archie, what do you *do* at the Bar?"

"Well, mostly now I just devil for a cranky old silk named Sir Gifford Kerr, on difficult points of law."

"Do you *like* it?" she persisted curiously.

"Strangely enough, I do, you know."

"I know what you could do, Archie! You could get Bracken's divorce for him, that would be sensational enough!"

"Not in my line of country, I'm afraid. It will come up in the Probate and Divorce Court. I'm in the Chancery."

"He'd pay *anything* to get that settled!" Virginia said.

"Well, it will be a nice plum for somebody, no doubt. His solicitors have already got their eye on the right fellow, you can be sure of that."

She looked at him a long moment.

"You wouldn't touch it with a barge-pole, would you!"

"I've never done a divorce case, that's all," said Archie uncomfortably. "It's a special sort of job. My work is all with trusts and equity. You see, we specialize, rather, at the Bar. We do go over sometimes, especially in Criminal Court jobs, but you have to know your ground. No one man can know it all."

"I see," she murmured.

"Besides, they'll take in a Leader, you know."

"What does that mean?"

"They'll engage a silk. A Q.C. Not just a junior like me. Somebody's going to land Bracken with a very stiffish fee, I expect. Just as soon not be the one. Can't marry his sister at his expense, what?"

"Do you know what I think? I think Bracken would let us use Farthingale to live in as long as we like."

"But that's impossible, I couldn't look him in the face with such an arrangement," he objected promptly.

"Oh, there you go again! It's very selfish of you, Archie, to let your own beastly pride make me so miserable! Just think, if I hadn't put my own pride in my pocket and practically proposed to you myself, you'd have gone on like this to the end of time and I'd have died a spinster!''

"Would you, by Jove? But there must have been countless other chaps who —''

"There *were,* idiot, but I didn't *want* them! I said *No!* Can't you get it into your thick head, I'm in love with *you!''*

"Well, God knows why, it is pretty thick, isn't it!'' He kissed her again. "I do believe you *are!''* he said then, rather dazed. "It's jolly good luck for me, but how is Bracken going to take it, when you tell him you want to marry a fellow who hasn't got a penny?''

"Oh, Bracken knows.''

"What?'' said Archie, startled.

"Bracken will have something all worked out for us, you'll see! He doesn't believe in all this nonsense about money either.''

"I say, Virginia — apart from everything else, you know, and even if you did have to wring it from me — I have been *hopeless* about you ever since the fancy dress ball!''

"Then why did you have to go on treating me like grim death and let me go home to America without a word?'' she demanded. "I very nearly never came back to England again!''

"Well, I thought that would be all for the best, you know.''

"You didn't *care* if you broke my heart!''

"My dear girl, such a thing never occurred to me! Besides —" He stopped.

"Well, what?"

"There was Edward. I knew he had so much more to offer you than I had, and I knew he was frightfully gone on you himself, and it wasn't my place to go barging in —"

"Archie, did you think I cared about the old *title?*" She glanced around cautiously, for you never knew if some gardener mightn't come in to nurse the roses and overhear. The greenhouse was empty, except for themselves. Virginia drew closer to him and locked her arms around his waist, a way she had always demonstrated affection for Bracken, who had learned to brace his diaphragm against it. It took the wind out of Archie. "I wouldn't marry Edward if he was the Prince of Wales!" she said extravagantly.

"Oh, well, in that case —!" said Archie, recovering, and a gardener did come in then, and backed out again, and they never heard him.

5

A marriage will take place early in June at St. Margaret's, Westminster, between Mr. Mortimer Flood of Belgrave Square and Lady Clare Campion, elder daughter of the Earl of Enstone . . .

Once more the house in St. James's Square was stiff with powdered footmen in blue livery and silk stockings, and little crowds gathered on the pavement near the door to watch dinner guests in evening dress alight from their carriages in the summer twilight. Dinah was to be one of the bridesmaids and as her presence was required in Town for fittings for her bridesmaid's dress, she and Bracken lost their week-end rides for the less satisfactory meetings which could be arranged in London. Eden and Virginia, who were not coming up till just in time for the wedding, remained at Farthingale entertaining some friends of Cabot's who had come to stay, so Bracken and Dinah had to take Miss French with them when they went to matinées and picture galleries and the Zoo. Once she let them walk in the Park for an hour while she was at the dentist's, and once she accompanied Dinah to tea at his chambers in Ryder Street, which was not much more than round the corner from St. James's Square.

Bracken noticed with relief that Dinah's clothes had evolved from the intermediate schoolgirl length and pattern to a style more suitable for a very young lady, now that she was allowed to wear Clare's hand-me-downs. Clare's things were of course twice too big for her, but Miss French was clever at altering them to fit, or more often making a whole new dress out of two of Clare's old ones. Bracken would have been very much touched if he had known how the gentle little woman contrived and labored to dress her darling so that the rich American who was so kind-hearted would be sure to see the wind-flower beauty which clumsy clothes might have obscured. Miss French in her deep secret heart was deliberately match-making. She had taken Bracken's measure long ago, and she wanted him for Dinah, who had not mentioned the existence of his wife. Miss French never allowed a hint of this daring ambition to cross Dinah's mind. But she noticed with satisfaction the way Bracken's eyes lingered on the girl in her charge, and her hopes grew daily and were stitched into every garment she worked at. She was glad too that the sewing-maid's time was occupied with Clare, for she was jealous of her own devoted part in Dinah's new grown-up look.

It was a season when everyone wore a bit of lace or chiffon tied around the neck with a filmy bow beneath the chin — an extravagant whimsy, because the perishable bows could be worn only once and often would not bear laundering. Dinah did not suspect that her *chiffoneries* had come out of Miss French's own money, as well as the shiny black braid lovingly sewn on by hand in a complicated scroll down the front of the overskirt of the blue and tan *polonaise* frock which they put together from two of Clare's. It wasn't everyone who could wear the trying *polonaise* or *princesse* style, which required a faultless carriage and form. Miss French knew that Dinah, hopelessly thin by Clare's robust standard of beauty, would soon have the fashionable Lent lily figure — what the French call *fausse maigre,* and which could wear anything.

Besides the blue *polonaise,* Dinah had for best an embroidered white voile with rose-colored ribbons and a fitted lace jacket, and the gossamer bow under her chin was always of an indescribable freshness, because it was made of the finest materials Miss French could buy. Dinah supposed that the money for these fragile accessories came of an interview Miss French had had with the Earl before they left the Hall. Only Miss French knew, indignantly, how grudging and insufficient Lord Enstone's response to her request had been — barely enough to provide what had to go underneath. Hats were most difficult of all, because Clare had not had very many to start with. But Archie got wind of this problem and contributed a pound, which was spent for a fresh wing and some ribbon, and Dinah, who discovered she liked learning to sew, achieved a very fair copy of a model in *The Queen*. To go with the voile they dressed up a discarded white brimmed shape of Clare's with tulle rosettes and one of her presentation feathers dyed pink.

Bracken perceived that Dinah regarded Miss French now as a friend rather than as a governess, and so he took notice of her in his easy way, which enslaved the dear soul still further. She began to feel that she simply couldn't bear it if, when her time came to go on to the next family — a spectre that lurks at every governess's elbow — she couldn't see Dinah safely into the care of this lighthearted, open-handed, understanding gentleman from New York. Miss French had her own opinion of Clare's choice, but it didn't trouble her much for she had never liked Clare, even in the schoolroom. She considered, with a defiant lack of charity, that Clare deserved Mortimer Flood. But to see Dinah sacrificed to a similar *mariage de convenance* would, she was sure, half kill her.

Victoria celebrated her eightieth birthday that summer at Windsor, and Flying Fox, the favorite, won the Derby, and at The Hague the Peace Conference was sitting — delegates from twenty-five Sovereign States of the civilized world, convened to discuss "the mitigation, at least, if not the abolition of war." The humors of the deliberations were somewhat grim, as when one of the Committees solemnly ruled by a large majority that the dum-dum bullet must be prohibited. In other quarters the opinion was expressed that the only practical guarantee of peace was the perfection of engines of destruction, and that a submarine boat which could blow up whole fleets with impunity would make maritime nations far more amiable to each other than any veto upon armaments. And Bracken wrote an article for the *Star* based on the assertion that the Conference would do better to concern itself, not with the conduct of war, but with its causes.

He had scarcely been surprised to learn that Lisl had by now disappeared from Biarritz with Serrano, making it impossible to serve the papers. Spurred on by Bracken's language, Partridge in an effort to save time applied to the judge in chambers for substitute service, and this was finally granted. Feeling that now they were getting some place, Bracken had a gala dinner at his club with a bottle of wine, all by himself, and wrote the news to his Cousin Sally at Cannes.

Within the week, near the end of a rather trying day at the Fleet Street office, Bracken's secretary came in and, carefully concealing his own surprise, said that a lady who gave her name as Mrs. Murray was waiting to see him. As Bracken described it later to Eden, the bottom dropped out of his stomach and Lisl walked in at the door.

He looked at her silently across the room, conscious of a faint surprise that she was really so beautiful, except — he had noticed it before — her nose was a little too sharp. She was tall, with a magnificent figure which managed not to seem heavy. She was dressed as always somewhat lavishly with a great deal of lace and ribbon and feathers. But whereas during the time she had lived as his wife in New York it had been in the best of a deliberately ornate taste, now it was sheer low Parisian gaudiness. She was dressed, he found himself thinking in that electric moment before either of them spoke, like a fairly high-class madam. Always sleek and confident to the point of felinity, she had now a subtle additional insolence, daring him. And while the familiar, exotic scent she had always used eddied towards him, there was something about her that he missed, without at first defining it. Then he realized that she wasn't wearing any diamonds. He saw with a still further and separate small surprise that even her ears, which had always been pierced for earrings, were bare of ornament.

"It is not a ghost, Bracken," she said, and he heard again with renewed aversion the slurred *r* in his name as she spoke it with the old mocking affection and the same clever smile, as though she had read your thoughts and found them indecorous. "You do not see things. It is Lisl. Have you forgotten already?"

He had come slowly to his feet behind the desk, making no gesture of greeting, no effort to return the smile.

"We have been looking for you," he said grimly.

"So? Well, I have turned up, like the penny. But perhaps I interrupt? I can wait. You take me to dinner, yes?"

"No," he said bluntly. "If this is absolutely necessary let's get it over." And he indicated the visitor's chair beside his desk.

"Ah, but how good it is to see one of your towering tempers again!" she sighed. "And I am dying for one of your cigarettes, too."

He noticed as she took it from his proffered case that her gloves were not clean. She had never used to wear a pair but once. He knew that his silence made it difficult for her, and did not speak. When he had held the match she sank gracefully into the chair, and he resumed his own and waited.

"There is no one in the world who can be angry as well as you can, Bracken," she remarked, two little jets of smoke coming out of her thin nostrils. Her curving painted lips left a red mark on the cigarette. "Even in a rage you are always a gentleman. This is an art I can appreciate. But you had many arts, Bracken." Her smile was knowing and intimate, her eyes met his boldly.

"I haven't time now to hear about my

accomplishments," he said. "You must have something more important on your mind. Let's come to the point."

"Ah, yes, you have the right to be angry," she conceded graciously. "But you were always big-hearted, Bracken. You always forgave me."

"I've had time to change," he reminded her briefly.

"You have had time to fall in love again, yes?"

"You rather cured me of that, Lisl."

She leaned forward, watching him.

"There is no one? In all this time?"

"Why should you care?"

"I do care. Because now I know what I threw away."

"Bit late, isn't it?" And then, as she was silent, watching him through the smoke of the cigarette as she had used to do, he added with an edge of impatience, "Why have you come here? What do you want?"

"Perhaps not quite what you think. You would never love me again, would you — not the way it was, though that is something to remember, yes?— but you could be kind, Bracken, as always you were, even when I was wicked. I know now how wrong I was. I am sorry. Let me come back. I will be good."

His incredulous surprise was so intense that it was like a clock ticking in the silent room, while he stared at her. He forced himself to answer sanely a thing he could hardly believe he had heard at all.

"That's impossible," he said, and found his lips were stiff.

"I shan't be any trouble to you now. Bracken — I tell you the truth. It is over with Hutchinson. Long ago. Since then I keep selling things to live — what I got from him, what I had from you — till now it is all gone. Lately I do not live very well. I have time to think — to remember — to regret. I come back to you. I wear sackcloth and ashes, but I am still your wife."

"That is all over too," he said. "And you are not, I think, telling the whole truth. Try again. What really happened?"

She paused to scrutinize him, her eyes full of the open appraisal she gave all men. She thought how well he looked, how fresh — how desirable. His lean, fine hands, so completely in repose, even now, under stress — his lean, long body, so at ease in its chair, so perfectly conditioned — his quiet, expensive clothes, worn with such casualness, his general air of unconcerned well-being — money did that for a man. Money — and love of a woman, to give him that ingrained indifference to all women but the one. She revised her plans a little.

"Well, you will get it out of me," she shrugged. "I make a clean breast. Hutchinson became impossible with his jealous rages. He was a dull man, Bracken, not like you, and clumsy —" Her wide, unembarrassed gaze slid from his eyes to his lips, ran over the breadth of his shoulders, rested on his hands, so that for the first time he stirred uncomfortably and felt the nerves at the back of his neck crisp with disgust. "He was noisy, and he bored me, and he made threats — it was so that I had no friends — I had to have peace — I had to save myself. So there was a man from the Argentine — young, handsome, so amusing — not rich — but very in love with me. I went with him."

"Mm-hm. Then what?"

"Wherever we went, Hutchinson came. I do not know how he did it, he bought detectives, I think. Always he followed. He did nothing, he was just there, and he watched. We tried everything to lose him. No. Finally it got on poor Jorge's nerves. He could not stand the watching. Even behind a locked door. Jorge could feel him — watching. So now Jorge is gone. With him go all my jewels. I have nothing. I make a mistake in Jorge, you see.''

''I see. And why not go back to Hutchinson instead of me?''

''I am afraid.''

He laughed.

''You aren't afraid of the devil!''

''That was once, maybe. Now I have been ill. I have been lonely and sad. I think of you all the time. I am penitent. I come home.''

''No, I'm afraid you don't do anything of the kind,'' he said quietly. ''I'm through, Lisl. You know that.''

If she had raged at him in the old way now, if she had tried to browbeat him, he could have hated her in the old way and been done with it. But when she began to wheedle, he felt a little sick.

''I don't think you quite understand, Bracken. I come on my knees to you. I was foolish. I was wicked. I was mad. Not now. Ah, Bracken, I make no nuisance of myself, I promise. I ask no questions, I make no claims. I know I have no right to these things any more. I ask very little, really — yes?'' Watching him narrowly, she shifted her attack once more. ''Well, then, if not under your roof — you have, perhaps, a little *ménage?* — then a simple place somewhere of my own, here in England where one feels so safe. You can afford that, yes? You will not miss the money — say, twenty thousand pounds? And so I make no trouble.''

"So that's it,'' he said, beginning to see.

"You would not like it to be known here in London that your wife is in want?'' she suggested softly, with her curving smile, almost as though she spoke words of love. "You would not like to have your wife go on the streets here — yes?''

With his eyes holding hers, he reached for the telephone and called Partridge's number.

"I have here in my office,'' he said clearly into the mouthpiece when Partridge answered, "a woman calling herself my wife who is unfortunately still entitled to use my name. She has just put it to me that if I give her twenty thousand pounds it will be unnecessary for her to go on the streets. Is that blackmail or isn't it?''

"Well, no, not quite,'' said Partridge cautiously. "Oh, dear, I'm afraid we shall have to cope with that. But you must not make appointments to see her alone —''

"I made no appointment to see her and I am not inclined to call in the office-boy as chaperon,'' Bracken cut in. "She is here. What do I do now?''

"Get her address, first of all. Has she a lawyer?''

"Shouldn't think so.''

"Tell her I will see her here tomorrow at three. Make it seem as though we were considering the payment of at least part of her demand. You are not to be present. Get rid of her now as fast as you can, and don't see her again."

"That's easy to say," said Bracken.

"And I had better see you before I see her."

"Dine with me, then. Seven o'clock tonight, at the club."

Partridge promised to be there, and Bracken hung up. He asked Lisl for her address, and wrote down the number in a dingy Bloomsbury street. "Lodgings?" he asked.

"Yes. Not very nice ones."

"You'll find my lawyer in the Middle Temple," he said, handing her the name and address on a slip of paper. "Go to see him there tomorrow at three. He secured evidence at Biarritz for divorce, which I intend to use as soon as possible. I will of course make some provision for your support." He rose and crossed the room to the door. "I have an engagement now. Please excuse me." He stood with his hand on the doorknob, waiting.

For a moment he thought she would not go. She sat looking at him from across the room, and her eyes had gone cold and unwinking, like a cobra's. Even without the mention of divorce, there was something in the look of him as he stood there by the door, the man she had once possessed with all his young ardor and loyalty, that told her quite plainly that now he belonged to some one else. It was not just that his love for her was ended. Somehow in his easy, confident carriage in the face of her proposals, in his added maturity, in his cool aloofness which could afford courtesy instead of anger, she read his love for some one else. But it was not Bracken she hated for that. It was the other woman.

She rose and walked towards him slowly, with her long, feline step, and he opened the door to the clatter of the outer office where a dozen people were at work.

"I shall find out who she is," she said, looking into his eyes, and went.

Bracken more or less felt his way back to his chair and sat for a while, staring blindly at the top of the desk where the pad lay with the Bloomsbury address written on it. Then he tore off the top page, put it into his coat pocket, took his hat and left the office.

Outside a fine drizzle was falling, and the air was warm and heavy. Bracken walked westward, unaware, along Fleet Street and the Strand, his hat still in his hand because he had forgotten to put it on. People glanced twice at his white face as he passed, crossing-sweepers paused to stare after him, cabbies pulled up sharply to miss him by inches, a policeman put out a hand and saved him from going under a brewer's team — he was unaware. Somewhere inside him a hammer was pounding — *let me come back — I am still your wife — I am penitent — you can afford that, yes? — I shall find out who she is* — I SHALL FIND OUT WHO SHE IS. . . .

Westward along the Strand he walked in the drizzle, past Charing Cross, into Pall Mall, through the corner of St. James's Square to King Street — bare-headed, unseeing, homing by instinct till he came to Ryder Street. Meakins, his manservant, opened the door to him, saying words still madder than anything he had heard from Lisl —

"Lady Dinah has been waiting half an hour, sir."

"Here?"

"In the drawing-room, sir. Might I suggest that you change your coat, sir? It's raining."

Bracken gave Meakins his hat, passed a hand across his hair, and turned silently towards the closed drawing-room door.

"I beg pardon, sir, but you hadn't ordered dinner for tonight. Shall I —?"

"No. I'm dining out. Not dressing. You may go."

"Thank you, sir."

Bracken opened the drawing-room door. Dinah was sitting in a corner of the divan, looking frightened.

6

The afternoon had begun badly in St. James's Square.

Miss French had one of her headaches and was lying down. Clare was having a luncheon for her bridesmaids, but the two youngest, Dinah and the younger Miss Norton-Leigh, were not expected to come because they weren't out yet, and therefore were considered only one degree higher than the flower-girl, who was seven years old. Evelyn Norton-Leigh was only fifteen, and gushed. Dinah disliked her, and felt degraded to be paired with her.

Alone in the schoolroom at the top of the house, waiting for her luncheon tray to come up, Dinah set her music-boxes out in a row and began to play them one by one. She had just got to the newest one, with its life-like trilling bird, when a voice behind her said,

"Boo! You never thought you'd see *me* today, did you! Oh, what's that? Let me see!"

Dinah's hand had gone behind her instinctively as she whirled to face Evelyn Norton-Leigh, whose idea of a joke was always to creep up on one unexpectedly. Evelyn made a grab and caught her wrist and snatched the silver box out of her fingers.

"It's a *music-box!* Oh, what fun, how does it work?"

"Give it back, Evelyn, you'll break it!"

"No, I won't, how do you start it? Oh, how *marvelous!*" By accident Evelyn's thumb had found the catch and the bird came up and began to whistle.

"Please, Evelyn, I'm always terrified he'll get caught! Let me have it!"

"Oh, *look,* you've got *lots* of them! Is that one *gold?* I never saw these before, where did you get them? Let's play them *all!*"

"I'd rather not," said Dinah desperately. "I don't play them very often, I just — hadn't anything else to do. Luncheon will be up in a minute. Are you going to stay?"

"Yes, all afternoon, isn't that marvelous?" Evelyn had set one of the other boxes tinkling. Then, still holding the silver one recklessly at an angle so that the flap which covered the grid hung ajar and all the works were upside down, she went on down the line till she had them all going — one for each Christmas and birthday and the bird was extra. "Oh, but none of them is as adorable as the bird!" she cried, and pressed the catch again. "Look, he even moves his wings and his beak when he sings!"

Dinah tried again to capture the box in Evelyn's hand, but Evelyn dodged out of reach, and since her consuming desire was to be one of the whispering, laughing group of older girls down stairs she seized the first excuse.

"I *must* show this one to Rosalind! The girls will simply *love* it! I *made* Rosalind let me come along to have lunch with you today for a surprise, and I'm *so* glad, I never *dreamed* you had anything as lovely as this!"

"No, Evelyn, please don't take it down there, I'd much rather you didn't —" Dinah followed helplessly to the top of the stairs, but Evelyn had already reached the flight below and scampered on, Dinah reluctantly at her heels. "It will run down, Evelyn, please give it back to me —"

They arrived breathless at the drawing-room door and Evelyn had all the other girls around her instantly, exclaiming over the whistling bird.

"Where did you get it?" Clare was asking,

and Evelyn said carelessly, "It's Dinah's. Hadn't you seen it?"

"Where did you get it, Dinah?" said Clare, and the girls, sensing tension, all turned to look at Dinah who had paused in the doorway.

"Bracken gave it to me."

"Bracken *Murray?*" squealed Evelyn's sister Rosalind. "That good-looking *American?* Well, I must say, Dinah, you do fly high!"

"Did he give you all the rest of them too?" demanded Evelyn. "She has lots more up stairs, there's even a gold one, but I like this the best. Fancy you not *knowing,* Clare, she tried to hide it from me too!"

Clare took the silver box out of Evelyn's hand.

"How long have you had this, Dinah?"

"He brought it back from America. It's just a gift."

Clare was looking at her coldly. Clare had had no gifts from Bracken, except a wedding present, but he seemed determined to spoil Dinah and turn her head. Or was it possible that he — Old jealousy stirred in Clare, and —

"Luncheon is served, my lady," said a powdered footman into the ominous silence.

"You and Evelyn run along up stairs, Dinah. I'll keep the music-box, I want to show it to Edward."

"Oh, please, Clare, it belongs to me! Bracken gave it to *me* —"

"Rather too expensive a gift, I'm afraid. We'll see what Edward says. Now run along, you two, I'll send for you later."

Nearly all the music-boxes had run down when they got back to the schoolroom. Dinah wouldn't allow them to be wound up again, but put them away in a cupboard and made Evelyn sit down to lunch.

"Well, I'm sorry if I made trouble," Evelyn remarked, obviously not sorry a bit. "But how was *I* to know you had secrets with Bracken Murray!"

"Oh, shut up, Evelyn, it wasn't a secret, it started as a sort of joke at Hamley's when I was a child, and he's just gone on sending them. I never thought what they cost, and I don't suppose he did either, he's got lots of money."

"What ever happened between him and Clare? Rosalind was *sure* Clare was going to land him once!"

"Perhaps he just wasn't in love with her."

"*Me-ow!*" said Evelyn, and laughed maliciously. "Well, I'd a lot rather have him than Mortimer Flood, and I bet Clare would too! Honestly, how she *can!* But I do think it would be very exciting to be kissed by Bracken Murray, don't you?''

''Is that all you think of when you see a man?'' Dinah asked sarcastically.

''Well, not *all!*'' Evelyn giggled. ''Bracken Murray is nice and thin, I'd hate a *soft* man, wouldn't you? I wonder who's going to get him finally? You'd better hurry up and come out, if you were fixed up a little, who knows! Some men *like* very young girls, and if he's given you all these presents it must mean something!''

''Oh, do stop it, Evelyn, he's known me ever since I was fifteen!'' Tears stood in Dinah's eyes. ''He's always been very kind to me, and we're friends, that's all, and I hope we always will be.''

''Do you let him hold your hand?''

''*No!* I mean, such a thing would never occur to him! And I think this is a perfectly beastly conversation and it's time we changed the subject!''

''Why, I do believe you're *blushing!*'' Evelyn cried, eyeing her cruelly. ''My goodness, Dinah, it's nothing to be *ashamed* of, I'd be wildly in love with him if he ever so much as *looked* at me! Those shoulders! And I like clean-shaven men, don't you, not so *scratchy!* Dinah, you *are* blushing, are you going to try to make him fall in love with you?''

''I wouldn't dream of such a thing and neither would he,'' said Dinah steadily, but her palms were wet. ''Have you been for another fitting? How do you think the hats are going to look? Mine is too big —''

She had no sooner got rid of Evelyn, who stayed for tea, than a footman came up to say that his lordship would like to see her in the library.

This meant Edward, because their father was still in the country — Lord Enstone hated London and had announced firmly that he would come up for the day of the wedding and give away the bride and would return to Gloucestershire the day after, and they could just get on with it. As she descended on the left of the curving double staircase which led down to the black-and-white marble tiled hall, Dinah was wishing that it had been her father instead of Edward. Lord Enstone was an indifferent disciplinarian and always got bored immediately after an interview began and one was likely to get off lightly because anything else was too much trouble. But Edward took himself seriously and behaved with pompous severity when one was called on the carpet by him. It came of having to handle all the people on the farms and so on.

He was inclined to treat everybody like a recalcitrant tenant who made a habit of leaky roofs. Dinah resented being bullied, and it always made her feel like fighting back, which wouldn't do, and so she was forced to take refuge in a blank-faced docility much more infuriating to her brother than tears or temper would have been.

Alwyn was sitting behind the sumptuous Empire desk with its green blotter and silver inkstand when Dinah entered the library. The music-box was in front of him, the bird invisible and mute.

Dinah closed the door behind her and approached the desk slowly, struggling for courage. Her hands were damp and cold, her knees shook, her tongue was dry. If he tried to take the music-box away from her she was going to make a scene. It was hers. It was part of the collection.

"Sit down, Dinah," said Alwyn, glancing up at her without a smile, and fixing his gaze again on the box while she crept silently into a chair at the end of the desk facing him. "How long has this been going on?"

"The music-boxes? He bought one at Hamley's for my sixteenth birthday. That was the first."

"How many has he given you?"

"One for each birthday and Christmas

since then — and this one.''

''But surely you realize a thing like this is much too valuable a gift for you to accept from him!''

''Well, I — he said about the first one that it didn't matter what it cost. This one was a — just a gift from America. I knew he had a lot of money —''

''Whether he can afford it or not is not the point. He's a married man, you know that. I told you myself.''

''He says — eventually there will be a divorce and — he will be free to marry again.''

''And you're fool enough to believe that? Now, once and for all, Dinah, I won't have you mucking about with a married man! It would spoil your chances to make a good marriage like Clare's, for one thing.''

''I don't want to make a marriage like Clare's.''

''You could do worse, you know. Besides, you'll never have Clare's looks, you might as well make up your mind to that! In any case, this Murray business is finished, do you understand? You will return the music-boxes to him, all of them, at once.''

''B-but what could I *say*, he —''

''Say? You know damn' well what to say! Tell him I have forbidden you to keep them, if you like.''

Dinah was trembling all over now, so that she was afraid he would see.

''Oh, but Edward, it's not like that at all, I can't think why you —''

''I suppose he's made love to you?'' He turned his stone-grey eyes on her, took note of her chalky face and the hands twisted together in her lap till the knuckles stood out. ''Just like his cheek to take advantage of you! I suppose you've let him kiss you. What about the governess? Is she in on this too, or just a fool? Where do you see him? In the woods? Have you ever been to his chambers here in Town? Well, answer me!'' And because she was silent and kept her eyes on her locked hands in her lap, he feared the worst. ''Speak up, now, and tell me what's going on here. Or shall I shake the truth out of him?''

''*No, no,* don't ever *dare* speak to him!'' Dinah was on her feet, and her voice rose in the high, quiet room. ''I shall *die* of shame if you say anything like this to him! I'm so *humiliated* to think my own brother could say such things, or *think* such things about a man like Bracken! You're *vile,* Edward, vile and nasty, to suggest there's anything *going on* between Bracken and me! We're *friends,* don't you know there is such a thing? He's good and kind and gentle, and he has a sense of humor and we laugh — *you* wouldn't know why we laugh — all you can think of is beastliness and filth! You aren't fit to black Bracken's boots, and if you do say any of this to his face I only hope he knocks you down!'' She snatched the silver box from the desk in front of him and made for the door.

''One minute, I haven't finished yet!'' His voice snapped after her, and she leaned against the inside of the door, sick and sobbing, clinging to the knob. ''Clare says it will spoil the looks of her wedding if you aren't present,'' her brother's hard, well-modulated tones went on. ''The day after the ceremony, however, you will return to the Gloucestershire house and stay there, incommunicado, until you come to your senses. You will leave all the music-boxes here and I'll have them packed and returned to him. In the meantime, I shall engage a new governess. Miss French has been lax, to say the least. Ask her to come down, I want to talk to her.''

''She's lying down with a headache.''

''I can't help that, I want this thing settled without delay. Tell her I'm waiting.''

While Miss French was taking her turn in the library, Dinah wrote a note to leave on the schoolroom mantelpiece:

Dear Miss French —

They're sending me back to Gloucestershire the day after the wedding and I must see Bracken once more, so I am going round to his chambers now to wait. It's nearly time for him to come back from the office. If they ask for me while I am away, please say that I have gone to bed and try to keep them out. He'll walk home with me, so I shall be quite all right, even if it should be after dark. Please help me, I must try and make him understand what has happened. It will be difficult for any sane person to believe.

DINAH

Then she put on the hat with the brave little wing, and slipped out of the house and round the corner to Ryder Street. It was beginning to drizzle and she had brought no umbrella, so she ran for the doorway and arrived there quite breathless. Bracken's man, about to depart for his evening off, let her in with barely concealed surprise and invited her to wait in the drawing-room, as Mr. Murray wouldn't be long now.

7

Dinah stood up as Bracken closed the door behind him, but her natural impulse to take refuge in his arms was blurred and frustrated by Alwyn's accusations. So she stayed where she was, across the room from him, and stammered.

"Oh, Bracken, I know I s-shouldn't have come here like this, p-please don't be angry with me, I had to see you!"

"Angry? Of course not, you're upset about something. What is it?" He came to her and took both her hands, felt how clammy they were and enclosed them comfortingly in his. But Dinah, confused and self-conscious for the first time, snatched them away and retreated to the other side of the divan, which brought Bracken very sharply into focus for he saw that something really serious had happened to her.

"I've had the most awful time with Edward," she was saying almost inaudibly. "I d-don't know how to tell you, but — they suddenly discovered the music-boxes, and then everybody went mad, I think."

"Discovered them?" he repeated, at sea.

"Miss French knew I had them, and so did Archie. But Clare and Edward didn't. Clare said they were too expensive for me to keep, and — and then Edward sent for me to the library, and — said the most horrible things — about us — about you and me." At that point, realizing that she had come to Bracken's chambers after all, and was alone with him there, shaken in her confidence of what such a thing might mean, and still aware of the warmth of his hands which had briefly taken hers, Dinah felt color flaming up in her face and hid it from his with a gasp of shame.

The clock ticked noticeably before Bracken spoke.

"What did Edward say?" he asked quietly, refraining with an effort from any movement towards her.

"I can't — I'd rather not —"

"Tell me what he said, Dinah. You'll feel better if you do. You know we can always say what we like to each other, why should you mind?"

With her back to him, she began haltingly —

"He said it was too valuable a gift for me to accept —"

"Perhaps I should have thought of that myself. What else?"

"He — said he wouldn't have me m-mucking about with a married man — because it would spoil my chances to make a good m-marriage —"

"Anything else?"

"He said I must return all the music-boxes to you, and — and —"

"Come on, Dinah, let's have it all."

"He — thought you'd been making love to me. He asked — if you'd kissed me —"

"You answered him on that, I hope!"

"But you had! That morning on the hill when you came back —"

"Oh, Lord!"

"He seemed to — to think I had come here to your rooms — alone — and now I *have!*"

"I'm very glad you have, too. Come and sit down quietly and let's get this straightened out."

Dinah looked at him, where he stood motionless by main force across the room, and at the divan beside him. Waves of embarrassment and shock eddied through her, complicated by Evelyn's frank remarks about him as a man. Dinah sat down on the edge of the nearest chair.

Full of pity and understanding, choosing every word and move with the greatest caution, Bracken perched casually on the arm of the rejected divan and said, without heat, "I'd like to knock Edward's head off, first of all."

"He's going to sack Miss French and send me back to Gloucestershire with a new governess directly after the wedding. This was my only chance to see you and explain —" She choked.

"Well, it isn't the way I wanted to say this," he began easily from the arm of the divan, "but I guess the time has come. We have got the evidence and a grant of substitute service, and my divorce is going through, I think. So if you'll just be patient and put up with Edward a little longer, I can ask you to marry me. Will that help?"

"Me?" said Dinah, on the merest breath of sound. "Ask — *me* — to —?"

"Well, who else would I be asking, hm?" he said sensibly.

"But — that morning on the hill when I said would you marry again and you said you hoped so — was that *me?*"

"It was."

"I — never even —"

"I'm probably breaking all the laws of the Kingdom to mention it, and of course we shall have to wait out the *decree nisi*. But anyway now I shan't have any this-is-so-sudden nonsense out of you, shall I? You'll have had a chance to get used to the idea gradually. And how does it strike you — as an idea?"

"Oh, *yes,* Bracken, but — I just can't — believe —"

"Why on earth are you so surprised? I've done everything I could to let you know!"

"I thought we were just friends. I — you haven't done anything — I mean, you've never — m-made love to me —"

"I've been a little handicapped." Without rising from the divan, he held out his arms. "Shall I begin now?"

For the first time since he had come in, Dinah smiled. He stood up carefully, and waited where he was while she came to him across the room, and then caught her close, for he could not have borne it another moment if she had not come.

"Bracken, your coat is *sopping!* You'll catch cold!"

"What? Oh — coat. Yes, I walked home. It is a bit damp, isn't it. You stay right here — don't move — I'll change it."

He was gone only a minute. When he

returned, shrugging into a coat from another suit which did not quite match his trousers, she was sitting in the corner of the divan again and the look she gave him was full of confidence and expectation. He sat down beside her, found the pin and took off her hat as though he had done the same thing a good many times before. With his arm around her shoulders she settled back against him with the utmost simplicity, saying, "How long will it have to be, Bracken? What does *decree nisi* mean?"

"Means I daren't move hand or foot for six months for fear of the Queen's Proctor."

"Who is he?"

"His job is to snoop round and see if he can catch me making love to somebody else before the divorce becomes final. If he can, he has the power to call the whole thing off. It's all very complicated, but the whole idea is to discourage everyone from even attempting to get a divorce."

Dinah counted on her fingers.

"But if you got the decree thingummy tomorrow it would last till Christmas!" she cried in dismay.

"And I shan't get it tomorrow. Not for weeks yet. It's probably just as well, because you're much too young to decide like this. Suppose in five years' time when you've seen something of the world some fellow should turn up that you like better than me?''

''There isn't any such fellow.''

''I sincerely hope there isn't.'' His arm tightened. ''But it is a risk, you know.''

''I wasn't going to marry at all, no matter what they said. But with you it will be all right,'' she said contentedly, her cheek pressed against the rough tweed of his coat.

''I shouldn't wonder if all girls feel sometimes that they'd rather not marry,'' he said thoughtfully. ''I certainly wouldn't blame them if they did. But most of them seem to outgrow it without my help.''

''You're quite wrong, Bracken, all the girls I know are dying to know what it's like. I get very embarrassed sometimes, at the things they say. Only this afternoon Evelyn Norton-Leigh was talking about you and she said —'' Dinah stopped suddenly on the brink of the abyss. But now, instead of blushing, she only wanted to laugh.

''About me? Do I know her?''

''Rosalind's sister. She's only fifteen.''

''Mm-hm. What did she say about me?''

Dinah shifted against his shoulder so that she could look up at him. She still wanted to laugh, now that she was here with him, so safe and so *usual,* and the events of the afternoon had already begun to seem like sheer nightmare from which he had wakened her with his voice and his reassuring presence.

"Evelyn said she thought it would be very exciting to be kissed by you," she reported solemnly.

"Oh, Dinah, have mercy —" He bent his head. Her lips were cool and closed and very ready. "I think I had better take you home now," he said, and then lingered to kiss her eyes and her hair. "Shall I come in and punch Edward's nose for him?"

But Dinah sat still, leaning against him, full of new sensations she was unwilling to part with. Her eyelids were drowsy from his lips, and she smiled. He smelled of tobacco and shaving soap and fresh air. His arms were hard and comforting, and she had a strange, floating feeling of being carried by unlimited strength, with nothing to worry about ever again.

"Tell me what you're thinking," he whispered, awed by her acceptance of his love-making, her sublime lack of shyness or surprise.

"You *feel* so heavenly," said Dinah, and she put an arm around his neck, pulling herself closer to him, burying her face against his chest as naturally as a kitten makes itself comfortable in familiar hands. "I was just wishing I never had to move from here again,'' she said.

He was silent, taking this in.

''Bracken.''

''Yes, sweetheart?''

''I — oh, say that again!''

He said it again.

''I just want to see Edward's face now, that's all!'' Dinah continued. ''He's never even thought of your wanting to marry *me*.''

''Yes, he has, and that's what's the matter with him! I told him I was going to, the night of the fancy dress ball.''

''You *did?*'' In her astonishment Dinah sat straight up to gaze at him. ''I remember — I was on the stairs. He looked so funny, I knew you'd said something, but I never dreamed — Oh, Bracken, 'way back then, did you —?''

''I have been in love with you, nobody else, ever since Thunderbolt dumped you at that gate. Remarkable, isn't it! When you were fifteen, it was even slightly improper. Don't you think I've behaved very well, on the whole?''

''Edward will never believe that, now,'' Dinah said.

''Do we care?''

Dinah came the nearest to a giggle he had ever seen her.

"Isn't it odd, Edward doesn't matter any more! When I came here I thought you'd be furious with him! I told him if he said any of those things to you I hoped you'd knock him down! But it doesn't really matter, does it!"

"Well, I don't say it wouldn't be a pleasure. Dinah, darling — I've got to know this. Shall you mind coming to America to live — some day?"

"I'd live in a tent in a desert if you were there."

After a moment's silent struggle he said, "It isn't quite as bad as that in New York. And now I must take you home, you know, this really won't do. Put your hat on, and I'll find mine." He loosed his arms and rose reluctantly and stood watching while she pinned on her hat in front of the mantelpiece mirror.

She followed him into the little foyer and as he set his hand on the doorknob he felt a tug at his sleeve.

"Bracken. Please kiss me like that again before we go."

Bracken obliged. And then, because his heart was choking him —

"What *would* Edward say?" he asked lightly, caught up his hat, and swept a bemused and radiant Dinah through the open door into the passage.

It was quite dusky in the street, and the rain had stopped. Bracken wanted to go home with her and tell Edward where to head in, but she insisted that she could slip upstairs without being seen, and anyway, she didn't mind anything now. But when the reached the corner of the Square she hung back. A carriage had stopped in front of the house and people in evening dress were getting out.

"Oh, bother!" said Dinah. "People coming to early dinner. It's a theater party tonight. Couldn't I stay with you until about eight-thirty and then they'd all be gone and I could get in without meeting anybody."

"Won't you be missed?" he asked doubtfully.

"I left a note for Miss French. She won't worry, so long as I'm with you."

"You'll get awfully hungry," he suggested.

"I'm hungry now. I couldn't eat any tea. Isn't there some place we could dine, like a tea-shop, where we wouldn't know anybody?"

"I suppose there are such places," he said, running his mind over Soho, where friends of Clare's would never be.

"Oh, please, Bracken, it would be such fun, and we may never have another chance like this!"

"We'll have lots of chances," he reminded her with amusement. "All the rest of our lives!"

"But not for *weeks,* Bracken, and it will be so long before I even see you again! After Miss French goes I shall probably have some gorgon that will even read my letters!"

"The woman tempted me," he murmured resignedly, and hailed a passing hansom and gave the name of a little French restaurant where he hoped he would not see anybody he knew. "We really ought to collect Miss French and take her along," he said with a last twinge of conscience as the cab turned the corner away from the Square.

"We can't get at her," Dinah said with some satisfaction. "I can't get in and she can't get out — not without being questioned. Not till after they've all gone to the theater. Anyway, she'll think we are having dinner there in your rooms, and that would be proper, wouldn't it, with your man serving it?"

"It would have been simpler, at least. But I let him go as soon as I came in." Bracken recalled suddenly that Partridge would be waiting at the club to dine with him, and decided that it was too late now, and gave himself up to the enjoyment of this unexpected windfall of Dinah's company, as she said gravely,

"Is there any way to save Miss French?"

"From getting the sack? Not if Edward's got the bit between his teeth!"

"It's our fault," said Dinah only.

"You're very fond of her, aren't you," he observed, and Dinah nodded without speaking and he saw that her eyes were full. "Then we'll save her," he said. "*After* he fires her."

"How?" She looked at him with a faint hopefulness. "She'll have to get another job as soon as she can. She had a sister who was ill for years and so Miss French wasn't able to put any of her money in the bank. She had to use it all. And she isn't — young, any more. I really don't know what will happen to her if she has to go, it's something I just — can't bear to think about."

"What do you think I'm here for?" said Bracken. "I'll buy her for you."

"Now, Bracken —!" She was half vexed that he should joke about it.

"It might look better if we called her a housekeeper after you're married, though."

"You mean I could have her *then?*"

"Why not?"

"Bracken, honestly, if I suddenly said Please give me the earth, would you say Why not?"

"Why not?" said Bracken, and took her hands. "Sweetheart, with me you are going to have the earth — as much of it as you can use. It's not considered good form to talk about money — is it. But mine was honestly made. I'm not ashamed of it. And they say money can't buy happiness. It's usually the people who haven't got it who say that. Sour grapes, Dinah. People can be happy without it, I don't say they can't. But with it, they can be happier."

Dinah sat looking down at her own hands held fast in his. Quite deliberately she raised them, and his, and he felt her lips and her tears on his fingers.

"Nobody ever loved anybody the way I'm going to love you," she said.

"Oh, God above, Dinah, it's such a *little* thing! Wait till I really get started!"

"It's not a little thing. It's Miss French's whole life. And to think I was almost afraid to mention it for fear —"

"For fear of what?" The words came almost sharply in his anxiety.

"The most I — thought of — was that you might be willing to give her a few pounds to — to sort of tide her over till she found something. And I was afraid —"

"Afraid of what?" he insisted.

"Well, it was because of something

Mortimer Flood said once — about Clare.''
She paused unhappily, and Bracken said,
"What was that?"

"He said — he meant to be funny, of
course, when he said it — and he said,
'Good God, the woman has begun to spend
my money before there's anything in it for
me!' And Clare blushed, and Edward sort of
snorted, and Father laughed, but I don't think
he liked it. Mr. Flood didn't seem to realize
that he'd said anything."

Bracken was silent so long that she looked
at him uncertainly.

"Have I made some kind of — mistake?"
she asked.

"Yes," he said slowly, and saw the
bewilderment in her face. "You were
afraid."

"I don't — know what you mean."

"And you are still afraid," he said, for her
eyes were wide and dark, and her lips not
quite steady. "Of me," he added without
emphasis. "I'm trying to think how I
deserved that."

Swiftly under his grave regard she rallied,
and began to smile. Her fingers curled closer
inside his.

"You don't deserve it," she said, "and I
apologize. I should have known I could ask
you straight out. I should have said —

Bracken, we must look after Miss French. Would that do?''

''Perfectly. Just kindly remember hereafter that you aren't marrying anybody named Flood.''

She leaned back luxuriously in the cab, her shoulder against his.

''I never thought I'd look forward to marriage!'' she sighed contentedly.

''And yet you find you do?'' he queried, smiling.

''Now that I find it's going to be you, I can't wait!''

''Of course you realize your father and Edward are going to raise Cain,'' he remarked.

''They can't stop us, can they?''

''Until you're of age, they can. Even then, the clergy will snub us because of the divorce. Shall you mind being married in a register office?''

''So long as it means I can live with you forever after I don't care *where* I'm married!''

''Thank you. Everyone is going to say that you're too young, and make a perfect ogre of me. We're going to be a scandal, Dinah, shall you mind that?''

''Bracken — would *you* rather not?''

''Not marry you? When it's all I've

thought of for years? I want you to know what you're getting into, that's all.''

''Do *you* want to know something, Bracken? Every girl in London, beginning with the Norton-Leighs, is going to wish she was in my shoes! Only this afternoon, Evelyn said that if you ever so much as looked at her she'd be wildly in love with you!''

''I'm glad you warned me,'' he remarked. ''I'll be very careful where I look. What did *you* say?''

''I wanted to kill her then, but now I'm sorry for her — because she isn't in a hansom cab on her way to have dinner with you. And I am. This is me, Dinah, driving down Shaftesbury Avenue with the man I'm going to marry! I'm all full of fireworks and rockets! Does it show?''

''Yes, it does. Most becoming.''

''And that's another thing. Do you think I'll look all right, when I'm fixed up a little? I'll never have Clare's looks, you know. I have to wear ruffles pinned across my front inside my bridesmaid's dress because I haven't got a figure. Maybe I shouldn't tell you that.''

''I might have guessed.''

''Bracken, I'll never be beautiful or clever. Are you sure you're not making a mistake?''

''Quite sure.''

"But I'm not at all the sort of woman I thought you'd marry!"

"What sort was that?" Bracken inquired with interest.

"You ought to have a princess, at least — beautiful and strange."

"But that's what I'm going to have."

She shook her head.

"I'm just me, Bracken."

"Some day — not in a hansom cab — I shall really exert myself, Dinah, and tell you all the things you are to me. Meanwhile, will you just take my word for it that you're everything I want in the world?"

They dined very well and unobserved at a corner table at Antoine's in Compton Street, and Bracken ordered champagne. Dinah said she felt as though they were married already, and Bracken suspected that the waiter was convinced it was a honeymoon.

"I've always wondered what people talked about after they were married," Dinah confessed as the meal went on. "I always thought they must run out of things to say. But now it all looks so *easy!*"

It was nearly ten when they got back to St. James's Square after a roundabout drive home because there was still so much to say. They would not be able to see each other again before she was banished to Gloucestershire,

651

except perhaps a few minutes at the wedding with everybody looking. Bracken was firm against stolen meetings from now on, feeling that he must pull up somewhere until after the divorce became a fact, or at least a *decree nisi*. He had laughed when Partridge cautioned him against becoming Involved, as Partridge put it, with another woman. He had laughed still more when Partridge explained further that by English law one adultery might make a divorce but two cancelled out and no divorce was possible. And it was just that sort of thing, said Partridge gloomily, that the Queen's Proctor dearly loved to ferret out. None of it made any sense. But at least the Queen's Proctor must not be allowed to take an interest in his meetings with Dinah. She might be permitted to see Virginia after she returned to the Hall, and they could send each other letters that way. Virginia would love carrying messages.

Bracken stood at the bottom of the steps and waited till the footman had let her into the house. Then he walked slowly back to Ryder Street, thinking what a day it had been.

As he put his key into the lock a man stepped out of the shadows on his right and said, "Mr. Murray?"

"Yes," said Bracken. "Who are you?"

"Inspector Evans, of Scotland Yard."

"Well, come in!" said Bracken cordially, beyond surprise. "Let's have a drink!"

8

When Bracken had turned on the lights and glanced at the man's card, he said, "Well, Inspector — what's on your mind?"

"I'm afraid it's rather a — difficult subject," said the Inspector delicately, and Bracken stared at him.

"Don't be tactful," he said. "Why have you come to me?"

"Are you aware, Mr. Murray, that a woman calling herself your wife has been living in a Bloomsbury lodging-house?"

"I am since this afternoon," Bracken admitted, while his insides went into a cold, tight knot. "Why?"

"You saw her this afternoon?"

"She came to my office. First I knew she was in England. We — haven't been living together."

"When did she leave your office today?"

"About five, I think it was."

"Did you accompany her?"

"No. I left quite a bit later. Why?"

"Have you seen her since then?"

"No. *Why?*"

"She has been murdered."

There was a silence. Then —

"Let's have that drink," said Bracken, going to the sideboard. As he handed the Inspector his glass he said, "Where and how? Or can't you say? Am I under suspicion?"

"It would be just as well if you can account for your time during the last four hours."

"Well, I can't."

"Can't?"

"Can't. So what's next?"

"I think I'd better warn you, Mr. Murray, that you're putting yourself in rather a serious position."

"Yes. What next?"

"I'm afraid I'll have to ask you to hold yourself available for further questioning."

"I'm afraid you will. Does that mean jail?"

"No," said the Inspector, and added reassuringly, "Oh, no," and left it at that.

"You mean not yet," Bracken suggested. "Mind if I get my solicitor around here before we go any further?"

"No objection to that," said the Inspector.

"You see, just to make it look worse," said Bracken, going to the telephone on the desk, "I had started divorce proceedings. Hullo, I say, Partridge — I'm frightfully sorry I didn't keep that appointment. Would you mind coming round to Ryder Street now? — Well, as a matter of fact, Scotland Yard is here, and I think I'm going to need legal advice. — Thanks very much." He hung up. "Lives in Dover Street. Be here in a few minutes. Do you think in the meantime you could tell me a little more about what has happened?"

"May I ask, Mr. Murray, why you are wearing a coat that doesn't match your trousers?"

"Oh, well, that I can explain. I got wet coming home from the office. Before I went out again in rather a hurry I changed my damp coat without stopping to change my trousers. It's in the other room, in case you want to examine it for bloodstains?"

"We aren't looking for bloodstains. She was strangled."

"In broad daylight?"

"Some time between six and nine P.M."

Bracken looked down at his own right hand, flexing the fingers thoughtfully.

"That wouldn't be easy to do," he said.

"Lisl is — was a tall, extremely able-bodied woman. It would be like tackling a wildcat."

"Unless of course it was some one she knew well," the Inspector suggested quietly. "Some one who could come quite close to her, perhaps take her in his arms, without arousing her suspicions."

Bracken nodded.

"Such as a husband. Yes, I can see that," he said.

There was a silence, while the Inspector sipped his whiskey appreciatively and Bracken sat staring into his own glass.

"Who found her?" he asked then.

"She had struck up an acquaintance with a woman named Levine who lived across the passage — a woman of rather questionable character," said the Inspector apologetically. "Apparently Mrs. Murray had confided in her. She knew that Mrs. Murray intended to see you today, and they had arranged to dine together so that Mrs. Murray could tell her about the interview. She heard Mrs. Murray come in about six o'clock and set her own door ajar to show that she was in and waiting to join her. A little later she heard Mrs. Murray's door open and assumed that she was coming to keep their engagement. Instead, she reached her own door just in time to see Mrs. Murray's door closing behind a man. She saw only his back.''

''Well?'' Bracken queried as the Inspector paused. ''Didn't she listen at the keyhole?''

''Since it appeared to her that Mrs. Murray had company, and she supposed it was yourself, the Levine woman says she went out to a place nearby where they had dined together before. Mrs. Murray did not join her there. When she went back to the house an hour or so later she knocked on Mrs. Murray's door and got no answer. She waited another hour, feeling, she says, vaguely uneasy — knocked again and still got no answer. Then she tried the door, thinking Mrs. Murray might have left a message for her inside. The door was not locked. Mrs. Murray was lying across the sofa, dead.''

''So Levine is ready to put the rope around my neck,'' said Bracken.

''No, it's not as bad as that,'' the Inspector objected mildly. ''But we would like to know —''

''Where I was at the time. No one could blame you for that. The Levine didn't happen to notice whether the man was wearing a coat that didn't quite match his trousers?''

''The passage was quite dark by then. Mrs. Murray's room was lighted. She saw his silhouette — a tall man with broad shoulders.''

"Six feet two, one hundred and eighty-five pounds. Or if you prefer, thirteen stone three."

The Inspector smiled indulgently.

"You needn't take too grim a view, Mr. Murray. Not yet."

"If I had ever wanted to murder my wife, Inspector — and I don't say I never have — I don't think I should have attempted it with my bare hands. Strangling — as I understand it — requires time. It almost requires that the murderer should, as it were, enjoy his work." In spite of himself his shoulders hunched nervously. "I just wouldn't have the guts," he said.

Partridge arrived then and was given a tall tumbler while events were explained to him. Tongue-tied in the presence of the Inspector, he looked guardedly at Bracken, who laughed recklessly and said, "All right, *tell* him! I can't see any sense in trying to be discreet about this thing. I'm in it just about up to my neck! What Mr. Partridge hesitates to mention," he added to the Inspector, "is that I asked him to dine with me at my club to discuss the interview with my wife which took place this afternoon, and then I didn't turn up!"

The Inspector began to look severe.

"I must say, Mr. Murray, you're not

making it easy for us,'' he said disapprovingly.

''Oh? I thought I was. Have another drink?''

''You're making it very easy for him to get a wrong impression, if I may say so,'' Partridge rebuked him. ''Surely you can say where you did have dinner.''

''At a pub in Kensington,'' said Bracken, too promptly.

''Alone?''

''Yes.''

''Is there some one there, such as a barmaid, who could identify you?''

''No.''

''You are not on oath now,'' said Partridge, frowning at him. ''But you may be. Where did you have dinner tonight?''

''Meaning you don't like the pub in Kensington? I'm afraid it's the best I can do.''

''Mr. Murray —'' The Inspector cleared his throat. ''Is it your firm resolve not to account for your whereabouts during those four hours?''

''Nothing firmer.''

And now, for the first time, the shadow of doubt dwelt on the Inspector's face, and Partridge looked quite apprehensive.

''About the divorce,'' said the Inspector.

"You mentioned, didn't you, that you had started proceedings. Was everything in order on that? Were there any hitches?"

"None. The evidence was quite clear against her," Bracken stated definitely.

"The case would have come up after the Long Vacation," said Partridge. "There wasn't much doubt of the verdict. He would have had his freedom. So you see there was no motive."

"But now there isn't any case!" Bracken pointed out wilfully and both of them turned on him looks of grave reproof.

Bracken stood on the hearthrug holding his glass, the evening with Dinah still bubbling in him like champagne, producing in him what seemed to him extraordinary clarity, complete detachment, utter reason, with regard to the fantastic circumstances he faced. He felt no grief for Lisl — only horror at the ugly thing that had happened to her. He did acknowledge a kind of guilt. She had told him she was afraid, and he had dismissed that as part of her game. But it was very fresh in his mind that the last words she spoke to him in the office were an implicit threat to Dinah.

"My dear Partridge — my dear Inspector Evans — can either of you seriously contemplate the possibility of my being such a blithering fool as to murder Lisl now? I'd have everything to lose and nothing to gain! You say yourself I'd have been free in a few months' time. Or do I seem to you the sort of man who could so hate a woman he once loved that he could lose sight of everything else in a brutal desire to choke the life out of her? Do you think perhaps I am not quite sane? Because if I am sane, I am not the man you are looking for! The man you want, Inspector, is the man who still loves her, who cares what she does, or has done in the recent past. A man who might even dread a reconciliation with me, if she came to see me as she did today.''

''Is there such a man?'' the Inspector queried alertly.

''I think there is. Name of Hutchinson. The fellow she left me for, several years ago.''

''Where was he last heard of?''

''That I don't know, except that she told me this afternoon he followed her everywhere she went after she had left him in his turn, for some one else. It seems most likely that he has trailed her to England. She said he had made threats. She said she was afraid of him. I blame myself very bitterly now for not taking her apprehension more seriously. Apparently she had good reason to fear him.''

"Well, that's something to go on with."
The Inspector rose, visibly relieved that
Bracken had been able to offer even this
glimmering hope of a solution which might
absolve himself. "We'll have to try to find
him. Could you identify him?"

"Yes, I could, though I haven't seen him
for three years. He's about my size, but
heavier — grizzled hair and mustache — he's
a Californian, so his speech would be
noticeable here."

The Inspector was writing down notes.

"Well, I think that's all for now, Mr.
Murray. If you will kindly come to my office
tomorrow morning at ten, I'll have the
Levine woman there. I want her to see you,
from behind. And we'll want to go into this
matter of Hutchinson further." He looked
back gravely from the doorway. "We're still
interested in where you were tonight, you
know," he said, and went.

When the door had closed Partridge said
worriedly, "My dear boy, you are asking for
it, you know, with that story about the pub.
What happened?"

"Not even for you, Partridge, will I name
names tonight."

Partridge looked still more worried.

"It is most indiscreet of you to be involved
with another woman just now."

"So you've said, and I didn't mean to be. Indiscreet is a most inadequate word for what I did this evening — and I won't part with it unless they've got me right up there on the gallows!"

"It won't come to that, of course, but —"

"You mean you hope it won't, but you aren't quite sure," Bracken grinned. "Hutchinson is their man. It could be Serrano, or it could be somebody since Serrano, but I'm betting on Hutchinson. Of course if they can't find him, or anybody else but me, it begins to be awkward. But I'm also betting on Scotland Yard. At least they didn't clap me in jail!"

"No," Partridge agreed cautiously. "But don't try to leave town."

"You mean I'm being watched?"

"Sure to be."

"And if I walked out of the house now and went to a railway station I'd be stopped?"

"You would."

Bracken sat down.

"Wherever she is," he said, "Lisl is enjoying this."

9

Dinah and Miss French went for their usual walk in the park the following morning, oppressed by the knowledge that Alwyn was interviewing gorgons in the library, and fortified by Bracken's promise that Miss French would go on his own payroll after Dinah married him.

When Dinah returned home the night before and ran up stairs to the top floor, lightheaded with love and champagne, she had found Miss French lying down in her bedroom which opened off the schoolroom on the opposite side to Dinah's. Miss French had been crying, and the room smelled of the Florida Water she rubbed on her head when it ached. Her only fault, she knew, was that she was a better judge of men than Lord Alwyn, and had trusted Bracken completely. For that she had got the sack, and it seemed that the long, affectionate friendship between her and Dinah was to be ended. But even then her anxiety was for Dinah and not for herself. She had not known until Lord Alwyn threw it in her face that Bracken had a wife, for Dinah had scrupulously refrained from discussing his affairs. The news had come as a shock to Miss French, and had shaken her confidence in him and in her own judgment of him. Lord Alwyn implied that Bracken had led Dinah on with hopes of his being free to marry her, and it was not until she heard Dinah's stammering, ecstatic account of the conversation in Bracken's chambers that Miss French saw how cruelly wrong about the whole thing Lord Alwyn was. When Dinah went on to tell how Bracken had said she would need help with the establishment and that Miss French should come to them permanently as a sort of housekeeper, the headache miraculously went, and they made cocoa on the schoolroom spirit-lamp and had a celebration with biscuits and fruit from the cupboard, and didn't go to bed till after midnight, there was so much to talk about.

As they were returning through Waterloo Place from their walk the contents-bills of the morning papers caught their horrified eyes. JOURNALIST'S WIFE MURDERED. MRS. BRACKEN MURRAY: SENSATION. Miss

French recovered first from a kind of paralysis of incredulity and bought a paper. They stood together on the pavement, Dinah reading over her shoulder — *found strangled in Bloomsbury lodgings — husband well known in Fleet Street — estranged for several years — further questioning of Mr. Murray as regards his whereabouts at the time of his wife's death —*

"He was with me," said Dinah in a whisper. "Why doesn't he *tell* them?"

"No gentleman would bring your name into it," Miss French said with conviction, and added a little dramatically, "He'd hang first!"

Dinah walked home in a haze, carrying the paper. In the front hall they met Alwyn, also with a paper in his hand.

"Oh, you've seen it," he said drily. "Well, I'm afraid your friend Murray is right up against it now."

"What will they do?" Dinah asked.

"Arrest him, I should think. Unless he has an absolutely watertight alibi for the time of the murder, and he doesn't seem to have one. You'd think an innocent man could say where he was, wouldn't you! *Somebody* must have seen him! Perhaps you will see reason now, instead of making a scene when I forbid you to have anything to do with him!"

Dinah turned and walked past her brother and up the stairs, followed by Miss French. She climbed the second flight slowly, as though she trailed a broken wing. Miss French went into her room to take off her hat, but Dinah stood still in the middle of the schoolroom floor, holding the paper and trying to think. *Further questioning of Mr. Murray — you'd think an innocent man could say where he was — he'd hang first — somebody must have seen him. . . .* I saw him, Dinah thought. I'm the only one who saw him. I could tell them where he was while his wife was being strangled. But he never will. If I don't tell —

Cold with terror, she saw Bracken in the dock, being tried for murder rather than mention her name, saw the wigs and gowns and solemn pageantry of the courtroom — Archie knew all about that — perhaps Archie could do something, perhaps Archie could save him — but Archie wasn't with him last night. There was only one person who could save him. There was only one way. . . .

Dinah's eyes rested on the door of Miss French's room, opening out of the schoolroom where she stood, with the key on the schoolroom side. Miss French's purse and gloves lay on the table where she had dropped them in her agitation before she went into her room. Dinah darted across the schoolroom, pulled Miss French's door shut on her and locked it.

"Miss French," she said against the panel. "Miss French, you've got to listen! I've locked you in — can you hear me? Will you please stay quietly where you are till I get back? I'm going down to Scotland Yard and tell them where Bracken was, so they'll let him go."

Miss French rattled the doorknob and said something Dinah couldn't hear. She raised her voice a little.

"You can't stop me, do you see? If they find out, it's not your fault, you couldn't stop me! And I'm going to pay the cab fare out of your purse, but Bracken will give it back to you!"

She snatched up Miss French's purse and ran out of the schoolroom and down the upper flight of stairs. The bedroom corridor was empty, but from the top of the lower flight she could hear Edward's voice in the drawing-room. Step by step she descended, screened by an angle of the hall, her feet cushioned by the stair-carpet, flitted to the outer door and heard it close behind her with a stealthy click. From the step, she remembered to turn to the left to avoid passing under the drawing-room windows, and caught a cab at the corner of Charles Street.

"I want to go to Scotland Yard," she told the driver as she got in. "Please hurry." She thought he looked surprised, but it was not so much at her destination as at her youth and evident state of distraction. Dinah did not know that people went to Scotland Yard for the sake of a lost umbrella much oftener than to rescue a lover from being tried for murder, and she felt that her mission must be suspected at once.

A large, benign constable stood at the gate of the big red building above the Embankment. He watched with interest while the very young lady with a wing in her hat paid her cab-driver and gave him a tip which wreathed him in smiles. Then the constable realized with increasing interest that she meant to enter Scotland Yard. He didn't get them like that very often here.

"Please," said Dinah, pausing before him, "I want to see some one about the murder."

"Which murder, miss?"

"M-Mrs. Bracken Murray."

The constable came to life. He led her into the entrance hall where a police sergeant sat behind a desk, and there was a whispered conference. The sergeant looked at her piercingly, as if he could not believe that he actually saw a girl in a blue *polonaise* with a wing in her hat standing where Dinah stood, and then he got up and went away. The constable gave her a chair and stood guard above her as though he thought she might try to leave.

The sergeant came back very soon and crooked a finger at her, saying, "Will you come this way, please, miss?"

She followed him to the lift and then along miles of upper corridors, and finally he opened the door of an office and motioned her inside and left her there alone. Presently an inner door opened and a tall grey-haired man with a kind smile approached her.

"Good morning," he said. "I'm Chief Inspector Jerrold. You have something to tell me about the Murray case?"

"Yes. Is he here? Please don't let him see me, he wouldn't want me to tell."

The Chief Inspector's smile went.

"First of all, will you please tell me your name?" he requested.

"I'm Dinah Campion. You can't arrest Mr. Murray, because he was with me last evening. My governess said he'd never mention that to save himself, so I — had to come."

"How long was he with you, last evening?"

"I went to his rooms after tea. I don't want you to think — you see, I'd never gone there alone before, but I was in trouble at home and I ran away to him because — because he's the person I love best in the world and I had to see him."

"And was he there when you arrived?"

"No, he was late, so I waited. His man let me in."

"What time did Mr. Murray come home?"

"Just after six. I heard the Palace clock strike while I was sitting there."

"And how long did you stay after he came in?"

"I was with him till nearly ten, but we weren't in his rooms all that time. It was his man's evening out and he'd gone, so we had dinner at a place in Compton Street. He — Mr. Murray wasn't out of my sight all that time. I don't want you to think — you see, we'd never done such a thing before, but I wasn't going to be allowed to see him again for a long time, and — he *said* we should get the governess and take her along, but that was impossible, and — I overruled him."

The Chief Inspector's smile was coming back.

"I'm sure you did," he said.

"So now that you know where he was, you'll let him go, won't you?"

"My dear child, he's not under arrest, you know."

"My brother said he would be, if he didn't have an alibi. My brother is Lord Alwyn, and I've got another brother who is a Junior at the Temple, but they weren't any good to Bracken because you see they didn't know where *I* was, last evening. I had to come here myself, didn't I?"

The Chief Inspector was seeing a great deal of rather blinding light. He was not a student of the peerage, but he could orient himself at once when he heard Lord Alwyn's name, and he was not surprised, in a way, that the honest, self-possessed young person in front of him had walked out of Debrett. She was young, but she was brave, and she was trying to protect the person she loved best in the world.

"Yes, I'm glad you've come," he said gently. "We had to ask Mr. Murray some questions, of course, and there was a certain amount of mystery about his whereabouts last evening, which is now happily cleared up."

"You — you haven't put him in jail?"

"Dear me, no, he's in the next room. Would you like to make sure?" He opened the inner door, through which he had emerged a few minutes before. "Come and see for yourself," he smiled, for while he believed her story he wanted Bracken's reaction to her presence there.

Three men stood up as she entered, among them Bracken. Dinah ran at him and clasped him protectively around the shoulders, crying, "Oh, Bracken, are you all right? I came as soon as I could!"

"Of course he's all right," said the Chief Inspector rather testily. "We haven't exactly had thumb-screws on him, you know!"

Bracken held her against him, looking bewildered and at the same time very proud.

"Dinah, what on earth have you been up to? How did you get here?"

"The paper said you hadn't got an alibi. So I locked Miss French in her room and came to tell them where you were last evening." She turned on the beaming Scotland Yard people with rather the air of a well-brought-up tigress defending its young, her arms still around Bracken. "Have you finished with him? May I take him away now?"

"Certainly, do what you like with him," said the Chief Inspector. "But first I must ask you to sign a written statement of what you told me in the other room, if you don't mind."

Dinah said she didn't mind, and the Chief Inspector explained that she must come into the other room with him and repeat her story before a stenographer. She left Bracken with a backward glance, safely in the company of Partridge and Inspector Evans, and followed Chief Inspector Jerrold into the room she had entered first. A quiet little man with a pad and pencil took down her answers to the Chief Inspector's questions, turning them into a statement as he went. Within a remarkably short time this was returned to her, typed, for signing. Dinah wrote her name with a firm hand, and the Chief Inspector led the way back to where Bracken was waiting, and said he was free to go. Dinah took his arm.

"Where's your hat, Bracken?" she asked in a motherly way.

Somebody gave Bracken his hat, and Dinah held out her hand to the Chief Inspector. Generations of graciousness were in the simple gesture.

"You've been very kind," she said, looking up at him. "Thank you so much for listening to me."

"My dear Lady Dinah, it was the greatest pleasure," he said gallantly, and when Bracken had said his own good-byes she led him away, still holding his arm protectively. Scotland Yard stood and watched them go, with fatuous smiles, for Dinah shimmered with romance.

They passed the desk in the entrance hall, where the sergeant said, "Everything all right, miss?" and Dinah smiled at him broadly and said, "Yes, thank you." And they came to the gate, where the constable touched the brim of his helmet and said, "Good morning, miss," and Dinah, holding Bracken's arm, said, "Good morning, and thank you."

Then Bracken spoke.

"Shall I call a cab, miss?"

"Yes, please," said Dinah faintly, and when it came she sank into the seat and pulled him down beside her as though how, at last, he was rescued. "Oh, *Bracken,* I was so frightened! What did they do to you?"

"Well, first," he said solemnly, "I was boiled in oil. And then I was drawn and quartered. And after that I was questioned on the rack —"

"Oh, if *that's* all," said Dinah, beginning to get her wind back, "I needn't have come!"

"Dinah, I haven't words." He took both her hands and kissed them, as the cab entered Trafalgar Square. "You were superb. Scotland Yard will never be the same again. Nor shall I."

"Nor will Edward, if he finds out!"

"I'm coming in now and talk to Edward."

"Had you better?"

"Yes, it's time."

"He's convinced you're in jail by now! Bracken, what *did* happen? Did you know she was in London?"

"Only since yesterday afternoon, when she suddenly appeared at the office. Gave me something of a shock, I admit!"

"She came —? But what did she *want?*"

"It was a form of blackmail. Partridge was going to deal with it. And then this other thing happened. Inspector Evans was waiting for me when I got home last night."

"Oh, Bracken, and I went to bed so happy!"

"So did I," he said. "God forgive me, so did I. They asked me to come down to the Yard this morning, and the woman who had found — found the body was there. She had seen a man go into Lisl's room, about six, and assumed it was me. When they asked to see my hat, I was sure she had seen Hutchinson."

"Who is he?"

"The man Lisl had been living with on the Continent. He is a Westerner and always wore a broad brim in New York. Apparently he still does. Anyway, my hat was wrong, and she said I was too slender for the man she had seen. How's that for a word?

Slender, she said!"

"I like thin men," said Dinah softly.

"All right, I'll see that you have one. In the meantime —" He took the flat jeweller's case out of an inner pocket, extracted the watch, and put the chain around her neck. "Let Edward make the most of that!"

"Oh, Bracken, do we *dare?*"

"You, after taking on the whole police force, talk about daring? Where on earth is this fellow going?"

The cabby, having had no directions, had simply followed his nose. Put right by a few words from Bracken through the trap, he soon brought them to St. James's Square and Bracken helped Dinah down, and they rang the bell. The footman looked surprised to see Dinah, whom he had admitted an hour ago with Miss French, and Bracken asked for Lord Alwyn, who sent back word that he would see them in the library.

But the library had no terrors for Dinah now, and she followed Bracken quite jauntily across the black-and-white marble squares of the hall floor, her fingers clasping the little watch which was their talisman.

"*Well* —" Alwyn began emphatically as soon as they appeared in the doorway, and Bracken cut in, speaking very softly, looking very bland, as was his way in a crisis.

"Now, before you say another word, Alwyn, let's get one thing quite clear. I am going to marry Dinah. I told you that two years ago, so you can't say you weren't warned. If you want to make a row about it, I am still going to marry Dinah. So why can't we talk it over sensibly?"

"Dinah is much too young to make up her mind," said Alwyn.

"I agree. That's why I am hoping that you will take a reasonable view of things and allow an ordinary engagement to exist in the ordinary way, at least till she has passed her eighteenth birthday. And by that I mean I must be free to see her, make her little gifts, take her around with only the usual amount of chaperonage, and no objections from you."

"But my dear fellow, you're in the midst of a bloody scandal!"

"Much as it may surprise you, Alwyn, I did not kill my wife. Even Scotland Yard says I didn't, now. What's more, they are well on the track of the man who did. The publicity is unfortunate, certainly, but it will blow over, publicity always does. And I fail utterly to see why you consider a marriage like Clare's to a man like Flood less objectionable than Dinah's, for love, to me. Incidentally, old boy — Dinah will have just as much money to spend as Clare ever will!''

Alwyn was uncomfortable. He had allowed his naturally domineering nature to run away with him, and he had been honestly horrified at the idea of Dinah's being involved in a *cause célèbre* — and he was touchy and resentful because Virginia Murray had had the effrontery to refuse him twice, and on top of that accept his brother Archie who had no prospects. But he had always liked Bracken, who was a very useful man on a horse, and he had a very wholesome respect for the Murray fortune.

''Well, you do see my position, don't you, old boy,'' he said placatingly. ''Of course you did mention at the ball that you were taken with Dinah, but it was hard for me to believe that you meant to follow through on it — Dinah is a sweet child, of course, but she isn't quite the wife I'd pick for a man like you.''

''Dinah has said something of the same kind herself,'' said Bracken. ''It's just possible that I see something in Dinah that both of you have yet to discover. But if she stays exactly the way she is now for the rest of her natural life, I shall be content.'' He put his arms around her, holding her close to his side. ''May we have your blessing,

Alwyn, or must we do the best we can without it?''

''I seem to have very little choice, since you've both made up your minds.'' Alwyn rose from behind the desk, shook hands with Bracken and kissed Dinah sketchily. ''Stubborn little beggar, aren't you,'' he said to her with a grudging affection. ''Always did have a mind of your own, dammit. Well, you've got him now, I hope you're satisfied!''

''Thank you, Edward,'' said Dinah in her usual docile tone, but her smile was wide and cheeky.

''Well, how about lunch, eh?'' queried Alwyn, ready to do the thing handsomely once he started. ''You'll stay to lunch, won't you, old boy? Have to celebrate this with champagne, I suppose!''

''That's very kind of you,'' said Bracken, and his fingers tightened excruciatingly in Dinah's ribs, with triumph.

''Oh, heavens, I forgot Miss French!'' Dinah cried. ''Edward, Bracken says I can have her after we're married, to help with the housekeeping, so don't you think it would be silly to sack her in the meantime? Can't she just stay on now, we've been such friends!''

''Very well, have everything your own way!'' said Alwyn, making as graceful a surrender as possible. "I swear it's got so a man isn't master of his own house any longer, the women run it all!"

"And may Bracken come up to the schoolroom with me and tell her — now, before lunch?"

"Tell her what? Oh, I see. Whatever you like, go ahead! Luncheon at one-thirty." Alwyn waved them out.

They took the two flights at a run, hand in hand, and arrived breathless at the schoolroom door where she stopped him, pointing towards the key still in Miss French's lock.

"She's in there," she whispered.

"Do we have to let her out right away?"

"You could kiss me first," Dinah suggested hopefully.

The publishers hope that this Large Print Book has brought you pleasurable reading. Each title is designed to make the text as easy to see as possible. G. K. Hall Large Print Books are available from your library and your local bookstore. Or you can receive information on upcoming and current Large Print Books by mail and order directly from the publisher. Just send your name and address to:

G. K. Hall & Co.
70 Lincoln Street
Boston, Mass. 02111